Praise for
TAINTED EVIDENCE
and
ROBERT DALEY

✳✳✳✳✳✳✳

"Mr. Daley understands politics from the White House to the station house, and he understands even more acutely the sinister politics of everyday life—of careerism and of love."

—*New York Times*

✳✳✳✳✳✳✳

"Elegant ... Daley engages the reader for pages on end.... TAINTED EVIDENCE is a superbly written novel of erudition as well as a window on our times."

—*Houston Chronicle*

✳✳✳✳✳✳✳

"Robert Daley draws masterfully on his experience."

—*Raleigh News & Observer*

more ...

BOOKS BY ROBERT DALEY

NOVELS

The Whole Truth
Only a Game
A Priest and a Girl
Strong Wine Red as Blood
To Kill a Cop
The Fast One
Year of the Dragon
The Dangerous Edge
Hands of a Stranger
Man with a Gun
A Faint Cold Fear
Tainted Evidence

NONFICTION

The World Beneath the City
Cars at Speed
The Bizarre World of European Sport
The Cruel Sport
The Swords of Spain
A Star in the Family
Target Blue
Treasure
Prince of the City
An American Saga
Portraits of France

ROBERT DALEY

TAINTED EVIDENCE

WARNER
VISION
BOOKS

A Time Warner Company

The characters and events in this book are fictitious. Any similarity to real persons, living or dead, is coincidental and not intended by the author.

WARNER BOOKS EDITION

Copyright © 1993 by Riviera Productions Ltd.
All rights reserved.

Cover illustration by James Steinberg
Cover design by Julia Kushnirsky
Hand lettering by Carl Dellacroce

Warner Vision is a trademark of Warner Books, Inc.

This Warner Books Edition is published by arrangement with Little, Brown & Company.

Warner Books, Inc.
1271 Avenue of the Americas
New York, NY 10020

W A Time Warner Company

Printed in the United States of America

First Warner Books Printing: March, 1994

10 9 8 7 6 5 4 3 2 1

Commit a crime and the earth is made of glass.

RALPH WALDO EMERSON

—BOOK ONE—

— 1 —

The 32nd precinct in Harlem, called the Three-Two by cops, is four blocks wide, thirty long, a rectangular box that extends north from 127th to 157th streets, bounded on the west by St. Nicholas and Bradhurst avenues, and on the east by Fifth Avenue. Where Fifth runs out, the boundary becomes the river—it's the Harlem River here but the East River further downtown where it bathes more genteel neighborhoods, same river. There are two bridges across to the Bronx. Felons escaping from the Three-Two sometimes jump into a car and are across in no time, and gone. The Bronx is a different command, different radio frequency, unfamiliar streets.

In the Three-Two live about 100,000 people, virtually all of whom are black. The police stationhouse on West 135th Street is one of the city's old ones, built in 1931. Out of it, going and coming around the clock, work about 250 cops, virtually all of whom are white. To those who live in the Three-Two a white face on the street, or in a car going by, means only one thing: cop. There are no tourists in the 32nd Precinct.

The Three-Two is divided into nine sectors; some previous commander ordered it, and it has stuck. There were and are about ten blocks to a sector, each one with a two-man car assigned to it around the clock. There are also footposts here and there when the manpower will stretch that far, individual cops sent out alone. Most of them stand nervously under streetlights for their entire tour, not budging, gripping their radios with both hands. Cops in the sector cars tend to feel responsible for them, and to honk or wave each time they drive by.

And there are nineteen detectives commanded by a lieutenant who work out of a squadroom on the second floor. All are men, sixteen whites, three blacks. These detectives work nine-hour shifts, four days on, two off. There are only two shifts a day, for at 1 A.M. the squadroom empties out and the door is locked tight, and night watch detectives take over responsibility for the precinct. The night watch works out of the Two-Five and covers all of Harlem, and if some egregious crime occurs during the night, the Three-Two detectives learn about it when they come to work the next morning—the paperwork from the night before is waiting for them, and they follow up on it. Egregious means homicides, all of which are investigated, and major armed robberies, particularly those in which someone is shot, but not burglaries. In the Three-Two there are too many burglaries and not enough detectives. The precinct's burglars operate almost with impunity, though without, it is hoped, realizing it.

There are too many homicides too, and homicides not only take preference, they take time. It is not enough to arrest the murderer. Unlike lesser crimes, even violent ones, which most often get plea-bargained away in exchange for derisory sentences, homicides have to be prepared for trial; public opinion being firm against murder, often they go all the way to trial. Only if you have an airtight case can you ever get a plea. Homicide, to detectives, translates into weeks of work finding evidence to bolster each case. Witnesses, many of whom are without fixed addresses, have to be found and persuaded to testify not only at the trial but at certain of the preliminary hearings. And if persuasion doesn't work they have to be found again and again and served with subpoenas. In Harlem most people prefer not to get involved. Some are afraid to testify, some are only afraid to lose time from work. People listen to the pleas and promises of white detectives, and are unmoved. Witnesses are always a problem.

On the night this story starts, insofar as any story starts at a specific time or even in a specific place, the oldest detective in the Three-Two squad was Dan Muldoon, forty-six. Muldoon, who had come to work two hours previously, sat now in a black unmarked Plymouth that moved through the streets of the precinct. His partner, Mike Barone, was driving. They were searching for specific individuals: a missing witness they had not been able to find for weeks; and any one of a number of regular informants; and the suspect in a particularly vicious murder, for they had information he had been seen again in the precinct.

Muldoon was a big, heavy man, divorced, no children. He had been a detective for twenty-three years, all of it spent in the Three-Two. He and Barone had worked together for several years and by now, in the manner of police partners, knew everything about each other. Although not agreeing on much, both of them, without a word being said, had accepted the partnership.

On the surface they were an unlikely pair, but many police partners were. They were as different in appearance as in style. Meeting Muldoon for the first time, one would note his bulbous nose, the broken veins in his cheeks. If close enough one would smell the beer on his breath, would note the stains on his tie, the garish sports coat buttoned taut over his belly. Some cops called him a hairbag, though not to his face. *Hairbag* is police slang for men who don't care anymore, who are waiting out retirement. But Muldoon, who had nothing else in his life except the police department, did care, at least in the sense that he had no intention of ever retiring. The emotions that drove him were the same as they had always been except that they had hardened. There was a good deal that Muldoon hated, and he was sometimes vocal about it.

The dress code for detectives was coats and ties. Muldoon each night was barely within the code. Barone each night exceeded it. Muldoon was a slob, Barone a fashion plate. He favored three-piece suits, silk ties, Italian shoes that cost money. He was thirty-five, tall, dark, his black hair combed straight back. Tonight's suit was a dark brown worsted. The gun in his belt did not show. He could pass for a stock trader, a lawyer; a notion that pleased him. Muldoon lived alone in an apartment in the Bronx that was dark and seldom clean. Barone was married with children, and owned a house in a suburb sixty miles north of the city. It had had to be that distant so that he could afford the payments on it. Like many other New York cops, he spent hours each day commuting.

Tonight the black Plymouth circulated slowly, up one street, down another. On Lenox Avenue the shops were closing; the two detectives watched the corrugated iron shutters come down one after the other, each with its own clamor.

The night got darker, the streetlights came on. By the time Barone next steered out onto Lenox all the shutters were down. They extended for block after block on both sides, walls of iron, inhospitable, hostile. Covered with graffiti too: names, slogans, obscenities. Barone, who was sometimes a fanciful man, thought of this graffiti as instructions in a language no one understood. Muldoon's emotion was disgust: These people fouled the place where they lived.

The car windows were open. The side streets were narrow and clumps of men stood about.

"The mutts are out," muttered Muldoon to his partner.

Cruising past them, studying each face, the two detectives were as concentrated as hunters. The social life of Harlem took place out of doors. It was what made tonight's job possible. But the light was poor, and in the shadows not all the faces could be discerned.

The perfume of the streets seemed to wash through the car.

It was almost tropical: spoiled food, unwashed bodies. The fetid odors of too many people crowded into too little space. The detectives inhaled this perfume as they looked for the men they wanted, and they listened for whatever else might happen: a scream, gunshots, the call of someone with information of interest.

As the hour got later, more and more people came out onto the streets, blocking sidewalks in front of houses, occupying stoops, whole corners. There were many women out now too, and even children. The detectives watched as people moved from group to group, watched them talking, gesticulating, sometimes concluding transactions—people who stiffened and fell silent as the black car approached. Attention always focused on the detectives, though not directly. Women pretended to ignore them. Some men pretended nonchalance, as if the car wasn't there. All avoided eye contact with the detectives inside.

Barone drove so slowly that the car was almost hovering. To the men in each group it must have seemed like a shark hovering, wondering whether to make a meal.

"Fucken mutts," said Muldoon.

When the detectives' car was well past, conversation and movement at last resumed. Muldoon saw this by turning around. Barone saw it in the mirror, and commented on it: "They all look guilty, don't they?"

"Throw them up against the wall," responded Muldoon. "Make them turn their pockets out. See what you find."

When Muldoon talked like this he worried his partner. "Now, now, Detective, we're not allowed to do that anymore," Barone said. Muldoon was sometimes rough with these people. Barone felt responsible for him, worried that he would do something to get himself in trouble—perhaps get both of them in trouble.

After so many years Muldoon knew every stoop, every storefront, every battered garbage can, almost every face. But so did Barone after a much shorter time. Night after night they moved through their long narrow precinct like predators pacing a cage. And they were predators of a sort. At any moment they might recognize someone and jump out and grab him, throw him in the back of the car, take him back to their lair.

But so far tonight they had found no one.

"Pretty quiet," commented Barone.

Suddenly Muldoon cried: "Stop, stop!"

He had spied one of the informants he was looking for, who, as it happened, was a midget. Spied him in a doorway. Saw him duck back into the building after spotting the black car. The little fuck was so small Muldoon almost missed him.

He was out of the car by now, quite swift for a man of his girth, lumbering across the sidewalk and up the stoop and into the vestibule.

"You little prick," Muldoon cried, smacking the cowering midget across the head.

"Don't hit me, don't hit me," whined the midget. And then, without drawing breath: "The dude is back. I seen him."

Muldoon, knowing who he meant, lowered his already raised fist and instead got money out of his billfold. It was his own money, not the department's. There was a department fund for paying informants, but to get at it required filling out forms, getting them approved by supervisors, then waiting months. Using his own money, to Muldoon, was a way of showing his contempt for the department and its procedures.

"Here's five bucks," he told the midget. "Tell me about it."

"Right," the midget said. The money had already disappeared. "I know where he is at." And he gave an address, a fifth-floor apartment off Lenox at 148th Street. "In the apartment, or on the roof."

"You're coming with us," Muldoon told him, wanting to exert maximum pressure on the little fuck, but the midget refused. He was only a midget, he whined, too small to defend himself. If anyone saw him with detectives he would be beaten up or killed as an informant.

"That's what you are," said Muldoon. "How much money have I given you so far, and what have you given me?"

In the vestibule the midget was clinging to the radiator. Lifting him, tearing the little fingers loose, Muldoon carried him out under his arm and threw him into the back seat.

When they reached the address, he ordered the midget to stay there until they got back, and he and Barone went into the building.

The case was this. Two months previously an old lady had surprised a burglar ransacking her apartment. She was found the next day bound to a chair, a towel stuffed down her throat, dead of suffocation. This turned a two-bit burglary that never would have been investigated at all into one of New York's two thousand homicides per year, all of which had to be investigated exhaustively. Muldoon and Barone worked hard on the case, and then Muldoon found the midget, who gave them the suspect's name, one of his names, said he knew him as Jonas. It was a start, and they began to winnow out the many Jonases on file, showing photos to witnesses, asking questions, winnowing it down, down, down until they were sure they had the right Jonas. They were also able to separate out this Jonas's left thumbprint from among the many prints Forensic had lifted. However, they were not able to find the suspect himself, and when they went back looking for the midget they couldn't find him either.

The building they now entered had been gracious in its day, but tonight was rank with strong odors, mostly urine and feces, and as they crossed its once proud lobby they were trying not to breathe at all.

Names and obscenities had been scribbled on every wall.

Muldoon, who did not like the look of the elevator, announced he was not getting on it.

"Five flights," teased Barone. "You'll have a heart attack."

"If it stalls out," said Muldoon, "you can stay in there a week, for all I care."

By the time Muldoon got upstairs he was panting. Barone

had waited for him. Muldoon rang the bell, then banged his
fist on the door.

"Police, open up."

"Who's there?"

"The white guys in suits," said Muldoon.

The door opened: a middle-aged lady with glazed eyes.

"We wondered if you'd seen Jonas," said Barone politely.

"I ain't seen him."

"Mind if we come in," said Muldoon, wading forward.
He did not wait for a response. The detectives had no warrant,
no right to enter, but the woman either didn't know this or
feared incurring their anger, probably both. In court, if it ever
came to court, they would swear that the woman invited them
in. Barone took the main room. Muldoon peered into the
kitchen, which was empty. He saw that the stove was stained
with grease and slime, the sink with sludge, and cockroaches
were climbing the walls. It almost made him puke. Sections
of the floor linoleum were curled or missing. The middle of
the kitchen ceiling had been broken open to expose pipes,
one of which was leaking. Someone had tied a dirty rag
around the leak. Water dripped through the rag into a black-
ened cooking pot on the floor.

Muldoon rejoined Barone in the living room. It was the
size of a jail cell but was crammed with people who were
sprawled on two decrepit sofas, and on the floor. Most of
them looked stoned. The room had two windows that were
not only closed but covered over with pieces of blankets,
pieces of rugs, overcoats. Drawn drapes, Harlem style. They
kept out unwanted light and noise. Also air. They kept in
odor that was close, like cheese that had gone bad.

Barone opened the door to the bedroom. Muldoon heard
him check the closet, under the bed. Muldoon checked the
other bedroom himself.

"These people live like pigs," said Muldoon when they
were again on the landing. "It's hard to have any sympathy
for them."

"You see the mirror?"

"And the razor blades on the coffee table."

"A little snorting party, I guess."

But the detectives were not there to enforce the narcotics laws, they had had no warrant, and they did not wish to test in court their assertion that they had been "invited" into the apartment.

The midget had said Jonas might be on the roof.

They went up two more flights of stairs, moving quietly. Carefully also, because there were no hall lights this high up and some of the steps were missing from the staircase. One could break a leg.

At the roof door the detectives took their guns out. If the murderer was out there he might have heard something. He must know that sooner or later the law would come for him.

He might start shooting at the first head that appeared.

Muldoon pushed Barone aside. He was senior detective and had the right to go first. "Fucken mutts don't scare me," he muttered.

But his heartbeat accelerated, his gun hand began to sweat. He had never been shot on a rooftop, but it could happen anytime. Tonight, for instance. He felt tense, but intensely alive, and he kicked the door open, banging it all the way back, and waited for a reaction, listening hard. He was about to step out into darkness, no streetlights or headlights, starlight only. There would be no normal human traffic to impose, or at least tend to impose, society's code of conduct on Jonas—or on anyone else who might be out there. The topography of this particular roof was unknown to him. There would be structures concealing who knew what, especially parapets to hide behind and shoot from.

There was no response to the door banging open.

Muldoon looked at Barone. They stared at each other a moment, after which Muldoon stepped out into the night.

Barone was right behind him.

Their heads darted around as they tried to check out simultaneously every direction from which shots might come.

In addition to having the normal clutter of rooftops, this

one was littered with discarded furniture—a sprung sofa, a doorless refrigerator, some broken tables and chairs—and with garbage in plastic bags.

Just then Muldoon spied movement.

It was in the shadow of the elevator housing. There was so little light that at first he thought it was someone sleeping, and then as it went on moving, that it was two people under a blanket making love. All these thoughts took only an instant. On Muldoon's part there was no hesitation, and he ran over and rammed his gun down six inches from their heads.

"Police, freeze," he shouted.

Too late he saw it was only a loosely tied garbage bag moving in the night breeze. When he turned around, Barone was smirking at him.

"It coulda been him," said Muldoon, acutely embarrassed.

"Yes of course," said Barone.

They checked the roof out thoroughly. Jonas was not out there. No one was out there. The guns went back into the holsters, and they paused to admire the view, or rather Barone did. To the south was the line of skyscrapers, to the east and west the two rivers. The city seemed ablaze with light.

"I love this city," said Mike Barone.

"It's a shithole," responded Dan Muldoon.

"I like the bridges the best. Look at the George Washington over there all lit up."

Instead Muldoon gestured toward the littered rooftop. "In Harlem, what do you do when you purchase a new living room suite? You carry the old one up onto the roof and leave it there. Same with your garbage. No wonder Harlem stinks the way it does."

They started down the stairs, and three flights below startled a young couple. The girl was about fifteen, the boy no older. To Barone the girl seemed young, innocent, pretty, and he said so.

"Innocent," scoffed Muldoon. "When I was going up she was going down—she was giving the kid a blowjob. Dumb bitch'll be pregnant in a month. She'll have five babies before she's twenty—from five different mutts—and be on welfare the rest of her life.''

This was possibly true and Barone nodded sadly. ''She was a pretty girl, though.''

As they continued to descend, their footsteps were loud on the stairs. ''You ever make it with a black woman, Mike?''

Barone grinned. ''No comment.''

Muldoon fell silent for a time. ''Ol' Mike likes the ladies,'' he said.

''The voice of envy talking,'' said Barone. ''Detective Muldoon hasn't been able to get laid in five years.'' They had reached the lobby and he glanced at his partner. ''If you'd get your clothes cleaned once in a while you'd help your chances a lot.''

Muldoon was stung, but said nothing.

''And about every decade or so you should buy a new outfit. Just a suggestion, you understand.''

Muldoon was trying to think up a suitable retort. ''Fuck you,'' he said, for nothing else had come to mind.

When they came to their car the midget was gone and Muldoon started cursing.

Barone only laughed. ''You didn't really expect him to wait around, did you?''

''When I find that fucken midget I'm going to cut his little balls off.''

They got into their car.

''Well anyway,'' said Barone, ''I sure did admire your technique up there on the roof—the way you got the drop on that garbage bag.''

''Drive the car,'' Muldoon said.

''Superb technique. I was awestruck. You should be in the police academy demonstrating it to recruits. They'd be awestruck too, I bet.''

Since he could think of no clever rejoinder Muldoon remained silent. He did not like to be teased, but from Barone he would take it, if it did not happen too often.

* * *

Several times in its existence the Three-Two, of course it wasn't the Three-Two then, was counted the richest and most desirable part of the island. It was called Harlem Plains, or the valley of Harlem. There were lush farms supplying produce for New York City, eight miles south. There were the estates and mansions of families that had been there since the days of the Dutch. Many people still had Dutch names. Well into the 1800s some kept slaves. There were hills and streams, and pure water to drink. There were magnificent views of the rivers. There was a blacksmith's shop and a small cluster of houses, and this was Harlem Village. There was a stagecoach line, but transportation to and from the distant city was mostly by steamboat, though only during the warm months, for in winter the rivers froze.

The cops who patrol the Three-Two today rarely know anything about its origins.

The Civil War freed those slaves who were left, and after two hundred years the soil was depleted anyway. The farms became run down. Many were abandoned. The former slaves stayed on, working at menial jobs, Harlem's first black colony, though an extremely small one. Shantytowns sprang up inhabited mostly by Irish immigrants who were considered lazy and dirty, shiftless, dangerous.

By the late 1800s the population of New York City was 1.1 million and growing. Waves of foreigners, usually poor and sometimes destitute, kept crowding in downtown near the docks. They brought with them disease and still more crime. They made people who could afford it want to get away. Harlem, the part of it that is now the Three-Two, became New York's first suburb. Tree-lined boulevards were laid out, wide streets. Elegant new brownstones were built from designs by the city's best architects.

The city engulfed its suburb. Between 1878 and 1881 three elevated railroad lines were pushed north into Harlem, and the real estate boom was on. Apartment buildings went up, some of them six stories high, skyscrapers. Residential buildings, it seemed, would never go higher. Each apartment had numerous large rooms. Everything was of the best quality, and the people who moved in were of the best quality.

Now real estate speculators began to bid up the price of lots. The rents went up and up and up. Too much was constructed in too short a time and in 1905 the boom collapsed.

Buildings stood empty. Banks foreclosed. Speculators short of capital lost everything. Others, to save what they could, rented for the first time to Negroes. They found they could get inflated rents from Negroes, who, because no one wanted them nearby, were used to paying more for housing than anyone else. Unlike the few already established in Harlem, who had lived mostly under the el tracks or on the marshes along the rivers or in other undesirable locations, the new Negroes moved into the newest buildings, into spacious apartments built originally for rich whites. And though the rents were high, they were able to pay them by renting out rooms or even parts of rooms to the hordes of immigrants arriving every day from the Deep South, ex-field hands for the most part, the uneducated and often uncouth sons and daughters of slaves, come to try life in the bright lights. These immigrants were mostly young. They frequently had only rudimentary ideas of sanitation. They had no families yet, they had no experience living in cities, and it was in Harlem that they first tasted their new freedoms.

Employment agencies proliferated, bringing women up on contracts, but not men. The women were able to find work as domestics, but often the men who moved north could find nothing at all. They could get menial jobs only, and not many of those. They couldn't even become prizefighters, for the state boxing commission had outlawed interracial bouts, and the sporting crowd had no interest in watching two blacks maul each other.

When they couldn't get work, many men went back where they came from, and before long there were more women than men in Harlem. Those men who were left were unable to support themselves, much less families. They lived off the women. They lived as a result with low or nonexistent self-esteem. Sociologists later wrote learned tomes about it. From the women's point of view there were not enough men to go around. Women learned to go after other women's men; it seemed to many of them that they had no choice. They acquired the reputation for being what was then called "loose." So the sociologists said. The emasculation of black manhood, the undermining of black family structure, is not a new thing. It existed from the very beginning.

Today's cops do know—vaguely—about black men, black women, and black families, but most are too young and incurious to know or care how it started.

Once the Negroes were solidly established in Harlem, the rest of the whites sold out and moved out.

Upon reaching New York the other immigrants had mostly started out in the sordid streets and narrow tenements of lower Manhattan, whereas the Harlem Negroes inherited parks, and tree-lined boulevards, and elegant buildings with huge rooms. Nonetheless, within ten years Harlem was a slum.

Wherever there is poverty there is crime, and so crime in Harlem was immediate, though not at the level that was to come, and it did not get the publicity that was to come. Blacks robbed blacks, blacks murdered blacks, and the white city took no notice. The newspapers were not interested. The news never left Harlem. Blacks knew better than to assault whites, however. It happened, but it was rare. Violence against whites was not tolerated, justice was always swift and usually draconian. It was not quite the Ku Klux Klan of the South, but almost, and the people of Harlem were aware of this.

Which meant that Harlem, for whites, was as safe as their own homes, safer. In the twenties it was the place white tourists came to laugh and drink and listen to the new jazz music. Harlem had the best speakeasies, and the best clubs, which were filled night after night by free spenders from downtown or out of town. Harlem was a tourist attraction of the first magnitude.

In 1937, after winning the heavyweight championship, Joe

Louis toured Harlem. This was not Louis's hometown, he was from Detroit. Nonetheless, there was an astonishing turnout, there had never been anything like it before. The streets overflowed with laughing, weeping Negroes, perhaps 100,000 of them, perhaps more, who seemed to see Louis as the first great hero black America had ever had or was ever likely to have. There had been others: Marcus Garvey, Frederick Douglass, even a fighter named Jack Johnson, who operated mostly abroad. But those men were the past and only dimly remembered. They were not seen in newsreels, heard on the radio—and they did not make headlines for smashing down white men. For the first time Negroes could hold up their heads.

In a sense Joe Louis, and the black reaction to him, was the first stirring of black manhood in the United States. Nothing happened right away. World War II came. After it, black athletes began to be accepted on professional teams. Also a tentative, nonviolent civil rights movement got under way in the South far from Harlem and seeming to have little to do with Harlem.

Harlem during those years was preoccupied with something else entirely, for a man had stood up calling himself Malcolm X, part of a religion called the Nation of Islam. Malcolm was a man of passionate oratory. He seemed to be preaching hatred of whites, and revolution, and a number of other fiery young men listened to him and crowded around him. The new religion acquired many converts. People began to call themselves Black Muslims and to take on Islamic names. But Malcolm got to be bigger than the leaders of the new religion wanted; he was shot to death in a hall where he had gone to speak—by his own people, apparently—before he could put his ideas into practice. This took place just over the line in the next precinct up, the Three-Four, into which blacks had begun to spread.

The Black Panther Party was formed. Its leaders preached outright violence against whites, particularly police officers, who were referred to as pigs—who began to be called pigs to their faces. Hatred of whites rose to new levels and in Harlem there were armed confrontations with the police. But the Panthers were infiltrated by undercover black cops and twenty-one Panthers went on trial for conspiring to murder cops and blow up police stations. It was the longest trial in New York history, the jury did not believe such a conspiracy was possible, and all twenty-one were acquitted. But the trial wrecked the Black Panther Party anyway.

Whereupon certain of the most violent Panthers formed an offshoot, called it the Black Liberation Army, and set out to prowl the streets shooting cops in the back. A few days after the end of the Panther trial they gunned down two cops here in the Three-Two. It was a balmy May evening. In a street outside the Polo Grounds housing project the two young officers, one white, one black, were returning to their radio car after responding to a routine call. Two black men fell into step behind them, pulled out guns, shot them multiple times in the back, and then when they were down yanked out the two service revolvers and emptied them into the still-writhing bodies.

This Black Liberation Army had even less of a program than the Panthers and was even more loosely organized, perhaps four hundred people in all, some of them wives, girlfriends, and more or less harmless hangers-on, but there were also about seventy-five heavily armed gunmen who roamed the country ambushing cops in San Francisco, St. Louis, New Orleans, and other cities, killing a number of them. In New York they assassinated four cops in all, and wounded a dozen others. Among those who survived, though as ruined hulks, were two who were machine-gunned as they sat in their radio car. This was in the Two-Six, the next precinct over. Most of these Black Liberation Army members were killed or jailed, but it took ten years.

A police department has a short memory—it is as short as a football team's. Today's players never heard of yesteryear's. But the Black Liberation Army has remained part of police lore to this day, partly because their outrages reoccurred for so long, mostly because photos and plaques commemorating the dead cops still hang in shrines in the stationhouses.

Harlem, meanwhile, continued to deteriorate. The heroin epidemic of the seventies became the crack epidemic of the eighties. Heroin had been mild compared to this. Heroin made people comatose. Crack made them violent. It gave a bigger high and a bigger drop and one needed repeated hits. It proliferated as heroin had never done. Before long it was being sold on front stoops, on street corners, in apartment house hallways, sometimes by children, sometimes openly. The police couldn't stop it, not in the Three-Two, not anywhere. No one could stop it.

There were more and more guns on the street too, more and more ripoffs. Mostly the crack dealers robbed and shot only each other, but they tended when aroused to spray whole areas, and upright citizens sometimes got caught in the crossfire. Crack dealers came to be the best customers gun dealers had ever had. They bought more and more guns, which became more and more exotic—and lethal. They became collectors, almost connoisseurs. And of course all new weaponry had to be test-fired, usually into courtyards or the air; you had to make sure the gun worked. On holidays gunfire became celebratory. A tourist—there had been no tourists now in sixty years—would have thought he was listening to a fireworks display. With so many bullets flying around they flew also into doorways, into open windows, they flew down streets, and inevitably they killed bystanders, some of them kids playing, some of them babies in carriages. For blacks in Harlem—blacks in America in general—life was bad and getting worse.

To the cops who patrolled the Three-Two it seemed that the citizens around them had become increasingly alienated from the rest of the population, meaning the white population, a separate society increasingly outside the mainstream. Whites seemed more and more hated, themselves of course included. This was not something told to them, nor had they worked it out intellectually. It was something felt. However little they knew of the history of Harlem, or of blacks in Harlem, they felt it more strongly every night. There were no Malcolm X's making speeches, no Panthers shooting at them, and a few of them wondered sometimes why not. How long could they be so lucky? What was coming?

Other cops never gave it a thought.

Muldoon and Barone, bored by a night on which so little seemed to be happening, pulled up in front of a Chinese takeout place and went inside.

Small as it was, the tiny store was fortified. Behind a kind of barred ticket window a Chinese woman took orders from customers waiting on line. The rest of the wall was steel, with a steel door set in it. This was one of the ways store owners tried to minimize the frequent stickups in Harlem.

Muldoon flashed his shield at the Chinese woman.

''Police.''

The detectives went inside and the steel door clanged shut behind them.

Three Chinese cooks were frying food at a long stove while steam rose around them. The walls were greasy and the odor was of cooking oil too often reused.

''You made a complaint about a robbery,'' Muldoon began.

The night before, one of the cooks had been robbed at gunpoint on the street. The takeout joint had closed and he was three blocks from the subway station on his way home to Chinatown. According to his statement, which he gave to night-watch detectives, the cook had recognized the perpetrator, for he had sometimes seen him hanging out on a certain corner.

Now Muldoon and Barone attempted to question the cook but all he did was bow and grin.

''Do you speak English?'' said Muldoon. ''You don't, do you?''

''I don't think he does,'' said Barone.

"Fucken guy," said Muldoon.

Using the woman as interpreter they offered to drive the cook up and down streets. If the perpetrator was from the neighborhood, they might spot him.

But an expression of fear had come onto the cook's face.

"Tell him," Barone said gently, "that no one will see him. All he has to do is point the guy out from the back of the car."

Eventually the cook seemed as afraid of the detectives as of the stickup man he might have to identify, but he followed them out to the street. As he got into the car he seemed to be trying to smile.

They drove up one street and down another.

In the Three-Two, street crime was mostly by locals. Muldoon knew this: the mutts blow the money in a crack joint and they're out on the corner again. If you go looking for them with the victim, often you find them.

Barone knew it too, but it continued to surprise him. "Before I came into this precinct, I worked only your better neighborhoods," he said as he drove. "If somebody ripped somebody off, he got out of the precinct instantly. No one waited around to get caught."

"The mutts here are not as smart as that," responded Muldoon.

At each clump of people they passed Barone slowed almost to a walk and turned to the cook.

"You see him?"

After thirty minutes, they returned the cook to the takeout joint. He had identified no one.

"I didn't think he would," muttered Muldoon.

"I thought he might," said Barone, as they resumed patrol. "We'll try him again tomorrow night."

By now everyone was out. In the warm night people hung over the windowsills talking to other people on the sidewalk below. People sat on stoops on camp chairs and swilled liquor out of bottles concealed inside paper bags.

"The colored are great drinkers," Muldoon muttered.

"The reason they have no money is, they drink it all. Those that aren't on crack."

Because Barone seemed to feel sympathy for these people, or pretended to, Muldoon finished his thought in his head: And when they get drunk enough, they piss against the walls. Animals.

Even the children were still out, some of them running beside the slow-moving black car chanting: "Poh-leece-man. Poh-leece-man!" Some were swilling from cans or bottles of soda which, in emulation of their parents, they carried inside paper bags.

The voice of Central came over the radio: "Man bleeding heavily, corner of St. Nicholas and 142nd, which car responding?"

Barone grabbed up the hand radio that had been lying on the seat between them. "Two-squad, Central," he said, holding it close to his lips. "We'll take that call."

He turned onto St. Nicholas Avenue and raced south, his gun already out and lying on the seat beside the radio. Muldoon's was in his hand in his lap. But when they reached the site there was no commotion of any kind. Mystified, they cruised on past. The grocery on the corner was still open, and a number of people had congregated near it, men and women both, some of them sitting in chairs. No one, as they drove by, called out to them or flagged them down.

Still expecting to come upon a disturbance, they continued down St. Nicholas for several blocks. Nothing. Finally Barone keyed the radio and asked Central for a clarification.

After a moment the same information came back a second time, same address too. Man bleeding heavily.

So Barone made a U-turn and went back. When they reached the corner again he slowed almost to a stop and they scrutinized the people on the sidewalk. There was still no commotion, and then they were past.

"Forget it," said Muldoon, "nothing there."

But Barone made another U-turn and a third pass, this time

pulling up to the curb and calling out: "Is somebody bleeding heavily there?"

"This man is," someone called back, pointing toward one of the chairs.

They got out and approached. The man in the chair was old, his face deeply lined, his hair white, and he had evidently had a nosebleed. There were blood spots on his shirt and a wad of toilet paper had been rammed up his nose.

"How you feeling, old fellow?" Barone said to him.

"Ah's feeling a bit better now, thank you," the old man said.

"Looks like you had a pretty bad nosebleed there. I think it may have stopped now though. Do you live near here? Do you have anyone who can take care of you?"

"Ah takes care of myself, mostly."

Muldoon had already turned to go back to the car. "Let's go," he said over his shoulder. "We're supposed to be homicide detectives for chrissake."

Barone put the hand radio to his lips and called in an ambulance.

"What's your name, old fellow?" he asked.

Barone, who had his notebook out, wrote down the old man's name: Eugene Mitchell. "What's your date of birth, Eugene? Where do you live?"

Eugene was only sixty-four, it seemed, not nearly as old as he looked, and Barone was surprised. But in Harlem, life spans were about ten years shorter than the national average.

Bystanders had crowded around wanting to get in on the excitement.

Having closed his notebook, Barone waited to see that Eugene got into the ambulance. Sometimes, if the cops didn't stay, the paramedics would refuse the patient and drive away.

"How'd you get the nosebleed, Eugene," he asked as they waited.

"Ah don't rightly know."

Barone decided to try to lift the old man's spirits. "I bet I know how you got it. You were humping your old lady, weren't you, Eugene.''

Eugene liked this idea, and he began to grin.

"Is that what you were doing, Eugene?" joked Barone.

The bystanders were all grinning.

"At your age? Eugene, I'm ashamed of you."

The old man was grinning too.

"I bet it wasn't your old lady at all," said Barone, for he saw that the old man was enjoying the attention. "I bet it was your girlfriend. She was too much for you. Am I right, Eugene?"

Barone was patronizing them, decided Muldoon, watching from a distance. They liked it. Everyone was laughing. They didn't even realize they were being patronized.

Barone said: "Listen to me, Eugene, you gotta take it easier. Young girls are too energetic. You stay away from them, you hear me? Or at least cut it down to only one of them at a time."

Eugene was still grinning, sitting up straighter.

"You gotta learn to avoid these strenuous exercises, Eugene."

Everyone was laughing. A bystander said to Muldoon: "Your partner missed his calling, man, he shoulda been a stand-up comedian."

Muldoon gave him a look, and resumed watching for the ambulance. Finally it came, backed up to the curb, and two paramedics got out. When Barone told them to take Eugene to Harlem Hospital, they nodded and walked him on board. Just before the doors closed, Barone called into the ambulance: "I hope you feel better, Eugene."

He got back in the car beside Muldoon.

"These people get a fart stuck between two ribs and they call 911," said Muldoon.

"Well," Barone said, "they don't have anybody else but us."

Now as he drove, Barone was looking for a patrolling radio car, because a form needed to be filled out on Eugene, and he didn't have one. Finally on 155th Street underneath the elevated road that crossed to the Bronx he came upon one of the precinct cars parked on the sidewalk in front of a defunct gas station. The interior light was on. Both cops were writing in their memo books. Barone, approaching from the rear, drove up onto the sidewalk and pulled to a stop beside them. They were so concentrated that they didn't see him until he was there, six inches away.

"Excuse me, Officer," Barone said into the recorder's window, "can you tell me where Harlem is at?"

The cop's head jerked up, startled. Then he grinned.

"You went through a red light, before," he said. "I saw it. Corner of 135th and Lenox. I'm going to have to write you a ticket."

The banter of cops in Harlem in the night. "But Officer," said Barone in a pleading voice, "it's my first time."

"Tell it to the judge," the cop said.

"You guys should be more vigilant," said Muldoon, talking across Barone. "We could have stuck one in your ear. You would've never known what hit you."

The cop thought this over a moment. "No one's looking to stick one in a cop's ear."

"When I came on the job," said Muldoon, "that's exactly what used to happen up here."

"Well," said the cop, "it doesn't happen anymore."

"It could start again," said Muldoon. "Anytime."

"You got an aided card there?" asked Barone. "Give me an aided card."

The cop handed one across.

Some nights, thought Barone as he filled in the card, there would be a murder, a victim on the floor, sometimes more than one, and they would work till dawn. Not tonight though. He filled in Eugene's address, date of birth, and the disposition: subject removed to Harlem Hospital. At the stationhouse later he would get a case number from the 124 man, fill it in, and toss the card into the box.

—2—

The offices of the elected district attorney of New York County, and those of his bureau chiefs and principal administrators, are on the eighth floor of a building at 100 Centre Street. The rest of the staff, more than 450 assistant district attorneys, many of them fresh out of law school but prosecuting major cases nonetheless, work out of offices on three other floors or else in other buildings, most of them nearby, into which, with the increase in crime and the increase in their own numbers, they have overflowed.

On the eighth floor there are anterooms and secretaries. On the DA's other floors and buildings there are sometimes neither, and everything must be shared. There is and has always been a disproportion in the allocation of law enforcement funds; the DA's office has never been given remotely the amount it needed.

The building at 100 Centre Street is huge, seventeen stories high and occupying an entire city block. One whole side of it is the prison known as the Tombs. Most of the rest is courtrooms, floor after floor of them. From the Tombs, barred corridors cross from the cellblocks to the courtrooms; they are called bridges, and in a sense that's what they are. They bridge the gap between crime and justice, between the mindless and the deliberative, between violence and reason, between man at his worst and what is perhaps the best that man can do.

Some years ago the Tombs became so overcrowded with felons and presumed felons, with psychopaths, perverts, and the permanently enraged, that it could not be managed or even repaired. Beds and plumbing were ripped off walls. Door mechanisms were wrecked by inmates or broke down. Whole cellblocks became unusable. The Tombs was closed by court order, its inmates removed elsewhere. But having been repaired—even in a certain sense redecorated—it has reopened and filled up again.

The front entrance of 100 Centre Street is for jurors, witnesses, complainants, defense lawyers, and those defendants not already incarcerated, who come in under the rotunda, approach security as they might approach the Pearly Gates, and then ascend to the place of judgment.

Assistant district attorneys, meanwhile, use a door around the side on Leonard Street. There are always armed cops on duty there to screen would-be visitors, and from inside the building the DA's floors are accessible only by certain elevators and stairwells which are kept locked and for which the assistants have special keys. These are not choirboys they are prosecuting, and they perform their job at a certain risk.

On this particular afternoon in one of the conference rooms on the eighth floor a dozen lawyers had met to consider the latest murders. There had been fourteen in Manhattan the previous week, about average. The meeting had gone on for an hour and would last at least an hour more. The three women at the table were variously dressed, whereas the men were dressed mostly alike although, since it was a warm afternoon and the DA's offices were air-conditioned only in the hottest summer months, some of them had stripped down to their shirtsleeves. Most, however, had gone no further than their vests. They were, after all, lawyers.

This was the weekly meeting of what its participants sometimes referred to jokingly as "the heinous crimes bureau"—

crimes that the city, meaning the politicians and the press, might be watching closely, and which, therefore, the DA and his bureau chiefs were determined to watch closely as well.

There were briefcases standing beside the chairs, and legal pads in front of each place. These men and women were the stars of the DA's office, and one after another they briefed each other on what had recently come in—the latest ways people had shot, knifed, strangled, bludgeoned, poisoned, defenestrated, decapitated, butchered other people in this city. Some of the cases were tangled. One could hear the speaker himself trying to make sense of a case even as he presented it. Sometimes there were legal technicalities involved, and the speaker was looking to his colleagues for advice. But other times whichever prosecutor had the floor was trying mostly to make his colleagues laugh, for some of these cases were so grotesque as to be funny.

At the head of the table sat Assistant District Attorney Karen Henning, presiding. She was thirty-eight years old, with blond curly hair worn short to set off her long, rather elegant neck. As a girl she had worried about her neck. She had hated her hair. She had wished for dark straight hair, as dark as possible, and it should hang down below her shoulders like those girls in her class she most admired. She had got over that. She had grown into an extremely attractive woman, and she knew it. She was a true blond, though her hair was darker now than it had been. She had blue eyes and a fair complexion—if something happened to make her blush, everyone nearby could see it. She had nice teeth and a fleshy mouth that her husband often told her was sexy.

"Who's next?" she said.

"Me, I guess," said Assistant DA Doug Van Horn, and he launched his case upon the room. "The deceased is not the deceased yet, but soon will be. He's got two in the head and it looks like he's going out."

"This was where?" Karen Henning said.

"Harlem, broad daylight," Van Horn said.

His manner indicated that this was a bizarre case, and

around the table the smiles came on, and the other assistants waited to hear the rest of it.

Karen sat with her legal pad balanced on crossed knees. Most assistant DAs joined the office fresh out of law school, but Karen had been already an experienced lawyer when hired. For this reason, and because the pressure was on to promote women, her rise had been rapid. As chief of the trials division, she was the highest-ranking woman in the district attorney's hierarchy—the token woman it sometimes seemed to her. Of the 450 assistant DAs, many now were women, but the other divisions were run by men, most of the squads were run by men, and in the normal course most of the best cases were routinely assigned to men to try.

"The defendant," Van Horn said, "is fifty-six, black, with a gray beard. He's got a Bible in one hand and an automatic in the other, and he stands on the sidewalk shouting: The Lord sent me to clean up the neighborhood. I am the law. He then pumps three bullets into the victim, a man he didn't know who had just come out of the building."

Karen said: "Any witnesses?"

"Five. An off-duty cop who happened to be driving by, two FBI agents on surveillance for a bank robbery, the building's super, and a bystander." Van Horn grinned back at his colleagues.

"Do you think you can win this case?" asked one of them, Mike Tananbaum, and everyone laughed.

"The super's not going to be much good to us," said Van Horn thoughtfully. "The defendant shot him next, and it looks like he's going out too."

"You still got a cop, two FBI agents, and a bystander," Tananbaum said.

"I'm not so sure," said Van Horn. "The defendant runs off down the street and the bystander starts chasing him. He's going to make a citizen's arrest, I guess. Unfortunately he's got a gun too, and as he's running after him he's firing away. This attracts the attention of the off-duty cop, who jumps out of his car and starts firing, but at the bystander, not at the killer. He and the bystander stand there firing at each other until they both run out of bullets. It's a standoff.''

"So you've got the bystander, anyway," said Tananbaum.

"Well, no. His gun being empty, he sprints right between the two FBI agents, never to be seen again."

Everyone was now laughing, even Karen.

"We don't know who he was, where he came from, nothing," said Van Horn.

"Who arrested the defendant?"

"The cop and one of the FBI agents have a fistfight over it. The cop wins. Knocks the FBI agent cold. The other FBI agent then tries to arrest the cop."

"And people wonder why we sometimes accept pleas," Karen murmured.

"In the stationhouse the defendant makes two statements," said Van Horn. "You'll like this. The first is: The revolution starts at four P.M."

"And the second statement?" said Karen.

"Give me liberty or give me death."

Karen was wiping her eyes. "Who's next," she said.

The meeting went on, relentless descriptions of crimes outrageous to the point of hilarity. Karen had a habit of twisting her wedding band as she listened.

In one case four men had stabbed the deceased; a fifth had shot him.

"So, what are we supposed to put in the indictment?" asked Tananbaum, whose case it was. "While four other guys were stabbing the deceased to death the defendant shot him to death? That's going to be some indictment."

"Did he die of the knife wounds or the gunshots?" asked Karen. "What does the ME say? Any witnesses?"

"There were no witnesses except for the two guys going through the deceased's pockets."

Again laughter.

"And a third guy who ran over and stole his sneakers."

The laughter lasted a considerable time.

Karen paged through the notes on the case. "This is the

same guy that robbed the health store in that other case," she said. "Another time he shot a guy in the chest. And he's only twenty-two years old."

"A victim of a deprived upbringing," said Tananbaum.

Van Horn said: "We should put him in a program."

"It's been a bad month," Karen said. She paused. "We're not getting dispositions." They all knew what this meant. There were too many murders for too few prosecutors, too few judges, too few courtrooms. However horrible these crimes, many would have to be plea-bargained away. Defense lawyers knew this too. "You've got to push harder for dispositions," Karen said. "In cases that don't mean anything, you're going to have to give a little."

Van Horn said: "The defense lawyers all want a lot, Karen. I've got one who won't plead unless I promise his client zero to seven."

"Keep trying," Karen said, and returned to her office. For the last half hour she had been checking her watch constantly. Now she stuffed her briefcase, grasped her handbag, and told her secretary she was going home. It was nearly 7 P.M., and other elements of her life demanded her attention—elements far more important, she told herself firmly, than her job.

She should have left the office ages ago. Fearing she was too late to take the subway she splurged on a taxi to Grand Central. Considering the tight budget she was trying to operate on, it cost a fortune, and she barely made the last train that would get her home in time, running down the ramp in heels, and just making it into the final car as the train pulled out.

The car was hot, all seats taken, the aisle narrow, three seats to one side, two to the other, elbows and newspapers extending outward, and she began to make her way through this car and into the next one, and then the one after that, and it was six cars before she could find an empty seat. She subsided into it and went to work on the folders she had with her.

The train again slowed.

"Bronxville," the conductor sang out. "Station is Bronxville."

Karen gathered her folders in her arms and joined a line of commuters waiting at the end of the car.

When she stepped down into the parking lot Henry was waiting with their small station wagon. He was a tall, sandy-haired man, forty-one years old. She dumped her folders in the back, kissed him on the cheek, and he backed the car out.

"We'll eat afterward," he told her. "We don't have much time."

"Did you pick up my things at the cleaners?"

"Yes." They drove a little way in silence. "The car's supposed to be serviced tomorrow," he told her.

"I'll drop it off on my way to the train."

Karen came in the door of her house and set down her folders and briefcase. Her daughter, Hillary, fifteen, was there waiting.

"Hurry up, Mom, we'll be late."

Backstage at the high school auditorium, the hem of Hillary's costume was not right, and Karen was on her knees lengthening it. Out front the seats were filling up with other parents, and Karen could feel her daughter's mounting tension.

"Hold still," she ordered.

Hillary began running lines of the play with a boy of about sixteen, whose name, Karen believed, was Randy.

Hillary: "I want to stay in Grover's Corners with you."

Randy: "Emily, we can be together . . ."

Hillary: "Mom, pull it down."

Karen, her mouth full of pins, gazed up at her daughter.

"Mom, it has to touch the floor."

Randy, ignoring both of them, concluded the scene: "Forever."

Karen began again on the hem. Finally she stood up. "There. You look terrific."

Hillary was looking around for a mirror, but there was none. "Do I really?"

"The audience will love you." Of course they will, she thought, they are parents.

"I hope so," said Hillary.

The other actors stood in a group on the other side of the stage, and Hillary went off to join them.

"Good luck," Karen called after her daughter.

The girl made no response. Karen didn't mind. Watching her, she beamed with pride and nervousness.

A little later the play began. Sitting in the audience beside her husband, Karen studied her case notes while waiting for Hillary's entrance. Not until the girl appeared onstage did Karen put her notes away. Thereafter she watched almost breathlessly, hanging on Hillary's every speech. She had to laugh at herself: one would think this the most serious moment of her day, so intent was her focus.

In another part of the auditorium her son, Jackie, along with two of his friends, also watched the play, though with much less reverence.

"My sister is the one who looks like a frog," one of the boys remarked.

"Mine's the one in the muumuu," said Jackie. "Anything for attention."

When the performance ended a crowd of parents and students milled around backstage. Karen hugged her daughter. "You were wonderful, darling."

Hillary was in a state of exhilaration and delight.

"In the first act you had me laughing and in the second act I was in tears," her mother told her.

"I thought you were going to forget the words," said Jackie.

"Who asked you, fatface?"

"No name-calling," said Karen.

It was midnight before she and her husband were in their room getting ready for bed. Henry Henning stood half in his closet folding his trousers over a hanger. His legs looked very long with no pants on. Very hairy too. His shirttails hung down over his boxer shorts. At her dressing table, watching him in her mirror, Karen was putting away her necklace, removing her earrings. She felt strangely excited. Her whole life seemed to her exciting. Her job was exciting. Watching her daughter tonight was exciting.

Once she had been in school plays herself, and she remembered them well, the tension of going onstage and then the exultation afterward, and the dreams she had had of becoming an actress. High school years. She gazed at herself in her mirror and remembered when her whole life was ahead of her but so far ahead she imagined she would never be able to wait that long. All that had happened since was then ahead of her: husband, children, her job, but she didn't know it and at times was filled with despair thinking it would never come. Or if it did she'd never get any of what she wanted. Instead she had got almost all of it.

Across the room her husband had begun humming. Their eyes met in the glass. In a moment, she knew from experience, would come a song of his own invention. Anticipating it, no longer a schoolgirl, pushing to one side her nostalgia but not her excitement, she began to smile.

"Have I told you this week that I love you?" Hank sang from the closet.

"You've barely seen me this week." She pulled a comb through her curls.

"Have I told you I miss you so much?" he sang, coming closer.

"Tell me again."

Putting his hands on her shoulders he began to nuzzle her neck. For a moment she watched him in the mirror, after which she closed her eyes and enjoyed it.

"Why are you so interested in me?" she said, standing, breaking away from him, starting to take her clothes off. "I'm an old married lady."

Watching him, not really expecting an answer, she undid the sleeves of her blouse, the buttons down the front. Hank hovered near her. All her attention was on him now and he knew it.

"Who said I'm interested in you?"

She moved away from him again, and continued undressing, her movements becoming more and more provocative. She got a nightgown out of a drawer. They were extremely aware of each other. All the while watching her, her husband too had been getting undressed, and when he came close to her she turned suddenly and bit his bare chest.

Then they were in bed in the dark, with nothing to be seen and only their voices and the movement of the bed to be heard.

"Sssh, the children will hear," murmured Karen.

"They won't know what it means."

The bed was squeaking badly. It made Karen giggle. "They're older than you think."

So he slowed what he was doing until the bed made less noise, almost none, his movements long and gentle now and oh so smooth, and his voice in her ear was almost a whisper.

"When we first started making love, every time I saw you I couldn't wait."

"Yes, I could tell."

"You always looked so cool."

"Cool? My knees were like jelly."

"Mine too."

"I was barely out of high school," she said. "Weren't you ashamed?"

"No."

"I wasn't either." She was writhing under him and could not have stopped if she wanted to. "You were the experienced older man."

"A junior in college."

"By now of course you're blasé."

"Do I feel blasé to you?"

"How can you still want to. It's been eighteen years." But it was becoming increasingly difficult for her to speak.

"Longer. We've been married eighteen years."

"Henry."

"Maybe the first time we did this I was more eager than tonight, but I doubt it."

"Do you want to know something? I'm in love with my husband."

"Maybe the first time it seemed more fabulous than now, but I doubt it."

"Don't—talk."

Later, her nerve ends still tingling, she lay awake, and it surprised her to realize how much, some nights, she liked to make love. Did other women her age enjoy it as much? Not from the way they talked. In her circle of women friends, suburban women mostly, the subject rarely came up, only occasionally, but from what they said, if you could believe them, they would most often like to pass. Usually she tried to say nothing at all, or if pressed agreed with them, though she didn't agree. Sex had its place, she would say firmly. But she would stop there. She didn't want some woman asking what she did, what Hank did.

In fact she could go days, weeks practically, sublimating it to her work, and to the needs of her children, submitting to her husband as necessary, sometimes with bad grace, and then a night like this would come along. How did you explain it? Was there something wrong with her? She shouldn't like it this much, perhaps. Tonight they had gone on and on, it had lasted almost forever, she had got all lathered up, and then at the end all the stars in the sky had seemed to fall on her at once. The sweat on her was only now drying, a sensation she luxuriated in, sweat honestly earned. Her skin still tingled. They had made love all different ways, she was embarrassed to count how many, including on her knees which she usually didn't like much, would do only when terrifically excited, but which sometimes, tonight certainly, aroused her beyond belief, she didn't know why, it didn't even feel that much nicer, except that presenting herself that way felt wicked. It stimulated her anew now just to think about it, her buttocks waving in the air, almost perverse, as if forbidden, him slamming into her. Anyway, terribly, terribly sexy.

Beside her, her husband slept peacefully, though she herself was in a state of sexual tension still.

— 3 —

In Harlem the day had been hot and the night had brought no breeze or coolness. As Barone and Muldoon moved through the dark streets, the windows were down and the hot air came in on their faces, their hands. Their shirts, their trousers were stuck to the seat. To stir in their seats they had to unglue themselves first.

The radio was lying on their coats on the seat between them, but it was silent. In the Three-Two all was quiet, no assaults, robberies, homicides so far. Again tonight Barone drove. Their pace was as slow as always. One could walk as fast. They eyed each group of street-corner idlers, studied each shadowy face. Any furtive movement would have stopped them, the hint of a crime being plotted or in progress, the glimpse of credit cards changing hands, or guns, or drugs.

"Fucken hot," said Muldoon. He had an open bottle of beer between his feet and a handkerchief on his lap with which he occasionally mopped his forehead.

There was a difference in the way they studied the groups they passed. Barone's gaze merely flicked from face to face, whereas Muldoon tried to lock eyes with anyone who would look at him. His cold hard stare was meant to intimidate the mutts, to reinforce the police presence in their minds if they had minds, a calculable weight on their lives and on their neighborhood. He dared any one of them to incur his displeasure, to step out of line in any way. Without the constant police pressure, himself and a few others, he believed, this place would become an even worse jungle than it was.

From time to time they crossed one of the sector cars on its rounds. Always the two cars gave each other horn toots, or brief waves of recognition. Muldoon felt sentimental about this. He was glad these other men were there. In a time of crisis, all you could count on was another cop.

Suddenly Barone braked hard and they jerked to a stop. "The one in the blue jacket," Barone cried, "grab him."

Both detectives threw their doors open, leaped out, and ran back the length of several parked cars, hands on their guns which, for the time being, remained holstered.

"You mutts up against the wall," Muldoon ordered.

It was two detectives against ten or more men—there wasn't time to count. Despite the odds no one questioned the authority in Muldoon's voice, or the right of two detectives, any two detectives, to jump out of a car and do what these two were doing. The men, all ten of them, moved sullenly to obey. They turned to the wall, their hands went up, and they leaned their weight against the bricks.

Barone had gone straight to a parked car, and then down on his knees to peer under it. After a moment he dragged out a kind of cloth purse closed by a drawstring, which he pulled open. He began nodding, and he showed his find to Muldoon: a small wad of money and a thousand or more crack vials.

Muldoon's face broke into a vast smile. "Well, well, well."

It was Barone's habit to watch in the rearview mirror after driving by each group of men—watch how they reacted after the car was past and they thought they were safe. It was a technique he had learned early in his career and it had brought him some good arrests. He took no particular credit for it, it was what a skilled detective did.

"The one in the blue jacket had this bag," Barone said.

"I saw it in the mirror. He dropped it to the sidewalk and kicked it under the car."

"Stupid fuck shoulda just stood there," chortled Muldoon.

"He shouldn't have tried to get rid of the evidence," agreed Barone. "We were already past, for God's sake."

Along with so much crack there ought to be a gun nearby, both detectives knew. At least one, maybe more, and additional money, the proceeds, unless the guy had just come out onto the street, which was possible. One by one Muldoon bent them over the nearest car, tossed them for weapons or money or drugs, then made them empty out their pockets onto the hood. Touching them was distasteful to him and he made sure they knew it. He found nothing. "Put that stuff back in your pockets," he told them one by one. "Now beat it. Scram. If I see your ugly face again tonight, I'll lock you up."

Barone, meanwhile, looked elsewhere for the missing gun or guns, and for the missing proceeds if any, and he started by feeling in under the fender wells of the nearby parked cars, patting the tops of the tires, feeling for whatever might be stashed there. When he found nothing, he moved to the curbside garbage cans, lifting the lids one by one, even stirring through the loose garbage on top. Next he went into the building where he felt atop the various ledges, and pushed at the letter boxes looking for a loose flap. But he found nothing.

They threw the man in the blue jacket, his hands cuffed behind him, into the car and as they headed back to the stationhouse, they began to interrogate him, Barone first, then Muldoon.

"What's your name?"

"Maurice."

"Maurice what?"

"Maurice Jackson."

Still watching the prisoner in the mirror, Barone said to Muldoon in a low voice:

"How much money in that sack?"

"Nothing. About $40."

Barone at the wheel was silent.

"In the old days," said Muldoon, "any cop worth his salt would take it."

Barone grinned at him. "There's no corruption in this department anymore."

"Not for years now."

"You can read it in the papers."

"And it's only $40."

Barone resumed talking to the prisoner. "How old are you, Maurice?"

"Twenty-two."

"You been inside before, Maurice?"

Maurice enumerated the various prisons in which he had done time. There was no point lying. The cops would call up his record.

"When you get out this time, you're going to be an old man, Maurice."

"I know that." For a moment all three men contemplated the vagaries of life: five minutes ago Maurice was imagining the night's profits, where he would go after work, who perhaps he might sleep with. Now he faced twenty years in jail.

"We could help you," said Muldoon. "You give us something, we give you something. That's the way it works."

Barone was driving even slower than before, making it last. "Give us something good," Muldoon said, "and maybe we let you go."

"You'd let me go?"

"You give us something, sure." Usually Muldoon would take whatever information the prisoner had, promising whatever it took, and then arrest him anyway. The deepest dungeon was too good for these mutts. He began to throw out names. "Give me one or the other, I'll let you go."

Maurice, obviously suffering, didn't know these people, he said. "Name someone else."

Muldoon went further afield: a major drug dealer named

Leroy. Or a man known as Assam who was believed to have killed a cop in the Two-Five a month ago. But Maurice didn't know them either.

"This mutt's not a dealer," Muldoon told Barone disgustedly. "He's a fucken mule. He's got nothing to sell. Let's take him in and lock him up."

Instead Barone pulled to the curb, where he spoke into the radio. "Two-squad holding one, Central. Request additional unit." After giving the address, he got out of the car to wait.

The surprised Muldoon joined him on the pavement. "What did you do that for?"

Within seconds three cars converged on the corner. Their drivers angled them in like the points of a star, and six cops wearing bulletproof vests and bulky with gear around the waist advanced on the detectives. One of them was a woman.

Negotiations began. Barone wanted to unload his prisoner. He wanted one of these sector cops to take him—take the arrest, do the paperwork, count the crack vials, take the prisoner to court.

The surprised Muldoon wanted to protest: Wait a minute, Mike, don't give that arrest away, I'll take it. But he was not quick enough.

The two pairs of male cops shook their heads, returned to their cars, and drove away. But the woman seemed interested. Her name, Muldoon remembered, was Maureen something— he was too far away to read her name tag—and Barone had been addressing his arguments principally to her anyway. He was practically courting her.

Muldoon hadn't had a good arrest recently. He needed one before some superior officer, the nigger lieutenant for instance, noticed and got on him. But it seemed beneath his dignity to insist on taking this one, not in front of a female officer—he didn't really think of Maureen as a female officer, but as "this young cunt."

While the woman's partner, a big burly guy almost as old as Muldoon, stared off in the other direction, wanting no part of it, Barone made his arguments in a low, persuasive voice.

Maureen was about twenty-three, and not long out of the police academy. It was a good strong arrest, Barone told her, and she hadn't had many of those yet. True, she'd be up all night doing the paperwork, perhaps taking the prisoner to court if she wasn't finished when the van came by, but he knew she was newly married and the overtime would surely come in handy.

"What about you?" Muldoon heard her ask somewhat suspiciously. "It would be a good arrest for you too."

"I want you to have it," Barone said, looking directly into her eyes.

Muldoon found himself imagining her with no clothes on. In the dim light she seemed to him gorgeous, and underneath all that gear she probably had a sexy figure. He supposed she wouldn't look twice at a man his age and girth, despite his knowledge of the streets and experience on the job.

Not long ago he was newly married himself, he heard Barone say. He remembered all the things you need to buy. If she would do him this favor, he would owe her one another day.

Finally Maureen grinned and agreed to take the arrest, and the prisoner was bundled across into the sector car.

Barone's gonna have her on her back before long, Muldoon thought enviously. I wonder if she knows it.

But as he watched the sector car drive off, he became angry. "Why did you give away our arrest?" he demanded of his partner.

The answer was exactly as he expected. "I can't work overtime tonight, I got a date with a lady."

They got back into the car. As they continued to circulate, Muldoon continued to burn.

Finally Barone headed back to the stationhouse. It was after midnight by then. They parked in front. Up in the squadroom Muldoon heard Barone on the phone to his wife. They lived way upstate in upper Westchester County. A number of other New York cops lived in the same town, Muldoon believed. Barone's two children were girls, six and eight. Muldoon had been up there once: a barbecue for the guys in the squad and their families. Bunch of fucken little kids running around.

Barone told his wife he wouldn't be home tonight, that he had an early court appearance and would grab a bed in the stationhouse dormitory. Muldoon overheard that much. But Barone spoke in too low a voice to hear the rest. He appeared to be sweet-talking her. Evidently she didn't believe in any court appearance, perhaps knew or suspected he was staying over to meet some woman.

Muldoon heard him say: "Kiss the little girls for me."

When he hung up Barone gave a sigh. "That's a highly suspicious woman."

"I wonder why," Muldoon said. There was irritation in his voice, but admiration too. "Let's go back out on the street."

"Why?"

They had about thirty minutes left in their tour.

"Something may happen," Muldoon said.

"I want to see how Maureen is getting on."

She and a uniformed sergeant were in the interrogation room, a windowless cubicle off the squadroom. They could see them through the open door. The rule said that drugs seized by a uniformed officer had to be counted in the presence of a sergeant. Maureen was seated at the table placing crack vials into empty bullet boxes. The sergeant was reading a newspaper, paying no attention.

"Have you fucked every female officer in this precinct, or what?" Muldoon asked his partner.

"Well," answered Barone with a grin, "not her." And he gestured toward the interrogation room.

"Yet," said Muldoon.

There were thirty women assigned to the Three-Two, up from zero when Muldoon was a young detective.

Barone got up and went in there.

"I'll take over now, Sarge," Muldoon heard him say.

The sergeant came out and went downstairs. Barone did not close the door, and the reason, Muldoon suspected, was to display his presumed triumph to the rest of the squad. Maureen had taken off her hat, her gear, the vest. She had blondish hair and a rather big bosom. Her uniform blouse looked stretched tight across it. To Muldoon she looked very young and very nice.

He saw Barone sit down opposite her and begin helping her put vials into bullet boxes, all the time talking to her in a low voice. The boxes held fifty bullets or fifty vials. When finished she would have to count only the boxes.

About twenty minutes later Muldoon looked in again. They had finished counting, but were still talking. Or rather Maureen was talking with great animation, while Barone, opposite, gazed directly into her eyes.

Muldoon decided to interrupt. "How many vials?" he asked, standing in the doorway.

"One thousand eight hundred and eighty-two," said Maureen.

"Maureen lives near me," Barone said. "Her father was a sergeant in the Five-Two. Both her brothers are cops too. That's why she came on the job herself. Her husband is a plumber. That's high-paying work. For the last several months she's been trying every way possible to get pregnant, but no luck so far."

Muldoon was offended by the reference to pregnancy. To him such private subjects should not be talked about to strangers or in mixed company. At least Maureen had the grace to blush, he noted.

"I really appreciate this, Maureen," said Barone, getting up from the table. "You working tomorrow night? I'll take you out after work and buy you a drink."

But Maureen was off the next two nights.

"Friday night, then," said Barone.

Maureen went back downstairs and the detectives—there were five of them in the squadroom at this time—straightened out their desks and prepared to sign out and close up.

"Quiet night," Barone commented, waiting his turn to sign. "Absolutely routine."

"Nothing happened," said Muldoon.

But just then the phone rang.

Muldoon took it. "Three-Two squad, Detective Muldoon."

The caller was a detective from the Four-One, across the river. He wanted any information they might have on a perpetrator named Lionel Epps. "Do you guys know him over there?"

Muldoon knew him, but pretended otherwise. "Would you spell that name," he said. "Has he got a B-number?"

He pretended to take this information down.

"I'll ask around," said Muldoon. In the police business you gave up information only in exchange for something else. He said carefully: "What's he supposed to have done?"

The conversation lasted some minutes, during which Barone stood attentively over Muldoon's desk. Finally Muldoon rang off.

"Lionel Epps is wanted in the Four-One," he announced, looking up.

"Homicide?"

"Yeah."

"Doesn't surprise me."

"The guy says he's become a major mover in the South Bronx."

Barone thought this over. "It's possible. Who's he supposed to have killed?"

"A dealer bigger than him. Rolled him up in a rug, shot him eight times, and set him on fire."

"Nice," said Barone.

"He's supposed to be taking over the entire division."

"I didn't figure he was that enterprising," said Barone. "Or that smart. Where is he supposed to be?"

"In the wind."

Barone nodded. "Came back here, most probably."

"Guy says he knows they're after him and that he's armed to the teeth."

"Dangerous, yes," said Barone. "That I believe."

The two detectives went back to the book and signed out. They were the last to leave the squadroom.

"What are we going to do?" said Muldoon.

"Look for him," said Barone. "We'll start looking tomorrow. If he's in the precinct he shouldn't be too hard to find."

They went down the stairs and out past the desk and the offices and stood on the stoop outside. The city was quiet and they breathed in the night air.

"Sleep well, Dan," Barone said.

Muldoon gave him a leer. "You won't be doing much sleeping, if I know you."

"I'm late," said Barone. "Maybe she won't have waited."

"For you they usually wait." In a way Muldoon was proud of his partner's supposed sexual prowess.

They walked across the street to their cars. "And tomorrow we'll look for Epps," said Muldoon.

"See you tomorrow," Barone said. "Go on home now, and don't drink too much beer when you get there. Try to get a good night's sleep for a change." There was concern in his voice. "You've been looking lousy lately." He put his arm around Muldoon and gave him an affectionate squeeze. "Good night, Danny."

"Good night, Mike."

Barone's thoughts as he got into his car were already focused on the woman who waited for him ahead. He started the engine and pulled out of the slot.

As he watched his partner drive away, Muldoon felt the loneliness come down on him hard. He was used to it. It happened every night once he had signed out and left the stationhouse, and tonight was no exception.

—— 4 ——

The village of Bronxville, one square mile, six thousand people, is one of the smallest and closest New York suburbs to the north, and one of the most exclusive. It is a place of steep hills and narrow streets under great old trees. It reeks of money. The houses are English Tudor, or Georgian, or French Château, and they are big, mansions most of them, built in stone or brick with slate or tile roofs, and full of turrets and gables, with leaded windows and terraces bordered with wrought-iron fences. The houses and the trees towering over them stand close together as if someone had jammed them in there, each on a piece of property that is too small for it. All of the lawns and plantations are impeccably tended by gardeners, the hedges and bushes cropped just so, the flowers of each season always in bloom.

The main street, called Pondfield Road, descends past the houses, passes several handsome churches, and then the police station, which is a noble brick edifice that puts the Three-Two stationhouse to shame. It passes the school which is a city block long and which, with its Gothic windows and tall chimneys, resembles the vast manor house of some English duke, and then enters the village proper, the shopping district. Two-story buildings stand at either side of the tree-lined street, and most of them are timbered in the Tudor style. Antique shops, art galleries, real estate offices. Chic clothing shops too, at least one of which sells maids' uniforms. The real estate agents call Bronxville the "Golden Square Mile" for obvious reasons. Though only about ten miles north of Harlem, it is, as they say, a whole world removed.

Karen Henning's house was on the outskirts of all this, and much less grand, a rambling Victorian that was in need of a coat of paint. She stood this Saturday morning in her kitchen making pies to go in the freezer. Today was her baking day, and her hands were dusty with flour. It was pleasant, mindless work. She thought of it as something to clear her head of the sordid details of her job.

When she and Hank were house-hunting they had searched this whole area, wanting to find clean air and good schools for the children. They had settled on Bronxville not to be among the wealthy but because they had found a house which, as it was in poor condition, they could afford. They had barely been able to make the down payment and even with both of them working they sometimes had trouble with the carrying charges. But it was good here, especially for the kids. She was under no illusions about Bronxville. Compared to New York, it sometimes seemed unreal. "We have no poor people, blacks, or crime," she sometimes remarked, adding with a laugh: "In every other way, our town is as typical as any place in America."

She was alone in her house this morning. Hank was playing tennis, Hillary was out on her bike, and Jackie, calling, "I'm going, Mom," had just gone out the front door. From the kitchen window she saw the car go by a moment later. The back seat was full of kids. Jackie was sitting beside Mrs. Price, who was driving, and he waved to Karen.

Not five minutes later her front doorbell rang. She went to it and an agitated woman she didn't know said: "Come quick, there's been a bad accident."

Instant, heart-stopping terror. Karen wore an apron over jeans and a sweater. Her hair and sleeves were white with flour and she went running out of the house behind the woman and her only thought was that Hillary on her bike had been hit by a car.

She rounded the corner and it wasn't Hillary, it was Jackie. Mrs. Price's car was wrapped around a tree and Jackie lay on the grass beside it bleeding from the face and moaning. She was vaguely aware that there were other moans besides his, someone else on the grass and bleeding badly: Mrs. Price. People were standing over her, and over Jackie too. And that the other boys, the ones from the back seat, stood close together as if afraid they were going to be blamed. And that ten or a dozen people had come out of nearby houses; they were gawking too.

She ran to Jackie, and those around him backed off. His face looked ruined, especially his mouth, and there was blood everywhere. She was on her knees and she lifted his head and cradled it.

"Mommy," he said, "Mommy."

"Mommy's here, darling, you're going to be fine."

His front teeth had been bashed in. She couldn't tell, there was so much blood. They looked bashed in to her. She did not want to look. It's not fair, she thought, those teeth are almost new, he only just got them. She wanted to weep or faint, but her child needed his mother, meaning he needed her calm. She wanted to cry out for Hank but did not even know where he was.

She looked up at the people standing around and said in a voice as calm as she could manage: "Did anyone call the ambulance?"

"It's on its way," someone said.

A police car turned into the street and a young cop got out. Karen heard him on his radio call for a wrecker.

First things first, she thought. It's not his son.

Next she heard him say to the crowd: "Did anybody see it happen?" No one had. He went over to Mrs. Price and bent down and tried to get her name, but all he got was moans. The woman's face was badly lacerated, Karen saw, and she glanced over at the car. The windshield was pushed out where the heads had struck it. It was splintered and opaque, and part was missing.

There was a picture stuck in her head of her twelve-year-old boy having to wear false teeth. She could think of almost nothing else. Now the cop was trying to move the bystanders back, though why? They weren't really close and not in the way. They would take two steps back and then, as soon as he had moved on, two steps forward.

He said to the other boys: "What happened?"

"The ball went in her lap," one boy said.

"Yeah, and she hit the tree," said another.

"Who threw the ball?"

The boys looked at each other. No one answered.

Two ambulances came. They loaded Mrs. Price into the first one, Jackie into the second. The wrecker was just pulling up. Karen got into the ambulance with her son and held his hand all the way to the hospital. He seemed to be at least partly in shock. From time to time he would look up at her and say: "Mommy." Otherwise he said nothing.

In the emergency room she sat holding his hand waiting for the dental surgeon. On the other side of the curtain Mrs. Price sometimes moaned, sometimes screamed as a doctor plucked shards of glass out of her face. Karen heard him say: "You're going to need some plastic surgery, I'm afraid."

The dentist came. He was very young. Karen wished he were older. He cleaned the blood off Jackie's face and she saw that his face was intact. Most of the blood had come from inside his mouth.

The dentist injected novocaine and while they waited for it to take effect he and Karen occasionally smiled at each other. She wanted to ask about Jackie's teeth but didn't dare. She could not accept the idea of a little boy with false teeth.

The dentist went to work. First he sewed up the inside of the mouth, all the while humming a tune of his own invention. Then he started on the teeth. He had his gear in what was almost a fishing tackle box, and he put bands on the teeth and began to wire them up. Karen could not look. She went outside the curtain, where she stood silently weeping.

"Mrs. Henning," the dentist called.

She wiped her eyes and went back in.

"We're one short."

"What?"

"There's one missing."

He peeled back Jackie's ruined lip and showed her.

It started her weeping again.

"Where could that sucker be?" the dentist said.

"I don't know."

"Do you think you could find it?"

"I don't know."

"If you could find it, I could stick that baby back in."

"I'll try."

"Find the car and you find the tooth. Of course sometimes they swallow it. Or spit it out on the grass."

She took Jackie's hand. "I have to go out and find your tooth, baby. I'll be right back."

He seemed calm, so she left him. She didn't want to leave him but had to. She ran out through the emergency room determined to find the tooth but with no idea how she was going to do it, and the young cop was there copying Mrs. Price's name off the admission form.

"Where was the car taken?" Karen demanded.

He looked at her in surprise.

"Please," said Karen, "please."

The cop began to look through his notebook. He seemed to take his time about it. Having found the page, he read off the name of the garage and she rushed out of the hospital, realizing only as she reached the street that she had no car. No money either. She ran up in front of the hospital and waited several minutes pacing and fretting until a taxi pulled up to let people out. She jumped in and gave the address of the garage.

The wreck was there. She made the driver wait and ran over to it. The side window had been shattered too and the floor was strewn with bits of glass, jagged little pieces, some of them bloody, and with junk that had fallen out of the glove box too. She pawed through all this and found no tooth, and started through it again and still found no tooth, and felt her eyes fill up with tears.

But she wiped them away and made the driver take her to the scene of the accident where she got down on her knees and combed through the bloody grass, back and forth, parting each blade, a tooth was so small, it could be anywhere. It could be on the floor of the ambulance, it could have been stomped into the turf by any of the bystanders.

But finally there the tooth was, standing straight up in the grass, the root bloody, flesh and bone adhering to it. She jumped up holding it triumphantly between thumb and forefinger.

She made the taxi wait outside the emergency room, the meter running, and ran in and handed the tooth to the dentist. She watched him disinfect it, holding it with tongs and dipping it repeatedly into a solution, but she looked away when he turned back to her son. She heard rather than saw him thrust it back where it belonged, heard the noise as he pushed hard, and then heard him wire it there.

He took her outside the room and gave her a vial of pain pills. "He's going to be in some discomfort when the injection wears off," the dentist said.

She asked the question that had tormented her for an hour. "Will he—will he lose his teeth?"

"We'll have to see."

It was only the answer she had expected, and it left her more tormented than ever.

"How—I mean—what chance is there?"

He had his toolbox with him and had set it down on a table. He was rearranging the contents.

"Often they take," he said. He was concentrated on his box, not her. She wanted to fling the box across the room.

"Even the one I just found?"

"There's a good chance." He looked up and smiled at her.

"Stop worrying. He'll be fine." He put his hand on her arm. "There's an excellent chance, really."

She felt tears in her eyes and she wanted to embrace him.

Instead she walked Jackie out to the taxi and they were driven home. Jackie was groggy and said nothing, and she sat with her arm around him, holding him close.

At her house she again asked the driver to wait. She took Jackie up to his room and put him to bed.

"I'll be right back, darling," she told him.

Having found her purse, she went out of the house to pay the driver. It took every cent she had.

When she went back to Jackie's room he had fallen asleep. She sat beside his bed staring at the battered twelve-year-old face, holding his hand and weeping. She was still there when she heard Hank come home. She went out and told him, and together they entered the bedroom and stood looking down on their son.

Jackie woke in the afternoon and she gave him a pill and a cup of broth that he drank through a straw. For supper she brought him more broth, and he fell asleep again. Hillary came home and was warned not to disturb her brother.

"Are his teeth going to fall out, Mom?"

"I don't know."

She and Hank went to bed with both doors open. She heard the boy several times in the night and got up and went to him and gave him pills or something to drink and sat with him till he had gone back to sleep.

— 5 —

There is a spaciousness about Harlem that is absent from the rest of New York. The parks laid out so long ago are still there, the boulevards are still wide, the downtown skyscrapers are so far off as to be out of sight and mind. There seems to be more air to breathe. One can see the sky in all directions.

Most of the gracious buildings of old Harlem still stand, and walking by, one can see how luxurious they must have been in their day with their decorated stoops and iron balconies and, in those places where doors remain, their once handsome doors. Many buildings have been abandoned, of course. Some have been torched, whether accidentally or on purpose one can no longer say. One peers up through scorched window frames at absent or partially absent roofs, at parts of the intervening floors inside. Such buildings have been condemned by the building department; their neighbors to either side, having been rendered unstable by the fire, usually have been condemned too.

Theoretically, condemned buildings must remain empty until demolished. Accordingly, the building department seals their doorways with cinderblocks, and over their windows nails sheets of aluminum that sometimes reflect the sun like mirrors. But in Harlem the theoretical does not hold, for the city condemns buildings quicker than it can take them down. In the meantime the cinderblocks can be staved in, permitting entrance, after which the sheet aluminum can be ripped off and sold, the window moldings too, and much else. Such buildings, once they have been broken open, make excellent sales outlets for drug dealers, excellent playgrounds for children.

Certain among them make excellent homes for the homeless as well, for electric wires can be plugged into hallway light sockets in neighboring buildings and strung across, providing current both for light and for electric heaters. This makes the condemned building habitable, more or less, and to otherwise homeless people even attractive, although at considerable risk of fire. The homeless move in, build fires on the floor, and perhaps cook something. For a time they can imagine they are living in a house just like everyone else.

When such buildings become inhabited, the police know it. But cops are not in the business of rousting squatters. They ignore them. It's not their job. It's the building department's job. To do a building inspector's work is beneath them.

Of the elevated railways that once laced Harlem like stitching, only two remain. On the west side heading north the Broadway subway still comes out of the face of what was once a naked cliff and crosses what was once Harlem Plains high up on trestles. Over on the east side the Metro North tracks emerge from under the street just as they reach the edge of Harlem. The street happens to be Park Avenue, which, a few blocks to the south, is the richest street in the city: its co-ops boast the highest maintenance charges, the most arrogant doormen. But the tracks there are under the pavement. In Harlem the trestles and their stanchions turn Park Avenue into blocks of darkness, among which move frightening shadows, prison bars of a sort. The noise and vibration of the trains shakes every thing and person nearby. Nearly all of the tenements and other buildings that face the track are empty and in ruins.

Beside the tracks between 127th and 128th streets, there

stood just such a row of condemned brownstones. The one at the southeast corner had collapsed or been demolished, and the city had put a chain link fence around the lot where it once had stood. But at some previous time the fence had been hacked through in places. The lot therefore was strewn with old mattresses, wrecked furniture and appliances, parts of cars, broken bottles——in addition of course to the piles of building rubble and the weeds. By day neighborhood children frolicked in this lot. It was their playground. Nights their elders used it as a garbage dump.

The other buildings on the block were supposed to be sealed and empty, but the middle one had been broken into, and a number of men, each in a separate room, were asleep inside. They were unknown to each other. One, a man who had been recently released from an asylum, had dragged a cardboard carton in from the street. He was never without his carton, and each time one disintegrated he was desperate until he had found another. He whimpered constantly. On this particular night he lay within his carton in a corner of the room he had chosen, which was on the ground floor, and he whimpered even in his sleep.

He had a name but no longer knew what it was.

One flight up lived a wino. He shambled out each day and pan-handled and when he had collected enough money he bought a bottle of cheap wine, the sweeter the better, and shambled back to his room and drank it. For a while after it was gone he sat in a corner talking to himself. Sometimes he dozed most of the day. The room reeked of the different wines, a sweetly sickening alcoholic odor, mixed with the stench of urine, and the place was crowded with empties. When the trains went by outside, the vibration sometimes caused bottles to roll across the floor.

The wino too had a name but had not heard anyone speak it in a long time.

On the floor above him slept a third man, a youth really, twenty-one years old. When awake he was exceedingly nervous, pacing the bare room, constantly approaching the window to peer down on the street through a place where he had pried up a corner of the building department's aluminum—he had made it curl outward the way the corner of a photo might curl in an album. He had been there three days without going out. At present he slept under a coat and some newspapers. His belongings in a sack served as his pillow, and he was surrounded by guns: handguns beside his head, a rifle and shotgun alongside his body. Above him part of the roof was gone, and his sleeping form was partly illuminated by moonlight. The trains blasting by his bedroom were only the width of the sidewalk away, but he did not hear them.

Down in the street a car slowly approached, gliding silently to a stop. He did not hear this either. The driver, who was Detective Muldoon, opened his door soundlessly, and just as soundlessly stepped out of the car. He took out a cigar and bit the tip off it, but did not light it. He was alone. Chewing on his cigar he leaned over the car door, his chin on his arms, and studied the building. But he kept glancing up the street, plainly waiting for someone. The time was well past midnight. He rolled the cigar around in his mouth.

Presently he reached into his car for a flashlight, checked that it worked, then went over to the doorway, where he pointed the light in past the broken cinderblocks, illuminating the vestibule in which there was nothing significant to be seen. Piles of rubble. Wrecked mailboxes hanging off the wall. Cockroaches surprised by the light: glittering black shells that skittered back into darkness.

Again Muldoon glanced up the avenue. It was Barone he was waiting for, who still had not come.

Turning, he walked up the sidewalk, and he studied what his flashlight showed him, mostly doorways, windows. Some were blocked, not all. Though heavy, he moved as silently as the beam of light he played over each building in turn. Finally he flicked the light off and returned to his car. Once again he was alone in the dark.

Another car entered the street some blocks up. He watched

it approach. It came slowly, silently, and glided to a stop in its turn. Muldoon went over to the driver's side.

"He's in there," Muldoon said.

Barone nodded. "Lionel Epps. Well—"

"Right, Epps."

"He's supposed to be heavily armed," Barone said. "You know goddam well he's violent."

"He's probably asleep."

"I tell you what you do," Barone suggested. "You call in Emergency Service. Let them do it."

"Those guys."

"That's their job. They got body armor. They got shotguns."

"We could take him."

"You take him, not me."

Muldoon said nothing. He studied first the building, then Barone. Both men had already signed out and were off duty.

"If you think I'm going in there, you're crazy," said Barone, but he sounded uncomfortable with the decision.

Muldoon still said nothing.

"I got another idea," said Barone. They were talking in whispers.

"What?"

"Get the prick out into the street so we can shoot the fuck."

"How?"

"You get some old newspapers," said Barone. "You pile them up in the vestibule, you take a match, you throw it in on top. As soon as it's going good you scream Fire. When the dickhead comes running out—"

"The whole block might go up," said Muldoon. "You'll have five hundred fire trucks here."

"I was joking, Danny. Christ, I really shouldn't joke around you."

"Let's see who else we can get," said Muldoon after a pause.

Barone nodded. "That's the best idea you've had yet."

Putting the car in gear, Barone drove off as quietly as he had come.

Muldoon went back to his car, eased his bulk behind the wheel. For a moment he merely sat there, listening hard. Nothing. Distant traffic noises. A siren. Faint music from somebody's radio, blocks away. Around him, except for the soft purring of his motor, the silence was as nearly total as one ever gets in a city. He put his car in gear and, holding the half-closed door in place, crept off. He was a block and a half away before he slammed the door shut and speeded up.

An hour passed, perhaps more. Lionel Epps slept on. A train went by, shaking the building, but he did not stir. Suddenly down in the street a car door slammed, and he was instantly alert, on his feet, gun in hand. He went to the window where he nudged the aluminum sheeting to one side. It was almost like parting curtains in a house in which people lived. He peered down: police cars with men pouring out of them, some in uniform, some not.

Epps's panic was instantaneous. He became bathed in sweat. His eyes glazed. He nearly fainted.

In fact there were two groups of cops, one at the corner, one in front of his door. They eyed each other suspiciously, and for a moment neither group moved. But Epps did not notice this, much less consider what it might mean. That one of the men was Muldoon and another Barone did not register. Epps knew them both, but was beyond recognizing them or anyone else. Then both groups started running. Some covered the back. Some entered other buildings. Some entered his building.

He heard all this as much as he saw it. He had been sleeping in his clothes: jeans, sneakers, a dirty T-shirt. He rammed guns in his belt, then ran to the back of the floor. His panic had already passed. The sheet metal had been half torn off the rear window too, but as he started to climb out onto the fire escape he heard voices coming up, voices coming down. He was trapped.

The cops combed the downstairs rooms first. They were led by Muldoon, whose cigar was now lit. He was smoking it, posing, pretending to be bulletproof, which he was not, behaving as if he were in charge, which was not the case either. As the later investigations would bring out—there would be many investigations—no one was in charge. All of the men present were detectives or police officers. Detectives hold no command rank, not Muldoon, not any of them, and there were no sergeants or above present. In addition, the men approaching Epps's sanctuary were all from the 32nd Precinct, whereas this building was in the 25th, so they were out of their jurisdiction as well.

Except for Muldoon, all had their guns out. They stepped over rubbish, peered into empty rooms, shone flashlights into the eyes of the other sleeping men to whom the condemned tenement was home.

The wretch inside the carton came awake. "What's up, man?" he whimpered. "What I done?"

"That's not him," said Muldoon.

They climbed. Their flashlight beams converged again: a face in a halo of light, but no saint. The dirty, unshaven, suddenly illuminated drunk.

"Keep going," ordered Muldoon.

They climbed another flight of stairs. In a moment they would come to Epps's room. In it he stood with his shotgun pointed at the closed door.

Muldoon stopped at each door in turn. He posed, cigar between his teeth. His lack of fear was probably real. "These mutts don't scare me," he had said often enough.

"This is Detective Muldoon speaking. You hear me, Epps. Come out with your hands up."

Muldoon kicked in the door. Epps was not behind this one, and nothing happened. He went on to the next.

"This is Detective Muldoon, Epps. Come out with your hands up."

He kicked open this door, and again nothing happened. No Epps, no shotgun blast. He went on to the next.

"You're surrounded, Epps. Come out with—"

He kicked the door open and Epps fired the shotgun. Muldoon went down and two other cops with him. They lay on the floor, covered with blood. A fourth cop jumped into the room and was shot. Epps threw away his shotgun and ran back through the floor. When he came to the rear room a cop was climbing in the window. Epps shot him, dove past him onto the fire escape, and shot down at still another cop climbing up toward him. Since he could see more cops in the courtyard, he decided to climb up, not down.

He ran out onto the roof. There were cops running toward him across the adjacent rooftops, one of them Barone. They were three roofs away, two. He shot, and kept on shooting. He had two 9-mm automatics, thirteen bullets in each clip and one in each chamber. More than enough. The cops were hiding behind a parapet, firing at him. Then he was past them, racing across more rooftops. He came to the last in the row and was forced to descend. Jumping out onto the front fire escape, he went down the steps two at a time, feet clattering, never a step missed, even in the dark. At the bottom he heaved himself over the railing, hung for a moment, and dropped to the sidewalk.

Of the cops Muldoon had been able to gather, five had carried hand radios. One of the five was now unconscious. The other four, some of them bleeding, were all trying to transmit at once.

"Shots fired, Central. Shots fired at this time."

"Officer down, Central. Officer down."

They were cutting each other off.

"Signal ten-thirteen, assist police officer."

"Two cops shot. Two cops shot." Actually the number was five. "Send ambulances, Central."

"What location?" Central shouted. "Give me a location."

These transmissions went into every radio car in the Sixth Division—Harlem. The sirens came on at once, the flashing lights. But no one knew where to go, and these cars too began transmitting, overlapping each other's voices.

"Location. Location."

"Christ, where are you?"

Finally one of the wounded cops managed to gasp out the address and be understood.

All sector cars from the Three-Two were already at the scene, though they should not have been. Two detective cars were there as well. The Three-Two was not being patrolled at all, meaning no further help could come from that direction, only from the two other Harlem precincts. The Two-Five had five cars on patrol at this hour, the Two-Eight, seven. All twelve cars responded. They responded instantly, sirens blasting, tires screeching. They converged from all directions at great speed, and also at great risk to themselves and to every other car or pedestrian abroad at that hour.

Epps on the sidewalk did not know which way to run. He stood amid el stanchions. He stood amid police cars, all double-parked, all empty. For the moment there were no cops, no pursuit. But he could hear the sirens coming, the squealing tires. Ramming his guns into his belt, he glanced this way, then that, prepared to run in any direction, but which one? The light he stood in was bizarre. Streetlights that cast strange shadows. Reflections off windshields. He knew he hadn't shot everybody. He heard the noise of the cops he had so far evaded. They were running, shouting, pouring out onto the sidewalk. He had no time left. He must run, run.

Suddenly a taxi came out of a side street. Its overhead light was lit, which meant it was empty. If it was or wasn't did not matter to Epps, who believed he was saved. Not that he could expect it to stop. This was Harlem, the middle of the night. Cabs didn't stop in Harlem at night for young blacks. Most cabbies wouldn't go into Harlem at all for anyone, some of them even by day, and few cabbies would pick up fares like Epps at any time anywhere in the city.

The cab approached Epps, coming fast. He was in the street waving his arms. The driver saw him. It made him come even faster. He swerved, had no intention of stopping, but Epps leaped out in front of him. The headlights were on him. He didn't dodge for safety.

The driver had no choice, he must stop or kill another human being. Habit prevailed. Brakes screeched. The cab slithered, stopped. Instantly the driver had it moving forward again. As Epps came alongside, the cab was already moving, spurting ahead. Whatever was happening, the driver wanted no part of it.

He was fast, but Epps was younger, faster. He wrenched the door open, though it almost took his hand off, and tumbled inside. "Drive, man," he screamed. He had his guns out again, one of them pushed into the nape of the cabbie's neck.

The cab, which was pointed toward the parked police cars, couldn't turn around. There were too many stanchions, too many cars. It could move in one direction only.

Cops had come out of the building, out of the alley. They were jumping off fire escapes. They were down on one knee firing at the cab. Epps was hanging out the window, his guns spitting. He was pulling triggers as fast as he could. Eight or ten cops were firing at the taxi, which rammed a stanchion and stopped. The crash sent Epps headfirst into the doorjamb.

Lights flashing, sirens wailing, the support cars came speeding up from both directions, and they sandwiched the cab. Doors flew open. Cops jumped to the street with guns drawn. Other cops out of the building ran up, and the cab's doors were torn open. They dragged the dazed and unresisting Epps out into the night, threw him over the front fender, whacked him in the head a few times with gun butts, twisted his arms back, and slapped handcuffs on him.

A moment later Muldoon reached the cab. He was breathing hard and blood was leaking down his face as he grabbed Epps by the hair. He yanked the head back as if to break the neck, and this was enough to throw light onto Epps's features.

"It's him," said Muldoon, and he hurled the handcuffed youth back onto the cab, which Epps struck with the side of his face.

More police cars were pulling up all the time. Some had come all the way from the South Bronx. Strange cops ran forward with guns drawn. The sidewalks began to fill up with spectators, though where they might have come from at this hour in this burnt-out area was a mystery. Ambulances arrived, all howling.

The excitement was nearly over. Guns had gone back into holsters. About thirty cops were standing around. Although the sirens suddenly went silent, the scene remained illuminated by dozens of flashing roof lights. The colors, thought Barone, were hallucinatory, impressionistic, phantasmagoric.

He had made his way down from the roof, and now pushed through the crowd of cops.

"You okay?" he asked his partner.

"Yeah," said Muldoon, but when he touched himself at the hair-line, he felt a lump which he squeezed, and a piece of buckshot popped out from under his scalp. The pellet lay in his hand and he scrutinized it.

"Read him his rights," said Barone.

Again Epps's head was yanked back by the hair. "You have a right to remain silent, fuckface," said Muldoon. "You understand that, mutt? You have a right—"

Barone watched. There was a half smile on his face though what it might have signified even he didn't know. He was unhurt, virtually unmussed. He wore a dark gray pinstripe suit that was still buttoned neatly over the bulletproof vest, plus the usual thin Italian shoes. His black hair was still combed straight back.

Muldoon too was wearing a vest. It looked somewhat shredded, Barone saw, but it had saved him. He never wore one normally even though regulations required them for all cops at all times. Tonight he had put one on at the last minute to please Barone, who had insisted on it.

"How's the cab driver?" Muldoon asked.

Aware that no sound or movement emanated from within the cab, Barone had bent to peer inside.

"He doesn't look too good, as a matter of fact."

Muldoon too peered inside the cab, after which the two men eyed each other briefly.

"I foresee a few problems down the road," said Barone.

"Problems?"

Barone nodded. "Problems."

"Fuck it," said Muldoon.

Paramedics, having thrown open their ambulances, were unloading stretchers, oxygen tanks, and other gear, were hurrying across the sidewalk into the building. They knew nothing yet about any cab driver, and in any case, cops came first.

A uniformed sergeant from the Two-Five pushed through the crowd of cops. "Who's in command here?"

"I guess you are, Sarge," said Barone.

The sergeant's jaw came out. "So what the fuck happened?"

"Good question."

"Come on, come on."

Barone said: "I think a crime scene needs to be established here, Sarge, don't you?"

The explosion of violence had lasted a few seconds only. It was now over, and in a short time would be difficult even to reconstruct.

But the night's work had just begun. There were notifications to be made, statements to be taken, a prisoner to be processed. In a few minutes a lieutenant arrived, superseding the sergeant, and a few minutes after that a captain drove up who superseded both.

The captain asked for a report. "Christ, what a ballsup," the lieutenant began.

Within an hour the captain too had been superseded. The street now swarmed with brass, all of them unhappy. An inspector from Division was there; and the borough commander, who was an assistant chief, two stars; and the chief of patrol, who wore three. The brass had been routed out of beds in distant suburbs. They were as grim-faced about being awakened as about the mess they were now forced to confront.

An assistant district attorney arrived from downtown in the back of a police car. It was Doug Van Horn, who worked for Karen Henning. He had been on duty, a job that fell to him about one night a month. He had been half asleep in his chair, half watching the small television set on his desk. Now he moved through the street taking down names, listening to explanations. According to the rules of the DA's office, whoever caught a case got to take it all the way to trial, and he was pleased. With so many cops shot this was a big case but it should be easy to win. It could make his career.

He was the only one in the street who was pleased. It was past 2 A.M. before the chief of detectives, who lived forty miles out on Long Island, was driven up, followed by the deputy commissioner for public information, who was coming from northern Westchester County, and who huddled immediately with his duty sergeant, for the sergeant, already on the scene, presumably knew something. Both men, as they conferred, anxiously eyed the small group of reporters and TV crewmen who also had gathered here in the middle of the night and who had been waiting with increasing impatience for a police spokesman to give them some kind of official report.

The police commissioner, likewise routed from his bed, had responded not to the scene but directly to Harlem Hospital, as had the mayor, and they sat side by side in a hallway for the rest of the night, waiting to see if the various cops on the tables upstairs would live or die. This was tradition. It was considered a political necessity. Meanwhile, the cops' wives and children had been picked up at home by patrol cops in radio cars and chauffeured to the hospital. One by one they trickled in, and to each one the PC and mayor murmured consoling platitudes while trying to look solemn and concerned.

But most of the wives were stony-faced, as if blaming the two officials for the night's events that had so altered their lives.

About 3 A.M., having spent more than two hours answering the increasingly irate questions of superior officers, Muldoon appeared in the emergency room to have his scalp stitched up. His detective's shield was still pinned to the lapel of his bloody sports coat.

The PC spied him leaving the emergency room and hurried across.

Muldoon was not a man to be intimidated by headquarters brass, any brass, including police commissioners, neither this one nor any other, especially not now. The role of headquarters, as he saw it, was to screw cops for the sake of political expediency, and he foresaw getting screwed over what had happened tonight.

"You're shot, man," said the PC, who had never seen Muldoon before and had no idea what his part in the shoot-out had been.

Muldoon eyed him. "I hit my head on a door."

"Well," said the PC, momentarily at a loss, "in that case, well, er, keep up the good work."

Muldoon gave him a curt nod and went out.

Barone was waiting outside in the car. He too had been answering questions for hours. Together they drove downtown and found a bar that was still open, where Muldoon stared into his beer alternately muttering and cursing.

"They're going to fuck us," he said repeatedly. "Bartender," he called, "gimme another one of these."

Altogether he drank five beers. Barone nursed one scotch and soda. After a time Barone stood up.

"Tomorrow's going to be worse," he advised. "Better go home and get some sleep. I'll drive you back to your car."

Muldoon's car was across the street from the stationhouse. Barone watched him carefully as he got into it. "You sure you're all right to drive?"

For an answer, Muldoon let out the clutch with a jerk. The

tires squealed, and he took off across 135th Street in the direction of the Harlem River bridges.

His two-room apartment was in the Fordham section of the Bronx. He let himself in, went straight to the refrigerator and pulled out a six-pack, then switched on the television and found himself a place on the sofa opposite. That is, he brushed old newspapers and other trash off onto the floor and sat down. The apartment had not been cleaned or even dusted in some weeks. He began working his way through the six-pack. About dawn he fell into a stupor that was akin to sleep.

By then Lionel Epps had been arraigned and held without bail, and a number of investigations had been ordered and were under way. What crimes had been committed, if any? Which regulations had been broken, if any? Who was responsible, and also, who could it be pinned on?—not the same question by any means. How had such a fiasco happened? Which procedures should be changed so that nothing like this could happen again? What was the city at large to be told?

The precinct commander was investigating, for he believed his job was on the line. The chief of detectives had men investigating, and he had already sacked the lieutenant who commanded the Three-Two detective squad. Phoned him up, woke him up, and when he had reached the scene told him to report to headquarters for reassignment. The borough commander was investigating also, as was the police commissioner himself. The PC had found a pay phone in the hospital corridor from which he dialed his chief of internal affairs. He woke him up and ordered him to get on it at once, to do it personally, to tell nobody, and to report to him only.

"Do you suspect corruption, Commissioner?"

"If there are any surprises behind this thing," the PC said in a level voice, "I want to know about them before anyone else does. Is that clear?"

And of course the normal pretrial investigation had been started by the district attorney's office.

Assistant DA Van Horn had returned to his office with a notebook full of names of witnesses. Some he had already

spoken to, some he had not got to yet. He waited to brief
Karen Henning. As soon as she came to work he sat down in
her office, they both sipped coffee, and he told her. Van Horn
had a way with lurid cases and long before his description
was over he had Karen shaking her head in disbelief.

"Can I ask you a question, Karen?" Van Horn said then.
"Is this my case, or what?"

There was a pause. Karen knew very well what he was
asking. It was a juicy case, would go all the way to trial,
would get a lot of ink, and looked easy to win. It was every
prosecutor's dream of a case. In a year or two Van Horn would
finish his commitment to the DA's office and go looking for
a job in the private sector that paid real money. He wanted a
case like this on his résumé.

Although she herself had no plans for leaving the DA's
office, Karen wouldn't have minded such a case on her own
résumé.

But fair was fair. "We have rules around here," she told
Van Horn. "Whoever catches a case gets to try it."

"Thank you," said Doug Van Horn.

They looked at each other. It was understood that in the
months to come he would brief her from time to time if she
asked to be briefed. He might come to her if he encountered
a problem of some kind. Otherwise she would not hear about
the case again until it was ready for trial.

"Who do you want to assist you?" asked Karen. Van Horn
was a skilled trial lawyer and she rather liked him as well.

"I don't know. I'll get somebody."

"Get whoever you want."

"I really appreciate this, Karen," said Van Horn, and he
went home to bed.

About a week passed before Karen was called into the office
of Chief Assistant DA Norman Harbison, the man to whom
she reported. It was Harbison, second only to the DA himself,
who made most of the decisions as to how the office was

staffed and run. He hired and fired, assigned people to bureaus, and sometimes overrode the decisions of the bureau chiefs and division heads. He made no attempt to be popular. He was a tall stoop-shouldered individual about fifty years old. Karen thought of him as a male version of a dried-up old schoolmarm.

"I'm taking over the Lionel Epps case," Harbison said.

No preliminaries. No: Hello there, Karen. No: Good morning, Karen. Just, bang: I'm taking over someone else's case.

She had never liked Harbison, it seemed obvious that he did not like her either, but he was her superior and she had to be careful how she appeared to him, how she addressed him.

"You shouldn't do that," Karen said.

"I've done it."

"It's Van Horn's case."

"Was. It's my case now. Please call him in and inform him of my decision."

"We have rules in this office," said Karen carefully.

"I made the rules, I can change them."

"Changing them is bad for morale." Her voice was rising and she warned herself to control it.

"People here do what I tell them, or they leave."

Karen, though she stood her ground, was silent. She wondered what Harbison's purpose was. He rarely tried cases himself. Was he thinking about his own résumé? Was he planning to leave for the private sector? Perhaps he wanted a big case to run on in the next election. Perhaps he imagined he could run against the old man who was his boss and hers as well. This seemed inconceivable on the face of it, but perhaps wasn't.

She could ask him none of these questions.

"Van Horn's counting on it."

"Please inform him that he's off the case."

"I promised him the case."

"Right, so it's up to you to tell him he's off it."

"He'll quit."

Harbison behind his desk was toying with a pencil. "So he quits. He'd quit in a year or two anyway."

"We can't afford to lose him."

Harbison shrugged. "These hot young lawyers. They don't stay. We can never keep them very long."

"He's the best trial attorney I have."

"I daresay I'm a better one."

"Are you?" said Karen.

"Your job is not to question my decisions. Your job is to do what I tell you to do."

"You want me to do your dirty work for you."

"He works for you. I'm ordering you to tell him he's off the case."

"Screw you, tell him yourself," raged Karen, and she turned and left the office.

The result was that Van Horn resigned on the spot, as did the man assisting him. Harbison as he took over could not get any of the trial attorneys to agree to assist him on the case. They all made excuses. He was having to run the office by day and work on the case at night. This gave Karen a certain smug satisfaction. She was sorry to lose Van Horn and she missed him, but as the days passed and dozens of new crimes were committed and came across her desk she put the Lionel Epps case out of her mind. She paid no attention to it in any way; it had nothing to do with her.

—6—

Police headquarters at One Police Plaza is a heavy brick cube of a building. It is fourteen stories high, thick walled, squat. Its windows are like gun embrasures, and it is without decoration or adornment of any kind.

The police commissioner's office is on the top floor underneath his helicopter pad. Actually it's a suite of offices housing about twenty secretaries in addition to himself. Most of the secretaries are sergeants and detectives, and most of them work the voluminous mail that pours in unsolicited day after day, opening and scanning each letter, stapling it to its envelope in case the postmark or the envelope itself should ever have to be entered into evidence, and routing it somewhere for action—or inaction as the case may be.

The PC's personal office is a big room but plain. The walls are plain, as is the ceiling, as is the floor—again all adornment has been left out. An institutional, undistinguished room. From his windows the PC has a nice view over Brooklyn and the East River, but cops, even those of exalted rank, know their city rather too intimately and are not deluded by views. The room does contain two ornate and gracious touches: the big desk at which Teddy Roosevelt sat when he was PC, at the end of the last century, only three years before he went

to the White House; and his portrait, painted at about that
time, hanging in its heavy frame on the wall opposite. Headquarters has been moved twice since Teddy's day; he never
worked here, and his desk and portrait do not seem to fit
such a bland, low-ceilinged room. In any case, one PC after
another has sat at his desk and gazed at his face, first in the
other buildings, now here, for almost a hundred years, and
perhaps this has caused some of them to think deep thoughts.

The incumbent PC, whose name was Charles Malloy, was
sitting at that desk today as his principal secretary, a deputy
inspector in uniform, announced the arrival of the chief of
internal affairs, Sydney Pommer. Pommer, who entered in
uniform, wore three stars on each shoulder.

"Yes, Syd?" Commissioner Malloy said, looking up. But
he did not get up, and he did not invite Pommer to sit down.
He did not like him, considering him pompous and self-
important. Slow, too. Pommer had been investigating that
mess up in the Three-Two for too long a time. If whatever
he had discovered was dire, then the PC should have been
told long ago—the other reports were all in. Most likely this
morning's meeting was a waste of the PC's time.

"I have that information you wanted, Commissioner," said
Chief Pommer and he glanced meaningfully in the direction of
the secretary. This was supposed to signify that his "information" was too sensitive to be divulged in the presence of a
third party.

Pompous, thought Malloy.

But he counted himself too experienced a commander to
display his true feelings, at least not yet, and with a nod he
sent the secretary out of the room.

"What do you have, Syd?"

The two men were very different. Commissioner Malloy
was a big florid-faced man. He represented the traditional
New York Police Department which, beginning in the middle
of the last century, had been dominated from patrolman level
to headquarters by men of Irish-Catholic origin. It was true
that in recent years the Irish-Catholic strain had run a bit thin.

The lawsuits had forced the department to hire and promote more minorities, and even women. But now, in the person of Charlie Malloy and in ninety percent of the new commanders he had promoted out of the ranks and was continuing to promote, the old Irish-Catholic ethos was back.

Malloy was in fact a throwback to the men who had bossed the department in the old days, and he had been chosen for this reason. His immediate predecessors had included a former judge, a former prosecutor, a former corrections commissioner, and a black police chief from out of town, all of them determined innovators. Malloy, when the mayor named him PC, was fifty-eight years old and, unlike these immediate predecessors, had worked for the same employer, meaning the NYPD, for his entire adult life. He had been, it was said, a cop's cop, a man other cops could depend upon. The principal accomplishment of the innovators, as he saw it, and as the mayor saw it too, had been to further poison department morale. Crime was up, response time was up, sick leave and retirements were up. The department simply didn't work as well as it should. The mayor had decided innovations had to stop for a while, and in addition he was a man who didn't like surprises. He had appointed Charles Malloy.

Pommer was smaller in stature than Malloy, darker in complexion, and he was a Jew. As commander of internal affairs it was his job to investigate other cops. Of course he had been pleased to reach three-star rank, but he was under no illusions, not then, not now. He knew Malloy didn't like him. The PC, to Pommer, was a closet anti-Semite. He knew why Malloy had appointed him to IAD: because it was good politics to have a Jew in the police hierarchy; and because internal affairs was a job none of the department's Irishmen wanted.

The religion and racial origin of New York cops was never very far from any cop's mind. Years ago the department had broken itself down into the so-called line organizations, or fraternal organizations, along strictly racial lines, and in a country that had lately become extremely sensitive to racial issues it sometimes seemed odd to outsiders that these organizations still existed, still had weight. There was the Columbian Society for cops of Italian extraction, the Steuben Society for Germans, the Shomrim Society for Jews, and so forth. There was the Guardian Society for blacks, and even the newly formed Jade Society for Asian cops, of whom there were almost none. The biggest and most important of these organizations was the Emerald Society for cops who still thought of themselves as Irish, who still called themselves Irish. The society had an insurance fund for widows, a scholarship fund for kids, and a bagpipe band that played its mournful dirges at the funerals of Irish cops slain in the line of duty. On St. Patrick's Day Emerald Society cops, meaning the bulk of the department, marched up Fifth Avenue as a group in the parade. Invitations to speak at Emerald Society communion breakfasts were prized by politicians. Detective Muldoon of the Three-Two squad was of course a member of the Emerald Society; so was the police commissioner.

Like most old-time PCs, unlike most recent ones, Malloy was not a college graduate, and he was sensitive about it, being careful to allude whenever possible to the time "when I was at Fordham." He had in fact audited some classes there when he made captain and first came into headquarters. He had imagined he might try for a degree, which supposedly would help his career, but when he was promoted to deputy inspector without it, he did not go back.

He had a strong New York street accent, useful when commanding cops, which he had been careful over the years never to lose. "So where are we with those yo-yos up in the Three-Two?" he said to Pommer.

Syd Pommer, on the other hand, had a law degree and a masters in business administration from NYU, both earned at night as he worked his way up in the department. He spoke like the educated man he was. "I've got a pretty good book on them, Commissioner."

"I told you to be discreet. Were you?"

"No one could have been more so, Commissioner." If

Pommer resented such a question, this did not show. When in the presence of Malloy, he was careful that nothing showed.

"How many of your men worked on this?"

"Two."

"You can trust them?"

"The Three-Two never knew we were there, Commissioner."

The PC doubted this. "Go on."

Pommer opened his notebook. "This fat guy, Muldoon, twenty-six years on the job, was apparently the instigator. Third grade detective."

The PC knew about Muldoon from the other reports he had seen. "Twenty-six years on the job and he's still a third grade," he commented.

"He was a first grade some years ago. Got flopped back to third for being drunk on duty."

The PC knew this too. "Great," he said. "Wait till that comes out in court."

"It may not," said Pommer, studying his notebook. "The record doesn't refer to it. The record says insubordination. I mean, the guy was a drunk, still is."

"What else?"

"We worked hard digging that up."

"I'm sure," said the PC dryly.

"Took us about a dozen interviews to run it down. It was only a rumor at first."

The PC was not interested in gossip of this nature.

"But we nailed it."

"Get to something important."

"Used to be married. Lots of very loud fights with the wife, by the way. Liked to knock her around, apparently."

The PC was not interested in this either.

"Cops from the precinct where he lived were always being called to intervene. The department chaplains took him in hand but it was too late, she divorced him."

Malloy stared impatiently into a corner of the room.

"Sounds like he should have been fired off the job years

ago,'' Pommer said. He was aware of the commissioner's impatience and in a sense was stalling for time. He was trying to figure out what Malloy meant to do with today's or any subsequent information that Pommer brought him.

"He made some good arrests over the years," Pommer said, studying his notes again. "You remember the subway token clerk murdered last year? He broke that case. Remember about ten years ago, the black councilman found in the trunk of a car—he worked that one on his own time and finally broke it. He's got a number of Excellent Police Duties, citations for bravery."

"How many civilian complaints?"

"You work Harlem you get those. The fastest way to the civilian complaint review board is as well known in Harlem as the fastest way to the welfare office."

"Corruption?"

"Allegations, Commissioner. Nothing proven."

"I want to know what relates to the current mess. The rest is a waste of my time. What about the other guy, the Italian?"

"Barone. He's a third grade also. Twelve years on the job. Went from the police academy to the Seven-Seven in Brooklyn."

The two men nodded at each other, but for a moment nothing was said. The department's biggest recent corruption scandal had occurred in the Seven-Seven. More than twenty cops were known to be involved. Six were convicted, one shot himself. To Malloy and Pommer both this meant the whole precinct was rotten, 250 men. Because policemen saw other men at their worst, they became cynics from a young age. Suspicion and conviction were the same.

"I know what you're thinking, Commissioner."

"Do you?" said Malloy dryly.

Nearly every officer in the 77th Precinct had been transferred elsewhere, and new men brought in. And after that Charlie Malloy was brought in, the PC reflected. He did not want any more corruption scandals. Not on his watch.

"Barone was already gone by then," said Pommer. "Went

into narcotics, got the gold shield, asked for the Three-Two and got it.''

Most of this Malloy already knew, but he mused about it. ''Learned to steal in Brooklyn,'' he said, ''perfected his techniques in narcotics, and is now ripping them off in the Three-Two. That's what you're thinking. What do you have to back it up?''

''Not a thing, Commissioner.'' Pommer was an expert at accepting rebukes and slights without showing emotion. Which was not to say he enjoyed it.

''All right,'' the PC said, ''you got nothing solid on either of them. What have you found out about the shoot-out I don't already know?''

''As I said, Commissioner, this Muldoon was the instigator. The other guy was just along for the ride, you might say.''

''Get to the point as quickly as possible.''

''Detective Muldoon was told the whereabouts of the perpetrator, Lionel Epps, by a confidential informant.'' Pommer looked up. ''An unregistered informant, I might add.''

This might be significant and it might not. In any case it was a detail, and someone else's job, not the police commissioner's.

''They're supposed to register them,'' Pommer said, as if this were something the PC did not know. ''A lot of them don't bother,'' Pommer added.

''What else do you have?'' said the PC impatiently.

''If he paid the guy he used his own money,'' persisted Pommer. ''There's no record of him putting in for department money.''

Though the PC began drumming his fingers on the desk, Pommer only studied his notes.

''That's enough to hang him on right there,'' Pommer said, looking up. ''Both of them, if you want.''

He was fishing for a reaction, but the PC gave none. He was in no mood to reveal his thoughts to Pommer, who seemed to have no idea of what this case represented in the large sense. All cases involving Harlem or blacks, if they reached the news media, were potential problems. Malloy had to know everything, be ready to brief the mayor if asked, be ready to respond to the press, if asked. He had to be seen to be on top of it. He didn't need to know about unregistered informants or cops beating up their wives.

Apart from that, five cops had been shot, and the morale of the department was paramount. He wanted cops to see him as a man who stood up for his men.

"By the way, Commissioner," Pommer said, "we ought to consider raising the amount of informant money we give the precinct detective squads. At present it's only a couple of hundred dollars a month. In a precinct like the Three-Two with many arrests, most of that money goes to paying citizens to stand in lineups with perps. They have to pay people off the street five bucks a head to stand in lineups. They could put detectives in the lineups of course, if they were black, but most of them are not."

The PC felt like asking Pommer what his name was originally. Pommowski? Something like that.

"There's no money left over to pay informants with," Pommer continued.

And spelling his first name Sydney, not Sidney. A total affectation. Probably so people wouldn't think he was Jewish.

"Get back to the shoot-out," said Malloy.

"The informant directs Muldoon to an abandoned building where the perpetrator, Epps, is holed up. This Epps is a real bad apple, by the way."

The PC waited impatiently.

"He and Barone decide they can't take him by themselves, they need reinforcements. The abandoned building is in the Two-Five, so they go to the Two-Five stationhouse and up the stairs to the squadroom. It's late. They find five detectives there about to go home. They don't know them, but they ask them to serve as backup."

This was possibly important. Why had no one else informed him about it already?

"The five detectives say: Who the fuck are you? You're not a boss. We're not moving without a boss. Get a boss."

Malloy the ex-street cop knew what this meant. The detectives had refused to move without a sergeant or lieutenant to lay it on if it went bad.

"Unfortunately," Pommer said, "there were no detective superior officers on duty in the Two-Five at that hour. Nor at the Three-Two either, by the way." He nodded several times. "The Three-Two squad has got only one lieutenant, only one sergeant, and they were both off that night."

"Get on with it," the PC said.

"They go back to their own precinct and they enlist every detective who's there, six in all, counting themselves. The uniformed shift is just changing, so they go out and wait by the cars and as the uniformed guys come out of the stationhouse they enlist them too. They're not going to go directly out on patrol after all, they're going to back up the two hotshots. They all agree."

For Pommer's benefit the PC decided to look pained, though as a young cop he might have done the same, probably would have. He was reasonably certain Pommer would not have, because Pommer had never been a street cop like himself, Pommer was a book guy. But to real cops the prospect of action was sometimes—meaning usually—irresistible.

"Five cars, Commissioner. Ten men."

"There should have been at least a sergeant there," the PC conceded. He said this principally for Pommer's benefit. But in fact crime and criminals did not operate on schedule. Cops could not always wait until the sergeant was there and everything had been completely thought out. The difference between him as PC and the idiots who preceded him was that he had been a real cop. He saw things from the cop's point of view, from the point of view of the street. In addition, he understood the importance of police morale.

Pommer said: "Muldoon tells them that all they have to do is surround the building and watch the fire escape and the roof. He and Barone will make the arrest, it will only take a minute.''

Pommer was practically chortling, as if he had again caught cops—any cops—with their hands out or their pants down.

Pommer said: ''This plan, which is no plan at all by the way, sounds terrific to everybody, and they all get in their cars and descend on the abandoned building. But during this time, unknown to them, the detectives back at the Two-Five have been having second thoughts.''

''I can imagine,'' said the PC.

Pommer said: ''The Two-Five detectives have figured it out that they can go arrest Epps by themselves, why the fuck not, it's their precinct, why do they need those fucks from the Three-Two?''

As Malloy saw it, the cops involved had only behaved like cops. What else did anyone expect? So far, Malloy approved. It was only later that the thing turned into a shambles. The eventual outcome was unfortunate and could cause problems in the future if he was not careful, but basically cops were cops and you knew that and accepted it.

''So what you have,'' Pommer continued, ''is two groups of cops trying to make a dangerous arrest in the middle of the night. They're not only not helping each other, they're in competition. They're trying to screw each other.''

The PC nodded. Most of this had never appeared in print and it would not sound very well in court, but if he were careful there was no reason it should reach either place. His object was to protect himself and protect his men. If anyone was to be disciplined it should be only Muldoon and Barone. But not much and not now. Not until after the trial.

Pommer said: ''The Three-Two cars and the Two-Five cars pull up almost nose to nose. Suddenly there's no time to elaborate on the plan—what there was of a plan. They see each other and they all start running toward the doorway to be first to arrest this violent sonuvabitch Epps who's waiting for them armed to the teeth. There are guys rushing in the front door long before anyone is in position in the back or on the roof.''

Pommer fell silent. The PC, as he turned this information over in his head, was silent also.

"You know the rest, Commissioner."

"Yeah, five cops in the hospital." It was a big case, that was the danger. Someone was liable to try to make it into something it wasn't.

He said: "Those notes you have there, did you make copies?"

"I'll have them typed up when I get back to the office."

"Give them to me," said the PC, reaching for them.

"But Commissioner—"

"What about your men, did they write anything down?"

After a moment Pommer decided to say: "I told them to hold off until I knew how you wanted to play this."

The PC was scanning the notes. "I'm concerned about possible Rosario material when Epps goes on trial," he said. "The most important single task facing this department is to convict the sonuvabitch."

Rosario material was the nightmare of every cop. Anything committed to paper during the course of an investigation had to be turned over to the defense, which could then use it to impeach police testimony. Or ridicule police testimony, if it came to that. Defense lawyers got their rocks off ridiculing cops on the witness stand on the basis of some asininity the cop had written down during the investigation. Some asininity such as Pommer's notes here. "This business about the drunken detective, for instance." The PC ripped a page off the yellow pad and crumpled it up. He was becoming angry. "The defense doesn't need to know that."

"I agree, Commissioner."

"If they find out, fine, but we don't have to tell them." He ripped off a second page. "The defense doesn't need to know about his ex-wife either." The PC was turning pages. "The 77th Precinct has nothing to do with the case." He tore the pad in half. "I would say the defense doesn't need to know about any of this." Getting up, he dropped it into the basket under his desk. "Do I make myself clear?"

"Suppose something goes wrong, and they come after us on this?" Pommer's entire investigation had just been thrown in the basket. "Demand to know what sort of internal investigation we did?" He was trying to make his questions sound intellectual. He was trying not to let his humiliation show. He was pretending to play the devil's advocate.

"You let me worry about that."

"Should I continue my investigation or not?"

"Stop it right where it is," said Malloy. As soon as Pommer had left the room he would put a stop also to any other investigations still in progress. He had read all the other preliminary reports, none of them nearly as complete as Pommer's.

"It could turn out that these are corrupt guys."

"We'll worry about that after the trial. For the time being they're heroes."

The PC began to lecture the internal affairs chief. He had five shot cops on his hands, he said. His red face was getting redder, even as Pommer's dark face got darker. The trial of Lionel Epps thus became of paramount importance to the department, the PC said. The morale of every cop demanded a conviction at all costs. For as long as the case pended there must be no suspicion that the actions of the police on that particular night had been anything but professional and above-board. Nothing must come out that might damage the prosecution's case.

Midway through this lecture the PC's tone changed, became that of a man talking to a friend and ally. He started walking Pommer to the door, he put his arm around him; the big man was almost hugging the smaller one. At his best there was a certain bluff heartiness to Malloy. He thought of it as his major positive attribute. On those occasions when he chose to employ this heartiness he imagined that others found him charming. He himself mistook his manner for charm.

"So how's Marge?" he asked Pommer. "We haven't had

a chance to even mention her yet. And the kids. Adam's at Dartmouth, I remember. How's he doing?''

This was another of Malloy's attributes: he remembered the names of his subordinates' wives and children.

Pommer mumbled suitable responses.

The case was now in the hands of the district attorney's office, Malloy said at the door. It had been assigned to Norman Harbison to prosecute. Norm Harbison, as Syd Pommer knew, was chief assistant DA. This proved that the DA's office was giving the case the importance it deserved. The police department could do no less. He himself was pleased that Harbison, the highest-ranking active prosecutor in New York County, and the most experienced as well, had the case, and he knew Pommer felt the same. And he thanked his internal affairs chief—for what, Pommer had no idea—and closed the door on him.

Which left Chief Pommer standing out in the hall humiliated, smarting. He was focused on Malloy. It seemed to him that the PC enjoyed humiliating people, himself especially. Each time Pommer got admitted to the royal presence, the PC found a way to do it, usually in front of others. But humiliation, Pommer told himself, bothered him only peripherally. In his thirty-two years as a cop he had been humiliated many times by many people but had usually managed to turn it to his advantage, which he would do again, he believed. His notes were gone, but he could replace them. Notes that related to a criminal prosecution. Destroyed by the police commissioner himself. It was unbelievable. Malloy had simply destroyed them. If Pommer spoke just a hint of this into the right ear it would cause a cover-up scandal and Malloy would be out on his ass. He might even go to jail. An incredibly stupid act by a stupid man.

But Pommer could not go to anyone with this, he realized. It would be his word against the police commissioner's. The mayor would side with the PC, would have to, since he had appointed him. Everybody would.

Chief Pommer needed additional ammunition, and he decided to get it by continuing his investigation of Muldoon and Barone. If he could prove them dirty, then he could bring them down, and Malloy their protector with them.

And in fact Pommer had a sense that Muldoon and Barone were dirty. Why? He had never spoken to them. Instinct, probably. He was chief of internal affairs. Nearly every cop with whom he came in contact was dirty; he rarely saw any other kind. He was a man who trusted this instinct. To him it never failed.

But the investigation would have to be invisible or nearly so, or the PC might spot it.

Suppose Malloy did spot it? But he wouldn't. It would be an investigation of such subtlety that even if he thought he had spotted it, he wouldn't be sure. He wouldn't be able to do anything. He couldn't publicly meddle in integrity matters anyway. He wouldn't dare.

For some years there had existed in each precinct one or more young cops recruited straight out of the police academy as "integrity associates." Pommer had appointed some. Others had been appointed by his predecessors. The cops around them did not know who they were. If they saw wrongdoing of any kind they were expected to report it to internal affairs, and an overt investigation would begin. Their names would never become known to their colleagues. This system did not work perfectly. Some of these integrity associates reported nothing. You never heard from them. They got sucked into that police brotherhood crap. They found they could not testify against another cop.

But others of them were responsible for some solid prosecutions.

Pommer decided to place an integrity associate in the Three-Two squad. Not many of these associates were detectives. It would take a little time to find the right man, one who could be trusted, and move him in there in a manner that would seem normal. He would place him as close to Muldoon and Barone as he could get him.

If Police Commissioner Malloy were brought down, the mayor would need a man of unquestioned integrity to replace him. He might look no further than his internal affairs chief. Why not Syd Pommer? Thirty-two years an honest cop. Why not New York's first Jewish PC?

—BOOK TWO—

— 7 —

Clutching a stack of dossiers to his chest, Norman Harbison, chief assistant district attorney and the man who would prosecute Lionel Epps, entered the DA's office.

To Harbison it was an imposing office, not because it was big, or because of the flags, the plaques, the oriental rug on the floor, but because of the man who now looked up at him from behind the desk. To most people, meaning those who didn't have to work for him, the DA was a revered figure, almost a legend. He had won eight straight elections, had held office thirty-two years.

"Yes, Norman?"

"I have a number of administrative matters—"

"I'm a bit busy today." Tall, thin, white-haired, seventy-two years old, the DA had a reputation for absolute political independence, for absolute probity as well, and he tended toward curtness, increasingly so as he got older, at least toward Norman Harbison.

"I'm sure you can decide without me, eh, Norman?"

But today, unlike other days, Harbison stood his ground.

The DA, who was busy signing letters, did not even glance up. "Something else, Norman?"

Harbison was there on a delicate matter. "Have you made any decision yet, sir?" he said nervously.

"Decision?"

"Kauffman, O'Reilly—I met with them last night."

"I see."

Now the DA did look up.

"They initiated it," said Harbison defensively. "I didn't call them."

"Of course."

"They asked me to come over, yes."

The DA looked at him.

"So I went over," said Harbison.

The DA leaned back in his swivel chair. He was nodding at Harbison who, after a moment, studied the floor.

"They asked me," Harbison forced himself to say, "what your intentions were."

"And you said?"

"I told them I didn't know."

"Kauffman and O'Reilly," murmured the DA, "the heart and soul of the Democratic Party." He swiveled toward his window. Outside on this gray winter day it had begun to snow. When he swiveled suddenly back, Harbison's eyes again dropped to the floor.

"They wanted to know," the old man mused, "after eight terms in office, if the incumbent district attorney of New York County might be contemplating retirement. Or is it you trying to retire me, Norman?"

"Not at all, sir. The party—"

"Do you think I'm too old to run again, Norman?"

"Of course not."

"Seventy-two years of age is the prime of life, as you'll find out one day."

When talking to the newer assistants on his staff, young men and women just starting out in the law, the DA could seem a kindly, fatherly old man. But to Harbison and the other bureau chiefs he most often seemed what he was— tough and manipulative.

Which was his mood at this moment, Harbison realized. He saw that this interview had become a confrontation, and that in provoking it he had made a mistake.

The DA came around his desk and put his hand on Harbison's shoulder.

"If I'm not thinking of retiring, I certainly should be, don't you think, Norman? You deserve your chance after all these years, don't you think, Norman?"

Harbison already had the answer he had come in here for. The old bastard had every intention of running again.

"You're loyal, hardworking, a fine administrator, an able lawyer—" The DA said all this in his kindly, fatherly tone, but he was walking Harbison to the door.

"Go to the committee for me, Norman. Start the process as if I'll run. That's the way politics works, keep them guessing. Then at the last minute, you can be ready to jump in. If I don't run, you're the man."

Harbison's humiliation went over into a kind of smothered anger. He was not some flunky to be ignored. At the door he made the only protest available to him. "I've been offered a job on Wall Street. A big firm."

"Which one?" the DA said bluntly.

He had the old man's attention now. He gave the name of the firm—the string of names of the firm's founders.

The DA was impressed despite himself—who would have thought such a firm would recruit Norman? His eyebrows rose slightly.

This reaction was almost imperceptible, but Harbison noted it and was pleased. "And of course they're offering much more money."

"How much?"

"More than twice what I'm earning here."

"Money isn't everything, is it, Norman?"

Harbison stood almost at the door, and the DA studied him. How long had Harbison been chief assistant? Eight or nine years? Was it that long already? When did he conceive the notion that he was qualified to become—might be elected—district attorney in his own right? For years the DA had seen Harbison as obedient, self-effacing, sharp-eyed, docile. The equivalent of the perfect butler. He made the house run smoothly and one hardly knew he was there. Most of the young lawyers were afraid of him. If the man were to quit, the DA himself might have to handle problems which at present never reached his desk. Harbison must certainly be prevented from moving to Wall Street, but he ought to be taught a lesson as well.

And so the old man repeated the name of the Wall Street firm—it was quite a mouthful—then remarked confidently: "That's not for you, is it, Norman? Civil litigation, a huge firm like that. I need you here running this office. And besides, you're my successor. Can't be my successor on Wall Street, can you?"

When he saw the air go out of Harbison he ceased to worry that he might have pushed him too far. This man doesn't want to be a rich lawyer, the DA told himself. He wants my job, which no one will ever elect him to, even if the idiots running the party nominate him one day.

Though he did not show it, the DA had become angry. Harbison must be punished.

"I've been thinking about that shoot-out last summer," the DA said. "The Lionel Epps case."

The abrupt change of subject seemed to Harbison to indicate that the DA bore no hard feelings. Much relieved, the chief assistant responded proudly, almost eagerly: "As you know, I'll be prosecuting it personally and—"

"I've decided to take you off it."

"Take me off it?"

"Not worthy of you, my boy."

"But I've been working on it for months, I've been announced in the press—my prestige—"

"—is great. We don't want to risk damaging your prestige, do we, Norman? You'll need that prestige if you run for my job in the fall."

Harbison attempted to keep his face a blank, but didn't

quite succeed. The DA saw this and knew he had guessed right. The Epps trial was vital to Harbison's plans. All those shot cops. Harbison was counting on weeks in the spotlight, followed by victory. It could be enough to make him attractive to the politicians, and maybe even to the voters.

"It's a messy case," the DA said. "We don't want to let you get messy, do we?" The DA was silently chortling. It wasn't often, he thought with pleasure, that one devised the perfectly appropriate punishment.

"I can convict Epps, win the case—"

"I'm sure. What do you think about letting Mrs. Henning take over?"

Harbison could only stand there, stricken, as the old man went to his intercom.

"Send Mrs. Henning in please."

Although his principal object was to put Harbison in what he conceived to be his place, the DA was now seeing additional advantages. By choosing Karen Henning he would appear to have given a prominent case to a woman in these feminist times and, who knows, it might win him a few extra votes in November. Not that he needed them. He had never been defeated and several times the Republicans had conceded the election to him in advance—did not even put up a candidate against him.

As he showed Harbison out the DA was talking almost to himself. "A woman might actually do better than a man," he told Harbison. "And if she fails, well, she was a woman."

"But sir—"

The door closed.

As Harbison went out through the anteroom he could barely see. As a result he almost bumped into Karen Henning coming in. The chief assistant had never before looked at her this closely. Previously he could not have told the color of her eyes nor what clothes she wore.

He had been aware of her principally because she was almost the only supervisor who dared resist his decisions.

Sometimes she ignored them outright, which was infuriating because he could do nothing about it. Women in these feminist times had become untouchable. It was the DA himself who had suggested her as chief of the trials division; Harbison had been obliged to concur. He had never thought the Manhattan DA's office an appropriate place for female lawyers, and for the most part had seen Karen Henning as a woman with a rather prominent jaw who probably wished she were a man.

At this moment for the first time he saw her also as a rival.

"Hello, Norman," she said curtly, and he nodded.

She was carrying case folders under her arm and she was wearing today a navy blue suit.

"I've asked him to give you the Lionel Epps case, Karen."

"What?"

"That's why he's called you in."

"But—"

"When he tells you, act surprised."

"But you—"

"I've made my decision. If you don't want it, tell him so. Don't tell me."

"But—"

"He's waiting for you."

As she entered the DA's office, Karen was trying to understand what Harbison had just told her, and to figure out what it meant, but there wasn't time. The old man was standing at one of his windows, but he came across to meet her.

"Ah, Mrs. Henning, thanks for coming in." He was a formal man. He had never called her anything but Mrs. Henning. He was formal toward the other supervisors too. It was a way of keeping them at arm's length, she supposed. Of course his age and prestige did that already. To his present staff he seemed a remote, unapproachable figure.

His manners were almost courtly—at least they had always been courtly to her. Now he took her hand and led her to the chair beside his desk. "Don't you look nice today," he said.

From a younger man a compliment of this nature might

have caused Karen to frown. From one this old, and especially at a time such as now when she was trying to sort out her confusion, she accepted it.

"Thank you," she said.

"And how is your husband?"

"Fine, thank you."

"And your lovely children?"

"They're fine too."

"How old are they now, anyway?"

"My daughter's fifteen and my son is twelve."

"Yes," said the DA. Having moved behind his desk he sat down and looked at her over steepled fingers. "What do you know about the Lionel Epps case?"

"That he shot five cops," she answered. "That jury selection starts in two weeks." She watched him. She wanted to ask: What's happened, what's going on here? But instead she said nothing.

"Five cops, yes," the old man said.

Karen tried to remember what else she knew about the Epps case, but her mind was whirling. There had been briefs written, motions argued. It was all vague to her. Since the day Harbison had taken over she had ignored the case entirely.

"Before that," she said, "the guy murdered one of his colleagues in the drug business up in the Bronx." Other details were coming back to her. "Cut his tongue out, wrapped him in a rug, and set him on fire, as I remember."

"So it was alleged. The Bronx jury acquitted him only last month."

"Previously he committed other atrocities in Queens."

"Evidently the lad has quite a temper."

"Queens couldn't convict him either."

"That leaves it up to us, doesn't it," said the DA.

"The evidence was overwhelming. Both times McCarthy got him off."

"Justin McCarthy, yes. Our famous civil rights lawyer. He'll be defending again. He'll be your opponent. I want you to try the case."

"Sir, it's Norman Harbison's case—"

The DA's voice got impatient. "Norman's got other things on his mind."

Karen fell silent.

"Justin McCarthy, the pride of the bar," said the DA in a kinder tone. "You're not afraid of him, are you?"

"No, of course not." What she was afraid of was being rushed into a courtroom without having had time to prepare.

She wanted to know what had gone on between the DA and Harbison, but saw that he had no intention of telling her.

"Justin McCarthy is the biggest lawyer you've come up against so far," the DA said. And then after a pause: "Of course you've beaten some very skilled lawyers, haven't you?"

She hated the patronizing tone but said nothing. Everyone patronized women around here. She did not have time for resentment. Her mind kept flashing from Harbison to McCarthy to herself. The trial was about to begin. If she took the case—did she have an option?—then the trial was already on top of her. Two weeks. Could she get it delayed? Probably not. She could ask for a continuance, but too many had been accorded already, all demanded by McCarthy. The many continuances had become as much a scandal as the five shot cops.

She wanted to refuse the assignment, or at least protest it, but once this old man had decided something, no one, to her knowledge, had ever changed his mind. She spoke carefully, choosing each word. "Norman's been preparing the case from the beginning. I can't—I mean I couldn't—" Realizing that she had begun to sputter, she stopped and tried to compose herself. "Two weeks is not enough time for me to prepare for trial—"

"Mr. Coombs was assisting him. You can have Coombs."

The old man had stood up. The interview was over. He was walking her to the door.

"You should have no trouble beating McCarthy on this one," the DA continued. "Probably get lots of ink, be on television every night. I see this as a real opportunity for you."

Those who resisted the old man's decisions were soon working elsewhere. "An opportunity," said Karen, but her voice was flat. "Yes. Thank you."

By the time she reached her own office she was in a fury. She had her division to run, there were two cases of her own that she was preparing for trial, cases that presented interesting legal questions and which, being rather short, would not cut into her time with her family. These were the case folders she had been carrying and she dropped them heavily on her desk. They landed with a thump and began to spill off and she had to lunge to grab them. It made her even angrier. She gave several loud sighs, then telephoned Harbison's office which was down the hall from her own. They were long halls—he must be nearly a hundred yards away.

Harbison would call her right back, his secretary promised, so she began to wait. As she paced she twisted the wedding band on her finger. She knew very well something was wrong between the old man and Harbison. That Harbison was suddenly out of favor was clear. That office politics existed was a given. If her own turf were threatened she would protect it, would have to protect it, but other people's turf was not her business. To get mixed up in an office feud was not in her interest. Most of all she wanted to protect her family life— her time at home. Now she saw herself working till midnight for the next two weeks, and probably throughout the trial as well.

She loved the law. She loved trial work, and matching her wits against other lawyers, usually men, and usually winning guilty verdicts. There was true evil in the world. She had seen it: the blood-spattered walls, the corpses that had been knifed, shot, bludgeoned. Stuff that had made her avert her eyes. She had prosecuted the perpetrators of such outrages. She had talked to them, studied them—human evil, men who nonetheless walked and talked and made flip comments just like everyone else. She had devoted her professional life to putting such persons in jail. Which gave her a good feeling when she had time to consider it. But this Epps business was not her case. To have had it from the beginning was one thing, taking it over now was quite another.

After fifteen minutes she phoned Harbison again, but he still wouldn't take her call. Angrily she marched down there.

As she barged in he was standing at his window looking out, so she realized he was wounded, and her mood softened.

She said: "Can we talk about the case?"

"No we can't."

"It's not my case," she said.

"It is now."

"If I'm going to try it—"

"Oh, you're going to try it, all right."

She stared at him a moment. She saw that he cared nothing about her, that for him she didn't exist, a realization that came as a surprise to her, though why? She wondered again what had gone on between him and the old man.

"You could always resign," he said.

Perhaps he wanted her to. Back him up by resigning in protest. But she loved her job, and the money she earned was needed at home. "If I'm going to try the case," she said in a milder voice, "I could use some help."

"See Coombs."

"Not Coombs, you. You've been working on it nine months, for God's sake."

He picked up his phone and spoke into it. "Get me Larry Coombs."

Karen tried to think what to say, what to do in the face of such rudeness.

"Larry," said Harbison into the phone, "I've asked Karen Henning to take over the Lionel Epps case. She wants to get together with you."

Karen knew Coombs. Each year dozens of law school graduates applied for appointments to the DA's staff. Interviewing them was one of the jobs performed by the senior assistant DAs, Karen among them. It had fallen to her last spring to interview Coombs. She had interviewed him twice and had recommended that he be hired, and he was. He was twenty-six, and from Yale, she thought. He was short, wore glasses, and had never tried a case. Also he was black. He wore suits with vests, or at least he did the few times she had seen him. She could picture his reaction to Harbison's strange phone call, his surprise. He would want to know what went wrong, why the last-minute switch, but probably would no more dare ask her for answers than she had dared ask the DA.

Harbison put down the phone. "He'll meet you in your office in ten minutes."

"Coombs wasn't even on the case in the beginning."

"If Coombs isn't satisfactory, I suggest you plead the case out."

"At the beginning you couldn't get anybody at all to work it with you, if I remember correctly."

"You remember wrong. You remember bullshit!"

Now I've antagonized him completely, thought Karen. How brilliant of me. "Norman, please—"

"No."

It made her set her jaw. "What happened between you and the boss?"

"Whatever happened between me and the boss," said Harbison coldly, "will remain between me and the boss."

They stared at each other. "You are something," Karen said, putting as much venom as possible into her voice. "You are really something."

A few minutes after she reentered her own office Harbison's secretary came in with the Epps case file. There were two expandable envelopes, each of them over four inches thick. She withdrew the contents of the first, and while waiting for Coombs paged through it.

Half an hour had passed. Diagrams of the crime scene had been spread out.

Coombs leaned over her desk pointing with a pencil. "The detectives came in here, led by this fat idiot Muldoon—you'll meet him—and boom, boom, boom, three cops are down."

"All right," said Karen.

"There are rules for arrests of this kind. Muldoon broke them all." Coombs glanced up at her. "Five cops shot altogether. It's a miracle they weren't all killed."

"Did he have a warrant?"

"Muldoon? Of course not."

Karen nodded.

Coombs said: "Legally they didn't need one."

"You know that, I know it, Justin McCarthy knows it," Karen replied. "But the jury won't know it. McCarthy will make a big thing out of it. He'll spend a week on it. Look, let's go up to the scene right now. Do you have time?"

"Of course," said the young man.

Of course, thought Karen. Well, what else could he say?

"The defendant leaps into the cab about here," said Coombs. It was late afternoon and the sun fell in ribbons through the el tracks above. "The cops then fire at the moving vehicle, which is strictly against department regulations. And—"

"Don't tell me," said Karen. The details were piling up in her head and she did not like any of them.

"They stopped it—hit the cab driver. Yeah, right in the head."

Karen said nothing.

"After that four of the wounded cops sue the department for damages."

Karen winced.

"Charging negligence, reckless planning, and I don't know what all else. The cab driver's wife has a suit going, too. It's a beautiful case, all right."

Karen gave a wry laugh. "Yes, a real opportunity for me."

Above her head a train went by. The stanchions seemed to shiver in the light, the sidewalk to tremble under her feet. She peered down the avenue. Three blocks south was the

125th Street station. Each morning, twenty minutes into her commute between the suburbs and work, her train stopped there for a few seconds. Each night on the way home, the same. Sometimes she looked up from whatever case she was poring over and gazed out at what she could see of Harlem.

Tonight she would board her train there. Her ride home would be ten minutes shorter. And she was starting home right now, she decided. She had had all she could take for one day. She would not go back to the office first. And although this decision was accompanied by a twinge of guilt, for she would be cheating the city out of a few minutes of her time, she made it right by promising to study the Epps case folders all the way home.

But she was a white woman in Harlem with gutted hulks of buildings to either side of the street, and she knew about violence firsthand.

"Will you walk me to the station?" she asked Coombs.

The young man's reaction was immediate. "Are you afraid some black guy will assault you between here and there?" he snapped. "Is that it?"

So she realized that her fear of Harlem—it wasn't really fear—had insulted him, and she thought: If he's that tender I don't want him on the case. I can't cope with him too. But he alone knew this case, apart from Harbison, who had no intention of helping. She needed Coombs, and so tried to make amends.

"I'm a woman, Larry." She gave him a smile. "I don't like to walk alone anywhere in this city."

His face had gone blank and she looked into it for a moment. Then he nodded and said: "My response was uncalled for. I'm sorry."

She put her hand on his shoulder. "We don't know each other yet."

And so Coombs walked her to the station. He even waited beside her until the train came into the platform. As it pulled out she waved to him from the window as she would have waved to her husband if she were starting a long trip.

* * *

New Rochelle to the northeast is another suburb close to New York. It is a serious city in its own right, seventy thousand people, with, therefore, more diversity than most suburbs. The downtown is not chic and there are neighborhoods where crime and violence are commonplace, where unemployed black men stand around on street corners same as Harlem. But there are country clubs and sprawling golf courses as well, and fronting on Long Island Sound are houses that could only be called mansions. But for the most part New Rochelle is a middle-class city, and a white city. Nice houses but close together. Tree-lined streets. Bronxville abuts it to the west.

In New Rochelle there is also a small, Catholic, liberal-arts college of modest academic reputation, and this was where Henry Henning, Karen's husband, was a professor of political science. As her train pulled out of the 125th Street station he was walking along one of the campus's well-tended paths toward his last class of the afternoon. He wore charcoal slacks and a tweed jacket and carried a briefcase in one hand and several books in the other.

Students greeted him as they passed, but he was concentrating on the class he was about to give and so his responses were distracted.

"Afternoon," he said repeatedly. "G'afternoon."

A student ran up from behind, slowing down to walk alongside him.

"Professor Henning?"

Henning recognized him. "Hello, Billy."

"Can I ask you about tomorrow's test?"

Henning frowned. "Why don't we wait and talk about it in class."

Together they entered the building, and then a particular classroom. Henning, as he stepped up onto the dais, saw that the seats were about half full. The students, boys and girls, were all about eighteen. He started by taking attendance, something the better institutions did not require, hadn't in years. It was the rule here though, as if to prove that in this place, if you didn't take attendance the students wouldn't come.

Attendance out of the way, Henning spoke about tomorrow's examination.

"There will be no obscure questions," he promised. He moved back and forth on the dais as he spoke. There were techniques for keeping the attention of teenagers, and he knew and exploited most of them. "The purpose is not to trick you. It's to make you consider one more time all we have been talking about these last two months." He looked out over the room. "And what is it that we've talked about so much?" He pointed to a girl student.

"Political leadership in the real world," she told him.

"Right. Especially a concept that may be new to some of you. Sometimes political leadership means hanging back. What about General Washington?"

Henning pointed to a second student.

"He hung back," the student said.

"Meaning?"

"He avoided a major battle because he feared that if he lost it, the revolutionary movement would collapse."

Henning liked kids, liked being revered by them, but the level of scholarship in this place was dismal. "For most of seven years Washington hung back," Henning said. "What about Lincoln?"

"He couldn't free the slaves immediately," a girl student told him.

He kept pointing his finger around the room, eliciting answers.

"It would have made the border states secede," a boy student piped up. "And he couldn't win the Civil War without them."

Everything had to be simplified for the students here or they wouldn't get it, much less remember it. He longed to go beneath the surface, to make them grapple with major ideas, but couldn't.

"Roosevelt?" said Henning. They did less well with this

one, so he explained it again. Roosevelt had had to find a way to keep England afloat until his own isolationist country got in the mood for war.

"What about Lyndon Johnson?" Henning looked for a raised hand and didn't get one. "Billy?" he said.

The boy wasn't sure of himself. "He didn't hang back," he offered.

"Right."

"He lost this country first, and the Vietnam war only after," the kid said.

It's the best I can hope for here, Henning told himself— that they learn to parrot some things back. He would never be able to make them understand what Vietnam once meant to the country. Vietnam had been, still was, Henning's war. He had joined the protest marches, ceremoniously burned his draft card, considered conscientious objection or fleeing to Canada. Fortunately he was in college and was never called. Many years had now passed, but he was still a militant liberal. His wife's views, unfortunately, were different. She actually liked putting people in jail. He imagined she had been tainted by contact with cops. To Henning, cops were right-wingers, rednecks, fascists.

"Washington, Lincoln, Roosevelt, Johnson," he said, "tomorrow's test will be about them. Guys with major problems. Guys not very different from you and me. Guessing. Hoping. Trying to work it out." It pleased Henning that the class had come with him this far at least.

"This is a political science course," Henning told his students. "But politics is not a science. It's an instinct, almost an art." He was talking only to himself, he supposed. "So is the politics in your own lives," he continued, "the politics of getting along with each other. Of giving something in order to get something." And with these remarks he left tomorrow's test for tomorrow, and launched into the material he had prepared.

His wife about then got off the train in Bronxville, got on the bus and rode home. She came in the door and called out, but got back no answer. Her mood was still what it had been an hour ago: frustration, anger, self-pity. Though the Epps case was not her job she was stuck with it. She had to tell someone, but the house was empty. She went into the kitchen and as she began dinner she waited impatiently for her husband to get home.

When the class ended Henning went back to the faculty lounge to check his mail one last time—in the box now lay a single letter. When he saw where it was from he took it into the men's room and opened it there. As he read it a big grin came onto his face and when he had finished reading he kissed it.

He left for home a few minutes later, stopping at the supermarket to buy $88 of groceries, because shopping was one of his jobs this week. When he came into the kitchen carrying bags, his wife was at the stove and Jackie was rummaging through the refrigerator. He put the bags down, gave Karen a kiss on the cheek, then turned to tousle the boy's hair.

"You'll never guess what happened today," Karen said.

But he interrupted her. "I had a letter from NYU."

"Mom, can I have a sandwich?" said Jackie.

"No, you'll wait for dinner." To her husband Karen said, "What did it say?"

Henning had begun emptying bags, putting groceries away. "There may be an opening for an assistant professorship in the fall."

"And?"

"I've got a good chance."

"Only an assistant professorship?"

"I'd take it. NYU is a great school. It's really a promotion."

Karen's son was pestering her. "When are we going to eat?"

She turned to her twelve-year-old. She looked at his teeth every day to see if they were holding. So far they were. "In about twenty minutes."

"I won't be an assistant professor long, believe me, and

even at the start there'd be more money. I could give up coaching swimming on the side," said Henning. He glanced down into the frying pan: pork chops. On the nights when he did the cooking he did not serve pork chops.

"A chance to do serious teaching," said Karen.

"A chance to pitch in the big leagues," said Hank.

He grinned and gave her a squeeze. Then: "I'm tired of kids who never learned how to study, who don't appreciate what I can give them. I'm tired of holding their hands. Give me some students who really want to learn."

Was teaching really what he cared about, Karen wondered. Or was NYU, if they took him, purely a chance to advance his career? As well as she knew him, she wasn't sure. Perhaps he wasn't sure himself.

"I'm hungry, Mom."

Henning went to the cabinet to make himself a drink, and though he didn't like pork chops, he didn't say so. He poured scotch over ice. "Want one?" he asked his wife.

"No thanks."

Both fell silent while he sipped his drink. "What were you going to tell me?" he asked her.

It was the opportunity Karen had been waiting for, and she opened her mouth to speak about the Lionel Epps case but nothing, to her surprise, came out.

"It's not important," she said. He was in an ebullient mood and her news would only dampen it. But also she was not sure he would understand why she should be so upset, or, if he did understand, accord her the sympathy she was looking for.

"No, tell me what's on your mind," Hank insisted.

So finally, somewhat hesitantly, she began. "Do you know the name Lionel Epps?"

"No. Should I?"

"This afternoon I became involved with him."

"Romantically of course," Henning interrupted. He grinned at her, raised his eyebrows.

She saw that he would turn whatever she told him into a joke.

She frowned, then said: "I can't stop thinking about him, I'll grant you that much."

Karen went back to her cooking, glancing at him from time to time.

"And your lives have become intertwined forever," Henning prompted.

"For the next couple of months." Then she added dryly: "After that, we may tire of each other."

"And you'll come back to me."

"If you're still here," she told him.

Henry gave her a hug, his attitude of banter dropped away, and he spoke with a certain feeling. "I'll always be here." After a moment he said: "What did he do?"

"Who?"

"Lionel Epps."

"Shot five cops."

"Oh, that Lionel Epps." Again he was making a joke of it, and again Karen frowned.

"Do you remember the case?"

"Vaguely."

"His lawyer is Justin McCarthy."

"The famous civil rights lawyer."

"Why does everybody say that?" cried Karen. "I doubt McCarthy cares about civil rights at all. I doubt he cares about the law at all."

Henning grinned at her. "Don't worry, you'll beat him." And he took a long pull of his scotch.

— 8 —

Two days later, promptly at 3 P.M. as scheduled, Justin McCarthy was shown into Karen's office. Waiting for this supposed titan of the bar, Karen had grown increasingly nervous, and in fact had just come back from the ladies' room where she had renewed the little makeup she wore, pulled a comb through her hair, and otherwise got herself together. Was she afraid of McCarthy after all?

She told herself no but was not so sure. She doubted he knew anything about her, had ever heard her name before today, whereas she knew all about him. Although she had tried and won major cases, she had not attempted to make them seem notorious as a means of attracting attention to herself. Whereas McCarthy seemed to search out notorious cases only——the more notorious the better. He was the great defender of unpopular people and causes. He had defended Vietnam deserters, militant Indians, black revolutionaries, men indicted as spies. He was admired by some, hated by many. Supposedly he worked such cases for no fee, though who knew. He worked them from little evidence, that much was clear, sometimes none, but he won verdicts. He got clients off. His pro bono work, he called all this, every lawyer should do some. And as Karen well knew, most did, they just didn't pick the cases McCarthy picked, and they didn't make speeches about them on the newscasts every night. He had sued major corporations on behalf of injured workers, and had extorted notable settlements, and however noble his press conferences and statements, he probably took money there. He had pleaded a number of scandalous divorce cases too, one or two in Hollywood, and if he didn't charge top dollar for that he was a fool.

All in all it was a puzzling persona, one that, to Karen, did not add up. But it was certainly impressive.

Now her intercom buzzed: "Justin McCarthy is here."

Coombs had asked permission to stay for the interview. "I want to get a look at the guy."

After hesitating briefly, Karen had decided to allow it. He was seated now in the corner as her door opened, and McCarthy followed her secretary in.

The lawyer was shorter than she had expected. He had white hair. Karen came around the desk with her hand outstretched but he stopped her by taking half a step backward as if stunned by her beauty. Then he stepped forward again, taking both her hands, not one.

"I had heard. I did not believe, I never thought—"

It was a highly theatrical entrance. The rest of him was theatrical too. The flowery bow tie. The flannelmouthed, flowery manner. The hint of an Irish brogue despite the fact that *Who's Who* listed his birthplace as Brooklyn.

He had been in Karen's office ten seconds and already her teeth were on edge.

She said coolly: "This is Assistant District Attorney Coombs, who is helping me on the case."

"Mr. Coombs," said the lawyer, bowing, "Justin McCarthy."

Coombs, who had risen to his feet, took half a step backward, mimicking similar awe. "I had heard," he said, "I did not believe, I never thought—"

It brought a smile to Karen's mouth, though she quickly erased it.

But McCarthy had wrung Coombs's hand, had ignored his remark, and had turned back to Karen, at whom he stared with exaggerated pleasure.

"Criminal law is a desperate business," he declaimed. "Ambitious young prosecutors, hardened older prosecutors. You must forgive my surprise, my delight, to have come upon this—vision."

"What's on your mind, Mr. McCarthy?"

"I thought, lovely lady—" McCarthy's mood shifted abruptly. In an instant it had turned exaggeratedly pensive. "—that perhaps you and I could reach an agreement."

Karen nodded. "You want to plea-bargain."

"I want—" It seemed to Karen that she had never heard so much earnestness in a human voice. "—I want to save trouble and expense for everyone."

Karen went back behind her desk and sat down. "But your client attempted to murder about twenty cops."

"Oh?" McCarthy feigned surprise. "I thought the indictment said five."

"Yes, the indictment specifies only five. In that respect you've already got off easy, it seems to me."

"Only five. Whew! That's a relief. You had me worried there for a moment."

"Put five young men in the hospital."

"But the facts of the case are what we have to consider, lovely lady. The facts, even if proven, do not necessarily constitute a crime."

"Really, Mr. McCarthy."

"I could think of numerous grounds—and you should be thinking of them too—on which the jury, any jury, might acquit."

"Like what, for instance?" In the face of such calm assurance Karen felt momentarily shaken. Was there something she had overlooked?

"For instance, American jurisprudence has always held that a man has an absolute right to defend the sanctity of his home. The courts have so ruled every single time."

"Which home would you be speaking of, Mr. McCarthy?"

"My client's actions could certainly be considered in defense of the integrity of his home."

"It wasn't his home, it was a condemned building."

"On that particular night it was his home."

"I doubt that particular argument will fly, Mr. McCarthy."

"But we can't be sure, can we? A jury might indeed be swayed by such reasoning if, let us suppose, it were put to them in a convincing manner."

"What other arguments have you considered?"

"How about not guilty by reason of insanity?"

"Insanity?"

"Temporary insanity. No one will doubt that my client was afraid. Twenty cops shooting at him. I would be afraid. Wouldn't you be? Fear is a form of insanity."

"Interesting."

"He was so afraid he didn't know what he was doing."

"He was trying to kill cops, that's what he was doing."

"Seeing all those cops with their guns drawn made him temporarily insane."

"I don't think so, Mr. McCarthy."

"Unfortunately," said McCarthy in a concerned tone of voice, "one never knows in advance how a jury will see things."

Karen looked at him in silence.

"Another possible argument is self-defense," said McCarthy.

Karen wondered if he had prepared for this interview. She had the impression he was firing off ideas as they occurred to him. But at least she should credit him with gamesmanship. He was giving her a lot to think about. On which line of argument would he base his defense? She would have to construct her own case several different ways just to be prepared for whatever he might do. Maybe that was his intention—to double or triple her workload.

"He had a perfect right to fire back," McCarthy said. "Otherwise those police officers probably would have shot him. A clear case of self-defense."

Karen had got over her original awe of this man. Her impulse now was to do something rude, laugh in his face, perhaps. But a number of past juries had accepted his preposterous arguments, not laughed at them. Reminding herself of this, she only studied him, while beginning to nod her head. "What sort of plea were you looking for?" she asked.

"Why don't we reduce the charge to, say, resisting arrest."

"You can't be serious, Mr. McCarthy."

"Ah, lovely lady, you're good at your job, I can see that."

Karen was twisting the wedding band on her finger. "May I ask you something, Mr. McCarthy?"

"Ask away."

"Why are you defending a thug like Lionel Epps?"

"Perhaps because he is not guilty of the charges against him."

"Come now, Mr. McCarthy."

"His guilt or innocence is for the jury to decide. It does not fall to you and me."

"The man is a thug, and you know it as well as I do. So why did you take the case?"

"At stake are issues vastly more important than mere guilt or innocence."

"Like what, for instance?"

"A society's worth is measured by its behavior toward its underprivileged." Karen had read articles about McCarthy in which he had expounded on this notion in some detail. He did so again now. The Constitution was real, he told her, the Bill of Rights was real. The rights of everyone were guaranteed, not just rich people, or educated people, or people of whom society approved. In defending the rights of Lionel Epps, one defended the very real rights of everyone else, including your rights and mine.

Karen interrupted: "A guy shoots five cops, he goes to jail."

"Perhaps it is the cops who should be in jail."

Where did this idea suddenly come from? "Why not use

your talents," Karen said, "to defend civil rights cases that deserve it?"

"Whenever the law persecutes a member of an oppressed minority, it persecutes us all."

"I see."

"Do you want to know the two most beautiful words in the English language, lovely lady?"

"Let me guess."

"Not guilty."

"You didn't give me time to guess," said Karen.

"You don't want to lose this case, now do you? Any of the arguments I have outlined might be sufficient to sway a jury. Certain of them swayed those juries in the Bronx, in Queens. And you haven't even had sufficient time to prepare."

This man was outrageous, Karen told herself. If he weren't so outrageous he would be funny. If he hadn't won all those acquittals he would be funny. But he had and therefore he wasn't.

"Why not accept a plea? I'll go a bit higher. Simple assault. How's that?"

She didn't know what reaction was called for. A man like McCarthy was a new experience for her. She decided to smile sweetly.

Which caused his face to break into a confident grin. "And if you promise not to ask for more than a year, I'll plead guilty to possession of an illegal handgun."

"You will?"

"I will indeed."

"He had four guns as I recall."

"When you don't have much of a case, you must accept the best you can get. Think of the time saved, the expense saved. Think of your career."

"I'm thinking of it," said Karen.

McCarthy's voice, his manner, had become seductive. "Remember the verdicts in Queens, in the Bronx," he murmured confidently.

Karen's head began nodding again. "A plea seems a good idea to me too," she mused.

"Your reputation, madam, is one of sound common sense."

"There is one plea I might accept."

"What plea, may I ask?"

Karen's mouth set like a suture. "Guilty to five counts of attempted murder of police officers."

And she showed him out.

When he had gone, Karen and Coombs stared at each other.

Finally Coombs said: "Quite a piece of work, isn't he?" He waited to hear Karen's reaction, but she showed none, merely went back behind her desk and sat down.

"The defendant shot five cops but it was due to either insanity or self-defense or while preserving the sanctity of his home——" said Coombs. "——you don't suppose he'd really plead such nonsense in court?"

"I wouldn't put it past him."

"But—insanity, self-defense? It's absurd."

"Depends what he can make twelve jurors believe."

There came a knock on the door. "The DA wants to see you as soon as you've finished with Mr. McCarthy," said Karen's secretary.

Karen threw Coombs a look. How did the DA know McCarthy was even in the building? Who was orchestrating all this? There were times, and now was one of them, when Coombs seemed her only ally.

She went down the long hall. This time the DA did not get up to greet her, nor did he invite her to take the chair beside his desk.

"I understand you just had a plea-bargaining session with your esteemed opponent."

"Yes, I did."

"And?"

Karen told him the gist of it.

Several times the DA nodded in a concerned way. "What's your instinct on this?" he asked when she had finished.

"We go to trial."

"Are you sure that's wise?"

"It's an open-and-shut case."

"No," said the DA, "in eight terms in office I've learned one thing above all else. There is no such thing as an open-and-shut case."

This was not what he had said when giving her the assignment a few days before. "I still say we go to trial."

"I see."

So did Karen. It shocked her that the old man considered a plea acceptable. Perhaps not the specific plea offered this afternoon, but some kind of plea, a compromise still to be worked out.

"I mean, we have to go to trial," she insisted. "The guy shot five cops. He fired shots at about fifteen others. We could have twenty counts of attempted murder here, if we chose. The city will be outraged if we don't go to trial."

"The city doesn't get outraged over very much, I have found."

Karen was silent.

"I want you to think this over carefully," the old man said.

"Well, we certainly don't accept any such plea as McCarthy offered today," said Karen, adding lamely: "Do we?"

For a time the DA only gazed at her. "An election is coming up in a few months."

The word *election* hung there between them. Karen was offended that such a consideration should enter into this discussion at all, and thought it showed weakness that he had mentioned it. Was there a split at the top of the Democratic Party? Was he in bad health? He was old, after all. What did the professional politicians know that she didn't? What pressure were they putting on him? After eight terms in office he suddenly felt vulnerable, that much was clear.

''McCarthy is tough,'' the DA mused. After a brief pause he added: ''And he'll turn this into a civil rights case. We don't need a racially polarized city, do we?''

Was he worried about the city going up in flames, or that he could be turned out of office as a result? She said: ''Do you want me to accept a plea?''

''Juries are unpredictable and it's a messy case.''

Karen was frustrated, possibly even appalled. She was extremely confused and perhaps the DA perceived this. In any case he seemed to decide to back off for the moment. ''Jury selection begins in a week's time,'' he said. He smiled at her as if fondly. ''See what kind of jury you get. We'll decide then.''

Once out in the hall, Karen almost ran in the direction of Harbison's office, and she walked in on him without being announced. Present in the chair beside his desk was his assistant, Goldman. Karen asked Goldman to leave and waited until the door closed behind him.

''I've just had a very unpleasant interview with McCarthy,'' she began, ''and after him with the boss.'' And she outlined the plea arrangement McCarthy had offered. ''You know the case,'' she concluded. ''Is there something I don't know? What do you think?''

The chief assistant had remained seated behind his desk. He said: ''Juries are—''

''Yeah, I know, unpredictable.''

''Five cops shot,'' said Harbison. ''Because they behaved like buffoons. Do we want the city to know that?'' His voice was dry, his manner cold. ''Besides which, McCarthy will start a race riot in court. Take the plea.''

''Take the plea,'' said Karen. ''I see.''

''Other than that I have nothing to say to you.''

''Norm—''

''Nothing whatever.''

''You intended to go to trial on it.''

''How do you know what I intended to do?''

"Can I ask you a favor, Norm? Will you please not lie to me. You intended to go to trial on it."

"That was me," said Harbison. "You are—you."

He gave a shrug whose meaning was only too clear. His own skill and experience would have been sufficient to convict Epps, whereas hers were not.

"Nice," said Karen. "Really nice."

When she got back to her office she found the Reverend Hiram Johnson sitting beside her desk. Who let this guy in, she thought, and what does he want? Johnson was a forty-five-year-old black man, extremely tall, cadaverous, wearing a brown suit, a huge cross hanging from his neck, the bottom of it reaching almost to his crotch.

"Reverend." She gave him a nod, sat down in her chair, and watched him warily.

"It's good to see you again," Johnson began. "I have been watching your career with great interest."

Karen doubted this.

"You have won many successes, all richly deserved."

"Thank you."

For a moment they gazed at each other in silence. Get on with it, Karen thought. What is it you want here?

Johnson said: "How strong is the evidence against this young man Epps?"

"Very."

"I understand you've been offered a plea by Mr. McCarthy."

"About twenty minutes ago. How'd you find out so quickly?" She watched the reverend's face and found her answer there. "Oh, I see. He told you. He's very clever, isn't he?" Obviously McCarthy had been to see the DA too. A new image presented itself to Karen: of McCarthy moving through the city gathering allies, natural ones or otherwise, so as to exert maximum pressure on the district attorney and on her as well, trying to stop the trial before it ever began.

"If you should go to trial on this matter," said Reverend

Johnson, "I'm worried about the possible reaction among my constituents."

"Constituents, Reverend?"

"Parishioners. The boy's been acquitted twice."

"Those were other crimes, other juries."

"In Harlem it sounds like he's being harassed by the law."

"Getting twelve people to agree is hard."

"Harlem is already an alienated community."

"Reverend, he shot five cops."

"A trial could cause demonstrations."

Johnson had about two hundred core demonstrators that he used. Men who were out of work and standing around. A few women, too. He brought them to sites in chartered buses. He paid them five dollars a head as they stepped off the buses and picked up the signs they were to carry in the line of march. It was his own money. He was a free-lance pastor who moved from church to church giving what he called "homilies," passing the plate afterward. Some of the signs he had drawn and lettered himself. Others he had had made. "Stop the War Against Black America" was a typical one. At the end of each march the signs were collected, for they could be reused. The signs didn't change from one demonstration to the next, whatever the nature of the protest, and the marchers didn't change much either.

"A demonstration would be out of my hands."

"We certainly want to avoid demonstrations," Karen said. I don't believe this, she thought.

"Those things can get very ugly at times."

Karen decided to say: "On television you always seem to be out in front of such demonstrations."

"I'm a man of God. I follow the dictums of the Prince of Peace." The holy man rose to his feet. "Think about it."

With the bemused Karen staring after him, Johnson went out, passing Coombs, who was coming in, in the anteroom.

Coombs glanced from Karen to the exiting Johnson and back again. "What did that guy want?"

"I think I've just been threatened."

"Think?"

"It was part of a sermon."

"Yes, all of Reverend Johnson's statements sound like sermons, and the reaction to them is purely religious," said Coombs. "The minute he opens his mouth people start praying."

It made Karen smile.

"Mayors, governors, city officials, they go down on their knees."

"Everybody's afraid of him."

"Because he knows how to put on demonstrations."

"No," said Karen, "because he claims that twenty-two percent of the city's population believes in him."

"Oh, they believe in him all right," said Coombs. "They've always had faith in men like Johnson." Coombs's grin broadened. "They've been disappointed time and again."

"He's a complete charlatan."

"He's full of shit, I think you're trying to say."

"He warned that if we put Epps on trial there may be demonstrations."

"It's possible."

"With him at the head of them, he seemed to say."

"It's possible."

Demonstrations had a way of turning into riots. Elected officials were terrified of them and so, whenever possible, they acceded to Johnson's demands.

"So what do we do?" Karen asked.

"We go to trial," said Coombs.

Karen looked at him. How young ne is, she thought. By now she had forgotten he was black. He was just another trusting young lawyer. She felt like his mother. The young, she thought, see the big questions as obvious, simple. She envied him.

Coombs was carrying an armload of dossiers which he now dropped on her desk.

"These are the cops involved in the case," he explained. "You going to interview all twenty or what?"

There wasn't enough time left to interview twenty cops in depth, which Coombs knew as well as she did. Karen began to feel a bit desperate.

Her secretary appeared again at the door. "The police commissioner wants to see you."

She had no time for the police commissioner, who had no power over her. He belonged to a separate arm of the system. Nonetheless, she felt she must try to fit him in. "All right, schedule an appointment tomorrow or the next day."

"No," said the woman, "he's here. He wants to see you right now."

Knowing she had twenty cops to interview, and other witnesses as well, Karen gave an exasperated sigh. Instead of dealing with her witnesses, she was obliged to fend off McCarthy, the DA, Reverend Johnson, and now the PC—what could the PC possibly want? This case was out of police hands. It had nothing to do with him any longer.

She could see him standing behind her secretary, big and florid-faced, the ex-street cop wearing civilian clothes that didn't quite fit. She had met him only once before. He was surrounded now by uniformed brass hats, six other high-ranking men in all. Quite an entourage, she thought. Forcing a smile, she rose to greet him.

"You fellows wait outside for me," the PC ordered his commanders. He then turned to Karen and demanded bluntly: "What's this about accepting a plea?"

"What plea is that?" Karen asked him.

"I happened to be in the building and I heard you're accepting a plea."

"You've been misinformed."

"If this case is lost—"

"Slow down," said Karen, still trying to smile. "What makes you think I'll lose it?"

"—you'll have a police revolution on your hands. I'll

speak to the DA. In my opinion, this case needs a man prosecuting it. A man who'll go all the way with it.''

She hadn't known that such Neanderthal types as this still existed.

''A man who thinks he can win it.''

''Commissioner, that's an outrageous thing to say.''

''That's why I'm here. To impress on you how strongly the police department feels about this case.''

''I feel strongly about it myself,'' Karen said tightly. ''Now if you'll excuse me—''

''I want your assurance that—''

She was trying to herd him out into the hall where his entourage milled about waiting for him.

''Remember my warning. I won't be responsible—''

Finally she succeeded in shutting her door on him, but as she stood closed up in her office she found she had sweated into her dress and was almost trembling.

The mayor and two assistants were in conference. When the mayor's secretary entered, leaning over to whisper in his ear, the police commissioner was already visible in the anteroom through the half-open door. The mayor could do nothing but nod that he be shown in. The two assistants remained in their chairs, but the PC, entering, ignored them and spoke directly to the mayor.

''May I see you in private, Mr. Mayor?''

''Lewis, Irving,'' said the mayor, ''we'll take this up later.''

The assistants gathered their papers and left.

''Mr. Mayor, there's a trial coming up.'' The PC was trying but failing to speak calmly. ''Lionel Epps,'' he said.

The mayor nodded. ''I know the case. Shot five of your men.''

''To cops it's the most important trial in the history of the city.''

''Yes, I can see how they might feel that way. What's eating you, Charlie?''

"The DA's throwing in the towel on it. The assistant who now has the case, Karen Henning—"

"Surprised me too."

"If that woman accepts a plea or loses this case—"

The mayor put his finger to his lips. "Ssshh. Half the electorate is of the gentler sex, Charlie."

"—I won't be able to control my men. How can a female even understand how important this case is to the department? I go to see her and she practically throws me out."

"Did you compliment her on her hairdo, on her fingernail polish?"

The PC did not answer.

"That's where you made your mistake, Charlie. She's a good-looking woman, isn't she?"

"I suppose."

"Good-looking women like to be complimented. You should take that into account."

The PC did not know whether the mayor was joking or not.

"All right," the mayor said, "what is it you expect me to do?"

"Make it plain to the DA that he is to go all out. Tell him to give the case back to Norm Harbison."

The mayor seemed to be considering this idea, but in fact he was stalling for time. His most immediate problem, he saw, was not the Epps case but his police commissioner. "What do you think happened there?" he asked. "Why the switch away from Harbison?"

"First of all the DA doesn't want Harbison getting that much ink."

If it was as obvious as this to the police commissioner, thought the mayor, it was obvious to everyone. "The party might get ideas about passing the torch to a new generation," agreed the mayor.

"That's right."

"Which means the old fart's going to run again," said the mayor. "I'm sure of it."

"Mr. Mayor, you're the only one who can turn this around."

The mayor shook his head sadly and got up to escort the PC to the door.

"The DA is an elected official, Charlie, and not subject to my orders."

"Mr. Mayor, you appointed me. I've always leveled with you. I don't want to be around the day that woman loses this case."

"In the last election my share of the black vote was down 12.2 percent. My share of the Hispanic vote declined by 7.7 percent. White women, on the other hand, love me. Let's hope none of them gets wind of this conversation."

The mayor had moved the PC out into the anteroom. He had his arm around him.

"Calm down, Charlie. She's competent, I'm told. Besides which, it's an open-and-shut case. I haven't practiced law in thirty years, but even I could get a conviction on this one."

Karen, at her desk, looked up at Coombs, who had been waiting patiently.

"I'll speak to these two first," she told him, and pushed across the top two files.

Coombs read the names on them and nodded: Muldoon and Barone. It was where anyone would start.

"Call their command, have them report here tomorrow morning," Karen said.

When she came out of the building to go home there were television crews waiting on the sidewalk. The blinding lights came on and she was asked about the rumor that the prosecution intended to accept a plea. She denied it as succinctly and coolly as she could.

"The trial will go forward as scheduled."

— 9 —

Tonight there were three detectives in the car. Barone was again driving, with Muldoon beside him and the new guy, Ritter, in the back. They were showing Ritter the sights of the precinct, of which there were not many, and most of those that existed were significant to themselves only. Such as 145th Street, for instance, where the drug dealers stood alongside their swanky cars watching men wash them by hand.

"See those cars at the curb? In the drug business, getting some mutt to wash your car out of a pail means status."

Such as the undertaking parlor on St. Nicholas—another status symbol—from which drug dealers liked to get buried when they met with accidents. "See that sign in the window: 'Because You Deserve the Best.' "

Back and forth. Up and down—the precinct was really quite small. The same few streets over and over. To Ritter they must all look the same.

"I had my first homicide in there." They had begun to point out specific buildings. "There was a knife in her back long as your fucken arm. Came out her left tit."

"Fucken mutt's girlfriend was in the can with his sister. He starts screaming that he has to piss, and they wouldn't open the door, so he starts firing his piece through the door.

Put a bullet through his girlfriend's ass. We arrested him. Mutt was fifteen years old.''

An entire people known to a certain group of men only by their crimes. By the most bizarre of their crimes. They were trying to tell Ritter this without actually telling him. Perhaps they didn't know it themselves. They imagined these were only stories. Tall stories that weren't tall. It was all true. Stories that were amusing, not shocking. No cop would be shocked. Stories that were meant to instruct as well.

"Threw him off the roof. He landed on some stolen bicycles, so we solved that case too.''

In addition they were setting themselves apart from Ritter—they had seen all this, and he had not. They imagined they understood what they had seen, which they didn't. No one did. No one could. But at least they had seen it, whereas Ritter, who had been a cop only four years, a detective only eight months, had come to the Three-Two from Staten Island. Staten Island was practically rural, for chrissake. He knew nothing about people who did such things to each other.

Barone had turned out onto Lenox Avenue, except that the street signs read Malcolm X Boulevard.

"What's Malcolm X Boulevard?'' inquired Ritter.

"Lenox,'' said Barone.

"They renamed the streets after these mutts,'' said Muldoon.

"Eighth Avenue,'' said Barone, "is now Frederick Douglass Boulevard, Seventh is now Adam Clayton Powell Jr. Boulevard.''

"Last couple of years you need a map to find your way around fucken Harlem,'' complained Muldoon.

They passed in front of the International Bar.

"Fucken International Bar,'' muttered Muldoon. "Nothing but Jamaicans in there.''

"Cowboys,'' said Barone. "Shoot first, ask questions later.''

Ritter listened respectfully, as young detectives should.

"Fucken triple homicide.''

'We've been looking for a certain witness for weeks,'' said Barone. "We can't seem to find him.''

Although Ritter was all ears, they fell silent, even as Barone pulled into the curb.

They locked the car and crossed the sidewalk to the bar.

"On Staten Island we never bothered to lock the cars,'' Ritter commented.

"Leave a police vehicle unlocked in Harlem, you don't know what you'll find when you come back,'' said Barone.

"Maybe nothing,'' said Muldoon.

"No car,'' said Barone.

"Or maybe some nice guy will have dumped a few bags of dogshit in on the seats.''

The barroom was long, narrow. The six or eight men at the bar went silent at once. Along the wall opposite were three widely spaced wooden tables, none of which matched each other in size, shape, or even stability. At them people sat drinking, mostly men, two or three women. They too went silent. Above their heads was painted a long, primitive mural of Caribbean scenes: villages, mountains, the seafront. In places chunks of mural were missing.

"Bullet holes?'' asked Ritter in a low voice.

"Of course bullet holes, what do you think?'' said Muldoon.

The detectives moved further into the silence. Ritter was glancing curiously around. Barone and Muldoon stood apart, facing in different directions, their hands on their hips, meaning near their guns, just in case. They were not afraid or even nervous. Nothing would happen to them in here. No one would dare.

Barone said to the barman: "Hello there, Wilfred, how ya doing?''

Wilfred was a huge man, bald, very black. His reaction was a grin that was overlarge, overly ingratiating.

"Everything quiet, Wilfred?

"Yes sir, chief.''

Barone reached over the bar and they shook hands. "Nobody shooting up the place lately?"

Wilfred gave a great obsequious laugh. "Not so's I've noticed."

"Not like the night of the trouble, eh, Wilfred?"

"That was some night, that was," conceded the grinning Wilfred.

The missing witness, as expected, was not present. Barone nodded in the direction of the other patrons, and led the way back onto the street.

As he pulled out into traffic he brooded about the case, as did Muldoon, but neither spoke.

"So what happened the night of the shooting?" asked Ritter.

"Three mutts DRT," said Muldoon.

"You mean DOA?"

"I mean DRT. Dead right there."

"I hadn't heard that expression," said Ritter.

"Fucken triple homicide," said Muldoon, thinking: Guy comes from Staten Island, probably never saw a fucken body in his life.

"Mutt pinches a woman's ass," said Muldoon. "Pats, pinches, feels—how the fuck do I know. The mutt she's with pulls a knife. The other mutt runs home to get his piece. He comes back and opens fire. Empties his gun into the bar. Blood everywhere."

"It was crowded in there," said Barone. "Twenty or thirty people at least."

"What was he using?" Ritter leaned intently over the seat.

"A fucken nine. You know the moral of the story?"

"Moral?"

"Don't bring a knife to a gunfight," said Barone.

"Mutt sprayed the fucken place," said Muldoon.

The new man peered out the back window at the diminishing bar.

Barone said: "By the time we got there, there's three on

the floor, right? Shoes, clothes all over the place. The blood was so thick we were slipping in it. We were splashing it up onto our pants legs. And clothing everywhere you looked. People tried to get away so bad they ran right out of their clothes. I never saw that before.''

"There's a mutt leaning against the wall by the door,'' said Muldoon. "The only witness still standing. I grab him, but he said he couldn't go with me because his leg's gone to sleep. I tell him: Well, wake it up and let's go. I look down and he's been shot through the leg. He didn't even know it.''

Ritter nodded. "And that's the guy we're looking for now, right?''

"He recognized the shooter,'' Barone said, as he steered into a side street. "Said he knew him as Chocolate Bar.''

Rows of brownstones passed by. Tonight no one sat on stoops in camp chairs. It was too cold. "How's that for a name,'' said Barone. "Chocolate Bar?''

"We put it in the computer,'' said Muldoon. "On Chocolate Bar you get about eight hundred hits.''

There were clumps of men on some of the street corners, though. They had lit fires in garbage cans or disused oil drums and they stood around warming their hands.

"Look at those mutts,'' said Muldoon. "When you arrest them you find they're wearing three pairs of pants.''

"I went back to the hospital,'' said Barone. As he drove by he studied the glowing faces. "The guy said he made a mistake. Not Chocolate Bar, Candy Bar. So we ran Candy Bar. Got another eight hundred hits. Yeah.''

"By now we had bits of description on this Candy Bar,'' said Muldoon, "height, weight, and so forth, from other witnesses we had found—who wanted nothing to do with the case, by the way. We put together ten possibles, carry the photos over to the hospital—''

"And the witness was gone,'' finished Ritter.

"Yeah.''

"Phony address,'' said Muldoon. "Fucken mutt.''

At the corner came another clump of black men. They

stood in threes and fours, maybe fifteen men altogether, no blazing fire here, men bundled up to the ears. Faces that stared back for a moment, then away.

"We've been looking for that witness every night since," said Barone. "If we can find him, and if he picks out a photo for this Candy Bar, it will give us a name, maybe an address to go with it. Maybe we can pick the guy up. Then maybe we can get the other witnesses to come in, have a lineup, maybe even arrest the sonuvabitch."

"Lotta ifs," said Ritter.

"Yeah," conceded Barone.

After driving in silence for a time, Barone said: "Making a case is so goddam complicated, so difficult. Finding witnesses, taking statements, making identifications, finding the perpetrator, finding the witnesses again, making your lineup—it's a wonder any cases ever get made at all."

The other two men gave no response.

"But sometimes you do all that work, and it all comes together, the case is there, ready for the DA, and it's such an incredible high—that's why you're in this job, looking for highs like that."

Muldoon stared at his partner's profile. Annoyed, he said: "You're one of these detectives think they're doing God's work. But all you're doing is shoveling shit. How many times I have to tell you?"

The car turned the corner, and they passed in front of a grocery that was still open. "Stop here," said Muldoon. His annoyance had gone over into a powerful thirst. "I gotta take a piss," he explained.

"You want anything?" he asked, getting out of the car.

"No," said Barone.

"Nothing, thanks," said the new guy.

As Muldoon lumbered toward the grocery he could feel Barone's eyes boring into his back.

"What about Fatso?" asked Ritter.

"What about him?" said Barone.

"If he needs to piss," said Ritter, "why not go back to the stationhouse?"

Barone pretended to be fiddling with the hand radio on the seat beside him. "He likes this place."

"I know these hairbags," said Ritter.

"Do you now?"

"I worked with some of them on Staten Island. One old guy, he was well over forty. Hairbag had bottles stashed all over the precinct. By the end of the tour he was always half pissed. I couldn't take it no more."

"You report him?" said Barone.

Ritter shook his head. "No. I told them I wanted out. Said I was tired of looking for maids who had run off with the silverware. I asked for a high-crime precinct. They transferred me up here."

"You'll like it here," said Barone dryly.

The more he thought about Ritter dropping in on them out of the sky, the less he liked it. One did not become a detective simply by asking. There were career paths. Of course sometimes a guy made a big arrest, or broke a famous case, and got the gold shield for it. But there were no big arrests or famous cases on Staten Island. Or if there were, Barone had missed them.

"Tell me something, Ritter, you got only four years on the job, right?"

"Four years, yeah."

"So how'd you make detective in only four years?"

After a moment, Ritter said: "I had a hook."

"A contract," said Barone. There were supposed to be no more contracts, no more hooks, but no one believed it. A hook was possible.

"Who was your hook?"

"You wouldn't know him."

"Where's he work?"

"Headquarters."

"What's his name?"

Ritter gave a name and Barone, though he nodded, remembered that Ritter lived in Brighton Beach, the most distant corner of Brooklyn, a commute almost as long as his own. Wouldn't a hook who could get him the gold shield also get him into a precinct closer to his house? There were plenty of high-crime precincts in Brooklyn.

Barone resolved to find out from friends in headquarters if anyone by the name of this hook existed. No point alarming his partner just yet. There was no telling how Danny would react. He could well go off the deep end. In the meantime Barone would watch carefully and keep his suspicions to himself. He would be careful for himself and careful for Danny too.

Inside the grocery, Muldoon had gone straight to the cooler. The grocer, who knew him, made no protest. Having lifted out a beer, the detective went through into the stockroom where he twisted off the cap and had a long pull. When he looked up the grocer was in the doorway watching him. Muldoon gave him a wave and again tilted the bottle.

Leaving the empty on a shelf he came out into the store, where he stopped at the counter and picked up a box of candies. The tag said $5. A customer had come in and stood waiting his turn. After studying the customer for a moment, Muldoon decided to say to the grocer: "How much for this candy?"

"For you, nothing," said the grocer, all smiles.

The grocer was a foreigner, some kind of Greek or Arab. Maybe a Polack, who the hell knew. "Oh, I must pay you for these candies," said Muldoon, watching the customer. Nothing had been said about paying for the beer.

"Please you take," said the grocer.

The detective nodded, put his money away, slipped the box into his pocket, and went out.

"That feels better," he said as he climbed back into the car. Breaking open the box he offered candy to the other two, who declined. Barone pulled away from the curb.

Suddenly Muldoon, who had shoved a candy into his

mouth, spit it violently out the window. "Fucken thing disíntegrated on me," he cried. He was still spitting, trying to clear his mouth. He was outraged. "Crumbled to fucken powder. It's fucken stale." He put on the reading light and studied the labeling. "It says here, 'Not for Resale,' " he announced. "This thing was put out by the Girl Scouts." His tone took on an even more outraged note. "The nerve of that mutt. He was gonna make me pay for this. I should have locked the fucken mutt up for fraud."

Barone was laughing. He thought that Ritter, who was silent, wanted to laugh too, but didn't dare.

"I don't see what's funny," said Muldoon huffily.

"You're right," said Barone, laughing. "It's not funny."

Later, they went out of their precinct into the Two-Six, which included Riverside Drive and Columbia University, and in a deli on Broadway and 115th bought hero sandwiches, tonight's dinner—most nights' dinner.

"This is how far you have to come on meal period," explained Barone to Ritter.

"No one who works the Three-Two would eat anything that comes from there," said Muldoon.

In the deli Muldoon grabbed a beer out of the cooler and drank it down while waiting for his sandwich to be prepared. He drank a second beer—concealed inside a paper bag—in the car on the way back to the stationhouse. When Barone stopped at a red light he opened the car door and disposed of the empty by standing it up on the pavement. When the light changed they drove away from it.

The detective squadroom on the second floor was a suite of offices that extended across the front of the stationhouse, seven small rooms, plus a holding cell that at this hour on this particular night was empty. The office at one end of the floor belonged to the lieutenant commanding the squad, who was no doubt in there now because his door was closed.

The office at the opposite corner had been made over into a kind of lounge. This was where the detectives went to eat their dinners. The two other detectives on duty tonight were already in there watching a basketball game on television. The lounge contained a table, some chairs, a terminally old fridge, and the inevitable filing cabinets along one wall. The TV was fixed to the wall above the fridge.

There was a coffeemaker on top of the filing cabinets. Barone poured out coffee for himself and Muldoon, but not for Ritter, who was in talking to the lieutenant, and they sat down and began munching their sandwiches. When they had finished they crumpled the bags and wrappings and tossed them into the bin.

They went out and sat at their desks, where Muldoon began typing up a DD-5 on a case he had worked on two nights ago, and Barone got on the phone.

Muldoon was a two-finger typist, and the typewriter, an IBM Selectric, was in poor condition. "When I came on this job," he complained to Ritter, who sat now at the adjacent desk, "we had these upright Underwoods with half the keys missing." He wanted to make it clear to the new guy how long he had been a detective. "Now we have these modern fucken electrics with half the keys missing."

Barone, on the phone, was talking to a woman. Muldoon attempted to eavesdrop, but his partner was talking in too low a voice.

The lieutenant came out of his office. His name was Whitfield. He was six feet four inches tall, and when Barone had hung up, which he did somewhat hurriedly, the lieutenant handed over the message he had received earlier. The two detectives were to report to Assistant District Attorney Karen Henning tomorrow morning at 9 A.M.

"Bring the Lionel Epps folder with you," he ordered.

"Who's Karen Henning?" asked Muldoon.

"She has the Epps case, apparently."

"Norm Harbison has the Epps case," said Barone. He and Muldoon had both been interviewed several times by Harbison.

"Not anymore."

"What happened?"

"Just be there," said Whitfield, adding over his shoulder as he went back into his office, "and be on time."

"Fucken mutt," muttered Muldoon in a low voice.

Lieutenant Whitfield had taken command of the squad shortly after the shoot-out and had been putting in new controls and procedures ever since, wasting everybody's time.

His departure was followed by a heavy silence.

Whitfield was thirty-five, Barone's age. Muldoon resented taking orders from a younger man, and from a black. Barone, Muldoon knew, resented Whitfield for a different reason. He and Whitfield had gone through the police academy together, and two years ago even took the sergeant's test together. According to rumor the test results were altered in some way to favor minorities. Whitfield with his altered score passed the test high, Barone in the middle. Whitfield was made a sergeant, and almost immediately took and passed the lieutenant's test for which Barone, still waiting to make sergeant, was not eligible.

That was the rumor. The police department ran on rumors, and Muldoon believed all of them. He had contempt for the men who ran the department, down to and including Whitfield, for they were gutless one and all in front of higher rank, and in front of politicians. The brass's sole function as he saw it was to exalt themselves by screwing cops.

Muldoon was studying the telephone message. "Karen Henning," he said to Barone. "You know this broad?"

"I think I had a case with her when I was in narcotics. Good-looking woman, if it's the one I think it is."

"Did you boff her?"

Barone grinned. "I don't remember."

Muldoon was envious not so much of Barone's supposed conquests, but of the ease with which he could joke about them and be believed. He himself, when he occasionally got wound up so tight he couldn't stand it anymore, went down to the Times Square area where he would find and go upstairs with a hooker.

"Want to go out into the street again?" asked Muldoon.

"On your feet, Ritter," said Barone, "time to go back to work."

The detectives signed out, went downstairs and got back in the car, and no sooner were they under way than another call came over the radio: a child teetering on a window ledge.

Barone grasped the radio. "Two-squad. We'll take that job."

"What are you, a social worker?" asked Muldoon. "You're a detective, for chrissake. Let the patrol guys handle it."

"Well," said Barone, "we're right there."

He pulled up at the address and they got out. There were two men in the doorway shivering and stamping their feet, but for Harlem the building seemed well cared for. A child, maybe four years old, was standing in an open second-floor window.

Barone tried the outer door, but it was locked. "You got your key," he said to one of the idlers, "open the door." When he flashed his shield, the man complied.

They went up the two flights, found what must be the door to the apartment, and Barone pounded on it, but no one answered. They went back down to the street, but when they again peered up at the window the child was no longer there. Perhaps he was watching television, or rooting in the refrigerator for food. If there was a refrigerator. If there was food. Obviously his mother had left him alone in there, which strictly speaking was not against the law. She might be in a crack den, or out getting impregnated by a new boyfriend. Or she might be at work—working hard to support her little boy.

They stood on the sidewalk peering up. There was a window guard in the window. Probably the kid was old enough to know better than to climb over it and splatter himself on the sidewalk.

But he might. One could envision still another of the ghetto tragedies of this nature.

It must be cold in there too, Barone thought.

They could call in the fire department. Firemen could go in the window and get the kid out. And do what with him? Besides which, the firemen as they worked would lord it over them—firemen lording it over cops. Then the mother comes home and her kid is gone and she goes berserk. Then what? How does she find him? She'd be sick with worry. She might even harm herself. Or harm the kid when she found him. What was the correct thing to do here?

Muldoon, who could see all these thoughts go through his partner's head, had already made his own decision.

Barone on the stoop addressed the same idler as before. "Do you know who that kid belongs to? Where's his mother? Do you know his mother? Is there a super? Does the super have a key?"

The idler answered the first two questions with "I don't know," after which he confined his responses to shrugs.

Muldoon took the radio out of Barone's hands. The kid did not become police business until such time as he was lying dead on the sidewalk. It was not the cops' job to make these mutts take care of their children.

Muldoon raised Central. "That job was ten-ninety, Central, unfounded."

He handed the radio back to Barone and returned to the car. Ritter followed. After hesitating briefly, Barone followed too. He did not know what else to do. Muldoon's solution seemed to him as good as any other.

At 1 A.M. the detectives signed out, and the squadroom closed down for the night.

Muldoon, Barone, Ritter, and the two other detectives went outside to their cars which were part of a row of cars backed into the curb opposite the stationhouse. All the buildings on this side of the street were burned out, condemned and empty. So were most of the buildings to either side of the stationhouse. The stationhouse was almost the only functioning building on the entire block. It was convenient in a way. The street had become a parking lot for the private cars of Three-

Two cops. The signs on the lampposts so proclaimed it: POLICE VEHICLES ONLY.

Muldoon said to Barone, "Want to go get a couple beers?"

"No, I can't tonight."

A number of patrol officers, all now in civilian clothes, were also moving toward their cars. As Muldoon grasped his door handle he saw Police Officer Maureen Whatever-her-name-was. He saw that she had changed into pants and a car coat. All the cops were calling good night to each other, getting into their cars and driving away, but not Barone and not Maureen. His partner had gone over to her, Muldoon saw. Now she was leaning her ass against her fender and Barone was talking to her. Now she grinned. Now she looked serious.

Now the two of them were looking toward Barone's car.

Muldoon let out his clutch. With a squeal of tires he was out of his slot and halfway down the street. The light on the corner was red but he went angrily through it, heading toward the bridge across to the Bronx.

"So how about that drink I owe you?" Barone said.

"I don't know. It's pretty late." She glanced around as if she wanted someone else to decide.

"We just got off work, so how could it be late?"

She seemed pleased to be standing here talking to him, but perhaps hoped this wouldn't go any further.

"Does your husband wait up for you?"

"Of course not. He's got to get his sleep."

"So we'll have a drink together. You'll get home twenty minutes, half an hour late. You slide into bed beside him, he'll never wake up."

"Some nights he wakes up."

Barone looked her up and down and liked what he saw. "If I were married to you I'd wake up every night."

She grinned. "No you wouldn't."

He took her arm and led her toward his car. This was the first test, the initial physical contact. How would she react?

Maureen, who might have snatched her arm back, only lifted his hand gently away, even holding it a moment before letting it drop. Although she had stopped him, from his point of view she had reacted very well indeed. In situations of this kind Barone was acutely attuned to whatever signals a woman might send, especially those she might not be aware of.

"All right, but I'll follow you in my car," she said. "So I can drive home from there. Where are we going?"

He led her to the Bronx Plaza Hotel near Yankee Stadium and they sat down in the lounge and ordered drinks, beer for him, a Bloody Mary for her.

"This is a nice place," said Maureen, glancing around.

"I wanted to take you to a nice place."

"I hope cops don't come in here."

"Right," said Barone solicitously. "We certainly don't want to start any foolish talk."

She looked apprehensive. "Oh, I hope not."

The Bronx courthouse was two blocks away, the precinct stationhouse not much further, so probably cops did come in here. "We have nothing to worry about," he told her. "No one comes here but ballplayers after the games." His principal worry was that the lounge might close soon, because it was empty except for themselves and the barman. He perhaps had very little time in which to work.

"And what we're doing is completely innocent anyway," she said, "isn't it?"

Barone grinned at her. "Unless you have designs on my person."

He got her to talk about her family. Once started she couldn't be stopped. She spoke of growing up in a police household, about her awe of her father and brothers, about how as a child she wished she were a boy so she could grow up to be a cop, and lo and behold by the time she did grow up it was possible for a woman to be a cop, a real cop on the street in a high-crime precinct like the Three-Two, and here she was, and she loved most of it, though not everything. On weekends they still gave her a stationhouse job, usually she was the 124 man, because she knew how to type, but she thought as time went on she'd be really accepted. She named one of the most decorated cops in the precinct, and, well, her proudest day so far was the day the decorated cop agreed to ride with her, because lots of the women in the precinct he wouldn't ride with.

"You went right home and told your husband," commented Barone.

"How did you know?"

"But he wasn't impressed. He didn't understand."

She sounded wistful. "No."

"He's not a cop," said Barone sympathetically, "how could he have understood?" And he patted her hand. She did not, he noted, recoil from his touch. "Is he a jealous man?"

"He has nothing to be jealous about."

"Sometimes men are jealous anyway."

"My father had a talk with him when I came on the job. He told him there would be nights when something happened and I would have to go to court, or work overtime, and wouldn't come home. He told him there might be nights when I would want to have a drink with some of the guys after work, and might come home late. He told him he had to accept that and not to be jealous and not worry about me."

Barone nodded understandingly. He patted her hand again, and when she did not immediately withdraw it, he let his own hand linger on hers. Then he began to play with her fingers.

This lasted only a moment before she frowned, excused herself, and marched off to the ladies' room.

After waiting until she was out of sight, Barone stepped to the front desk where he showed his shield and asked for a room.

"And I want the special rate. You got a special rate for cops, don't you?" With the courthouse so close and all, cops must have to stay overnight here all the time.

The clerk gave him a rate.

"You can do better than that, can't you?" said Barone. "Look how late it is. Why don't we do it on the arm, and I'll owe the hotel a favor?"

The price came down again. Not all the way, but it came down. Clutching the key, Barone made it back to the table just as Maureen reappeared. She had combed her hair, he saw, and had perhaps washed her face. But she did not sit down, the first wrong signal so far.

"I better be going."

He had perhaps misjudged her and would be stuck with the room. Well, he'd just give the key back and say he changed his mind. "You're sure you don't want another drink?"

"I'm sure. I've got a long way to drive."

"I know. I live near you, remember? I wish we could drive it together."

She smiled at him. "That would be nice, wouldn't it?"

Barone put money down and they put their coats on and walked out past the desk to the street.

"It's a pity you have to go," he said.

"It was really nice getting to know you."

"We could do it again."

"Yeah, I'd like that."

They looked at each other, and neither moved.

Maureen laughed. "I didn't know what you'd be like."

"I'm like most cops."

"You have such a reputation in our precinct."

"Undeserved, I'm sure."

Again both were silent. "I've decided not to drive home after all," said Barone. It was best to get this out in the open now. Let it weigh on her. "I've taken a room in the hotel."

"Oh, I didn't know that."

"I've got court in the morning."

They stood looking at each other.

"I should go," said Maureen.

"Can I kiss you good night?"

"What do you want to do that for?"

"I feel very close to you, somehow."

"I feel close to you too."

"I've been wanting to kiss you for an hour." It was better to ask permission, make her think she was the one in control of whatever might or might not happen. "So can I?"

The question made her smile. "Sure."

She seemed to offer her cheek, but when he turned her chin, her lips were there. They were quite fleshy lips with her teeth behind them but closed up tight, and then after a moment they opened and he felt how sharp her teeth were, and then her tongue. Barone thought he could tell a lot from a kiss, and this one told him he had only to press on a bit further.

"You don't really have to go, do you?"

"Maybe not."

"You don't really want to go."

"No."

He took her hand and they went back inside. The clerk, watching them get into the elevator, shrugged.

The bars Muldoon drank in after work were those frequented by other cops, who came from many precincts. Some nights he found men he had drunk with before, some nights not. They ordered bottomless pitchers of beer and recounted stories that became more righteous, more obscene, more heroic, sometimes funnier, certainly boozier as the pitchers emptied and the night wore on.

One of Muldoon's bars was on the West Side, and another, tonight's bar, was in the Fordham section of the Bronx. He sat over a pitcher of beer telling a cop from the 19th about the triple homicide in the International Bar. The 19th was a rich man's precinct on the Upper East Side. Cops from outside Harlem, he had found, made a more appreciative audience than other Harlem cops. They were more likely to see the ironies involved, to understand to what extent blacks in Harlem were animals.

"Three mutts DRT," Muldoon told him.

"You mean DOA?"

"You fucks from the Nineteenth," Muldoon snorted, thinking: Only precinct this joker ever worked, probably. Probably never saw a fucken corpse in his life. Like Ritter tonight. Still a virgin. "In Harlem it's DRT. Dead right there."

He squinted at the other cop through smoke.

"Thing happened to me once," the other cop ventured.

Muldoon ignored him. "I grab the witness. I look down and he's been shot through the leg. Mutt didn't even know it."

Muldoon signaled the bartender for another pitcher.

They stood in the center of the room caressing, kissing.

"You got quite a handful there," said Barone. "Two handfuls."

"Would you like to see them?" said Maureen throatily. "You could see them if you want." She pulled the sweater off over her head, disarraying her hair slightly. Her arms went behind her back. She hunched her shoulders to make the bra slide down her arms. "There," she said proudly, and shook them at him.

Barone liked that. He liked a woman who was proud of her tits. "You're gorgeous," he said.

She grasped him by the ears, pulling him forward. She was grinning almost as if drunk. She pulled his face up close and slapped his face with them, right cheek, left cheek.

He undid the waist of her slacks. Her off-duty gun must have been in her pocket, for as the slacks slid downward her gun fell to the floor. This gave him a start. He picked it up. She stood in her underpants. He stood fully dressed holding her gun. They began laughing.

"Someday in some hotel room," Barone said, "one of these things is going to hit the floor and go off, killing a guy's partner. He's going to have some tall explaining to do."

"Or she will," said Maureen.

She came into his arms and rubbed herself against his clothes. Reaching back he deposited the gun on the dresser behind him, then embraced her. His hands began to move all over her body.

"You know what I feel like?" she murmured. "I feel like being really bad." And she bit his ear.

He loved this. Each time he was with a woman he was amazed at how smooth their bodies were. Smooth all over. He loved the way their bodies felt. He loved the way they looked and smelled. They all reacted in a different way and said different things, and he loved that too and was amazed each time. He got his hand down inside her underpants and through the thicket and into what for him was the core of the solar system. Her clit was as thick as his finger and hard and she was very wet. Her eyes closed, she was thrusting against him, and for the longest time seemed to forget to breathe.

To undress he was obliged to step back. She watched him, watched him drop each article of clothing. Breathing more or less normally, no longer quivering, she was smiling now, confident, a bit avid, a bit impatient. And, something unusual in his experience, she seemed as curious and as intent on watching him undress as a man would be watching a woman.

"Do you have a rubber?" she asked. "Let me put it on you. I'm really good at putting them on."

He handed it over, and she knelt in front of him.

"Don't I know how to do it?" she said. "There. I'm terrific at it, right?" She gave her work a friendly pat.

For him this first part was always the best part somehow. He pulled her to him.

But once they were in bed in the dark it all changed. Her body, especially that special part of it, was exactly the same as other females' he had had, encompassed him in exactly the same way, reacted exactly the same, no different, and although she made a good deal of noise there was no more conversation. It was like a road he had already been down, he was not amazed anymore, there were only small surprises left, and not many of those, it was almost anticlimactic, automatic, and he knew he hadn't gained any ground, that he understood the world, life, himself, no better than before, that next time it would be as if this time had never happened, he would have to start anew.

"She's lying there in a pool of blood in front of the lockers. Fourteen years old."

The other cop stared with glazed eyes into his glass. He was perhaps no longer listening. Muldoon was not aware of this. The story he was telling was as real to him as life, perhaps more so. As a story it was not even particularly unusual, not for Harlem, merely recent and on his mind, but it had acquired its own momentum and would go forward.

"Kid that shot her, he's fourteen too. They all got guns in that school."

"Any witnesses?" interrupted the other cop.

"An accident, he tells us." Muldoon had begun to slur his words. "Said if you don't have a piece in that school, you're nobody."

"Gotta find the witnesses. Crucial."

"Find the fuck sold him the gun," Muldoon said. "That's who I'm gonna to find. Kid gave us his name."

"Who?"

"Can't find him. Fucken mutt. The girl was pregnant, did I tell you that? Autopsy showed it. Fourteen years old. When I find that mutt I'm going to blow him away."

"It would fuck up your case."

"Everybody beats the case. You want to win the case, shoot the prick."

"All right, shoot him then."

"It's what he deserves."

"What will your partner say?"

Muldoon's head felt thick. He missed Barone. He wondered where he was and what he was doing. In bed probably. All Barone cared about was cunt. Muldoon experienced jealousy and anger at the same time. "My partner does what I tell him," he muttered drunkenly. "I'm the boss."

Barone reclined against the headboard. Maureen lay heavy in the crook of his arm. Because of the heaviness he assumed she was asleep. He had begun to worry about her father and her brothers. The police society had its own commandments. One didn't fool around with another cop's wife or girlfriend. Or with another cop's daughter or sister. Cops were armed, they got angry, and they tended to have old-fashioned ideas as far as daughters and sisters were concerned. He didn't want to be accused of ruining Maureen, or Maureen's marriage. If she got caught, who knew what she might say. It wouldn't be the father who came after him. One of the brothers, more likely. Or both brothers. Tonight was perhaps a mistake. He wished Maureen would wake up and go home. He wanted her to be in her own bed asleep for her husband to find when he got up in the morning.

He moved his arm jerkily, but Maureen only purred and nestled closer. Perhaps he was exaggerating the degree of risk. Whether he was or not, he wanted her to go. He hankered to be alone now. He wanted to feel she was no longer his responsibility. He needed to get some sleep as well. It must be 4 A.M. by now, and in a few hours he had to be downtown at the district attorney's office.

He jostled her again. "Wake up, Maureen. Shouldn't you be getting home? Wake up."

More purring.

He would never actually tell her to leave, but if the idea did not occur to her he was considering leaving himself, even though this room was both comfortable and, now, would have to be paid for. He could tell her he must get back to the precinct. There was a bunkroom off the squadroom. If he had a late date or a day tour or court appearance in the morning, he sometimes slept there. Two double-decker bunks and hardly enough room otherwise to turn around. No blankets or sheets of course, but he kept a sleeping bag in his car. However, he hoped that in a few minutes Maureen would get up and leave. The dormitory room was really small, tended to be airless, and if there was anybody else in there it was almost impossible to sleep.

—— 10 ——

In her kitchen Karen and her husband talked it out. She was dressed, ready to leave for work. Hank was in pajamas and still rubbing sleep out of his eyes. Until she got a handle on this case, she told him, it would have to be his job to feed the children, get them off to school, give them dinner at night as well. Hank agreed. It was still dark out. The lights were on in the kitchen. Since she didn't know what time she'd be home, she'd take the car to the station. Hank could catch a ride to the college with someone else. He agreed to this too, and she kissed him and left the house.

As she crossed the back lawn to the garage, the sun was just coming up. It caught the tops of the bare trees, and the air smelled clean. At the station she stood on the platform in the low cold light amid men in dark overcoats and white shirts. They all seemed tall to her, tall men reading tall newspapers. Executives who wanted to get to work early.

The train came in. It was crowded. She could get only a middle seat. Her arms felt pinned to her sides. The air in the car smelled stale. She was surrounded by newspapers that kept rustling. On her lap were the personnel folders on Detectives Muldoon and Barone, whom she would interview that morning, and she studied them, not looking up again until the train was crossing the bridge over the river into Manhattan. The water below was brown and she looked down at it and tried to work out how the interviews should go.

At Grand Central Station she went down into the subway. The rush hour had not started yet and she got a seat. She sat with her briefcase on her lap, enjoying what was probably the last quiet moment of the day. Centre Street, when she came up into the air again, was empty too, only a few people, lawyers probably, hurrying toward their offices. The principal business in this neighborhood was trials. In addition to the courtrooms in her own building, there were others across the street, and still more in the imitation Greek temple next door, the original courthouse, built early in this century. The federal courthouse was nearby too. But the courts would not convene for two hours or so. The sidewalks were bare of all the courtroom guards, bondsmen, jurors who would clog them later.

She went into her building past the cop on security duty, whom she greeted by name. He was drinking coffee from a cardboard cup and looked tired, ready to go home and to sleep. She rode upstairs in an empty elevator and unlocked her door off an empty corridor. Her secretary's desk was unoccupied. She left both doors open but from the corridor could hear no sound.

Now in her office she got out other folders and paged slowly through each of them, trying to memorize the details of a case that was extremely complicated—a winnable case certainly but bulky and unwieldy because it involved so many people. Plus an opponent, McCarthy, who would throw in extraneous arguments, outrageous arguments, all of which would have to be defused instantly by her. Never mind the facts. McCarthy would try to fog up the jurors' minds. It would be her job to see this did not happen.

Her secretary came in at 9 A.M. and shortly after that announced the arrival of Detectives Muldoon and Barone, both of whom were some minutes late.

Karen's door was closed by then. ''Send for Mr. Coombs, please,'' she directed her secretary. ''I'll take Detective Muldoon first.'' This was proper; Muldoon was both the senior man and more central to the case.

Karen came around her desk smiling, and stuck her hand out. ''Good morning, how are you?''

Muldoon no more responded to her smile than to her greeting. He wore a plaid sports coat that was mostly green, and a striped shirt that was mostly blue, and a flowered red tie with stains on it. Her hand was out there and he looked at it. Finally he gave it a brief shake. His hand was fat and moist. He was not used to shaking hands with women, apparently. Karen frowned. Muldoon was her principal witness and already she was put off by him.

She sat down behind her desk and looked at him, noting his bloodshot eyes and the red veins in his nose.

Coombs came in.

''This is Mr. Coombs,'' said Karen. ''He was working with Mr. Harbison, so you know each other already, I believe.''

A brief nod by Coombs. No reaction whatever from Muldoon, who looked at him, then away. Coombs took the chair in the corner.

Muldoon had not yet made eye contact with anyone. This man may only be nervous, Karen tried to encourage herself. Some cops distrust lawyers. It's automatic with them. Muldoon doesn't know me after all, probably doesn't know what I want from him.

If he was nervous then her first job was to put him at ease, and so she began to speak of past cases he had worked on— this was information out of his file. She asked questions, tried to sound admiring. He answered with grunts or monosyllables and continued to avoid eye contact.

Karen kept smiling, stayed outwardly cheerful.

Muldoon interrupted her. ''Would you mind telling me what this is all about.''

''I want to go over the Epps case with you. Jury selection starts next Monday and—''

''I've been all over that with you people.''

''Well, not with me personally—''

"A hundred times."

"Well, once more won't hurt, then."

"Norm Harbison knows all about it."

"Yes, I've talked to Norman. He's busy on something else, I'm afraid."

"Look, lady, I got homicides I'm investigating."

"I'm sure," said Karen.

"See Harbison. It's in his notes."

Karen had inherited no notes. Harbison had apparently made none, nor would she make many herself, perhaps none. The case folders contained official police reports, the defendant's police record, minutes of his previous trials, hospital reports and photos and diagrams, the grand jury indictment, copies of the various briefs and motions, and no notes, plans, or strategies by Harbison. This seemed to her normal. Unwilling to provide the defense with foreknowledge of his strengths and weaknesses, he had determined to keep his Rosario material to an absolute minimum. Which was all to the good, though hard on anyone inheriting the case.

She began asking Muldoon specific questions. Though she was stubborn about it she got only more grunts and monosyllables, plus a few bored sighs. There was still no eye contact. Certain details Muldoon claimed to have forgotten. Or else he answered:

"Ask Harbison."

"I need to have some idea how you are going to respond to these questions on the stand," Karen explained politely.

"On the stand I'll tell exactly what happened."

"Yes, and exactly what was that?"

"You don't have to worry about me on the stand, lady."

But she was already worried.

"Do you know how many trials I've testified at?"

"I'm sure it's a great many." Be calm, Karen ordered herself, you need this man. "You'll be cross-examined—"

"I been cross-examined before. About a thousand times. I laugh at those guys."

I can't afford to antagonize my chief witness, Karen warned herself.

"The defense lawyer is very good," she said, "he's—"

"Those jokers don't worry me."

A silence fell between them. Finally Karen said: "Are you feeling all right?"

"Fine."

"You're not ill?"

"If I was ill I wouldn't be here."

"I thought you might be ill."

"Do I look ill to you?"

"No," said Karen bluntly, "you look hung over."

Muldoon gave a derisive snort. "What would you know about hangovers, lady?"

"Well," said Karen, studying him, "I've had a few."

"Me, never."

"I doubt that, somehow."

"You don't know a goddam thing about it."

If he is this hostile on the stand, thought Karen, he will lose the jury, and he may lose me the case.

"Can I ask you a favor?" she said, wearing a forced smile.

His impatient gaze flickered across hers. Then he was staring out the window again.

"I'd like you to wait in the anteroom a short time while I meet your partner."

No response from Muldoon.

"After which I'll want to talk to both of you together." She came around the desk. "It will only be a few minutes." She ushered him out with the best grace she could muster, and invited the second detective to enter.

She stood in the doorway as Barone moved past her. It was a wide enough doorway, but he came through it closer to her than he should have. He almost brushed her breasts with his arm. She looked up sharply. Though it might have been an accident, she was in a mood to consider it deliberate. These men, she thought angrily, who are they? Nothing but cops.

They were subordinate to her in this situation, and she resolved to make them know it.

When she turned, Barone was standing behind her, his hand outstretched.

"Mike Barone," he said cordially.

Calm down, she told herself. Maybe it wasn't deliberate at all. Maybe you're only imagining things.

His smile seemed pleasant, and compared to Muldoon he seemed to want to be friendly. Karen had no choice but to smile back, to declare a truce in a war he did not know had been declared.

"Karen Henning," she said, and as she shook hands with him she realized she knew him. She remembered him on the witness stand some years back: a tall young man with dark eyes and nice hands.

"We've worked together before," Barone said.

She went behind her desk and he took the chair facing it. "We have?" she said. She was not looking for a friend but for a cooperative witness. "When was that?"

"About six or seven years ago."

"Remind me."

A series of robberies of midtown jewelry stores. As he described the case now, he downplayed the investigation and arrest, which had been extremely skillful on his part, accentuating instead the prosecution and trial, which had been extremely skillful on hers. A not-so-subtle dose of flattery. He used the word *we* a lot. We did this. We did that.

"Do you remember?" he asked her.

It had been her first major trial, her first important conviction, which he hadn't needed to know then, nor now either. "Vaguely," she answered. "There have been so many cases since."

She remembered that he had made an excellent witness, but that his presence had made her a bit uncomfortable. There had been something too ingratiating about him. He wanted to be liked, and worked hard at it. He had exuded understanding and warmth. She had put him on the stand the first day, and he was so good the defense attorney did not bother to cross-examine him, and after three hours he was finished and she had sent him back to his command.

"After I testified, I came to the trial on one of my days off just to watch you work. You were terrific."

This too was flattering, if true. It made warning bells go off. Karen was cynical enough to ask: "What day was that?"

"The alibi witness was on the stand. Did you dismantle that guy! Did you ever!"

Remembering, Karen grinned.

"He claimed the defendant was unknown to him," Barone continued. "You got him to admit they had been in juvenile hall together. You had the papers to prove it. Then you asked him if they were not perhaps even related to each other. You had the papers to prove that, too."

Karen laughed. "Married to cousins but they didn't know each other."

"You had the courtroom in stitches."

"He was such a jerk."

There was no way Barone could know all this unless he had been there. Karen found that she accepted the flattery. To break down the alibi witness that day was fun, and she had done it beautifully, and now Barone had given the experience back to her.

They beamed at each other. But after a moment she looked down at his folder, pretending to study it while preparing to get this interview back onto a businesslike plane.

But when she looked up at him he was smiling at her, so she said: "I didn't see you there that day."

"You were busy."

"Why didn't you come up and say hello afterwards?"

"You didn't need me bothering you."

If true, this was extremely thoughtful.

She glanced down at the folder again, seeing the details of his life printed there, the names of his wife and children, his date of birth. Michael J. Barone. He was three years younger than she was.

"Well," she said, "let's talk about the Epps case, shall we?" And she began to ask questions.

Barone answered freely, or seemed to, seemed entirely forthcoming, had no difficulty remembering details most cops didn't notice, or else had forgotten: exact time and sequence of events, direction of movement, degree of available light, number of shots fired. As the interview continued she felt almost elated, for she imagined she had found a witness the jury would believe and that she herself could rely on, and against whom the memories of other witnesses could be cross-checked.

Thirty minutes passed. Although she toyed with a pencil throughout, she wrote nothing down. Finally she ceased questioning him and sat back in her chair.

"Your partner is a hard man to interview," she said.

"Danny? Why do you say that?"

"It's like pulling teeth."

"He just doesn't feel he knows you yet."

"I was wondering. Were the events of that night traumatic to him? Some cops after shoot-outs can remember nothing. When they try their minds go blank." Karen had encountered this syndrome before. "Is it something he just can't talk about?"

"Nothing shuts up Danny. You got the wrong guy. Try him again. I'll help you."

A few minutes later she invited Muldoon back into the room, and this time it went better. In the presence of his partner, he was somewhat more voluble, though still basically surly. He was often impatient with her and her questions, and as she took him through the night of the shoot-out he did not bother to hide it. Sometimes he could not remember details, or did not want to, and when this happened Barone prompted him. It was clear to Karen that Barone was the leader, though probably if you asked, Muldoon would claim the opposite. And probably Barone would listen and say nothing.

Finally she dismissed the older detective but held Barone,

who sat expectantly in his chair as she paced her small office and tried to decide how to proceed.

"Danny's going to make a great witness," said Barone, "what did I tell you!"

If Detective Barone wanted to help as much as he pretended, there was an unusual area she could lead him into. It would save her a lot of time. But she didn't know how he would react. Abruptly she made her decision. "I want to ask you about the other cops involved," she said. "I'd like you to tell me what you know about them."

"No problem, fire away."

She decided to mention the wounded cops first. "Police Officer Pierce?"

"Excellent cop."

She waited for him to say more, but he did not.

"Police Officer Boylehart."

"Another excellent cop."

"Police Officer Wiendienst."

"A great cop also."

"All right, Detective Barone. I suggest you sign out and go back to your command."

Barone, who remained in his chair, grinned up at her. "Ask me something hard."

"I'll phone the precinct, advise them you're on your way."

"I'd really like to help you," said Barone. "But I don't know what kind of information you're looking for."

"Look, Detective, I've been handed this case with very little time to prepare. I go to trial on it in a few days. There are twenty officers involved, I have to interview them all, and apart from their names I don't know who they are or what part they played, or what questions to ask them. You could save me a lot of time, but if you're unwilling, fine, go back to your command."

Barone glanced at his watch. "It's past lunchtime," he noted. "Why don't we go out to lunch and discuss it?"

"No thank you. You may go."

"You have to eat."

"On the contrary, I rarely eat lunch."

Barone nodded understandingly. "In that case, let's go through those names again."

"You mean that?"

"Yes."

Perhaps it was best just to get rid of him. Then she thought: Why not test him? See if he really wants to be cooperative. Ask him the hardest question first. "Let's start," she said, "with Detective Daniel Muldoon."

"This is off the record, right?"

"Yes," said Karen. "What can you tell me about him?"

"Danny's not a lush exactly, but he drinks a lot of beer. He's been divorced many years. And he's lonely and he's a slob. But he's an extremely astute investigator." Barone paused. "If anything I say ever gets back to him, I'll consider it a terrible betrayal of confidence."

"Is he honest?"

"You mean did Danny ever accept a free cup of coffee? Probably. Anything worse? I don't know. Not since I've been there."

Karen nodded. Barone had become truculent in the telling, a reaction she both understood and admired. The loyalty of a cop toward his partner was, to them, more sacred than the marriage oath, and she knew this. To them it represented a more perfect love, and who was to say they were not right. It was a love she had never experienced herself and did not entirely comprehend, but she knew it was there, and she respected it.

"Why don't you ask me the same question about myself," Barone said. "Or don't you dare? Am I honest?"

They stared at each other, and then Barone's expression softened and he grinned up at her again. "Give me the Miranda warning first, of course."

Karen turned away to keep from smiling. "We'll come back to Detective Muldoon in a moment," she said. "Tell me first what you know about the other men: Pierce, Boylehart,

Wiendienst? I don't want to be surprised in court. What will Justin McCarthy know about them, or be able to find out about them, that I should know?''

The prospective jurors, some of whom had been collecting in the corridor for some minutes, began to enter the big room at 9 A.M. as ordered. The clerk came along the corridor wading through them as he neared his door, which he opened with a key. They followed him inside where, one by one, they handed over the summonses they had received in the mail, and he inscribed their names in his ledger and asked them to take a seat. Some of them wanted to know what the procedure was, how long they would be here, but the clerk only kept repeating: "Please take a seat. You will be notified.''

The newspapers came out onto laps, the crossword puzzles, the books, the knitting. Some who had thought to bring none of these things stared at the floor or ceiling, or paced up and down, or tried to strike up conversations with neighbors, provided the neighbor seemed to come from the same ethnic or economic background or was the same sex or age. For most people this was as close as they had ever stood to crime and corruption, so conversations were rare. It was as if in talking to someone one risked becoming a suspect, or perhaps even convicted.

It was a large room containing about two hundred chairs in rows, but by nine thirty it was overcrowded, the air a bit close. People stood or sat in boredom and discomfort in the equivalent of a schoolroom for which there was no textbook and no teacher. Prospective jurors were still trickling in, summonses in hand, to the great irritation of those who had come on time and who saw by now that there was much more boredom and discomfort ahead. They had known this when the summons had arrived in the mail, but then it was only theoretical. Now it was real. They saw that they would be waiting it out minute by minute for some days.

After about an hour the clerk stood up and called for their attention.

Since this was the most exciting thing to have happened so far, the silence was both immediate and total.

"Those whose names are called," he announced, "will go out in the hall and line up by twos."

He called about sixty names. Those called acted as if they had won something. They grinned, became sprightly, gathered belongings, and made for the door. For them the wait was over, at least temporarily. For the others it began again.

In the hall the sixty prospects were led like schoolchildren to the elevators, where most of them pushed and shoved to get aboard the first car, though this was impossible. Eventually they piled into several.

On the fourteenth floor they were led two by two along the corridor and into a courtroom where they were told to take seats in the spectator section. The jury box was empty and there was no one on the bench. In the well sat Karen and Coombs at one table, McCarthy and an assistant—and Lionel Epps—at another. All were facing forward, did not turn around, and it was not clear to any of the newcomers whether they were important or not. The two tables, it was noted, were piled with dossiers.

But presently a door behind the bench opened, everyone was ordered to stand, and the judge in his robes strode out and onto his dais.

Attention now shifted to this man. When he had sat down, he looked them over like specimens, while nodding his head slightly. It made them look around at each other. They saw what he saw, though perhaps did not attach to it the same significance. As many faces were black or Hispanic as white. Their overall numbers would now get reduced, and in the process the proportion of whites would diminish and that of minorities would increase.

The judge began to make a speech. He spoke of the Constitution, of the Bill of Rights, of due process of law, of the historical significance of trial by jury, of the right of every man to a swift and impartial trial before twelve of his peers.

The judge's name was Birnbaum. He was about sixty, somewhat stout, and there was a slow and ponderous weight to his words. He fancied himself an orator, which he was not. He liked to make this same speech each time, which his listeners did not know, and the reaction was the same each time too. They soon stopped listening. They began to fidget, to stare at their hands.

"The purpose of jury selection," the judge intoned, "is to ensure as far as possible an impartial trial." He paused and surveyed the sixty faces, most of whom avoided his eyes. "This is a case of attempted murder of police officers by the accused. Here I must emphasize that the accused has only been accused. He has not been found guilty yet. It is up to you men and women to decide if he is guilty or not. Your word goes." This declaration was followed by a theatrical chuckle. "It is you men and women who are the decision makers, it is not the lawyers, it is not me."

He paused again. "Now we will interview you in small groups to see whether you are suitable to sit in judgment in this case. The interviewing will be done by the prosecutor, Mrs. Henning. Mrs. Henning, will you please rise and face the prospective jurors? This," the judge said, "is Mrs. Henning. And the defense lawyer is Mr. McCarthy. Will you please rise and face the jurors, Mr. McCarthy?"

Karen had simply looked out over their heads, her face expressionless. McCarthy grinned, bowed, gave them a friendly wave.

"Thank you, Mr. McCarthy," the judge said, cutting the lawyer's performance somewhat short. "You may sit down."

He waited until McCarthy was back in his chair. "And this is Mr. Lionel Epps," the judge said. "Please stand, Mr. Epps."

Epps wore a well-cut blue suit and horn-rimmed glasses. He looked an upstanding young black businessman. Or a young black lawyer, perhaps, indistinguishable from Coombs, who was seated nearby.

"Mr. Epps is the defendant in this trial," the judge said. "His guilt or innocence will be decided by you the jury after you have heard the evidence."

When Epps had sat down, the judge continued his speech. Karen at her table was doodling on a legal pad—she had heard it all before.

"Not all of you here will serve on that jury. Some of you will be disqualified for cause—maybe you're a friend or relative of the defendant or of one of the lawyers—and others by peremptory challenges—maybe one of the lawyers thinks you'd be too sympathetic to the other side." He gave another theatrical chuckle.

"Each side has twenty peremptory challenges. If you are rejected you won't know which side challenged you or why— the clerk will simply send you back to the central jury room. Now would those of you seated in the first row please file into the jury box. Just fifteen of you. That's all. That's enough. You, sir, please return to your seat. You'll get your turn next. We won't forget you." Several people laughed.

Judge Birnbaum turned his swivel chair so as to address the jury box specifically. He looked the prospects over, perhaps making the same head count Karen was making from her table. Eight whites, seven blacks.

"This will be a long trial," Judge Birnbaum said, "perhaps two months. Those who would find this an impossible burden please raise your hands."

All the white jurors raised their hands, and most of the blacks.

The judge, who could not have been surprised, decided to show irritation early. "I'm not going to excuse people who just want to get out of jury duty," he said. "You have a civic responsibility. Juror number one, what fairy tale are you going to tell me?"

"I'm a computer salesman, Your Honor. I work on commissions. Two months—"

"Come up here."

Judge Birnbaum questioned him for some time. He wanted details of the man's employment, expenses, financial status.

But finally he seemed satisfied. "Excused," he said. "You may go back to the central jury room and wait for some other trial that may not inconvenience you so much." He managed to impart considerable sarcasm to the word *inconvenience*.

Again the judge swiveled toward the jury box. "And you, madam?"

She was a white housewife. "I have preschool children, Your Honor, and no help."

He questioned her too. How many children, what were their ages, where did her husband work, how much did he earn, what relatives might be available to help.

But finally: "Excused."

To the next man he said: "What is your profession, sir?"

The prospective juror was white, middle-aged, and wore a conservative—and expensive—business suit. He was, he said, a stockbroker. "I won't be able to serve, Judge."

"A stockbroker. I see. You are, I take it, a man of means."

"Not really."

Fixing him with a baleful eye the judge began one of his backup orations. "Justice—our entire system of government—depends on each of us serving as jurors if called. Do you hear me, sir? I am not going to entertain frivolous excuses."

For a moment the juror remained silent. He did not wish to serve and, whatever the law said, had no intention of serving.

"I know the case," he said. And he added truculently: "The guy is definitely guilty."

The judge gave him a hard stare, but the juror stared back just as hard. The judge had no choice. "Excused," he said with a sigh.

Hours passed, and after that, days. New batches of sixty people entered the courtroom, filed into the spectator section, listened to the judge's unchanging speech, then moved in groups into the jury box and were examined. But the results remained distressingly similar.

A few of the prospective jurors made no protest, or their protests were overruled, and these were then examined singly by Karen Henning for the prosecution and Justin McCarthy for the defense. Karen wanted people who seemed to be upright citizens. She wanted no one who had served time in jail or in drug treatment centers, or who spoke poor English, or who seemed to have a short attention span.

McCarthy's questioning was eclectic, and at first his strategy was not clear.

"Tell me, my good man, who do you feel commits the most crime in this city?"

The man he was addressing was white, a retired postal worker. "Well, er, young black guys, as I understand it."

"May we approach the bench, Your Honor?" said McCarthy.

The conference at the bench lasted nearly ten minutes, even though McCarthy, who was whispering, made his point at once.

"Challenged for cause, Your Honor. Obvious prejudice against young black defendants like my client."

"Wait a minute—" said Karen.

Their heads were close together but they kept glancing over at the juror they were discussing.

"I'll allow it," decided the judge finally.

"That should cost him one of his peremptories, Judge," said Karen.

"You're excused, sir," said the judge to the prospective juror. "Continue, Mr. McCarthy."

McCarthy moved back toward the jury box.

The first juror that both sides agreed upon was a female welfare clerk; she would become forewoman of the jury. The next two were men, a sanitation-truck driver and an elevator starter. Since all three were municipal employees, their salaries would continue for as long as the jury sat. All three were black.

It took a week to empanel these three. Since for a trial of this length two alternate jurors would be necessary, making fourteen in all, the process of jury selection obviously had a long way to go.

Karen was in court until it closed each day, then went to her office. In addition to selecting a jury she had her division to run. There were always subordinates waiting for decisions, however late in the day it might be, plus reports to study, memos to read and to write, and phone calls to return. Cops who had taken part in the Epps shoot-out would be waiting. She tried to interview at least two superior officers each night too, men who had reached the scene after the shooting stopped. What had they seen or heard that was not in their brief, cryptic official reports? By the time she got to them the normal working day was long over. The offices along her corridor were all empty, the entire building still.

She reinterviewed Muldoon and Barone separately. Muldoon this time was a little less taciturn, a little less surly than before, though still plenty of both. But the details he provided remained the same in the retelling, which to say the least was heartening.

Barone was as forthright, as accommodating as ever, or so it seemed. She took him over the events in chronological order, and then in reverse order, as if she were only trying to understand better. This was a technique she sometimes used, a kind of disguised cross-examination, which Barone perceived at once. It made him laugh. Muldoon had never noticed, whereas Barone twitted her about it in a good-natured way.

They worked very late on that particular night, which caused Barone to suggest dinner again, but she refused.

"All three of us," Barone said, for Coombs sat on his usual chair in the corner.

"No, thank you."

"You can't speak for Larry," Barone told her. "Larry's hungry, aren't you, Larry?"

"The defendant," Karen said, "is coming across the roof-top shooting. Then what happened?"

When Barone suggested he go out and get sandwiches and something to drink, she rejected this idea too. But a few minutes later she cut the interview short. Annoyed at Barone and at herself, she announced she was going home, stood up, and started stuffing papers into her briefcase.

Barone said good night and left, but when she came out into the corridor he was waiting there for the elevator. They waited together. She kept glancing around hoping Coombs would make it a threesome, but he was in the men's room or somewhere and did not appear. In the elevator Barone said nothing all the way down. I'm being foolish, Karen told herself.

Then they were out on the street together and Karen was looking for a cab.

"I have my car," Barone said. "I can drive you up to Grand Central, if you like."

Which meant he had taken the trouble to find out that she took the train each night. Did he know her address too?

"No thank you, I'll take a taxi."

"I go right by it."

She gave him a kind of half smile. "Thanks anyway."

"Well, good night, then."

There was an idea Karen had been mulling over for an hour. She had only a moment now or he would be gone, not enough time to decide properly.

"I'd like you to report here tomorrow evening," she said. "In fact each evening this week." The other patrol officers in the case, men she had not yet met, would speak more freely, she told herself, if Barone was present too. She did not have time to make small talk with each one, to be friendly, to handle them casually. Alone in a room with two lawyers they might freeze up. Lawyers to cops were not thought of as natural allies, but as natural enemies. She knew this. Lawyers were capable of putting cops in jail. With Barone present it would be better.

"So will you come in?" The moment this question was spoken Karen was angry at herself. Of course he would come in; she didn't have to ask his permission, just request him through channels. He would have no say in the matter.

"What time do you want me?" Barone asked.

As he went off to get his car Karen stepped into the street. Peering downtown she tried to spot an approaching taxi, but she knew there would not be many in this area this late. She was afraid she would still be standing here when Barone came by in his car—but to her relief a taxi appeared, and she waved to flag it down.

She got home at night later and later, and her husband began to grumble about it. He had to make the beds mornings, clean the house, do the shopping, cook for the children every night. He had no time to prepare his classes, he said, or to work on the monograph he was writing. He had not complained for the first few weeks, but enough was enough, it wasn't fair.

She mollified him as best she could.

One night she left the building late as usual, and rain was pouring down. She stood at the curb under an umbrella and the few cabs she saw went by full, their splashes sometimes coming up onto her shoes, and then a dark car pulled up in front of her, not an expensive car, a Toyota or something, not new either, and the driver, reaching across, threw open the door.

"Get in," Barone said. "You'll get soaked standing there."

She hesitated a moment, then furled her umbrella and entered the car.

"What time is your train?"

She told him.

"Don't worry, we'll make it."

"I hate to impose on you this way." To ride to the station with him was not a good idea.

The wipers were sweeping back and forth, but with two people in the car the windshield fogged over. Barone was driving with one hand, clearing the glass with the other. Karen produced a handkerchief. "Let me do that for you."

She had to lean across him.

"That's much better. Thanks."

They said little more until he had pulled up in a bus stop in front of Grand Central.

"You have about fifteen minutes to spare," he said, glancing at his watch.

She grasped the door handle. "Well, thanks again."

"Why rush?" he said. "You're more comfortable here. It's full of perverts and homeless in there."

"Lots of commuters too."

"More panhandlers than commuters at this hour."

"I want to make sure I get a seat."

Their breathing had fogged up all the windows. They were alone in a kind of opaque cocoon. No one could see in. She was surprised at how intimate it felt.

"How old are your children?"

She told him.

"You got pictures of them there?"

"You can't possibly be interested in my children."

"We're friends, aren't we?"

What was she supposed to say to that?

"I want to know everything about you."

She looked at him sharply.

He laughed. "You know you want to show them to me."

Finally she drew them out of the wallet in her handbag. He studied the photo of her daughter for some time.

"She's a beautiful girl," Barone said, handing the photo back. "It's very unusual for a beautiful mother to have a beautiful daughter."

It was a nice thing to say but not very subtle. She sat

breathing inside the opaque windows. She heard traffic go by in the street, people go by on the sidewalk. They couldn't see her, nor could she see out. She was extremely conscious of the man beside her, and supposed he was conscious of her. It felt as if something were about to happen, which was absurd. She was in a car parked on 42nd Street in the rain.

"I have to go." She opened the door and got out, and Barone rolled down the window and called to her, saying she had forgotten her umbrella. He handed it out. "Good night," she said. "Thank you for the ride." The rain had stopped, she saw. They were under an overhang anyway. She went into the station and down the ramp and boarded the train.

When she came into her house it was late and she was terrifically hungry so she went into the kitchen and Hank came downstairs and immediately wanted to know how long this would go on.

"How long will what go on?"

"Your coming home this late."

"I'm trying to unload these other two cases I was working on," she said. "Once I get them out of the way, and once the trial starts, it will be better, I promise."

She stood in the kitchen eating a bowl of cereal. Her dinner.

She was shortchanging her children, Hank told her, not to mention her husband. She nodded contritely, but it didn't stop him, and when he continued to press her she got angry.

"I didn't ask for this case."

"You could have refused it."

"That's ridiculous."

"You took the case because you wanted to."

"I took the case because I was ordered to."   .

"You could have said no. I'm sorry, no."

"I'd have lost my job."

"Then you'd have lost your job."

"May I remind you who brings in half the money around here."

"Right."

"More than half."

"You like being in the spotlight, that's why you took it. Your name is in the paper. You get interviewed on television."

"I've been interviewed on it exactly twice. I'm stuck with this case. There was nothing I could do."

"All you think about is your career."

"That's not true."

"Your career is more important to you than your children, more important than me."

"That's an outrageous thing to say."

"You're teaching me more about career women than I ever wanted to know."

"I never wanted this case."

"You never do anything you don't want to do."

She said: "Why don't you stop before you say something that's completely unforgivable."

It ended there, both of them speechless, glaring at each other. "I'm going to bed," snapped Karen, and she did.

She heard him come to bed later. She lay facing the wall, and as the mattress sagged on his side she did not budge. It was her own words that still rang in her ears, not his. She was the one who had said something unforgivable, not her husband. She could patch this up, but it would have to wait until morning, she was too angry to do it now.

The sixty-mile drive home took Barone under sixty minutes. Most of it was on superhighways, but by no means all. One good thing about being a cop, you could drive as fast as you wanted. The Toyota was four years old with close to 100,000 miles on it, but he had it up to eighty-five most of the way. He kept the engine in good shape.

He lived in a small house on a small piece of ground two blocks behind Main Street in a town that was too far out of New York ever to have been called a suburb. It had been a farming town once, dairy farmers apparently, who also grew corn for the animals and for the summer visitors. The village itself was very small, only a few shops. Some of the families had been there since the Revolution, or even before. The Presbyterian church had a graveyard beside it that was the oldest Barone had ever seen, the stones worn smooth by centuries of rain, but you could read dates from the late 1600s, and the same few names appeared over and over again, the Hoyts, Meads, Keelers, Benedicts—the families that had founded the place and kept it going for hundreds of years. The history of the town was buried there beside the church. But after World War II—perhaps before—the farming had become uneconomical and had died out, and it had been a depressed place at the time Barone came into it and bought his house, after the birth of his first daughter. He had been living in Queens then. He had come to this town because other New York cops lived here already.

The town was rising in the world now. Too much so. More and more major corporations had been moving their world headquarters north out of New York City into the near and even the not-so-near suburbs. They moved them within commuting distance of the more distant towns, Barone's and others. Real estate developers had not ignored the trend. They had moved into Barone's town and begun building houses. The town was becoming a bedroom community at last. It had had to build a new school, and had even hired a five-man police force—Barone had met them, a bunch of shitkickers who knew nothing and who looked up to him as if he were a ballplayer or an actor, or some other star. The town taxes had gone up too, in fact up and up and up, and now totaled almost ten percent of Barone's salary. He had a floating mortgage and with the interest rates, that kept going up too.

He had been short of money for as long as he could remember, but as he came in the door, singing out: "I'm home," his wife started in on him right away, and the subject she had in mind was of course money.

"You don't give me enough."

He was standing in the hallway, had not even taken his overcoat off yet. One of his little girls was clinging to him. He lifted her and nuzzled her neck until she giggled.

His wife was not going to let it lie. "I need more money."

He put the child down and off she ran, back to the TV most likely, which was not such a wonderful idea, the kids watching so much TV, but what could you do.

"I can't make ends meet on what you give me."

It was not an argument yet because Barone chose not to argue back. Instead he moved to embrace her. "What's for dinner?" he said. He liked to soothe people, calm them down, make them forget whatever was bothering them.

"Spaghetti," his wife said truculently.

It was best to avoid confrontations altogether, if possible, or at least as long as possible.

"No problem, I like spaghetti."

"It's all we can afford," his wife said, "on what you give me."

"I give you every dime I can spare," he said.

"You don't give me enough."

"How much do you think detectives get paid?"

"I need more."

"I don't have more."

"I went and got a job." Her eyes glanced off his and away.

"What?" He didn't think wives should work, not his wife anyway, and she knew it.

"In the stationery store in the village."

She would not meet his eyes.

"It's only mornings while the kids are in school," she said defensively.

"How much are they paying you?"

She told him.

"That's minimum wage," he said, at the last moment trying to get the derision out of his voice. He took both her hands. "You're worth more than that."

"Well that's all the job pays."

He was silent a moment.

"Can we eat now?" he asked gently.

"You expect dinner to be ready as soon as you come home, but half the time you don't."

"Don't what?"

"Don't come home."

Now we're getting close to what this conversation is really about, Barone thought. To Barone it was still just a conversation, not an argument. He said: "I always phone you when I'm not coming home. When I have to go to court or something I always tell you."

"You tell me stories."

"If I get off work at 1 A.M. and have to be in court at nine, it doesn't make sense to drive all the way out here."

"This is your home."

They still stood in the hall just inside the front door. He had not been able to advance any further into the house. He said: "If you think I prefer a sleeping bag in that airless little room off the squadroom instead of cuddling up with you in our bed, you're mistaken. Come on," he said, moving again to embrace her, "You've seen that room, remember, when you were in the stationhouse. Of course I'd rather be home if possible."

She shook him off. "You keep rubbers in your wallet."

He looked at her.

"You think I don't look?" she said.

The expression on his face had not changed, he believed. No start of surprise, no guilt. "I keep those for you," he said, and gave her a leer. "In case you want to do it unexpectedly sometime."

"Huh," she snorted. "When did that ever happen?"

"What about in the parking lot in the back of the car that time?"

"That was years ago."

"If the mood suddenly takes you, I want to be ready."

"I don't believe you."

He said: "And I don't want to leave them around the bedroom for the kids to find."

He saw she wanted to believe him. Wanting to believe was not very different from the real thing, and just as good usually.

"They're too young for learning about rubbers," he said gravely.

"True," she admitted.

"And you won't go on the Pill—"

"They make me bloat."

"—or get fitted for a diaphragm."

"It's always my fault," she said. "Everything's my fault."

"Of course it's not your fault."

His daughters were going to be pretty girls, but his wife was a plain woman, and he had chosen her in part for her plainness, and also because she had been born into the same tradition as himself.

"No one is accusing you of anything," he said.

She was small and dark, with a big nose and thin lips, and he put his arms around her and kissed her on the forehead. He had understood in advance what kind of woman she was and what marriage to her would be like. Not exciting perhaps, but solid. She would make a home for him and for his children, and be grateful for the opportunity.

He took some bills out of his wallet and gave them to her. "I'll try to give you more money," he told her. "How about fixing dinner now, and then tonight maybe we can—" He gave her another leer, and watched her go obediently toward the kitchen.

He went out the side door into his yard. There was not much grass underfoot. One of the trees had a swing hanging off it. There was a concrete barbecue he had built, and a redwood table he had built that they ate picnics at sometimes when the weather was warm, and some other trees, and no room for much else.

Still in his overcoat he sat down on the swing and waited for dinner. Marriage was serious, he had been taught. A man flirted with the good-looking women and bedded them if he could, but women like his wife made better wives and mothers because they were not tempted in other directions. That was the tradition. Also, other men would be less likely to go after them and you would not have to worry if you left them home alone from time to time.

He found himself comparing his wife to Karen Henning. A career woman, not a housewife, and with a high-powered New York job, not part-time in a stationery store in the sticks. And of course far better-looking and better dressed. Good figure too. She seemed to him as exotic a creature as he had met recently. In fact he had never known anyone like her. Except that all women were women first, and differed from each other only in small ways. If you touched the right button they all reacted the same. The difficulty was to find which button it was.

He looked at his house, which was bigger now than when he had bought it. The family room had been added on. He had built it himself, with the help of two other cops. The trouble was, you build a nice addition because you need the space, and the town raises your taxes on you.

He could certainly use some extra money.

When the alarm went off Karen reached over and silenced it, then lay for a moment unmoving in the dark. Hank was awake too, she could tell, though he did not move either. She had much to do today and wanted only to dress quickly and catch the early train, but instead she reached out and stroked Hank's thigh. When he did not respond she reached a little higher and noted that he was responding after all. When his arms came around her she broke loose and peeled his pajama bottoms down. Off came her nightgown. She really didn't want this, but it had to be done, she did love him though he wasn't being fair, and it was her job (it was always her job, or so it seemed) to make this marriage whole again, and after a time she got on top of him and began to rock gently back and forth. Presently his arms pulled her down and he cried out.

"Why don't you make the coffee and toast," she whispered into his neck, "while I get dressed." And she kissed him briefly and got off.

When she came into the kitchen the coffee was perking, the toast was buttered and on the table, and Hank was smiling happily. He even kissed her on the nose as he served her. She was much relieved, but also somewhat puzzled by him—by men in general who could be bought off so easily. She ate quickly and left the house.

But as she rode into the city she began to think about her late nights, her taxicabs to Grand Central, and about Barone waiting around for her with his car, and she became increasingly disquieted. As soon as she was advised that the DA was in his office she went in to see him and asked that a car be assigned to take her to the station on nights when she would be working late.

"I'll have them assign a car to you," the DA told her.

But she continued to press her explanation. At present she was dependent on taxis which were rare some nights, she said. Or else she had to catch a ride with anyone going in her direction.

"I understand," the old man told her.

"It makes me very uncomfortable."

"You were right to come to me."

"So if you could have a car for me—"

"I'll take care of it right away."

"Thank you." She turned to go.

"How's jury selection going?" he asked her.

"Everything's going very well," she told him, and they smiled at each other, and she left the office.

She took his question to mean he hadn't looked at any of that yet. Good, she thought.

—11—

In court Karen interviewed a prospective juror, a secretary in a midtown ad agency. Karen's questions were brisk and brief, and the woman's answers were the same. Name, age, marital status, education, employment. The woman seemed intelligent, unbiased, and most of all she was willing to serve. Instinctively Karen trusted her. After a few additional questions she decided to accept her as a juror.

McCarthy in his turn asked the same preliminary questions again. It was as if he had not even been in the room until now. At her table Karen doodled impatiently on her pad. McCarthy took his time. He had all the time in the world.

By then six jurors had been seated, three men, three women, all of them black. The secretary whom McCarthy was addressing at present was white, and Karen waited to see what would happen. So far none of the white men or women she had accepted had been approved by McCarthy.

"And have you ever been arrested, madam?" he asked.

"You have to be a criminal to get arrested."

"Any speeding tickets?"

"One, once."

"Cop nice to you, was he?"

"He gave me a ticket."

"Cost you some money?"

"I think it was $50."

"Make you hate cops, did it?"

"On the moment."

"On the moment. I see. Any police officers in your family?"

"No."

"Ever know any police officers personally?"

"Well, I once dated a cop."

"Yes. And how well did you get to know him?" McCarthy had turned his back on the woman. He was looking straight at Karen, and he was almost leering.

Karen stood up. "I must protest this line of questioning, Your Honor."

The judge looked thoughtful. "No, I think it's fair in a trial like this. Please answer the question, madam."

Karen sat back down.

"I think we went to the movies three times."

"Come now, madam," said McCarthy.

"What are you insinuating?"

Karen stood up again, and Judge Birnbaum nodded at her. "I would ask you to be careful here, Mr. McCarthy," he admonished.

"He's wasting our time, Judge," Karen said.

"Continue, Mr. McCarthy."

For a moment McCarthy was silent. "Your friend the police officer," he said to the woman, "honest, was he?"

"I went to the movies with him three times."

"Yes, you said that. Let me rephrase my question. If you learned about someone who had fired shots at policemen, would you say that made him a bad person?"

"Are you kidding?"

Another conference at the bench. Again McCarthy spoke in what was almost a whisper. "Excused for cause, Your Honor," he said urgently.

"There is no cause whatsoever," said Karen.

"Obviously a law-and-order fanatic," said McCarthy.

"If you ask questions like he asks, those are the answers you are going to get."

The judge looked from one to the other.

"Your Honor, I protest," cried Karen. "This is what he always does. He's systematically excluding white jurors."

It was a protest she expected to lose. The Supreme Court had ruled that the prosecution could not exclude jurors by race. The defense, however, was permitted to do so.

"That will have to be one of your peremptory challenges, Mr. McCarthy," Birnbaum ruled finally. "You have six left."

Content with her small victory, Karen started back to her table, but McCarthy, although the judge's ruling had gone against him, remained at the bench, arguing for what he called "fairness." Peremptory challenges were the defense's only weapon against the awesome power of the state, he declaimed. The defense could not afford to spend one of its few peremptories here. With flowery eloquence he argued, and although Karen and even the judge attempted to interrupt he could not be shut off. As soon as one line of argument ended, he started another. He used up an enormous amount of time, as he had done on nearly every prospective juror so far. Only when Birnbaum got angry did he stop.

"You have six peremptories left, Mr. McCarthy. Now get on with it, please."

The next prospective juror was a retired textile manufacturer, Jewish, a donor to liberal causes, who admitted to an abiding distrust of the police, but who had no valid excuse not to serve. Although a less than perfect juror from the prosecution's point of view, Karen decided to accept him too, for there were, relatively speaking, so few whites in the juror pool at all, and even fewer able, as this retiree was able, to accord this trial two or more months out of their lives.

However, in his lengthy questioning McCarthy managed to badger the man to the point where he muttered something that was not understood and that he would not repeat but that McCarthy was able to categorize as a possibly racist remark against blacks.

"Excused for cause, Your Honor," said McCarthy at the bench, and though Karen protested vigorously, Judge Birnbaum let him get away with it. The Jewish juror was excused and it did not even cost McCarthy one of his remaining peremptory challenges.

One month and two days after jury selection started, the box was filled.

"Ladies and gentlemen," Birnbaum announced with a pleased smile, "we have a jury."

Karen's eyes panned from face to face. Six men, six women. A subway motorman, two receptionists, a tow truck operator, two postal workers, an elevator starter, a bus driver, a welfare clerk, a sanitation worker, two secretaries. Ten blacks, two Hispanics.

The two alternates were white women, but they would not become part of the jury unless one of the others fell ill or died.

Of course Karen had watched as the jury was put together day by day. She had known what the final result would be. But that was theoretical. Now it was official, could not be changed. It was a legally constituted jury. It sat as constituted, as solid as a slab of cement. It stared back at her, and it was so racially unbalanced that she feared its opinions, its prejudices. She feared what it might decide, and she twisted her wedding band with her fingers and muttered: "How did I let this happen?"

"It is against the law to exclude jurors for racial reasons," said Coombs beside her, "and you obeyed the law."

"The trial begins at nine A.M. tomorrow," intoned the judge on his bench.

"All rise," called the bailiff.

The judge left the courtroom.

The jurors filed out of the box, and Karen watched them go. "Those people are just as capable of rendering an honest verdict as anyone else," she said grimly. She said this not so much to Coombs as to herself. She told herself she believed it.

Her opening statement to the jury would come in the morning, and she stayed late at the office to work on it. Several drafts existed—she had been putting it together off and on for days. It had to be immensely strong. And clear. It had to be clearer than clear. She had to make the jury see Lionel Epps shooting down cops. She had to make the jury see what her case would be and believe she could prove it.

She was writing on a yellow legal pad. As she worked she worried about Justin McCarthy, and his possible tactics, and she kept crumpling pages and throwing them away. It took hours before the final draft satisfied her. It never satisfied her, but ultimately she got so groggy she could hardly focus her eyes, which made that particular draft the best she could do, and she put all the lights out and left the office. At Grand Central she caught a local train home—the expresses had stopped running.

Hank had the car today. She had to take a taxi home from the station. When it pulled up in front of her house she saw that every window was dark, her house was dark. She crossed the lawn and had just put her key in the door when a car pulled into the driveway and stopped and she looked and saw her daughter, Hillary, get out. Hillary, who was supposed to be doing her homework, or else should be in bed asleep.

Karen came out of the shadows and marched toward the car. She passed her daughter in the middle of the lawn and continued on.

"Hi, Mom," said Hillary to her back.

The driver saw Karen coming. In a squeal of rubber he backed out of the driveway, spun the steering wheel, and was gone.

"That's just Greg," said Hillary.

Karen had returned to the door stoop. "I saw who it was. In the house."

"What's the matter, Mom?"

"What's today?"

"Thursday."

"What time is it?"

"About ten o'clock."

"Eleven thirty. Your father and your brother are at a basketball game. Who gave you permission to go out?"

"Greg called and—"

"Who said you could go out?"

"Well, no one."

"Right."

"You weren't here," the girl said guiltily.

"You know what the rules are."

"I called to ask you," Hillary said, "but your switchboard was closed."

It was Karen who felt guilty now, but she ignored it. "You're not allowed out without permission, you're not allowed out school nights at all, and before you get into a car I want to know who's driving it." She felt guilty enough to add: "I thought we could trust each other."

"You know Greg. What's the problem?"

"Greg's sixteen years old. When did he get his license?"

"Yesterday," said Hillary. "But he's a good driver."

"I won't have you in a car with him when I'm not here."

"That's not fair," Hillary accused, "because you're never here."

The girl went sullenly past her into the house. As Karen was about to follow, their station wagon pulled into the driveway. Hank got out on one side, Jackie on the other.

"We won, Mom," Jackie cried out.

By the time Hank reached her side Jackie was already inside the house.

"Just getting home?" her husband said, gazing at her briefcase. This too made her feel guilty. She found herself trying to hide it behind her skirt.

"Hank," she said, "Hillary was out on a school night."

Hank looked puzzled. "She was doing her homework upstairs when I left."

"She went out without permission."

Hank nodded.

"In a car driven by a sixteen-year-old boy."

Hank said: "I shouldn't have left her alone tonight."

"You had Jackie's basketball game to go to."

"No, it's my fault."

"It's not your fault."

"Whose fault is it, then?"

"All right, I was late," Karen said. "I couldn't help it."

Hank said nothing. He didn't accuse her of anything. But he didn't look at her either, much less touch her or kiss her, and they went into the house.

They got ready for bed. Hank in pajamas carried some magazines across the room. He got in on his side and began reading.

Karen said: "Do you think I was too hard on her?"

"Was she too hard on you?"

Their eyes locked. Karen's mouth hardened, but Hank said nothing further. Presently he returned to his magazine.

Karen put a bathrobe on. "I'm going to talk to her."

She padded down the hall to Hillary's room, knocked, and went in. Hillary lay with her hands behind her head in the halo of light that spilled in from the hall. Karen sat down on the edge of the bed.

"I know you tried to call me," she began.

There was no response from the girl who, instead of looking at her, stared at the ceiling.

"I get home as early as I can, but some nights—"

Still no response.

"Supposing something had happened to you?" said Karen.

"Nothing happened to me."

"But suppose something had?" She could imagine her daughter crushed to death under a car—or disfigured or maimed. After what had happened to Jackie it was easy—her fault because she had not been home. It was all too vivid and brought tears to her eyes.

"If anything happened to you—"

Karen turned away and began silently weeping.

"Oh, Mom." Her daughter sat up and embraced her. "I'm sorry, Mom."

Because she was so tired and overstressed, and because children never understood how much you loved them, Karen wept. "You don't see, you can't imagine—" she said. "If anything ever happened to you—to you or Jackie—I would die."

—BOOK THREE—

The jurors were in the box, the spectator section was filled, as were the lawyers' tables, and there were courtroom guards standing about. Karen from her table looked over at Lionel Epps, the reason everyone else was here. He wore another three-piece suit—he seemed to own a number of them. During jury selection he had worn a different one every day of the week. He wore his usual horn-rimmed glasses as well.

He looked as studious and responsible as anyone could wish. "Look at him," Karen murmured to Coombs beside her.

"Straight out of the pages of *GQ*."

It made Karen smile.

"Who pays for them?" asked Coombs.

"McCarthy, maybe. Or maybe he bought them himself with some of that drug money he earned."

Coombs said: "He should have been made to come to trial in his shoot-out clothes: sneakers, jeans, and a dirty T-shirt."

Karen had prosecuted cases where the defendants, represented by legal aid lawyers, did come to court in their shoot-out clothes; the juries usually convicted such men in fifteen minutes.

"Here we go," she said to Coombs, and she rose to begin her opening statement.

She was dressed in a navy blue suit that brought out the blue of her eyes, set off her blond curls, and hid what she took to be the imperfections of her figure. Her skirt came to her knees and she wore matching blue shoes with medium heels in which it would not be uncomfortable to pace back and forth in front of the jury. She had thought a long time about what to wear this first day of the trial. The jurors would soon be familiar with her entire wardrobe. They were mostly familiar with it already, though not with this suit which she had saved until today. It was well made and fit her well. She wanted her appearance to seem as careful and as thought out as the evidence she was about to present. She believed that the image the jury would have of her this first day was important. These past weeks of jury selection had been preliminary. There was a new Karen before them. The past did not count. The trial started today.

"This is a very simple case," she began. She stood in front of the box making eye contact with each juror in turn. "The defendant is a violent, dangerous young man. He was heavily armed. He fired on police officers who had come to arrest him on suspicion of other crimes. He intended to murder them so as to make his escape. He wounded five, and you will meet them. There were no extenuating circumstances . . ."

The jurors listened. She paid strict attention to their reactions. She outlined the entire case clearly, concisely. Though focused on the jury, she was aware that there were spectators in the courtroom too, rows of them behind her, and she glanced that way from time to time. Up front sat a number of newspeople, some of whose names she knew. This was not unexpected; they had been interviewing her, or trying to interview her, for days. She knew they could turn the trial into a circus if they chose. She hoped they wouldn't, but Justin McCarthy might see to it that they did.

About half the remaining spectators were black. This was unusual—a full courtroom was already unusual—and they were so silent and intense that they seemed to her threatening. The black congressman from Harlem was in attendance. Probably he was just showing solidarity and would be gone tomorrow. But the Reverend Johnson was there too, and might intend to come every day. His expression was somber. Sitting up straight he looked as tall and cadaverous as ever, and around him sat his claque, grim-faced men and women. No one of them cheered or hissed or made any noise at all, their deportment was entirely correct, but to Karen they constituted something menacing of which she was half afraid. Later, if the trial seemed to be going badly for their side, their number might swell day by day. It might overflow into the halls outside the courtroom, they might picket the building outside in the street. It had happened during other trials.

She spoke for thirty minutes, then sat down, and Justin McCarthy rose in his turn, and she watched him.

". . . These sad events took place in the Thirty-second Precinct in Harlem, which most years leads the city in murders," McCarthy began. "Which most years, if the truth be known, leads in police corruption as well. Some of you may live there. If so, I'm not telling you anything new."

"Objection," Karen said. She had risen immediately to her feet.

It was unusual for one side or the other to object during opening statements, and to do so was not always wise. After days or weeks of boredom the jurors wanted only to hear what the case was about; they could be angered by interruptions that might seem to them trivial. But Karen had decided to put McCarthy on notice at once: She would not tolerate carelessness with facts, but would call it to the jury's attention every time.

She spoke loudly and clearly. "These sad events, as Mr. McCarthy terms them, did not take place in the Thirty-second Precinct at all, but across the border in the Twenty-fifth."

McCarthy gave a dismissive wave of his hand. "I stand corrected."

"As for Mr. McCarthy's characterization of the level of

corruption in the Thirty-second Precinct, his statement is not true. He has no statistics to back it up.''

Another dismissive wave of McCarthy's hand. He simply went on with his opening statement. During the exchange between the two lawyers, Judge Birnbaum did not speak at all.

Now McCarthy strode along in front of the jury box. His bow tie was theatrical. So were his white suit and his wild white hair and his gestures. So were his words.

"Let me talk about police corruption for a moment."

Sometimes he was difficult to track, as if his thoughts wandered, but he seemed to be building toward something. He maintained a certain tension. The jurors felt this. Karen felt it herself. He never came near the subject of Lionel Epps, or the five wounded police officers, or the evidence of the case that was to be tried. Instead for more than an hour, mostly in quiet, understated tones, he contented himself with denouncing the New York Police Department.

"Do the policemen who move among you seem honest to you? Or do they watch drug deals going down on door stoops and street corners and do nothing? Do they seem like gentlemen to you? Do they seem caring? Or do they barge into your apartments on any pretext or none, supposedly seeking some suspect you never heard of who isn't there? Do they repeatedly and willfully violate your homes? Do they jump out of cars and make honest citizens spread-eagle themselves against walls and search them, for no legitimate reason, and sometimes steal what they find in their pockets?"

At the prosecution table Karen squirmed. These were only rhetorical questions. A lawyer was allowed great latitude in an opening statement. For the most part there was nothing concrete she could object to, and an outburst on her part risked turning this nearly all black jury against her. And so she kept silent while McCarthy continued.

"What are your true feelings," he asked rhetorically, "about this army of occupation that patrols your streets? This white army?"

Not only did the jurors seem to listen attentively, but certain of them nodded agreement at one or another of his points, and Karen observed this, and as a result became worried anew about how this jury would see her witnesses, about whether such a jury would believe her witnesses.

At long last McCarthy focused on the crimes of which his client was accused: "This trial is about a bright and loving young man—no previous convictions—who found out about a certain area of police corruption. He found out about it and he hated it and protested against it, and he sought to find a way to stop it. As a result he became a victim of police harassment. He was made to sell drugs for police officers. It made him sick to his stomach. He sought to expose this corruption, these corrupt police officers, he wanted to send them to jail. But he never got the chance, for a horde of them descended on the place where he was peacefully sleeping, intending to murder him in his bed. But he is young, alert. He woke up, appraised the situation, and quite properly defended himself . . ."

He went on in this vein. His client was innocent by reason of self-defense, he declared. This white-haired white lawyer actually told the jury that Epps had had a perfect right to shoot down five cops. As the jury received this astonishing statement Karen studied their individual faces, but was unable to read them. The faces were blank. But certainly no one looked away. No one seemed to reject the argument outright. No one reacted with obvious disagreement, much less with disbelief.

"And so at the end of this trial you will acquit my client of the charges of which he is accused on the grounds that he acted exactly as you yourselves would have acted—he fired on those police officers only to save his own life. He acted in legitimate self-defense."

And there you have his case, thought Karen: self-defense. The schemes and rebuttals she had prepared against other possible arguments could be discarded, all that work into the garbage. She knew now what her opponent's case would be, and had only to arrange her own case to fit it.

* * *

"And what was your post that night, Doctor?"

"The emergency room."

"And were any emergency cases brought to you that night?"

"Yes."

"A gunshot victim?"

"Yes."

Karen's first witness was one of the surgeons who had worked on the wounded cops. She intended to examine all five, one after the other, two from Harlem Hospital, three from St. Luke's.

"Who was that victim?"

"A cop."

"He had been shot, Doctor?"

"Yes, shot."

Her questions were as short and low-keyed as possible. It did not pay this early in any trial to seem overly dramatic. "Can you describe his wound or wounds?"

The surgeon did so.

"And can you describe the procedure you performed?"

He did so. Karen wanted the jurors to hear the sirens, the shouts and panic, but not from her. They should see cops on stretchers being run into operating rooms, but as described by the surgeons who were there. They should see cops bleeding, their uniforms being cut off them, the instruments probing for bullets. But she thought it essential that the blood, bullets, agony be brought into the courtroom by this surgeon and the ones who would follow, not by herself.

"No further questions."

McCarthy rose, slowly approached the witness box, and there hesitated, as if searching for the exact information that needed to be elicited.

"Tell me, Doctor, were you asked also to treat the defendant, Mr. Epps?"

"No I was not."

"Wasn't he wounded too?"

"I don't know."

"You don't know." McCarthy made a show of trying to digest this information. "Twenty cops firing shots at him, but you don't know."

"No."

"Wasn't the defendant a human being?"

"Yes of course."

"Don't human beings have a right to medical attention if they are hurt?"

"Yes of course."

"But he was black, so that made him less of a human being."

"Not at all."

"But you didn't treat him?"

"No."

"You didn't even think to ask about his condition?"

"No."

"Why was that?"

The surgeon watched McCarthy pacing, and did not answer.

"Of course, you were busy," offered McCarthy.

"Yes, I was busy."

"Too many cops to take care of?"

"Yes."

"And they take precedence over ordinary human beings."

The surgeon did not answer.

"Especially in Harlem they do?" said McCarthy. "Is that not correct?"

Again no answer.

"Answer me!" shouted McCarthy. "Is that not correct?" Feigning enormous disgust, he returned to his table. "No further questions," he said as he sat down.

Karen tried always to be home for supper, and to spend time with her children before and after. She would ask about events at school, help them set the table or put the dishes in the dishwasher. But as soon as they were in their rooms she would curl up on the sofa to study reports, motions, transcripts, minutes. It all had to be committed to memory. She had to be able to come out with the vital fact or detail at a moment's notice. She was like a violinist preparing a concert piece; she had to get the notes out of her head and down to her fingertips. She had to be able to play them instinctively, without conscious thought, and she had not had nearly enough time to prepare. For a perfunctory case, yes. A habitual offender in ragged clothes and a legal aid defense lawyer who hadn't had time to prepare either, yes. But this was not a perfunctory case, and McCarthy was not a perfunctory opponent.

She would work very late, until finally her husband would come down in pajamas.

"You owe the city eight hours a day, no more."

"I'll be up in a few minutes."

He would leave her. Each night she sat on, studying, memorizing, considering her strategy, revising it and then re-revising it, the light over her chair the only one still burning in the house.

Afterward she had trouble sleeping. The physical tension became so intense that she took up jogging again. She hadn't jogged in years. She got up an hour earlier, put on a sweat suit and sneakers, and jogged through the still-dark streets. When Hank protested she invited him to join her, but he refused. She ran and ran.

The streets were narrow. There were no sidewalks. The jogging ended when a car came around the corner too fast and in the dark sent her sprawling into the bushes.

So she joined a health club off Wall Street, the same one to which Jill Herman, her former college roommate, belonged. She didn't tell Hank. After court, after her other duties were taken care of, she pumped the stationary bike, rowed, walked the treadmill. And talked with Jill. Sweating and red-faced she listened to Jill's marital problems; Jill listened to her frustrations and worries about court.

"This should have been a three-day trial," Karen railed. They were in adjacent shower stalls by this time, the water pouring down. "McCarthy then decides that the only way to win is to make it into a crucible of black-white relations. He's going to turn up the heat until there's an explosion." Sometimes Karen had her head outside the shower curtain. Sometimes, trying to be heard through the partition, she was almost shouting. "It's infuriating what he's doing. And according to the rules there's almost nothing I can do to stop him."

"I'm sure you're worrying needlessly," said Jill as they were drying themselves off.

"Am I the only one who sees how important this trial has become, how much is at stake? What the reverberations might be? It's not just Lionel Epps who's on trial. Blacks are on trial, whites are on trial, the NYPD is on trial, women are on trial, I'm on trial—Lionel Epps is the least of it." Karen had wrapped the towel around herself. "Nobody sees it yet. They will before it's over."

"You're exaggerating," Jill suggested.

"Am I?" said Karen.

But as she rode the train home she was in a good mood. It had been a vigorous workout. She felt purged of physical and emotional tension both. She gazed out the window at the streets of Harlem, and then at the dark countryside rushing by, and all her muscles tingled and she felt full of confidence. Of course she'd beat McCarthy, how could she not? She was just as good a lawyer and had a stronger case.

". . . You crept along the hall, Officer Wiendienst, kicked open the door and then—"

"He had a shotgun. He blasted us. Me and two other guys went down. An inch to the right and—"

Although she had Muldoon and Barone standing by each day, she had decided to present three of the five wounded cops next, saving the final two until the end of the trial. The first of these men was Wiendienst, who sat on the stand wearing what looked like a brand-new, beautifully pressed uniform.

"No further questions."

As McCarthy approached she noted how warily the witness watched him.

"Officer Wiendienst," McCarthy began, "isn't it the case that you went there that night not to arrest Lionel Epps, but to murder him?"

Wiendienst was more than surprised. He was almost speechless. He spoke only one word, but it took him some seconds to get it out. "No."

Karen was on her feet. "Objection," she cried. "No evidence has been introduced to support this line of questioning."

"—to murder him, to silence what he knew of police corruption in the Thirty-second Precinct."

"Sustained," said Judge Birnbaum.

"Absolutely not," gulped the witness.

"Whose idea was it to murder him?"

"Objection!" said Karen.

"Mr. McCarthy, please," admonished the judge.

As the questioning continued Wiendienst began to avoid eye contact, to display the evasiveness people associate with guilt. He began to look like a dishonest cop. To Karen this was a manifestation of his anger, of the contempt of most cops for lawyers. But the jurors might see it differently.

McCarthy: "Tell me, Officer, have you ever engaged in corrupt acts as a policeman?"

"No, sir."

"No? But other cops have?"

"Not that I've ever seen."

McCarthy turned away from the witness. He was grinning at the jury and nodding in disbelief. "I need new glasses, Officer," he said. "Who is your eye doctor—so I'll know not to go to him."

In the jury box this caused a certain nervous laughter, which evidently embarrassed Wiendienst. In any case, he blushed.

"No corruption, Officer?" continued McCarthy. "Not one teeny-weeny bit?" He became suddenly angry. "Come now, Officer, some of these jurors live in the Thirty-second Precinct."

The jurors' laughter this time was more sustained.

"I've heard about corruption," answered Wiendienst stubbornly, "but I've never seen any."

"Was the defendant, Lionel Epps, running drugs for corrupt police officers in the Thirty-second Precinct?"

"I doubt it," Wiendienst said.

"Was he forced to run drugs for them from the age of fifteen to avoid being arrested? And now he wanted out. He wanted to testify against the Thirty-second Precinct. Is that why you and your friends went there that night to murder him?"

Karen, who had been raising objections all along, was again on her feet. "Objection, Your Honor. This is outrageous."

Judge Birnbaum: "Sustained."

But McCarthy was playing for effect, not answers, and the judge's ruling did not immediately stop him, though the rules said it should have. "To murder him so as to silence him forever?" snarled McCarthy, as he made his way to his seat. "No further questions."

So Karen rose for redirect. "Did you know who the defendant was, Officer?"

"No."

"You had never seen him before?"

"No."

"Or heard his name before?"

"No."

To her dismay the traumatized Wiendienst would no longer make eye contact with her either. She feared he seemed just as evasive now as when questioned by McCarthy.

"Then you could not have been part of a plot to murder him, could you?"

"No."

"And the other uniformed officers, did they know who he was? So far as you know?"

"No."

"You were there to help arrest him?"

"Yes."

"And that's all."

"Affirmative."

"There was no plot to murder him?"

"None that I knew about."

"There was no plot to murder him?"

"No."

From there she went over much the same ground she had covered the first time. She was obliged to do this to blunt, or attempt to blunt, whatever effect McCarthy's charges may have had on the jury. Her questioning had to take time. It had to occupy space. It had to have weight so that weeks from now, when considering the verdict, the jury would remember it. But for her and for the jurors it made for a tedious afternoon.

At the health club later she sounded off to Jill. "Do I simply assume the jury will disregard McCarthy's tactics on their own? Or do I go after him—at the risk of boring the jury to death? There are constant decisions to be made. I can never be sure what's best."

"One of the girls in my tennis group just discovered she's pregnant," Jill interrupted. "Do you want to fill in for her?"

Karen started to say no. If she accepted, then on one night a week she would get home even later than at present. She felt guilty about what Hank was going through, and his resentment made her feel even more guilty. But each night after court her neck and shoulders were stiff and she had a headache. She blamed McCarthy, but she blamed Hank too. The workouts helped. To play tennis would help even more. Tennis would free up her body, free up her mind. She preferred mindless physical activity to facing the complications at home.

"Sure, which night?" she told Jill. Let Hank carry the load for a while longer, she thought. She had needs too, and for once she was going to give in to them.

Karen: "Were you present in the stationhouse when the raid was being planned?"

The second wounded officer, Pierce, was on the stand. He said: "In the stationhouse, yes."

"What, if anything, was said about the defendant?"

"That he was wanted for questioning in connection with something in the Bronx."

"Anything else?"

"That he was probably armed and probably dangerous."

"Was anything said about killing him?"

"No."

"Nobody said: Let's murder him, or, Let's silence him."

"No."

Karen went on with it, hammering just as hard as McCarthy but in the opposite direction. "Nothing about shoot to kill, or shoot first and ask questions later?"

"No."

"You were present from beginning to end?"

"Yes."

"You're certain? Maybe some of the cops were off to the side plotting to kill the defendant but you didn't notice."

"There wasn't time. We had just come out of the stationhouse to go on patrol. Five or six different cars. There was almost no planning. The meeting lasted about two minutes."

Karen walked away and McCarthy came forward. Under cross-examination, the witness became immediately wary, and after that so obviously hostile that he began to seem, or so Karen imagined, less and less credible to the jury.

McCarthy: "Why the haste, Officer?"

"Detective Muldoon was afraid he'd get away. He said he was slippery and had got away before."

"He called him a slippery black bastard, is that it?"

Already Pierce was avoiding eye contact. "A slippery something. I don't remember what."

"Slippery black bastard sound about right?"

"I don't remember."

"Slippery nigger, maybe?"

"No."

"Let's murder him, or, Let's get him? So he can't tell what he knows about police corruption in the Thirty-second Precinct. You didn't hear that?"

"No."

"How about 'assassinate him.' Let's assassinate him?"

At the prosecution table Coombs leaned over to Karen: "McCarthy has discovered the word 'assassinate.' "

"And he will now beat us to death with it," Karen responded.

McCarthy had turned to the bench. "Would the court please order the witness to respond to the question?"

" 'Assassinate' is not a cop word," muttered Pierce. "I never heard a cop say 'assassinate' in my life."

McCarthy nodded as if with understanding, and then paced for a moment. Pierce's eyes never left him. The witness resembled a man tracking the movements of a snake.

"I suppose," McCarthy said conversationally, "you're still another cop who has never witnessed police corruption in the Thirty-second Precinct?"

"If you mean personally, no, I never have."

Again McCarthy nodded. "Have you spent your entire police career in that precinct, Officer? Would you say your loyalty is entirely to the Thirty-second Precinct and the men assigned there? Would you testify to whatever lie was necessary to uphold the 'honor' of the Thirty-second Precinct?"

Karen was once more on her feet. "Objection, objection."

"Sustained," said Judge Birnbaum. "Save that kind of thing for your summation, Mr. McCarthy."

Karen remained standing. "Would Your Honor please instruct the jury that Mr. McCarthy's questions are not evidence, that only testimony counts as evidence, and that no testimony whatsoever has been advanced to support any of the supposed crimes Mr. McCarthy may be alluding to."

"Ladies and gentlemen of the jury," murmured Judge Birnbaum, "the prosecutor is correct. Mr. McCarthy's questions are not evidence. The jury is entitled to consider them as, shall we say, whimsical."

"Whimsical, Your Honor?" sputtered McCarthy. "Whimsical?"

"Well, yes, whimsical."

When she got back to her office during the noon recess Barone was there seated in her anteroom reading a magazine. "What's happening?" he cried, jumping up. "How's it going?"

She looked at him. "McCarthy is accusing you all of intending to murder Lionel Epps."

Barone, who knew this from the newspapers, started to laugh. "Again?" he said.

She said: "A ridiculous charge perhaps." She watched him. "Unless he can prove it."

Barone was still laughing.

"It's not funny."

"I know it's not funny."

"He says he ran drugs for you."

"Me personally?"

"All of you."

"He's got balls, doesn't he. But don't worry, no one's going to believe him."

"Oh no?"

She glanced around but saw no sign of Muldoon. Both of them were supposed to be standing by. "Where's your partner?"

"Danny went out for sandwiches. He'll be back in a minute. Tell me really, how's it going?"

"Fine." What else was she supposed to say?

Karen's secretary handed her a message from the DA and she glanced at it: he wished to see her as soon as possible.

About what? Karen wondered.

"So when do you think you'll put me on the stand?" said Barone.

"I'm not sure," said Karen vaguely. "Soon."

"Sitting here all day is hard."

She looked at him—really looked at him—for the first time that day. The nice suit that fit him properly, which was rare among policemen. He must spend all his money on clothes, she thought. She liked his dark eyes. The white teeth. The smile. His smile was quite appealing. He had a way of focusing in on her—on whoever he was talking to, probably. She didn't flatter herself, he must do it with everyone. But unless she wished to be rude, the warmth he exuded, and his apparently sincere interest in her, were difficult to resist.

"Are you really so anxious to get back to Harlem?"

"Yes."

"Why?"

"It's a fascinating job. Harlem is a fascinating place."

She became preoccupied with the telephone message in her hand: she worried about what the DA might want.

"I'm interested in the people," Barone continued, "there's something new every day. Crazy things, sometimes." Seeing that she was not listening, he stopped.

"I'm sorry," said Karen. She gave him a smile. "I have something here that I have to attend to immediately."

She went out and crossed the hall and went into the DA's office and stood before his desk with her hands crossed in front of her skirt. She felt—and imagined she looked—like a schoolgirl who had been called on the carpet. The DA was eating a sandwich.

"Have you had lunch?" he asked her cordially.

"Not yet, no." In fact there would be no time for lunch today, had been no time for lunch since the trial began.

The DA finished his sandwich and wiped his hands on a

paper napkin. "I've been reading the minutes each night," he said then. "You've been doing a fine job. I have no complaints on that score at all."

"Thank you."

The DA hesitated a moment, then said: "There's a lot of pressure on me to accept a plea."

"Political pressure?"

The DA gave a half nod, conceding this.

"From where?" asked Karen.

"That should not be one of your concerns."

She tried not to see him as old. But he was old. She didn't think he looked well either. Was he worried about his health? He doesn't care about right and wrong anymore, she told herself. He just wants to be reelected one more time.

"I've tried about thirty murder cases to verdict," she said. She had decided to fight for her point of view from the start. "I've won all but two. I can make the jury see this case clearly."

"Are you sure?" asked the DA with a smile.

"I can make them see through McCarthy's tactics."

"I asked if you were sure."

"Of course I'm not sure."

She looked at him. He was tall and thin. His white hair was thin. Strands of it hung over his ears. He needs a haircut, she thought.

"Would McCarthy plead to first-degree assault?" he asked her. "A five-year sentence, perhaps."

"His client shot five cops," she said.

"You have a nearly all black jury. Your jury is an unfortunate one."

"There was nothing I could do about that."

"Probably not. I'm not accusing you of anything. Just stating the facts."

Karen watched him carefully. "We have to believe in the jury system," she insisted. "I know it's not perfect, but it's the best we have."

"Sometimes it's not good enough."

"The correct thing to do," said Karen stubbornly, "win or lose, is to try the case to verdict."

The old man frowned, then became suddenly decisive. "We don't want to lose this case. It's as simple as that. Will McCarthy plead to assault?"

"I don't know," said Karen in a voice that could hardly be heard. "I could ask him."

"Five years," the DA mused. "Maybe more. It would be an acceptable result."

To Karen it wouldn't be acceptable at all. "I can win this case."

"Try for more, but accept first-degree assault."

"We can't abandon a case every time we get a jury not to our liking."

"A good theme when speaking to a seminar of young lawyers."

"You should give me credit for the ability to read a jury. I've read this one."

"Have you?"

"I can make this jury see through McCarthy."

"It's turned out to be a bigger case, and also an uglier one, than I ever thought. The racial thing. We don't want demonstrations in the street. And it's come at a bad time. I'll have to ask you to give in to me on this one. Talk to McCarthy."

She went back to the courtroom. The jury box was empty, the judge not yet on the bench. People were milling around. She forced herself to go over to the defense table and lean over McCarthy.

"Can I see you in my office later?" It was the most she could make herself say. The end of the day would be soon enough to end the trial. She could not bear to end it immediately. She would carry it forward as far as she could. If she could keep going until the end of the day she could perhaps talk to the DA again, plead with him, beg him. Perhaps something would happen to change his mind.

But McCarthy's face had brightened. "I sense that you wish to discuss a possible plea."

Without answering she started back to her place. But McCarthy, all bow tie and teeth, came after her.

"We can talk now," he said. "Why subject all these people"—he waved his hand in a dramatic gesture—"to a long, uncomfortable, and possibly unnecessary afternoon?"

Karen felt as she imagined men must feel on such occasions. She wanted to punch him in the middle of his grinning face. "After this afternoon's session will be soon enough, Mr. McCarthy," she said, and sat down.

He stood over her grinning triumphantly but she did not look up. He had just turned back to the defense table when Coombs came dashing down the aisle. The noise of running, unusual in a courtroom, caught her attention. She wondered why he was running. Reaching her, he whispered urgently in her ear.

"The boss has had a seizure of some kind."

Karen jumped up and, together with Coombs, rushed out of the courtroom.

Once in the hall she too started to run. The elevators leading to the DA's floors were at the other end. It was a long hallway and there were people in it who glanced at the two running figures in surprise. Coombs had his key out and they got into the elevator and started down.

On the DA's floor everyone was out in the hall. Assistant DAs in shirtsleeves mingled with secretaries. Everyone was moving, gesticulating, talking excitedly. With Coombs close behind her, Karen ran past people who tried to speak to her, one of them Barone, and into the DA's anteroom, which was empty, and then into his inner office, which was overcrowded. She recognized Norman Harbison, and the old man's secretary, Betty, who stood with her knuckles at her mouth, and a number of others.

The DA lay on the floor with his tie undone, his shirt ripped open. His glasses were askew, and his face was blue. Someone was pounding on his chest. Karen recognized Dr.

Goldberg, one of the assistant medical examiners. He must have been in the building to testify.

Goldberg stood up, his eyes glancing somewhat wildly around the room.

"He's passed away, I'm afraid."

It was a euphemism Karen hated. She stared down at the corpse on the floor. Why not come out and say it, she thought. The DA is dead.

"Heart attack?" someone offered.

"I assume so."

Karen, who was having difficulty swallowing, said what anyone would say under the circumstances: "I was talking to him less than twenty minutes ago."

Someone else murmured: "I have an appointment with him twenty minutes from now."

"It's cancelled," another voice said, and someone gave a bizarre laugh.

She stood looking down on the late district attorney of New York County. More and more assistant DAs in shirtsleeves crowded into the office and did the same, and for a time no one said anything more.

The news spread throughout the building. The assistants were all flooding downstairs, and most judges, Karen's among them, responded by adjourning their trials for the day.

When Karen got back to her office McCarthy was waiting for her. To her he was still all bow tie and teeth, and his thick briefcase sat beside him on the floor. She had to step over it to get to her desk. McCarthy's assistant, she saw as she sat down, a lawyer named Rosenstiel, occupied the chair in the corner, the one she had come to think of as Coombs's chair.

The DA's body had been removed from the building by then. The paramedics had come and gone. They had spread their body bag on the rug and she had left the room, not wanting to see what came next. The DA had been transported to the morgue where an autopsy would be performed. Karen had witnessed autopsies. She did not wish one on the old man.

Less than half an hour ago she had bent close to McCarthy's ear—and been unable to tell him that the trial was over. Now she faced him somberly.

"Sorry if I've made you wait," she said.

"I've been waiting for beautiful women all my life," said Justin McCarthy. "They are moments that I savor."

Karen gave this comment what it deserved. She ignored it. "The DA just died."

"Yes, I heard. How sad. What did you wish to see me about?"

For a moment Karen only looked at him. This man was probably the best known lawyer in the country. Famous? Notorious? Either word fit. Civil rights lawyer? Maybe. He certainly took many civil rights cases, of which Lionel Epps's was not one.

She wondered who was paying him. Not a street thug like Epps. Did anybody pay him? Did he care about money, or only about seeing his name in the newspapers?

When he forced the law to the wall, did he do it for the law's own good, because somebody had to and he had appointed himself? Perhaps he saw courtrooms as an extension of the political arena, neither more nor less. He was expressing his politics. Or perhaps he hated the law, taking his pleasure in thwarting it. All right, she could understand people maybe hating the law, which was an imperfect system that did not always work. But what about justice? Justice was not a system but a concept, and as such it was perfect. Did he hate justice too? But a person who hated justice was a perverted human being, possibly a monster.

Perhaps he was merely the type of man who liked to spoil things, the way some children liked to mess up other children's castles in the sand. Perhaps to spoil something big in a big way made him feel like a big man.

"I asked you this once before, Mr. McCarthy. Why are you defending a thug like Lionel Epps?"

McCarthy gave what could only be called a wolfish grin—

all his side teeth showed. "But madam, it's those cops who ought to be on trial. Those cops were trying to murder my client."

Perhaps he got his kicks by bending the law over his knee, by breaking its back and tossing the remains aside. Which quite often was remarkably easy to do.

"If they had wanted to murder him, I'm sure they could have managed it, don't you think, Mr. McCarthy?"

McCarthy did not answer, but his wolfish grin remained in place. Presently he said: "You invited me here to negotiate a plea, I believe."

"A plea? Why would you expect me to go for a plea?"

"Because the DA ordered you to," McCarthy said smoothly, adding: "His dying wish, so to speak."

Karen was stunned. Was he guessing? He was too confident to be guessing, and it was too easy to imagine the DA meeting with him behind her back. As she pictured McCarthy and the DA negotiating in a closed room, she fought to control her face, to show no emotion, but felt her color come up and knew she had failed. The dead giveaway, her cursed face. Two men in a closed room had come to a decision, and even then she wasn't told.

"I could possibly be induced to accept a plea," McCarthy said smoothly. She saw him glance over at Rosenstiel, who so far had not spoken a word. "The right kind of plea. Some degree of assault, possibly."

Her composure was gone and she fought to regain it. "Plea?" she managed to say.

"What sort of plea did you have in mind, madam?"

It had all been decided and she was the last to know.

In fact nothing had been decided. The district attorney was dead, the orders he had given her had died with him.

"You can't possibly know what the DA and I talked about," Karen said.

The wolfish grin slowly faded. First the side teeth disappeared, and then all of them. "How will it look if an assistant district attorney is exposed to the public as rejecting the last order of this—this titan, this icon?''

"Don't threaten me, Mr. McCarthy. Until such time as a new DA is appointed, the decision is mine. In the case of *The People versus Lionel Epps*, no plea will be accepted.''

"You're experiencing grief, aren't you?" said McCarthy. "I can understand how you must feel. Your beloved master is dead and these other matters must seem of little moment to you. You have my condolences, madam.''

"I suggest you get back to your client.''

"You're not yourself,'' said McCarthy. "We'll have an opportunity to talk tomorrow.''

"Yes,'' Karen said grimly. "Every day, in fact. In court.''

The DA's funeral took place in St. Patrick's Cathedral. Karen sat with the bureau chiefs and other principal administrators in the row just behind the family. The cathedral was full. Most of the other assistant DAs were present, and so were most of the political, financial, and business leaders of the city.

After the service Karen stood with Coombs on the church steps. They watched the coffin being slid into the hearse. They watched the cortege drive off.

Below them various dignitaries crowded around Norman Harbison on the sidewalk. The mayor was there, shaking his hand. The police commissioner, Reverend Johnson, and some others waited their turns. It was obvious that everyone considered him the DA's heir apparent. The assembled TV crews were filming every handshake.

"The governor hasn't appointed him yet,'' Coombs said.

"He looks pretty confident,'' murmured Karen

"That's because he's such a jerk.''

"Hush,'' said Karen with a smile. "You're talking about your future boss.''

"I hope not.''

"Who else could it be?''

"You, maybe."

The idea shocked Karen.

"It would only be until the election anyway," said Coombs.

Karen had never imagined herself as district attorney. A judgeship was certainly possible one day. But DA was a political office and she was not a politician.

"Where are we, in April?" said Coombs. "In six or seven months you'd have to run for election."

Karen laughed. The idea seemed to her preposterous, so the laugh was genuine.

"You'd make an attractive candidate," Coombs told her, "and the politicians like to win elections."

The governor would appoint Harbison, Karen decided, or else some political crony. "You're crazy," she told Coombs.

As they started down the steps Harbison, who had finished shaking hands, came toward them. He looked smug, it seemed to Karen, obviously pleased with himself.

"The DA was such a great man," he said when they came together. "Well, I guess we'd all better get back to work, hadn't we?"

The DA's official Cadillac drew up at the curb. "Sorry I can't take you back in my car," Harbison said, "but I've asked the PC to ride downtown with me. We have a lot to discuss."

Police Commissioner Malloy was part of a group further along the sidewalk. Harbison called across to him. "My car's here, Charlie, if you're ready."

— 13 —

Detective Muldoon took the stand. His direct examination, which lasted five hours, went about as Karen had expected. His syntax was poor and some of his answers rambled, but she took him over important points several times until satisfied that the jury understood and would remember. However, he avoided eye contact throughout, preferring to stare at the ceiling or the floor. He never once looked at her, or at the jury either.

This made him, from the prosecution's point of view, a less than perfect witness, a concept that did not occur to him.

That night in her office she tried to speak to him about it. "Tomorrow you'll be cross-examined by Mr. McCarthy," she began.

Muldoon said nothing.

"If you could look him in the eye when you respond to his questions," she said, "it would make a better impression on the jury."

Muldoon still said nothing.

"And you should look at the jury from time to time so they know you're sincere."

"I've never had any trouble convincing a jury I was sincere."

She nodded and tried to think of an approach that might reach him.

"I never lost a case yet where I testified," Muldoon said.

Though she doubted this, Karen decided not to dispute it. "Eye contact is important," she persisted.

"Lady, the only thing important is I tell the truth of what happened."

She judged him to be a fragile personality who could be pushed only so far. Testifying at trials was a large part of what he did for a living and he believed himself an ace at it. She pushed as hard as she dared.

"The truth by itself is not always sufficient," she said. "If the jury doesn't believe you, the defendant will walk. You wouldn't want that to happen, would you?"

"Lady, he won't walk. Not after I get through with him. Put the sonuvabitch where he belongs."

"You mustn't seem angry or vindictive on the stand. Try to be impersonal."

"Impersonal? The sonuvabitch shot me."

"A detached, professional attitude is what you should try for."

He became huffy. "My attitude is always professional."

"You have to be believed."

"They'll believe me."

"Have you ever had a case with Mr. McCarthy before?"

"No."

"What do you know about him?"

"I know everything about him."

"When he examines you, I want you to look him in the eye and treat him with respect."

"Why? Because he's a lawyer? What is it with you lawyers? When someone's a degenerate you don't hold back just because he's a lawyer. If I see a chance in court to show him up for what he is, I'll take it."

"That might be counterproductive," said Karen.

Muldoon said nothing.

"I'm not asking you to respect him personally, but as an officer of the court. Because that's how the jury wants to see him treated."

Muldoon again did not answer.

Karen said: "Well, would you do it as a favor to me?"

"Lady, you may be asking the impossible."

"Promise me you'll try."

Muldoon not only looked her in the eye but actually smiled. "All right, for you I'll try."

Barone, who was present, put his arm around his partner. "You're going to do what she asks you, right, Danny?" To Karen he said: "He'll be fine. He's going to be a great witness."

As the two detectives were leaving, Karen called Barone back. He stood in front of her desk. "Talk to him for me, please," she said.

They looked at each other. "I'll talk to him," Barone said. He grinned at her. "Ask me something hard," he said. "I'll do that for you too."

She waited until he had gone out before she let a smile come on. He was always cheerful, and could usually make her cheerful too, and she liked having him around.

Barone and Muldoon had dinner in a bar. The owner liked cops and would give them something off on the bill. They ordered beef stew, which was the night's special, and beer, and when they were finishing up Barone said: "All right, let's prepare your testimony on the stand tomorrow. I'm Mc-Carthy, and I say to you, Answer my question, asshole."

"He won't call me an asshole in court."

"He'll imply it. How will you react?"

Instead of answering, Muldoon said: "What's between you and this broad?"

"Nothing. Let's go on. Answer my question, asshole."

Muldoon was mopping up the last of his stew. "The trial is not a game," he said.

"No it's not."

"You want to play games, play them by yourself. Are you getting into her pants or what?"

"No," said Barone. "She's got a husband and kids and no interest in me."

"Then why are you taking her side?"

Why indeed, Barone asked himself. "Because she's a nice woman," he said. But his feelings were stronger than this, and he knew it. "I like her," he said. "I admire her. I don't want to see her lose the case, and the key to the case is you. McCarthy is going to needle you, goad you, insinuate you're a crook. Now put the beer glass down and let's go over how you're going to react."

McCarthy said: "And did you have a warrant for Mr. Epps's arrest, Detective?"

Muldoon in the witness box gazed at the ceiling and said in a bored voice: "You already asked me that question, counselor. Several times in fact. You know something, you may be boring the jury out of their socks."

The white-haired defense lawyer turned and spoke with some asperity to the bench. "Will Your Honor please instruct the witness to respond to the question? Yes or no."

Muldoon did not wait for instruction. "We didn't need a warrant according to law. How many times I have to tell you?"

It was his third day of cross-examination. The first two had gone exactly like this one.

Justin McCarthy said: "If the suspect had been a stockbroker, would you have got a warrant, Detective?"

For two days McCarthy had cross-examined him. The same questions over and over again. At the start of each day Muldoon was careful that his contempt did not show.

But then McCarthy would push him too far. He was a New York City detective and he could not just sit there and let this hump continue to impugn his honor and the department's honor. He could not continue to take the snide insinuations.

If he did, the jury might believe them true. Since he was confined to the witness box and restricted to direct answers to questions put to him, there was no way he could fight back except to let his feelings show for the jury to see. The jury would see that he was telling the truth and would believe him.

"Suppose he had been a violinist with the New York Philharmonic, Detective. Would you have got a warrant?"

Muldoon in the box studied the ceiling and did not answer. The button that held his sports coat closed seemed ready to pop. He imagined he looked gray-haired, imposing, authoritative. In fact he looked only hostile.

"But because he was an underprivileged black youth, a member of an oppressed minority, no warrant was necessary. Is that it, Detective?"

"He was wanted on suspicion in another case."

"On suspicion. Twenty cops armed to the teeth to pick up one black youth on suspicion. Or was the object to silence him once and for all?"

Muldoon studied the wall, while McCarthy paced. "You had a shotgun, is that correct, detective?"

"I left it in the car."

Muldoon could not bring himself to make eye contact with the white-haired fuck. If this seemed evasive, it could not be helped. He was doing his best.

"What was loaded in it?"

"Double O buckshot."

"That's enough to blow a man's face right off him, isn't it?"

"I left it in the car."

"Blow a young black youth's face right off him. No one would even know who he was—had been, and no story of police corruption would ever come to light. Isn't that right, Detective?"

"Objection, objection," cried Karen.

"But you left it in the car. Are you sure of that, Detective? Yes, you left it in the car. Are you sure, Detective?"

"Sustained," said the judge finally.

As Muldoon waited for redirect examination, he was still fuming.

Karen rose and approached the witness box. "Were you armed at all, Detective?"

Muldoon decided to look her in the eye. "I had my service revolver in its holster."

"You take the gun out, Detective?"

"I didn't have time."

"Which means?"

"We went through all that on direct."

"Yes," she said. "Please answer the question, Detective."

"I kick the door in and the f—the defendant fires a shotgun right in our faces. The cops with me are all on the floor screaming in agony."

"You couldn't get your gun out, is that correct, Detective?"

"There was a wounded cop on top of me thrashing around. He was bleeding all over me."

"You couldn't get your gun out?"

"I couldn't get it out."

"You had one gun, Detective. The defendant had how many?"

"We recovered four guns. Two handguns, a rifle, and a shotgun."

At the defense table McCarthy jumped up. "Objection, Your Honor. This line of questioning is inflammatory."

"Oh, I'm terribly sorry, Mr. McCarthy," said Karen. "Really sorry."

Muldoon in the witness box knew sarcasm when he heard it, but thought it too subtle for a degenerate like McCarthy. It was too subtle for the jurors too. Those people would see what they wanted to see: that the cops had tried to shoot down one of their innocent young black boys without provocation. In this city everyone dumped on cops.

Muldoon watched the two lawyers go at each other.

"I certainly did not wish to seem inflammatory," said Karen. "How can you ever forgive me?"

"I accept your apology," said McCarthy.

"Inflammatory," Karen cried. "You've taken every opportunity for the past month to inflame the jury with every prejudice known to man."

They were shouting at each other.

"Let me explain to you, Mrs. Henning, under the law—"

"Don't you lecture me on the law, Mr. McCarthy."

"I am defending an innocent man."

She walked away from him. "Inflammatory, huh!" she snorted.

"That's enough by both of you," said Judge Birnbaum mildly.

At the end of the day Muldoon was told to return the next morning. He and Barone had dinner in a place in the Bronx that was half bar, half restaurant.

"You've got to try harder with your attitude," Barone said.

"He never laid a glove on me. I wiped him out."

They were eating hamburgers, french fries, and sliced tomatoes, and were drinking beer. This owner liked cops too. Every cop in the city knew such places.

"He's a good lawyer," Barone said, "and tomorrow you're still on the stand."

"That white-haired fuck."

Barone was trying to decide how to proceed. From the other side of the partition came the noise of glasses, of loud conversation.

"Listen, Danny—" He hated to lecture his partner each night, and so far it hadn't done any good.

Karen, meanwhile, had reported to Harbison, as requested. She found him in the late DA's big office. There were cartons on the floor. The flaps were all laid back and he was unpacking them. As she watched he carried an armload of stuff to the DA's desk.

"You moved in here pretty quickly, didn't you?" she said, glancing around the office. "He's not cold yet."

"Until the governor appoints an interim DA I'm in charge."

"Yes, I know that." She handed him a sheaf of papers. "Here are the minutes of today's action as you requested. Runs, hits, and errors."

"Not too many errors, I hope." Harbison gave a weak smile, as if he had meant this to sound amusing. But Karen did not find it so.

"The trial is not going as well as I hoped," he commented as he placed books on shelves.

Karen was focused not on him but on her trial. McCarthy's game, obviously, was to rouse the jury to a racist fever, and she was trying to think of a way to stop it and him. Unfortunately, the bar association's rules of professional conduct permitted nearly all of what McCarthy was doing, or at least did not expressly forbid it. It was a gray area. She could complain to the court, but presumably Judge Birnbaum had already decided in favor of McCarthy, for he had done nothing to stop him up to now. Her complaint would be taken as criticism, and judges did not like to be criticized. It would make him angry, and if it made him angry enough all his decisions would start going against her—a sure way to lose the trial.

All these thoughts were going through her head. Harbison said: "As soon as I get straightened out here, you and I will have to have a talk."

Karen gave him a look. "Sure," she said, and nodded to him and went out.

Across the table at dinner Karen's daughter was beaming about something.

"I went out for cheerleading, Mom."

The girl looked around as if everyone should greet her news with excitement.

But this did not happen. Although Hank said dutifully: "That's wonderful, sweetie," Karen chose to remain silent.

"Hilda and Sharon are going out too," Hillary added. Hilda and Sharon were her best friends.

"Why would you want to be a cheerleader?" asked Karen, keeping her tone amused. She wanted what was best for her daughter, wanted her to set her sights high, find a goal that appealed to her and go for it. Almost anything in life was possible for her daughter. There were no limits today. Hillary did not, as in the past, have to be satisfied with cheerleading.

"Cheerleading is fun, Mom."

"Why don't you go out for the girls' gymnastics team or the volleyball team," Karen suggested.

"Because she's boy crazy," said Jackie.

"Shut up," Hillary said. "You twerp. Because I don't like gymnastics or volleyball," she told her mother.

"Isn't cheerleading, well, rather passive?"

"Cheerleading is hard. You have to learn a lot. It's really very hard."

At the head of the table Hank watched and said nothing.

"Well, is that the way you see yourself?" asked Karen. "As a girl who—as someone—who stands on the sidelines and cheers for boys?"

"You were a cheerleader in high school, weren't you?" asked Hillary.

"No. In high school I was interested in my grades, in choosing a college, in—"

Hillary jumped up and performed the school cheer. Her feet hopped, her fists punched the air.

Go blue, go white
Go Bronxville, fight, fight—

The others stared at her.

"I guess I'd feel better," Karen said, "if you went out for something more, you know, active."

"Cheerleading is fun, Mom. Fun, fun, fun."

Karen looked at her.

"Why does everything have to make a statement with you?" the girl cried. "It's fun."

She ran out of the room and up the stairs.

"She's in the attic," said Jackie, after a moment. Everyone listened to the noise she was making.

"Eat your dinner," said Karen.

"What's she doing up there?" said Hank.

"Sounds like she's rummaging through trunks."

"I thought you told me you were a cheerleader in high school," said Hank.

"Well, I wasn't."

She resumed eating, and after a moment the others did too. The noise from the attic stopped and they heard Hillary running down the stairs again.

As she reentered the dining room, she was holding her mother's old cheerleading sweater to her chest.

"What's this, Mom?"

After staring at the sweater in surprise, Karen started to laugh. "That was in junior high school."

No one was conceding her the distinction, which only made her laugh harder.

"It was a different world then," she said when she could speak. "Women didn't have the opportunities they have now."

She saw that this explanation was not accepted either.

"You're right," she said, gazing fondly at her daughter. "It was, well, fun."

Rikers Island lies in the East River between the Bronx and Queens, a flat sand dune of an island, an almost perfect oval about a mile long, half a mile wide. In an earlier age its shores were equidistant from adjacent land at all four points of the compass, but La Guardia Airport's north-south runway was pushed out further and further into the water, until one end abutted and nearly touched the island. This is as close as the island or anyone on it gets to the mainstream of the American dream.

Nothing can be seen from the air to disclose the island's function. Arriving and departing passengers look down on a number of substantial buildings, some roadways, and a bridge across from Queens. All this where once only sea grass grew. The whole resembles an apartment house complex, which it is not, even though it is home to twenty thousand people, none there because they want to be. Rikers Island is a conglomeration of prisons, nine in all.

There are no guard towers or enclosing walls, only a series of chain link fences topped by barbed wire; the different prisons seem to have been separated into compounds. The roads are as wide as boulevards, and here and there attempts have been made to plant trees, hedges, and even flowers, but in the sandy soil nothing much grows. Most days, depending on the wind, the adjacent runway is in use every thirty seconds for takeoffs and landings, and the noise in the cells under the planes is stupendous, and virtually constant. When the tide is right, the island and its prisons crouch under the stench given off by the mud flats and by the raw sewage floating by.

This is not a nice place, but it is not Devil's Island. The skyscrapers of Manhattan are visible from some of the cells. Offshore there are no violent currents to sweep men away, no ravenous sharks to prevent escapes, of which there have been a rather large number, more than the corrections department likes to admit. Men have been released by mistake too. The wrong papers are presented and out they go. It happens. These are prisoners who come and go frequently in any case. Sometimes detectives or district attorneys come out and drive away with some individual. The blue-and-white corrections department buses load up groups of inmates each day and drive them to courtrooms. The buses are heavily reinforced with steel mesh windows, they are locked up tight, and of course all have been trashed inside.

The men on Rikers have been arrested but not yet tried; or tried but not yet sentenced; or have pleaded guilty to reduced charges and are waiting to be released; or have been sentenced and are awaiting transport to one of the heavy penitentiaries upstate: Attica, Greenhaven—one of those. Rikers has its share of fights, beatings, riots, knifings, homosexual assaults, overdoses, same as all prisons, but the men incarcerated here are not doing what cons call hard time.

Or rather, most are not. About 60 percent live in dormitory rooms, only about 40 percent in cells. The racial breakdown is 57 percent black, 35 percent Hispanic, 7 percent white, 1 percent "other." Of course whites and Asians who get in trouble with the law are more likely to be able to make bail.

The nine prisons are known euphemistically as "facilities," of which Facility No. 1 is the oldest and the worst. It is all cells, and that is where the most violent or notorious of the inmates are kept, sometimes in punishment cells.

It was where Lionel Epps had been held for the ten months since his arrest and was being held during his trial, and that same night at about the time Hillary Henning performed her school cheer for her mother, Epps was on the telephone trying to call his lawyer.

Inmates were allowed one phone call a night. There was only one phone in Epps's section of Facility No. 1. It was on the wall in a corridor and the men were lined up waiting to use it. To call their lawyers, to call a loved one. One phone call each. They had looked forward to this call all day.

Epps seemed to be taking an inordinately long time. The men on line behind him were jostling each other and shouting at him to hurry up.

The guards, who supposedly kept order but in fact did nothing, noted that no one dared jostle Epps himself.

There is a hierarchy in all prisons, and it is based on fear. There were violent criminals on Rikers, career criminals too, but they did not stay there long. Anyone sentenced to more than a year got moved upstate, leaving behind the many burglars and petty drug dealers who came and went. Epps had been arrested late the previous spring and now it was spring again. He had been there longer than most of the other inmates, time enough to establish himself at the top of the food chain.

He was not a big man. If a boxer he would have been a middleweight. He worked out with weights every day. He rarely spoke and had no intimates. His eyes seemed to smolder and he would sometimes stare at one of the other inmates for a minute or more. There seemed to be an invisible line around him. Step across the line and he would lash out with his fists, or with whatever weapon came to hand. No one knew where that line was. Cut into a queue ahead of him, tell a joke he did not understand, accidentally invade what he counted as his personal space—do this and he would beat you senseless, or until pulled off by guards, after which he would retreat to his cell and stare out, saying not a word.

No one knew what caused the violence, or when it would erupt.

Tonight Epps had dialed McCarthy's office number. He had once asked for his home number but the lawyer had refused to give it. Now the phone rang many times in what sounded like an empty office. But despite the lateness of the hour, someone finally answered. Epps gave his name, and was put on hold. With increasing impatience he waited, while behind him in line the jostling and yelping increased, until Epps turned with the phone at his ear.

"Shut the fuck up," he shouted, and for two or three minutes the jostling stopped and the others fell silent.

At the time that this call came in McCarthy was seated at his desk with his chair tilted back and his feet up, sipping from a glass of the Irish whiskey which he favored, and which was as much one of his affectations as his bow tie or his flowery manner. Present in the office were two law students from NYU, both twenty-three years old, who worked for him as interns. They worked without pay and were glad of the chance, for it made possible nights like this, which they treasured, nights when the great man would pour out whiskey for himself and for them and sit back and pontificate on the tactics that had made him famous.

"Success is all in getting the jury you want," he was saying as the phone rang in his secretary's office. He felt quite mellow by then and the noise of the ringing made him frown. "Don't answer it," he said, and then continued his line of thought. "If you can empanel the jury you want, you'll get the verdict you want, you can count on it."

"There's nothing in between but the trial," said one of the law students.

"An extremely astute observation," said McCarthy.

The phone continued to ring.

"And once the trial starts, what do you concentrate on?" asked McCarthy rhetorically. After taking a long pull at his whiskey he said: "One of you answer that thing, or it will never stop."

Both law students jumped up but it was the tall one with the thick glasses who went out to the secretary's desk and spoke into the phone.

In a moment his head came back into the room. "It's your client."

McCarthy's feet were still up on the desk. "When the trial starts, what do you concentrate on?" he repeated.

"Well, the evidence, obviously," said the other student, who was short with big ears.

"That may be what they teach you in law school," said McCarthy, "and if you prefer an entirely undistinguished career, that's exactly what you should do."

The young men looked confused.

"You have to understand that nearly all of your clients are guilty. The evidence will only convict them. Sometimes overwhelmingly so. No, you stay as far away from the evidence as you can."

"But—"

"On the other hand, if you want to win verdicts—"

The two young men waited for the wisdom that was to come.

"Once you empanel the jury you want," said McCarthy,

"you have only to play to their prejudices, their preconceived ideas. For instance, most people are only too willing to believe all policemen to be sadists and crooks. If your client looks respectable enough, most juries, the kind of jurors you want, are perfectly willing to believe your client didn't commit the crime at all, the cops did. And not only that. What did those dastardly cops do next but try to pin it on that honorable young man who is your client, on trial now for one reason and one only, because the police framed him."

McCarthy was nodding his sagacious white head and staring into his glass.

"Speaking of clients," suddenly remembered the tall student, "your client is still on the line."

"I have nothing to say to him," said McCarthy with a dismissive wave of his hand. "Tell him I'll see him in court."

The law student went out to the secretary's phone.

"You have to know when to hang up on your clients," said McCarthy to the other one. "That's very important for a lawyer."

They heard the phone go down in the other room.

"Leave it off the hook so he can't phone us back," called McCarthy. And then, when the student reentered the office: "And how did my client respond when obliged to contemplate his relative standing in this relationship, his and mine?"

Evidently the law student did not want to answer.

"Do not be embarrassed," said McCarthy. "You may repeat what he said word for word."

The student hesitated. "He said: You tell that fuck—"

McCarthy laughed. "Tell me what?"

"I don't know, I hung up."

"You'll make a lawyer yet," chortled McCarthy, and he poured more whiskey into all three glasses.

On Rikers Island the enraged Epps had dialed again. When he got a busy signal, he ripped the phone box off the wall, and the receiver on its cable out of the box. There would be no more phone calls for anyone that night or even that week probably, perhaps longer. The prisoners in line behind Epps became as angry as he was, and without a word spoken rushed him.

Epps began swinging the receiver on the end of its cable. It was a vicious weapon and men went down. Other men reached out for it and ripped it out of his hands. Epps drove his fists into faces, broke out of the melee, and ran for the latrine where he ripped a sink off the wall and began flailing away.

In court the next morning an angry McCarthy approached the bench. Karen joined him. The spectator area was full as usual, and Muldoon was already seated in the witness box, but the defendant was not in court, nor were the jurors in the jury box.

"During the night," said McCarthy, "my client was assaulted in jail by other inmates—the police appear to be behind it."

"Come now, Mr. McCarthy," said Judge Birnbaum.

"They're trying to kill him even in jail," declared McCarthy. "Release him on bail so we can arrange guards to protect him from the police."

"Can we get on with the trial please, Judge?" said Karen.

"No we can't," raged McCarthy. "I haven't told you the half of it yet. Not only was my client assaulted, but all of his court clothes have been slashed and are unwearable—six Brooks Brothers suits."

"A pity," said Karen, laughing.

"What's so funny?" demanded McCarthy, turning on her.

"They were nice suits," said Karen.

"Judge," continued McCarthy, "he certainly can't come to court in prison garb."

"The jury might get the wrong idea about him," said Karen.

Muldoon watched all this.

"I require a week's recess, Your Honor."

"A week?" said Judge Birnbaum.

"Time to outfit him in new clothes. May I ask the court for the money to pay for them?"

"I don't see where that's the court's responsibility, Mr. McCarthy."

"The court remanded him to jail in the first place."

"I have a suggestion, Judge."

"Yes, Mrs. Henning?"

"Let whoever bought him the first six suits pay for them."

The judge looked thoughtful.

"I've already spoken to the press about this," threatened McCarthy. "The press will know what to do."

"Mrs. Henning?" said Judge Birnbaum.

Karen had been holding a sheaf of papers; she tossed them into the air in disgust.

The court reporter, who was transcribing the colloquy on his machine, looked up in surprise.

McCarthy pointed a finger at him. "Let the record show that Mrs. Henning displays her contempt for these proceedings by throwing her papers in the air."

"No," said Karen, "let the record show that Mrs. Henning threw her papers in the air to show her contempt for certain lawyers, who are a disgrace to their profession."

Leaving McCarthy sputtering, she walked back to her place.

"Bring in the jury, please," called out Judge Birnbaum.

All waited until the jurors had filed into the box. The judge then addressed them: "Something has come up and I am going to declare a recess until next Monday morning. I will admonish you again: Do not listen to television reports about the case, or read news reports about the case. Do not talk to anyone about it. Do not talk about it even among yourselves."

The bailiff held open the jurors' door and they filed through it. Muldoon got down out of the witness box, and the entire courtroom slowly emptied out.

— 14 —

Barone was waiting when Karen, accompanied by Coombs, drove out onto Rikers Island the next day. The tide was out and his nostrils sucked in the odor of the mud flats. The entire island smelled like a latrine.

They followed a corrections department captain into Facility No. 1, passing through a number of barred enclosures. Jail doors clanged.

"It really stinks out here, doesn't it," Karen murmured once. And then, when a jet went over at rooftop level: "Listen to that."

They were led along barred corridors to a point where they could look down into what was some sort of common room. There were TV sets high up on the walls, all blaring. Inmates were milling about, talking, arguing, shouting. As always inside jails, the noise level was stupendous. Every thirty seconds another jet went by overhead.

"They don't have much privacy," murmured Karen to Barone.

"Most of them don't know what privacy is," he said. "They don't miss it."

Barone already knew the facts of Epps's brawl. He was

surprised that Karen had wanted to come out herself, verify it all firsthand.

"Any more than they miss good food," said Barone. "Most of them think prison swill is terrific."

If he himself were confined here it wasn't privacy exactly that he would miss, Barone believed, though a person certainly needed a place to go where he could be alone from time to time. He watched Karen, such a good-looking woman, as she continued to peer down on all those men. More than the privacy he would miss silence. A person had a right to silence, for noise could drive one mad. At times, Barone reflected, one craved silence as much as one craved solitude, maybe more. But in this steel world there was no silent place to which one could retreat. A world of bars. A man could not pass between them, only sound could. A prison, especially this one so close to the runway, was an ocean of swelling and receding sound.

If you were in the business of arresting people, these were not thoughts to brood over. Barone was not without sympathy for the prisoners, but he had no illusions either. They were lawbreakers one and all, and most of them were not going to change until too old or sick to commit additional crimes.

He said, pointing: "See that wrecked phone there?"

Karen nodded.

"Epps was on the phone trying to call his lawyer. There was a line of men behind him waiting their turn."

Karen nodded again. He could see her picture it.

"McCarthy refused to talk to him."

"You mean Justin McCarthy wouldn't take the call?" said Karen. She grinned. "Justin McCarthy? The famous civil rights lawyer? It's not possible. I can't believe it of him."

Barone liked her a good deal at that moment. "So Epps ripped the phone off the wall," he said.

"Look out," said Karen.

"The inmates behind him laughed and went back to their cells," joked Barone.

"A fight started," said the corrections captain earnestly.

"Epps was losing it," said Barone, "so he ran down this corridor here into this latrine." He pointed and led the way.

"You're sure of all this?" asked Karen, following.

"Well, I was out here all day yesterday and again this morning. I interviewed the guards, and after them about twenty inmates. You wouldn't believe how nervous everyone was. Yeah, I'm sure." They had given him a consultation room next to the infirmary to use as an office and had begun bringing men in. The prisoners, all of them young blacks, were worried about being disciplined. So were the guards. The guards were blacks also, and only a little older. They were undereducated, underpaid, some with prison records themselves, he believed. He had had to joke and cajole—get each man to trust him—before he could get them to talk. It had taken patience and enormous amounts of time, great skill too, he thought, but he did not say so to Karen. He hoped she would realize it without being told.

"All right," said Karen, "Epps in the latrine does what?"

"He rips that sink there off the wall to use as a weapon." The sink, broken into two pieces, lay on the floor.

"He's very strong, isn't he," commented Karen.

"He just shook it until all the pipes broke," said Barone.

"Caused an immediate flood," said the corrections captain.

"To which the guards reacted with their usual poise and tact," joked Barone.

He had made Karen smile, he was pleased to see.

"Epps is whaling away," Barone said, "the guards are clubbing people, the water is up over their shoes—what a mess."

"While this was happening," said the corrections captain, leading them into a cellblock, "part of the group ran into his cell, this one here, which was open."

"And bye-bye the wardrobe," said Barone.

Karen laughed, and gazed at him. He thought for a moment she might not be entirely immune to his charm after all.

"If you really want to hurt this guy, what do you do?" Karen murmured.

"Right," said Barone.

"I guess he was pretty fond of his new clothes."

"He had never had clothes like that in his life."

At present the cells on the block were open and empty. They all peered into the one that had been inhabited by Lionel Epps: a toilet without a seat, a bunk, a pallet of a mattress. No personal belongings. Epps had been moved elsewhere, obviously.

Karen got back to business. "McCarthy says the police assaulted him."

"That's ridiculous," said Barone, surprised.

"Normally there are no police officers inside the facility," said the corrections captain.

"The police were trying to kill him," said Karen.

"Nobody would believe that," said Barone.

"No?" said Karen.

The corrections captain led them into the punishment block. The cells were occupied and the cell doors locked.

"Move quick," said the captain. "They see you're a woman they're liable to start flashing you."

A din had already gone up. Men were at the bars trying to peer down the corridor after Karen. They were calling out, banging on the bars.

The captain led. Karen looked uncomfortable, Barone thought. She looked like a woman who had entered a men's room by mistake. She was standing in a domain in which she had no business.

They reached Epps's cell. He was already at the bars, and he stared out principally at Karen. After a moment she nodded at him in recognition. He did not nod back. He wore the prison uniform. There was no shirt and tie, no Brooks Brothers suit, and the horn-rimmed glasses were absent. It's good she sees him like this, Barone thought. Sees him looking like what he is.

Karen gazed at him, and Epps stared back. His eyes were hard, unyielding. Two people who know each other, Barone reflected. One of them was inside the bars, one outside, and he imagined Karen's head filling up with emotions she could not sort out: something about men who had to be kept in cages. Barone had experienced such emotions more than once. Men who were primitive, feral, dangerous. More dangerous than beasts. But man was designed to be free. A man's imagination needed room to soar. Men did not belong in cages. Yet when they behaved like this man, what else were other men to do with them?

He saw that it was Karen whose eyes dropped first.

They left the island in two cars and once across in Queens stopped at a coffee shop on Ditmars Boulevard, taking a booth, the two men on opposite sides of the table sliding across the plastic to the wall, leaving Karen with a choice to make. Sit beside Barone or beside Coombs.

She seemed to hesitate, then slid in next to Coombs. It was a small thing, not worth thinking about. Nonetheless, Barone was disappointed. What did she think would happen if she sat next to him? That he would press his leg against hers under the table? He wouldn't do a thing like that. She kept her eyes down on the menu.

The waitress came and stood over them. They ordered coffee and it was served and they drank it.

She and Coombs reached the office first. Barone came in a few minutes later because he had stopped to buy the afternoon newspaper, which he handed across saying: "Look at this."

He leaned forward to read it over Karen's shoulder. Her hair smelled nice, her skin too, but he felt uncomfortable being so close, so he moved back, even though Coombs had leaned over her other shoulder and was reading too.

The front page headline read: ASSAULT ON EPPS IN JAIL. And then in smaller type below—*McCarthy Accuses Police*.

Karen, reading, seemed to get silently furious. When she had finished she got up and walked to the window.

"So now the jury knows why court recessed yesterday," she said.

"But they can't possibly know," Barone said, trying to make her lighten up. "The judge ordered them not to read the papers."

"There are legal remedies," offered Coombs.

"Sure," said Karen, who had not cracked a smile. "I can question each juror when court reconvenes."

"Sneak any peeks into the papers over the weekend?" joked Barone.

She looked at him, not finding him a bit amusing. He decided to drop the comedy.

She said: "They either say no and perjure themselves—"

"Didn't happen to glance at the television, did you?" said Coombs, taking up the unappreciated joke.

"—or yes," continued Karen, "and we have an immediate mistrial. Another month picking a new jury. A second month to get as far into the trial as we've come."

"It's what McCarthy would do," said Coombs.

"I'm not McCarthy."

"No, you're not," said Barone quietly, but she ignored him. There was no reaction of any kind.

"Stalling is his major tactic," said Coombs. "He stalls until everybody is so sick of the trial they just want it over."

"Do you realize the cost of this thing already?" said Karen. "A new trial would last all summer."

"How about till Christmas?" said Coombs.

Karen smiled and gave a brief laugh. "I can certainly see the humor in all this. We're caught, aren't we? We ignore the whole thing. There's nothing else we can do."

Just then her phone rang, and she picked it up. As soon as she realized who was calling, and why, her breath seemed to catch. Barone saw this, and wondered what it was. After listening a moment she put her hand over the receiver and looked from him to Coombs.

"Would you excuse me a moment, please?"

Barone got up and sauntered out of the office, but Coombs, no doubt supposing that he and Karen had no secrets from each other, stayed.

Karen was still holding her hand over the receiver. "Larry—" she said to him. Barone saw this from the hall.

Looking surprised, Coombs too left the office.

As the two men paced the corridor, they could hear Karen on the phone. She seemed to be trying to keep her answers as brief and cryptic as possible, which was mysterious, to say the least.

"The trial is in recess until Monday," they heard her say. "I'd rather not take time away from preparation right now, though . . . Well, under those circumstances."

After hanging up she came out into the corridor. "I have to go out," she told Coombs. She looked at Barone too, but seemed to be trying to keep her face as expressionless as possible.

"Something's gone wrong," Barone said.

"No, no," she said quickly. "It's a personal matter."

She left them and crossed the hall to the DA's office— Harbison's office. They heard her speak to the secretary.

"Is Norm free? I need him for just a minute."

"Gone for the day. He'll be phoning in, though. What shall I tell him?"

They heard Karen hesitate. Finally she said: "It's not important."

She came back into her office for her handbag and coat. Coombs was gone by then, but Barone, who had lingered, followed her in.

"You're upset," he said. "I wish I could help."

"I'm not upset." And she smiled at him to prove she wasn't.

"Something wrong at home?"

"No." Wherever she was going, she had decided to take her briefcase with her and was stuffing things into it.

"I have my car," said Barone. "Let me take you wherever you need to go."

She gave him an abstracted glance. "That won't be necessary," she said, and strode toward the elevator.

Watching her go, Barone decided she didn't like him very much.

In the street Karen hailed a taxi and asked to be taken to the Wall Street heliport.

The helicopter was already waiting, its rotor idly turning. It had the New York State logo on its side. There were two pilots, one of whom came down to help her up into the machine. She shook hands with that one on the tarmac, and with the other one once she was inside the cockpit.

"I've never ridden in one of these things before," she said nervously as she strapped herself in. That she was under considerable tension had nothing to do with this being her first flight in a helicopter, and everything to do with the interview—and the possibilities—that lay ahead.

"The flight will take about fifty minutes," the pilot said.

She hardly heard him. Don't get your hopes up, she warned herself.

In a moment the helicopter lifted off. In the air it tilted and seemed to skitter along at rooftop height. She was terrifically conscious of its speed. Finally it lifted. It flew up the East River and curled around the tip of Manhattan Island, and below them now was the Hudson, with the suburban towns to either side. Then the towns ended and she looked down on the heavily forested Hudson River Valley.

After a time Albany came into view ahead, and then the state capitol building. A middle-sized country town with a huge building in the middle of it. A monument to some politician's grandeur. Not the present governor. Another. She had never seen the capitol building before, but recognized it at once. What else could it be?

The helicopter set down on the capitol grounds. An official met Karen under the rotor and led her into the building.

"The governor's waiting for you upstairs."

She was put in the governor's waiting room, handed some

magazines, and her nerves got worse. She wondered if she looked all right, but could not afford to go to the ladies' room to see—the governor might come out at any moment. She wondered if she wore the proper clothes. A tweed suit. Brown shoes and handbag. If she had known this morning what today would bring she might have dressed differently.

Waiting, Karen leafed through a magazine and did not see a thing in it. Finally the door opened, but it was not the governor who came out, it was Norm Harbison.

Harbison did a double take—he was that shocked. "What are you doing here?" he said.

The secretary's console lit up. "The governor will see you now, Mrs. Henning," she said.

Karen was as shocked as Harbison. She didn't know what to say, and so said nothing.

She went past him into the governor's office.

The governor in shirtsleeves was at his desk, but he got up and came toward her. There were flags behind the desk, and plaques on the walls. Karen was trying to see and remember everything. Or perhaps she was merely bewildered and unable to focus. There were two aides in the room, but seated some distance back, almost in shadow. One had a notebook open on his knee. She was introduced to them; neither said anything at all.

She was directed to take a chair in front of the desk. This was followed by a silence, as if the governor didn't know what to say or do next.

He then asked if she was comfortable in that chair. She said quite comfortable. He asked if her flight up the Hudson had been comfortable. She said yes, very comfortable. They nodded at each other.

The governor began to apologize for bringing her up here on such short notice. He said it was incumbent upon him to appoint an interim district attorney as quickly as possible. No matter how she tried to concentrate, Karen was having difficulty tracking him. He said something like that, perhaps not those exact words. He did actually use the word *incum-*

bent. He said how important the appointment was that he would have to make. One of the most important of his administration. Haste was important too. He spoke about ships without rudders. He said he didn't mean haste, actually. But the appointment had to be made with all due dispatch. At no time did he say he was considering appointing Karen, and because of this her nervousness left her and she became annoyed at herself. It was precisely because of the haste that she had dared to imagine she was really a candidate. How silly can you get, she thought.

There was another rather long silence.

"That's some trial you have on," the governor said.

"Yes it is."

"I read about you every morning in the papers. I see you on the TV news broadcasts every night. You handle yourself very well."

"Thank you."

"Tell us about yourself," the governor said, indicating with a sweep of his hand the two silent aides.

She was now almost at ease. This interview wasn't going to lead to anything. She was able to smile. "Where would you like me to start?" At least tonight she could tell her children she had had a ride in a helicopter.

"I'm told you are the third-ranking assistant in the office. Is that correct?"

"Fourth or fifth, the others might say. It depends who does the ranking."

"And the highest-ranking woman."

This was irritating. To be accorded special consideration because of her sex was always irritating. "Well, the others are all men," she said.

"So tell us about yourself."

To talk about oneself without self-consciousness was not easy, and afterward, after she had left the office, Karen would be able to remember little of what she had told him, apart from certain details about her children.

"When I finished law school I was almost nine months

pregnant. I thought I wasn't going to make it to graduation. The day I took the bar exam my husband was out in the hall with the baby so I could feed her from time to time.''

"Then you joined the Manhattan district attorney's office?''

"No. I couldn't leave my children while they were so small. I worked part-time in a small law office in New Rochelle until our son—our second child—was old enough for kindergarten.''

"So you've been with the DA's office how long?''

"Eight years.''

The governor had nice eyes. They were brown. He wasn't a handsome man, but she liked his face.

For a time he did not speak. He appeared to be studying her.

Then: "As I told you, appointing an interim DA is a priority item with me. I've been interviewing candidates for the past two days. Someone recommended you.''

They gazed at each other. "Someone I trust,'' he said.

Obviously she wondered who it could have been. Just as obviously she did not ask.

"What do you think of Norman Harbison?'' the governor said.

And that's the real reason I'm here, she thought with disappointment. He wants to pick my brains about Norm. He's already decided on Norm. He's just trying to check out Norm as much as he can.

"Well, Norm is chief assistant.''

"Yes, I know that.''

"Norm certainly knows everything about running the office.''

"I'm sure he does.''

After another pause the governor said: "Is that faint praise, or what?''

It was her chance to disparage Norm, perhaps turn the governor away from a man she did not like or trust. She was reasonably certain it was what Norm would do in her place.

"Faint praise?" she said. "I didn't mean it that way. Norm has run the office for many years. He does it very well."

"What kind of man is he?"

"He's conscientious, hardworking."

"Is he a good trial lawyer?"

"He used to be. He doesn't try many cases anymore."

The governor stood up, so Karen stood also. The interview was over.

"I asked you up here this afternoon to sound you out," he said. "Suppose I appointed you district attorney, would you accept?"

Was he serious? Karen did not think so. "If the answer were no," she said, "I could have saved myself and the state a helicopter ride." But his question, she was convinced, was merely a display of his innate politeness—a way of easing her politely out of his office.

"And your family?"

"My family would accept also."

"It would be just an interim appointment—until the November election."

Karen shrugged.

"Of course you could run for a full term in November."

Another pause. The governor looked over at the other two men in the room, but again neither spoke.

He escorted her to the door. "May I ask what your feelings are about the law?" he said.

Karen glanced behind her at the two men. The question made her somewhat embarrassed.

"About the law?"

"Please," said the governor.

"I'm afraid I'll sound like I'm preaching."

"Not at all."

"I love the law."

"Yes." The governor smiled warmly. They had reached the door but he was suddenly in no hurry to show her out. "Go on."

"Between us and barbarism what else is there? Religion?

For the time being, I don't know why, religion—our religious leaders—seem to have failed us. The law is all we have to hold us together. We have nothing else to hold on to.''

''Well put,'' the governor said. For a moment she thought he was going to applaud her. Instead he looked questioningly over at the other two men.

''Gentlemen?'' he said.

One of the aides nodded his head. Neither spoke.

''I'm pleased to hear you speak of the law that way,'' the governor said. ''I'm a lawyer myself, you know.''

He showed her out. ''Thanks for coming in,'' he said. ''You may be hearing from us.''

In her kitchen Karen prepared dinner. Her husband was at her shoulder. Hillary came and went as she set the dining room table. By this time Karen had convinced herself that she was being seriously considered—it was what she wanted to believe—and that she should warn her family. Talking about it made the possibility more real to her, and it was important to know what Hank's reaction would be.

''You did what?'' Hank said. ''You went where?''

''I'm being considered as district attorney. Maybe I am. I'm not quite sure.''

''That's exciting, Mom,'' Hillary said. ''That's really exciting.''

Henry did not find it so, apparently. He seemed to be thinking out what to say and how to say it. This was only what Karen had expected, and she watched him closely, and then her smile faded and she bit her lip.

''You don't seem too pleased at the idea.''

''Of course I'm pleased for you,'' Hank said carefully. ''Proud of you too. But—''

''But?''

''I'm a bit confused. Have you thought this out? As DA how many lawyers would you be in charge of?''

''About four hundred fifty.''

''Prosecuting how many felony cases a year?''

"Fifty or sixty thousand. I'm not sure."

"It's a twelve-hours-a-day, seven-days-a-week job, wouldn't you say?"

Karen handed a platter to Hillary. "Put this on the table, honey."

"Are you sure you have your priorities straight?" Hank said. "Your children might begin to ask: What about us?"

"Oh, Hank."

"I thought you were talking about spending more time at home, not less."

"I know, I want to."

"What you give up today you don't get back next year or the year after. They'll be grown and gone."

In the face of such pressure Karen became annoyed. "I couldn't very well refuse the governor's summons, could I. He hasn't offered me the job and probably won't. Even if he did, it would only be until the election."

"No, if it's gone this far there's a good chance you'll get it," Hank said.

This reaction, in the midst of all her other conflicting emotions, caused Karen a certain elation, but also a certain fear. Of course he was right about lost time with the kids. If it happened. If it did, what were her priorities? But if it didn't happen it wouldn't be a problem; naturally and humanly she did not want to face unpleasant decisions unnecessarily. Not this far in advance.

"You've earned it," Hank said. "But—"

If Hank believed she had a good chance, then perhaps she did.

Although the possibility suddenly became more real to her she felt obliged to say defensively: "I'll never get it."

"Karen, I'm carrying a full schedule of classes, I'm coaching swimming, I have to finish the monograph I'm writing and then find a publisher for it, because that's how you get ahead in the academic world. I won't be able to take up much of the slack."

She was imagining herself as district attorney, and did not

want to let the idea go just yet. "We could employ someone. There would be a good deal more money."

"We employed people before and it didn't work out too well."

"I was thinking of a housekeeper, perhaps."

"Wouldn't you have to maintain a New York City residence as well?"

"Yes."

"By law."

"Yes."

"A housekeeper and a New York apartment. That takes care of the extra money, wouldn't you say?"

Karen fell silent. She felt guilty and confused. Mostly guilty.

"It would certainly turn our lives upside down," said Hank, "which maybe is what we want right now, I don't know."

Opposition from Hank was only what she had expected. Nonetheless she didn't know how to cope with it.

"Once you get the appointment, you're stuck with it," Hank said. "The party will put you up in November and you won't be able to say no."

"Let's talk about something else, shall we?" said Karen. "Kids," she called out, "dinner's ready."

During dinner she interrogated her children. She asked them about schoolwork, about cheerleading, about anything she could think of. She concentrated on it, and scarcely looked in the direction of her husband at the head of the table.

But when she and Hank were getting ready for bed, the original discussion resumed.

"I'd be very proud of my wife as district attorney," he said. "It's just—you better think it out carefully. Decide right now how much your children need you. And—"

Hank was hanging up his trousers. Karen was rummaging through a drawer for a clean nightgown. "And what?" she said.

Hank glanced all around him as if looking for someone else.

"I don't know—is there anyone else around here who needs you?"

Karen tried to smile, but it was thin. "I'm sure he won't appoint me."

"You're an ambitious woman," her husband told her.

Karen was reduced to tears of guilt and frustration, but kept her face in the drawer, determined he would not see them.

"I don't blame you for that," he said.

He came over and put his arms around her, but she shrugged him off.

"Let's see what happens," he said.

— 15 —

The call came over the radio at one minute past 10 P.M.

Muldoon had just entered the grocery and made a beeline for the beer cooler. He had left Ritter and the radio in the car, or so he thought, but in fact Ritter had come in behind him. He didn't realize this until the radio went off in Ritter's hand.

In the absence of Barone, who was still working for the DA's office, Muldoon had found himself paired with Ritter recently. The black lieutenant had said to him, "Give him the benefit of your expertise." Muldoon had thought: Why not? His private name for Ritter was the Virgin. For some nights now he had been trying to serve as the Virgin's mentor, instructing him on the precinct and all, even though he did not entirely trust him.

Actually there were two radio calls while they were in the grocery, but the first was of no concern. Fucken cardiac arrest in the Two-Five. All it did was alert Muldoon to Ritter's presence. Immediately he changed direction. He made a right angle turn like a soldier, away from the beer, and headed now for the toilet, which was in the stockroom, calling over his shoulder to the grocer:

"Just want to use your facilities."

As he watched his urine splash into the bowl, Muldoon

reminded himself to be careful with this Ritter. He was not sure of him. Too stiff. Too observant. He wanted to see the fucken guy do something he was not supposed to do. That was the only way to tell whose side he was on, headquarters' side or the side of his friends.

Muldoon had just come out of the toilet when the second call came over. He was halfway across the stockroom, his fingers still working at his fly. Ritter was in the doorway watching him.

"Report of a ten-thirty," the radio said. "Armed robbery in progress. Man with a knife."

The address was given: the St. Nicholas project, an area four blocks square and constituting almost half of Sector One. There were thirteen high-rise, low-rent apartment buildings in there, but Muldoon recognized immediately which one.

"On the grass in front of the door," continued Central in a voice of no particular urgency. "Which car responding? K."

Muldoon came out of the stockroom so fast he nearly knocked Ritter down, grabbing the radio out of his hand and keying it while running. "Two-squad responding, Central. K."

"Two-squad responding, ten-four," acknowledged Central in the same bored voice.

Their car was double-parked outside and Muldoon threw himself behind the wheel. Ritter barely got in before Muldoon took off with a squeal of tires.

By the time he reached the corner, which he took on two wheels, Muldoon had the car up to sixty. Speeding downtown, he had the accelerator floored, and to get around intervening cars he was sometimes out in the face of oncoming traffic. He had the siren on, and also the magnetic red light which was stuck onto the dashboard between them and which was flashing in their faces like repeated gouts of blood. They had about ten blocks to go. With the constant swerving, braking, accelerating, the light kept bouncing off the dashboard. Muldoon was driving one-handed. He had the other clapped on top of the light trying to hold it in place until Ritter, who looked terrified, slapped his hand away, crying: "You drive, I'll hold the light."

This was the most dangerous work cops did, which Muldoon well knew, but the object was to get there fast. On the radio he could hear other cars responding. They would be rushing to the scene too. If you got there fast enough, the witnesses would still be there. The perpetrator was often still there, and you could grab him, case closed.

The driveway into the project was narrow, and Muldoon at great speed turned into it. The turn almost capsized him, he had to correct and then recorrect. The driveway was lined with parked cars, making it only a single lane wide, and the end of it was stuffed with emergency vehicles: two radio cars and an ambulance, all with roof lights turning. Muldoon very nearly bounced off several of the parked cars, and at the end with his brakes jammed on he slid into the rear corner of one of the radio cars, hammering it forward into the side of the ambulance.

As he jumped out he gave all this barely a glance but ran toward the door of the building.

There were some uniformed cops standing around, some civilians too, most of them peering down at a pool of blood on the cement walk. The blood measured ten or twelve inches in diameter which, Muldoon knew from experience, was a lot of blood. You seldom saw more than that. It meant someone had been wounded deeply, perhaps fatally. Leading away toward the door there were drops of blood every four or five feet.

Muldoon sized all this up with a glance, and he said to one of the uniforms, "How far did he get."

"He collapsed in front of a door on the second floor."

Muldoon was peering all around, trying to absorb whatever details he could.

"He was trying to get back to his apartment," the cop said.

Muldoon knew this without being told. The wounded ones

always tried to get home. Standing over the blood he asked himself what else he knew. That the crime took place right here. That there were probably witnesses. If you could find them. Maybe these people standing around, maybe not. If you could convince them to talk. He didn't know much. What was the motive? Drugs? Robbery? Domestic violence? The perp ran off in which direction? Which of these possible witnesses was it worth spending time on? All this and more he did not know.

"Whatta ya got?" he said to the cop, for perhaps the cop had heard something, interviewed someone already, though he doubted it. Cops were not that enterprising. Their way to handle a crime scene was to wait for the detectives to show up.

Before the cop could answer, here came the victim out of the building, on a stretcher between two paramedics. The guy was not in a body bag, not covered over, which meant he was still alive, so that was where the investigation would start, it took precedence over anything the cop, or even one of the witnesses, might be able to tell him.

Muldoon lumbered off in the direction of the victim, leaving Ritter to handle the rest of it. The paramedics were moving fast and they had the angle on him. They had the stretcher in the ambulance and the doors closed before Muldoon reached them. The ambulance was already moving and its siren came on as Muldoon, running now, yanked the doors open and heaved himself in.

The paramedics looked up, startled. They were only paramedics, not doctors, which was good. Doctors rarely rode these ambulances, interns once in a while, but when they did they could be counted on to give detectives a hard time. It became a turf war. They did not want detectives inside their ambulances. One time one of them kicked the door open and shoved Muldoon out. The ambulance was moving at the time, too.

The light was dim inside but Muldoon could see that the victim was bleeding all over the cot. The paramedics were

working on him, but without much success. One of them had
a wad of cotton or gauze pressed over the wound, which was
in the left side. The blood was leaking out from under his
hand and dripping onto the floor, each time with an audible
splat. The victim's face was gray, if a black guy's face could
be said to be gray. He looked unconscious. But often you
could wake them up and interrogate them, even the dying
ones, get them to answer questions.

Muldoon, who had his legs spread for balance and his
hands braced on the roof, spoke to the paramedics first, and
quickly. "Where you guys from?" It was an important question. He needed to know how much time he had, for no one
was going to let him interrogate the victim once they got him
on the operating table. It had to be done right now in this
ambulance, or not at all. He hoped they were not headed for
Harlem Hospital which was right around the corner. They
weren't. This ambulance was from St. Luke's, good, a longer
ride.

Muldoon crouched down beside the victim's head. The
ambulance was making time, careering around the corners,
and maintaining balance was difficult. He was gripping the
bars of the cot with one hand and shaking the victim's shoulder with the other. He was being gentle about it, he believed.
"How you doing, man," he said several times, still shaking
him.

Finally the eyes opened.

"What happened, man?" Muldoon said.

"Dude stuck me."

The eyes were half glazed over. It was a look that Muldoon
recognized from other nights, other victims.

"Who stuck you, man?"

"I tell him his woman have a big fat ass, and he stick me."

The eyes kept going in and out of focus.

"Try to remember his name."

Muldoon could tell as accurately as any doctor which victims would live, which die.

"Why'd he have to stick me, man?"

"You know him, don't you?" Muldoon said. This guy is on the way out, he thought. "What's his name?" Muldoon said, thinking: Come on, come on, in two minutes you'll be dead, so how about giving me his name before you go.

"You know him from somewhere," Muldoon insisted.

"I knows him, but I don't know his name."

"How do you know him?" There was a long wait for each response. "Tell me how you know him."

"Dude live in my building."

"Where in your building?"

The silence this time was the longest yet. Then: "Somebody tell me he live on the top floor. Yeah."

There might be eight or ten apartments on each floor, maybe more. "Where on the top floor?" said Muldoon. "Where?"

Though the eyes had closed, Muldoon continued shaking him, repeating his question several times. He stopped only because he thought the guy was dead.

The ambulance careered into the hospital entrance and stopped with a jerk that nearly threw Muldoon over backward. The doors were yanked open from the outside and the stretcher was run into the hospital. Because he had work to do still, Muldoon followed. He didn't even know the guy's name yet. Once inside he inhaled the hospital odors that were as familiar to him as those of the stationhouse. Though the victim was out of sight now, he knew exactly where he had been taken, exactly where to go. He figured he came into this place, or Harlem Hospital, three nights a week at least, sometimes several times a night. He couldn't count how many men he had watched die.

There were a number of emergency operating rooms—not real rooms but cubicles closed off by curtains. Muldoon kept parting curtains, sometimes surprising people, until he located his victim. The doctors were working over him, four men in all. He supposed they were men. They wore gauze masks and green hats and those loose green smocks, so you couldn't tell. A technician with a clipboard was in there going through the

guy's clothes, and in a moment would come out with what
Muldoon needed. Meantime he watched the surgeons, not the
technician. He watched the knives rise and fall. The victim
was being stabbed again but didn't know it. When the technician came out past him, Muldoon let the curtains fall back.
The final moments of another ghetto tragedy were being
played out. Tonight he had no desire to see it.

The technician had the victim's effects in a manila envelope, which he handed over.

"How's he doing in there?" Muldoon asked. He didn't
expect an answer and didn't get one. The technician only
shrugged and moved off. Muldoon upended the envelope on
a countertop and stirred through it. Some loose change, some
keys, a pocketknife, a handkerchief clotted with snot, a cheap
watch, a wallet containing four dollars. No contraband, anyway, no weapons, no drugs, no credit cards in someone else's
name, so maybe he was a decent enough guy. Muldoon's
notebook came out and he copied down what he needed:
name, address, date of birth, and so forth, then poured everything back into the envelope.

One of the surgeons came out through the curtains.

"How's he doing, Doc?"

"You the detective?"

"That's me," said Muldoon. "Whatta we got, murder, or
only assault?" This detail too he needed to know.

"Oh, he's down the shitter."

Muldoon said: "That's one of those highly technical medical terms, isn't it? Would you mind couching it in words a
layman can understand?"

The surgeon did not crack a smile.

"He rolled a seven," Muldoon said. "Is that what you're
trying to tell me?"

Still no smile.

"Post the vacancy sign," said Muldoon. "That's your
message."

The surgeon's eyes went skyward.

"He still in the picture, or what?" demanded Muldoon.

"We're doing all we can to save him," the surgeon said, and he walked away without looking back.

Two uniformed cops had ambled in a few moments before. They were glancing around, not knowing where to go.

Good, thought Muldoon, seeing them. They'll give me a ride back to the crime scene. And he beckoned them over.

Turned out they had been the first officers on the scene so they needed the victim's particulars also, and Muldoon handed over the manila envelope.

"Be my guest," he told them. He watched them open it and peer inside. "Watch out for the snotty handkerchief," he advised. Needing the ride, he was being nice to them. "What else do you need?" he asked. He was anxious to get back to the crime scene. He intended to go up to the top floor and knock on every door. Hope somebody did something nervous. That would give him the correct apartment, after which he would improvise. You broke a case like this in forty-eight hours or never. Often it was two hours or never. He sensed he had very little time. Right now the perpetrator was probably packing a bag. If he had any brains he was. In a few minutes he'd be out of the precinct, and then they'd never find him. Assuming that the victim died they'd never even identify him.

"I need a lift," Muldoon told the two cops. "Let's go. You can look at that shit in the car."

He led them out of the hospital, spotted their blue-and-white, and climbed into the recorder's seat in front. Though Muldoon did not outrank him, the guy whose seat it was let him do it. Civilians didn't realize that detectives outranked nobody, and neither did most cops. Without protest the cop got in the back.

"Your partner found a girl who may have seen it," said the cop who was driving.

Though he said nothing, Muldoon was surprised. He had worried that Ritter would not know what to do. That by the time he got back there the possible witnesses would have vanished.

When the car pulled up at the scene all the other blue-and-whites were gone and Ritter was standing on the curb waiting for him. There was no sign of any witness. Ritter had sent her back to the stationhouse in a radio car, he said.

"She actually saw it?" said Muldoon. He had turned and started toward the building.

"She was coming along the path," said Ritter, who was hurrying to keep up with Muldoon. "She knows the guy lives here somewhere. She's terrified. I doubt she'll identify anyone."

At the doorway stood two black detectives. Their shields hung from chains around their necks. "You can't go in there," one said.

"Who the fuck are you?" said Muldoon.

"Housing Authority police. We been detailed to safeguard the crime scene."

Muldoon was fixing his own shield, identical to theirs, to his lapel. They were New York cops same as himself, but they belonged to a different police department.

"It happened in a Housing Authority building," the other detective said, "it's our case."

"It happened outside your building."

"Same thing."

"It's a fucken murder," said Muldoon. "Murders revert to us."

"We heard he was still alive."

"By now he's cashed out, you can count on it."

"We're only doing what we been told."

Muldoon turned to Ritter. "Go back to the stationhouse and get the witness. Hold her here until I call you." Plucking the radio out of Ritter's pocket he said: "Gimme that," after which he gestured toward the taller of the two detectives. "Sherlock and I are going upstairs and make an arrest. Come on, Sherlock," he said to the tall one, and he brushed past him and entered the building. Not to his surprise, the detective followed.

"What's it all about, man?" the detective asked him in the elevator, but he made no answer and they rode up to the top floor in silence.

There were only seven apartments. Muldoon was glad enough to have a black detective at his side. People would be more willing to talk to him in the presence of one of their own. He began ringing doorbells.

"There's been an accident outside," he said to whoever answered the door. "We're trying to find out if anyone saw it. Did you just come in, by any chance. Did you see anything."

In two of the apartments no one was home. No one answered his ring and when he put his ear to the door he could hear nothing inside. Two other apartments were occupied by young women with small children. The women told him they were alone except for their children. They appeared to answer his questions frankly, without tension, but he asked the little kids if their daddy or uncle was home, just to make sure.

In the fifth apartment he hit pay dirt, he believed. A big man answered and seemed tense. He admitted he had just come in from outside. He was aware of the commotion and had seen the pool of blood, he said. What happened out there? he asked.

But there were perfect creases in the man's trousers. Noting them, Muldoon reasoned that he must have just put them on. He hadn't even sat down in them yet. He admits he's just come in from outside, Muldoon reasoned, it's eleven o'clock at night, and he changes into a fresh pair of pants. Why? Because there was blood on the other ones, that's why. There was no other conceivable explanation. Which meant that this guy was the perp. Had to be. Inside the apartment, if he had a warrant, Muldoon would find bloodstained trousers and a bloodstained knife. Of course he didn't have a warrant. Nonetheless, the murderer was this guy in front of him.

Muldoon kept him talking but couldn't trip him up on his answers, nor would the man invite him into his apartment. Without a warrant and with Sherlock the Housing Authority cop at his elbow Muldoon felt he could not just barge in, much as he wanted to and nearly did.

Finally he let the guy go and when the door had slammed shut he continued on along the corridor to the final two apartments. There were men in each, four men in all, and Muldoon gave out his fairy story and then interviewed them. They were all forthcoming. He noted nothing suspicious.

When he had finished he went to the far end of the corridor, as far from the suspect's apartment door as he could get, and got on the radio to Ritter. Tried to, rather. He was talking right past Central trying to make contact with Ritter who surely must be on the radio by now, either en route back with the witness or already waiting with her downstairs.

He was talking in a low voice that would not carry as far as the apartment in which the suspect was probably pressed against the door listening hard to find out if Muldoon was still out there ready to grab him.

But Ritter did not answer any of his repeated calls.

There was an alternative. Muldoon might have gone downstairs himself, found Ritter himself, but he had no intention of leaving Sherlock alone in this hallway, either to screw up the case or grab the arrest for himself.

Keying the radio again, holding it close to his lips, almost whispering, he tried to make contact with whichever detective was monitoring the radio back in the squadroom. Someone was supposed to be monitoring it there at all times, but at the moment no one was, apparently, for no answer came back.

Finally he made contact with the uniformed desk lieutenant downstairs in the stationhouse. He asked him to send out a radio car to find Ritter and tell him to bring the witness up to the top floor in the building.

Muldoon settled down to wait. He was standing where he could watch both the elevator and the door to the suspect's apartment. The minutes passed exceedingly slowly. He had nothing to say to Sherlock and did not want any talking out here anyway. Fifteen minutes went by. Thirty. Where the fuck was Ritter?

The answer was downstairs on the sidewalk with the witness but without a radio, and waiting to be told what to do. Two uniformed cops found him and sent him up.

Muldoon lit into him as soon as he stepped off the elevator. "You call yourself a fucken detective?" he hissed, and he launched into a series of whispered, strident curses.

Ritter simply took it and said nothing.

Muldoon turned to the witness, the girl. She was very young, very black, and, he saw at once, very scared. When he tried to question her she blurted out: "It was dark, I didn't really see nothing."

So Muldoon took her out into the stairwell and sat down with her on the steps and talked to her quietly for ten minutes or more. He told her the perpetrator was a murderer, she didn't want to live in the project alongside a murderer, did she? Who knew who he might murder next. She was the only one who could put him in jail where he belonged. And she needn't be frightened. She could make her identification from out here in the stairwell, for Muldoon had noted that there was a small square window in the stairwell door. He pointed to it. The guy would be on the other side of the door in the hall. He would never see her face, he said.

"He'll see me through the glass," said the girl.

"No," corrected Muldoon. "We'll cover it over so you can see out, but he won't be able to see in." In his pocket he had a DD-5 form which he unfolded and held over the window. "You'll be perfectly safe," he told the girl. "My partner will be with you the whole time."

Ultimately she said she didn't know if she could identify the guy, but she'd try.

Muldoon decided to march the four nonsuspects past the window first. He believed he was about to break this case wide open but he was worried about it standing up in court. The lawyers had so many rules now they could get a case

thrown out on almost any technicality. Show a witness only
one mug shot, for instance, and no matter how firm that
witness's identification might be, that case would get thrown
out instantly, and never mind what outrage the hump in question might have committed.

So he knocked on the first of the two doors and asked
the two men to step out into the hall with him for he had one
or two more questions. They were agreeable and he moved
them to a point where they could be seen through the window.
No reaction from behind the door. He thanked them and
knocked on the second door and did the same. Again no
reaction.

All this time Sherlock was at his elbow, saying nothing.

He rapped on the suspect's door and made the identical
request. The suspect did not want to come out into the hall
but he was trying to appear innocent, so what the hell else
could he do?

This time Ritter rapped sharply on the door, the signal.

"I'm going to have to ask you to come to the stationhouse
with me," Muldoon told the suspect.

"Am I under arrest?"

"No." There was no sense wrestling the guy to the ground
and putting cuffs on him if it was not necessary. "But I'll
arrest you if you prefer."

"Just let me tell my woman." He started to go back into
the apartment.

"No," Muldoon said, taking no chances with the guy,
"call her out here and tell her."

When he came out into the street Muldoon saw that a cold
rain was falling. He called in a radio car and told the two
cops to take the suspect back to the stationhouse and hold
him there. He said that he and Ritter, who was walking the
witness back to her apartment, would be along shortly.

He waited for his partner in the car. The rain was coursing
down the windshield. Presently Ritter climbed in beside him
and he started the engine and backed carefully past all the

parked cars and out of the long narrow driveway and into the street.

Muldoon had no intention of going back into the stationhouse any time soon, and told Ritter so. "Let the fuck sweat," said Muldoon happily. "The more nervous he is, the more he's likely to blab something when we start interrogating him. Also, the later we start interrogating him the more overtime we can pile up." He grinned at his partner. "There is absolutely no corruption in this department anymore, as you know. The only corruption we can still work is overtime."

Muldoon was feeling great. Nobody else could have broken this case as quickly and solidly as he had. He was feeling really well set up. Proud. And thirsty. He would have given his teeth for a beer. But the stores in the precinct were all closed now and he did not want to step into a bar in front of Ritter.

So he sat behind the wheel and they cruised up and down streets. The mutts were out even tonight in the rain. They were standing under overhangs or in doorways, but they were out. To say he didn't understand these people was an understatement. Early in his career he had tried, but it was impossible, he gave up. Nowadays he didn't even bother to try.

They passed a woman in a raincoat walking her dog. It was some kind of miniature, a schnauzer maybe, really tiny. Slowing almost to a walk Muldoon rolled down his window. "Hey, lady," he called. "Your dog shrunk. You better get him in out of the rain before he disappears." Chortling at his wit, Muldoon rolled the window shut and speeded up.

He felt good even toward Ritter tonight. If the guy really was working for headquarters, let him report the way Dan Muldoon had broken this case. Let him check the overall clearance rate for homicides in the Three-Two, as far as that goes. He would see it was the highest in the city, thanks to the detectives assigned there, of which he was the most experienced and the leader.

They came up on a man walking along, and on his head he wore a wok. He was using a wok for a rainhat.

"Look at that," said Ritter.

"What do you call those things?" said Muldoon.

"That's what you call a wok. It's a Chinese cooking pot."

"I know what it's for, for chrissake. What do you think I am, some kind of jerk? The name of it slipped my mind, is all."

But he was in too good a mood to stay mad at Ritter. "These people wear the most astounding things on their heads sometimes," Muldoon said as he turned into the next street. "Berets. Cowboy hats. I saw a guy wearing a German helmet once. I saw a guy wearing a Mexican sombrero that must have been five feet in diameter." Muldoon began laughing. "It was wider than he was tall."

They could see the rain pouring down in front of the headlights.

"It's really quiet," Ritter said presently.

"We've had our investigation for tonight," Muldoon told him confidently. "Rainy nights, snowy nights, icy cold nights, the mutts don't do much. The crime rate goes way down."

They came up again on the man walking along under the wok. He had advanced several blocks from where they had spotted him the first time.

"I'm going to have some fun with that guy," Muldoon announced, and he stopped the car and jumped out. "Hey you," he called.

The man had stopped and turned around.

"Get that thing off your head."

The man whipped off the wok and held it under his arm.

"Don't you know you're not allowed to wear a wok around here?"

"Yes, sir, I mean, no sir."

"This is a no-woking zone," Muldoon said. "Can't you read? See that sign on the corner?"

"Yes, sir."

"It says Don't Wok."

"Yes, sir."

The light on the corner changed. The man peered through the rain. "Now it say Wok."

"All right," said Muldoon. "When it says Wok you can wear it, but when it says Don't Wok you can't."

Muldoon as soon as he had climbed back into the car burst into laughter. His belly shook with it.

Ritter only smiled. In addition to everything else, the guy had no sense of humor, Muldoon decided.

He steered into 135th Street and parked diagonally in front of the stationhouse and they went upstairs, Ritter right behind him, and he began looking for his prisoner but couldn't find him. He looked in the interrogation room and in the cage, he ran down the stairs and looked in the cells. The guy was nowhere.

Ritter was standing in front of the desk when Muldoon came out from the cells.

"They say some Housing detectives came and took him," Ritter said.

"What?" said Muldoon. "What?"

He lumbered up the stairs and burst into the squadroom. The lieutenant's door was closed. Muldoon banged on it, threw it open, and barged in.

"What the fuck did you do with my prisoner?"

"Calm down, calm down," the lieutenant said. "Two Housing detectives came and took him."

"You gave them my prisoner?"

"The victim didn't die," the lieutenant said. "It's their case. There was nothing I could do."

For some minutes Muldoon moved back and forth cursing. The lieutenant merely watched him, he said nothing. At the end of that time Muldoon stormed out into the squadroom. The other four detectives on duty at that hour sat at their desks watching him.

Muldoon went straight to the logbook and signed out. Ritter came up and put his hand on his shoulder, but Muldoon shrugged it off.

"Hey, guy, I'm really sorry."

"Fuck it," said Muldoon. "What the fuck do I care."

He went down to his car and drove off in the rain.

—16—

Today Justin McCarthy wore a bright blue suit with a red bow tie that was twice normal size. Pacing, he said: "So how did you know where the defendant was, Detective?"

Karen glanced across at the defense table where Lionel Epps listened intently. He was wearing a new, dark brown suit someone had bought him over the weekend.

"Did he send you a letter, Detective Muldoon? Perhaps he telephoned you."

The witness box to Karen looked too small for a man of Muldoon's girth.

"I'm sorry," said Justin McCarthy. "I forgot—there was no telephone in that abandoned building, was there."

Muldoon glanced at him, then away.

"So how did you know, Detective? How did you know?"

"A confidential informant told me, that's how."

McCarthy seemed to leap on this. "What was his name?"

Muldoon's gaze had shifted to the wall above the jurors' heads. "His name is confidential."

"You knew where Lionel Epps was because you were dealing drugs with him, and you went there to silence him, isn't that the simple truth? There was no informant, was there, Detective? That's something you made up afterwards, isn't it,

Detective?'' From the beginning of this rather long accusation Karen was on her feet. "Objection," she cried again and again. "Objection."

"Sustained," said Judge Birnbaum. "Jury will disregard."

But the jurors had heard McCarthy's charges, and perhaps believed them. Karen studied every face, trying to read it, an impossibility. They were just faces. Impassive faces. The faces of a people who had suffered for centuries and had learned to show nothing. In any case, she did not see the skepticism she was hoping for.

Because she could not allow McCarthy to score cheap points or to have the last word, she rose to reexamine Muldoon still again.

"Without telling us his name, Detective, please describe this informant."

"When he wasn't in jail and when I could find him he was good. He knew what was going on in the street."

"He's what you call a habitual offender, I believe."

"Right."

"Not a nice fellow."

"No."

"You had searched for the defendant about two weeks, I believe."

"About that." Muldoon was looking a bit more relaxed. But he was still wary, even with her.

"For about two weeks you tried to find the defendant and couldn't, because he had not been seen on the Manhattan side of the river for months, is that not correct?"

"That's correct."

"But now he was hiding out on the Manhattan side, and the informant was able to tell you he was in that abandoned building we've heard so much about, is that not correct?"

"That's correct."

"And you went there with other police officers to arrest him, and he shot five of you, is that not correct?"

"That's correct."

"Shot you all down without warning?"

"That is correct."

When court ended for the day Karen returned to her office where she stared out the window. Did the jury believe that there was no informant? That Muldoon was secretly a rogue killer? Did the verdict now hinge on producing this informant in court?

Coombs sat in his regular chair, a legal pad on his lap, and watched her and said nothing.

"I guess we have to put the informant on the stand," said Karen finally. She had known from the start that this would be a problem. Harbison and Coombs had interviewed him months before, but he had been back in Attica when she took over the case. She knew about him only from Coombs. Getting him down for an interview had proven complicated, and she had let it go, hoping he would never be needed. With so little time to prepare she had been obliged to cut corners, one of them the informant.

"McCarthy knows very well the informant exists," said Karen bitterly.

"He also knows we don't want to put him on the stand," said Coombs. "That's what he's counting on."

"Now we have to put him on."

"You better have a look at him first."

"Is he that bad?" said Karen.

Rastar Williams was a tall, shambling black man about forty years old. Escorted by Detective Barone, handcuffed behind his back, he marched down the long corridor that led to Karen's office. The corridor was otherwise empty. The two sets of heels went *tap-tap*. The only windows were at either end of the corridor, giving the light an almost metallic quality. There was a metallic sound to the footsteps as well.

They went into the office.

Karen was at the window. Coombs sat in the same chair as before. Barone placed Williams in the chair facing the desk, then took up position beside the door, and Karen walked over and sat down in her chair. Noting that Williams was still in handcuffs she gestured to Barone that they were to be removed. He did this. Williams, flexing his hands, suddenly looked dangerous. She glanced at Barone, whose hand was on his gun, then at the dossier on her desk, from which she selected Williams's yellow sheet. It was three pages thick, and she glanced at it, then put it down.

"You've been in jail rather a lot, Mr. Williams," she began.

"This time when I get out, I'm going to get a job," Williams said thoughtfully. "A life of crime don't suit a man my age."

"Yes. Do you know a detective named Muldoon?"

"I calls him Mull. He going to help me with some charges I got."

"Why would he do that, Mr. Williams?"

"Something I told him."

"Do you know a man named Lionel Epps?"

"Mull know him too. Mull say to me: Tell me where he at, and I help you with that rape charge."

As a throwaway line, this one would be difficult to beat, Karen decided. It was enough to make any normal person flinch. But she had learned to smother such reactions.

"I figured, that rape charge stick, on top of what I already got to do, I won't never get out."

Barone grinned and said to her: "Very few police informants are as handsome and personable as this guy."

Even at heavy moments such as this one, Barone had the ability to make her smile. "Did Detective Muldoon promise not to arrest you?" she asked Williams.

"That's the way it work. Don't you know that?"

"But you're in jail at the moment."

"Somebody else arrest me one week later."

Karen nodded. "All right, let's go over your—your career in detail, shall we?"

She questioned him for two hours. She was methodical about it, thorough. At the end of that time she could be reasonably certain of what the truth was, but not at all certain how a man like this would behave on the stand. His mind wandered, he fancied himself a comedian, and he had a three-page sheet.

She stood again at the window. Coombs sat in the same chair. Barone and the prisoner had gone out.

Karen's secretary stuck her head in the door. "Mr. Harbison is asking to see you."

Karen nodded, but did not immediately move. She was trying to decide what to do about Rastar Williams.

"Do we put him on or not?" said Coombs.

"It will make McCarthy's day," Karen said.

"When he sees this guy take the stand, he'll have an orgasm."

"He'll rip him to shreds on cross."

"But we have to put him on," said Coombs.

"Let me think about it a little longer."

"We'll be taking a chance either way."

Karen said bitterly: "Everything those cops are testifying to is absolutely true, and McCarthy is making them all sound like liars."

Coombs said nothing.

"Let me go see what Harbison wants," Karen said.

But the door opened and Barone came back into the room.

"Where's your prisoner?" asked Karen in surprise.

"I asked your secretary to baby-sit him for me," said Barone. "And she said she would."

Karen went to the door and peered out. Rastar was on his knees on the floor beside the desk, handcuffed to the pipe that came out of the floor. Her secretary was out in the hall as if trying to get as far away from the prisoner as possible.

"I brought this guy down here early in the case," Barone said. "Mr. Harbison had a pretty thick file on him. I've been wondering—you don't seem to have it there."

"I have this file," said Karen, waving it.

"I remember it as being thicker than that. I'll ask Mr. Harbison about it, he may remember."

"I'll ask him myself," said Karen somewhat sharply. "You just worry about your prisoner." She felt under pressure from all sides, including from Barone.

Her rebuke had come out stronger than she intended. Barone's reaction was stronger too, or seemed so. He looked hurt. His smile disappeared, and he nodded at the floor several times. Why was he so vulnerable to her displeasure? She watched him turn and go out. He only wants to help, she thought. She heard him unhook his prisoner and say: "That's enough praying, Rastar, on your feet." And then to her secretary: "Don't touch the radiator, unless you want to get AIDS." This seemed to Karen too rough a joke, but it made her smile anyway.

She went across the hall to see Harbison. When she entered the big office the acting district attorney was seated behind the late DA's big desk.

"You went to Albany," began Harbison. "Why wasn't I informed?"

"You went there too. You didn't inform me."

"I asked you a question."

"I thought I had answered it."

"Why wasn't I informed?"

"As a matter of fact I went to your office to tell you, but you were out."

"The governor wanted to see me," said Harbison.

"He wanted to see me too."

"What did you tell him about me?"

"Your name hardly came up," said Karen.

"But it did come up."

"I praised you."

"Well, I hope you did. What else did you talk about?"

"He asked me about myself and—"

"And?"

"How the office worked."

Harbison said nervously: "Like clockwork, I hope you told him." After a pause, he said: "I expect to be appointed district attorney in the next few days, and to run for election in the fall.

I want you to know that I intend to increase your responsibilities and your pay by appointing you chief assistant in my place." Harbison gave her what looked to her to be a false smile.

She decided to say nothing.

"I'd like to think I can count on your support," he said, and gazed at her expectantly.

She felt as sullen as a teenager, a mood she blamed on him. "I don't want to be chief assistant," she said. "I want to try cases."

Harbison walked her to the door. "We can talk about that. So can I count on your support?"

"If the governor appoints you, sure."

As the door closed behind her she realized she had forgotten to ask him about the Rastar Williams file.

The weekend came again. In the backyard patio Henry Henning was cooking lunch on the barbecue. It was a chilly day on which to hold the first family cookout of the year, but they had planned it and were going through with it.

"We'll leave about four," Hank said.

Dressed in jeans and a big sweater, Karen reclined on the chaise longue with her case folder open on her lap. "Okay," she said.

"We don't want to get there too early, but not too late, either."

Hank was working with a big fork. Eyes half closed against the smoke, he was turning meat. The two children stood beside their father close to the fire.

"You're awfully pensive," Hank said.

"I don't think I could ever get it."

"Get what?" said Hank, teasing her.

"You know. I can't stop imagining myself district attorney. I'm sick of myself."

Jackie was peering down at the grill. "Ugh," he said, "I hate spareribs."

"I'm making you a hamburger," his father told him. "If you get it, do you get a limousine?" he said to Karen.

"Yes."

"Can I ride in it?" asked Jackie.

"Only if you're in handcuffs."

Hillary sat down on the edge of the chaise longue. "Our civics teacher talked about your case in class, Mom. He said we should all be proud of you."

"Well, are you?" Hank asked his daughter.

"Of course. Mom, can I sleep over at Sharon's tonight?"

"Is her mother going to be there?"

"Sure, what do you think."

"I'll phone her. But you'll have to stay with your brother till your father and I get home from NYU."

Hank began spearing ribs onto plates. "This reception tonight is vital."

"I know," said Karen. She got up and moved toward the picnic table.

"I'm as nervous as a damn kid. The chairman, the dean, all the biggies will be there."

"You'll impress them all."

"They have a real political science department there."

Karen decided to switch roles. She was a wife and mother first, everything else after. As the luncheon progressed she made herself forget her ambitions and her case, listen attentively to the concerns of her husband and children, focus wholly on this backyard, on this family, her family, and she realized she was happy.

"I want that job so much," said Hank.

"You'll get it. I know you will."

"I need new leotards, Mom," said Hillary. "The ones I have you can practically see through."

"Who would want to?" said Jackie.

The four of them were seated around the picnic table. Across from them smoke was seeping out from under the lid of the grill.

"Why don't you two be nice to each other once in a while?" said Karen lazily.

* * *

The cocktail party took place in the faculty lounge off Washington Square. The Hennings were there, drinks in hand. Karen wore a black dress and looked very nice, very feminine, she hoped, not like a prosecutor at all.

"This is Professor Kuhn, chairman of the department," Hank said to her. "And Dean Blake."

Around them clustered a group of educators, and she was trying hard to remember their names: Blake, Kuhn, Fortman, Stone—there were too many. She did not dare call anyone by name for fear she would get it wrong and hurt Hank's chances.

"Are you *the* Mrs. Henning?" asked Dean Blake.

Watch out, thought Karen. But she smiled and said: "Which Mrs. Henning is that?"

She gave an anxious look at her husband. She knew what was about to happen and worried about how Henry would take it.

"I've seen you on TV," said Blake. "That's some case you're prosecuting."

"And she's going to win it too," said Hank proudly.

Other men clustered around. Gradually Hank got moved into the background. All attention was now on Karen. She saw how her husband watched her, how his eyes began to narrow.

"What's a man like who shoots five cops? Psychotic. Actually evil?"

"A druggie?"

"How could he shoot five cops and not get shot himself?"

The questions, the comments became more and more intense. These professors who considered themselves students of the city were in the presence of someone whose knowledge was real, not theoretical, who stood right in the crucible. They clustered around her, demanding information and insights.

Dean Blake reappeared with two men in tow. "This is Professor Pleasance, Mrs. Henning. And Professor Dilger."

"How good a lawyer is McCarthy?" Dilger wanted to know.

Pleasance was a black man. He said: "The scenario McCarthy is suggesting is, historically, not implausible."

"What do you mean?" asked Karen, though she knew very well what he meant.

"That the cops went there to murder young Epps. Any truth in it?"

"None whatever," said Karen.

"Yesterday some cops shot a black kid who was stealing oranges," Pleasance said. "It was in the paper."

"That was in Brooklyn," Karen said defensively. "I'm not really familiar with it."

"In your case it was the black kid who shot the cops. You get my meaning?"

"No, I'm not sure I do."

"There are parts of this city in which McCarthy's charges do not seem farfetched."

The group around Karen seemed only to increase in size, but the questioning was dominated by the black professor. For the most part the others only listened. Pleasance seemed genuinely concerned about where the truth lay, but skeptical about Karen's answers. At times she found herself making what amounted to short speeches.

A little apart from the group stood Henry Henning. Seeing that he was alone, Professor Kuhn came over. "They've abandoned you, I see," Kuhn said, and gave a chuckle. "That's what comes from having a famous wife."

"Yeah," said Karen's husband.

The result was that he stared out over the wheel and did not speak to his wife all the way home.

"Hank—" Karen said once.

But he did not answer.

The car pulled into the Hennings' garage which was cluttered with bicycles, lawn mowers. Getting out of the car Hank stumbled into a garbage can. He reacted angrily.

"This place is a pigsty," he snarled. "I thought you were

going to get the kids to clean it up. Get someone to clean it up.''

Knowing the quarrel was not about the garage, Karen went around the car to him.

"Hank, I didn't do anything. I wasn't responsible for what happened."

"That was my chance to make an impression on those people. I hardly even got to talk to them. I want that appointment."

"It wasn't my fault, Hank."

"I deal with the minds and souls of young people. That's important too. You're beginning to overwhelm me. I feel half suffocated."

"Hank, Hank."

She embraced him. After a moment his arms went around her. They embraced amid the garage clutter, under a cone of light.

In Albany in the governor's office a conference was in progress. The governor's two top aides, the same two Karen had met, were present, but they had moved up much closer to his desk. One was a boyhood chum of the governor, the other a political crony since early in his career. Neither had ever been elected to anything, and their names were scarcely known outside of Albany.

"Harbison seems to have been the choice of the late district attorney," said the boyhood chum.

"Who's dead," commented the governor.

"He's the mayor's choice as well."

"The mayor is not a friend of this administration."

"There are some other possibilities we could interview."

"What about the woman?" said the governor.

The two aides looked at each other. "Well, she's qualified, I guess," said the second aide.

"You guess?"

"Can a woman manage all those ambitious young prosecutors?"

"Can a woman deal with cops and criminals on such a high level?" said his partner. "Successfully, I mean?"

"Come on, come on," the governor said impatiently. "We have women mayors now, a woman on the Supreme Court, we have women police commissioners."

"Mayors are elected," the governor's boyhood chum said. "A woman mayor fucks up, no one gets blamed. It's the electorate's fault."

The second aide said: "A woman on the Supreme Court does not have to manage a multimillion-dollar budget and an office that size. All she has to do is give her opinion once in a while."

"Which women like to do," the boyhood chum said, and they all laughed.

The second aide said: "It's true that there have been one or two women police commissioners or police chiefs in your smaller cities. Usually it didn't work out."

"Law enforcement is an all-male club," said the other man. "In New York it is, anyway. A woman might not have the authority necessary."

"You appoint a woman and she fucks up," said the second aide, "guess who gets blamed?"

"A man might fuck up too," said the governor.

There was a long, thoughtful silence.

"I don't know," said the governor. "Somehow I lean toward the woman. She impressed me more than Harbison and—"

More silence.

"Her name is in the papers every day," said the governor.

"True, she's had a lot of ink."

"And we need someone who can win in November," the governor said.

"You're saying she'd make an attractive candidate," commented his boyhood friend. "Whereas Harbison—"

He stopped there, and no comment derogatory to Harbison was ever made.

"Yeah," said the governor, "exactly."

The discussion went on a long time, but the governor's men saw the way he was thinking and accepted it and encouraged it until at the end the governor may have imagined that to appoint Karen Henning was their idea, not his, and in any case a much stronger idea than he had thought at first.

"My gut feeling—" the governor said.

The outcome became inevitable.

"And one half of the electorate would stand up and cheer," said the governor. He had said this, or something like it, several times in the past hour, and his aides saw that he had almost decided.

"True," one said.

"Women, gentlemen, that's the trend," the governor said.

"All right, when do we announce it?"

The governor hesitated. "This Lionel Epps case—any chance she'll lose it?"

"None whatever."

"You men have studied it much more than I have," the governor said uncertainly.

"The guy shot five cops," said his boyhood chum.

Any second thoughts the governor may have harbored evaporated, and he sighed with relief. The decision was made at last. "As soon as possible, then," he said.

It was a risk to put Rastar Williams on the stand, but an even greater risk not to, Karen decided. Above all, given the composition of her jury, she must seem to be holding back nothing, hiding nothing.

And so the door at the corner of the courtroom opened and Rastar Williams shambled in, took the stand, and was sworn. Since the district attorney's office had no funds for outfitting witnesses in Brooks Brothers suits, he was wearing the clothes in which he had last been arrested: frayed chinos and a dirty sweater. He had a short attention span, and as Karen began to examine him his concentration wandered.

She had his arrest record in her hand and began there—
better that she bring it to the jury's attention than McCarthy
later.

"Mr. Williams, were you convicted of assault with a
deadly weapon as a teenager? And of four counts of burglary
at the age of twenty? And of two counts of armed robbery
two years after that?"

Williams seemed proud of his arrest record. "Ain't many
people been in as many jails as I have."

"After which you moved into drugs, I see." Karen began
reading from the pages in her hand. "Possession, possession,
sales to an undercover officer, sales, sales—"

"Liquor stores was getting too dangerous."

Karen's face was impassive but inside she was squirming,
convinced that putting Williams on the stand was right, but
worried about what such a man was likely to say under cross-
examination by McCarthy.

"Are you awaiting trial on charges of rape and sodomy at
this time?"

"I'm up here listening to you at this time."

The courtroom broke into laughter that caused Judge Birnbaum to begin banging his gavel.

Karen waited until the courtroom was silent again. "And
do you know a man named Lionel Epps?"

"I knows him."

"Do you see him in this courtroom?"

"That's him over there."

"Indicating the defendant," said Karen. "Now, Mr. Williams, please tell the court how you happened to make the
acquaintance of the defendant?"

"We dealt dope together. He would get it, I would sell
it."

"And how long did this last?"

"Until I went to jail the time before this. When I come
out, I go looking for him. I need some money real bad."

"And did you find him?"

"In that building where he was holed up. He send me out to get some food."

"And in the street, did you run into someone you knew?"

"Detective Muldoon. Last person in the world I wanted to run into. He grab me. I say: How you like it I tell you something you like to know?"

"Meaning the whereabouts of the defendant?"

"He want that Lionel Epps worse'n he want me."

"Mr. Williams, have you been promised anything—a lighter sentence, for instance—in exchange for your testimony today?"

"No, but I'm, you might say, hopeful."

Williams, as McCarthy approached, was grinning vacantly at the ceiling.

"You say you dealt drugs with the defendant," McCarthy began. "These drugs were furnished to him by the police, I believe."

"Could be."

Karen: "Objection."

But McCarthy plunged ahead with his next question. "He was being forced to deal drugs for corrupt police officers, was he not?"

Judge: "Objection sustained."

"Could be," said Williams.

"Answer will be stricken," said Judge Birnbaum.

Karen on her feet cried out with outrage. "Will Your Honor please instruct the jury once again that Mr. McCarthy's whimsical questions do not constitute evidence."

Judge: "The jury is so instructed."

Unabashed, having turned back to the witness, McCarthy continued: "According to this rap sheet you're a dangerous criminal, Mr. Williams, is that not correct?"

"I don't know why I'm so bad."

"Yet you say the police wanted the defendant more than they wanted you. Why is that? Is it because they only wanted to arrest you, whereas they wanted to murder him, silence him forever?''

"Objection," shouted Karen.

Judge: "Sustained."

McCarthy ignored them both: "Would you say you're in such trouble that you would do anything the police told you, in hopes of a lighter sentence—perjure yourself, give false testimony—"

But Karen was still on her feet, still shouting. "Your Honor, I demand to know his reasonable basis in fact for the wild allegations he is making in this courtroom."

"Reasonable basis in fact" is a legal term, and a long one to shout without taking a breath, but in her fury Karen got it out.

"I am defending my client," McCarthy said.

"Allegations that are wild beyond belief."

"The prosecutor is completely out of bounds. I demand an immediate mistrial," shouted McCarthy.

"Wild, wild, wild," shouted Karen.

McCarthy must have thought he was losing ground. "Your Honor," he said in a milder voice, "this is a matter to be discussed at sidebar."

Both lawyers approached the bench and a conference began, but when their voices began to rise, perhaps carrying as far as the jury, Judge Birnbaum led them out the door behind them into his chambers.

There Karen repeated her demand. She wanted McCarthy ordered to disclose his reasonable basis in fact.

"If he has one," she said.

"Of course I have one."

"I think the court has a right to hear what it is, don't you, Judge."

"I've been concerned myself as to what your reasonable basis in fact may be," said Birnbaum mildly.

"All in good time, Judge."

"That's a nonresponse, Judge," Karen said, "you can't let him get away with it."

Birnbaum looked from one of them to the other.

"Give me a chance to present my witnesses first," said McCarthy reasonably.

"He's got no reasonable basis in fact," cried Karen. "None at all. I want him put on the stand under oath to be questioned by you and cross-examined by me."

This was an extreme solution. It could happen. It did not happen often. The jury would not be present in the courtroom and would never know it had taken place. But McCarthy, if he gave the wrong answers or no answers, could be cited for criminal contempt. Which at the very least might slow him down for the rest of the trial.

Birnbaum appeared to be considering such a hearing.

McCarthy said: "May I advise Your Honor that if ordered to respond to questions under oath I would refuse to obey, citing the attorney-client privilege, the work product doctrine—"

Birnbaum was nodding his head.

"And perhaps one or two other doctrines I might ask my students to look up for me." And he grinned all around.

Impasse.

Karen knew it was an impasse. Birnbaum would duck today's confrontation with McCarthy, and also any other confrontation that came before him for as long as he served on the bench. To Karen, judges were gutless. There were exceptions, but Birnbaum was not one of them. Judges in her experience were motivated not by notions of justice, but by fear of being reversed on appeal. The audience they played to were the law journals and the judgment of their peers. No one else was looking at them, and no one except prosecutors, defense lawyers, defendants, and a handful of courtroom habitués—an extremely small group—ever knew what went on in their courtrooms. Most judges preferred verdicts of acquittal. An acquittal meant they were in the clear, the case was over, there could be no appeal. A guilty verdict, on the other hand, would be appealed. The judge's decisions and conduct of the trial would be scrutinized, and if the appeals court found error by the judge, it would reverse the conviction.

Karen said: ''I want him forewarned that if he goes on with his present tactics he'll be held in contempt.''

McCarthy gave her a bland smile. He had defied many judges in the past, as Karen knew, and Birnbaum also knew. He had gone to jail several times, and had appealed, and in a day or a week had come out more notorious, and in certain quarters more of a hero, than ever. It was the judges who looked bad because he had proven publicly that they couldn't hold him.

Karen knew that Birnbaum was not going to be very stern, would not forewarn him about anything.

''I suggest you try to curb your—your enthusiasm a bit, Mr. McCarthy,'' Birnbaum said. ''Now let's go back to court, shall we?''

The first person to learn of Karen's appointment was the governor's driver, a New York City detective who prided himself on his big ears, he sometimes said, and who happened to be waiting in the governor's outer office. The detective excused himself to the governor's secretary, hurried down the hall until he found an empty office, and dialed Police Commissioner Malloy in New York. In the NYPD, information is power. The detective knew this; he succeeded in getting the PC on the line, and he passed on what he had.

''Are you sure?'' said Malloy.

''They called in the press officer. I heard them do it. They told him to schedule a press conference for an hour from now.''

''All right,'' said the PC. ''Thank you. I owe you one.'' And he hung up.

Information could be power for the PC as well. The problem was knowing how to use it, and he sat for some seconds drumming his fingers on his desk. Then he jumped up, called for his driver, ordered some subordinates to join him in the garage, and took the private elevator down to his car. Malloy may have been a rough man, but he was not stupid nor was he always unpolitic. If Karen Henning was to be DA, even on an interim basis, then she had become important in his life. He assumed she did not like him—had she not thrown him out of her office some weeks before? Was there some way he could make use of this hour's information to rectify the situation at least partly?

Together with his entourage he set out for the criminal courts building.

By then court was over for the day, and Karen and Coombs had returned to her office where she dropped her dossiers on the desk and sank wearily into her chair.

A moment later Norm Harbison came in. It was time for a conference, he told her, but they waited in silence as Karen's secretary brought in three coffees in Styrofoam cups and passed them around.

As soon as she had gone out, wasting no time on idle preliminaries, the acting DA said: "I've been reading the minutes each night. In my opinion you could lose this trial."

"One can never be sure how juries will decide," said Karen. She realized what was coming, realized she was in for a fight with Harbison, and so sat up straighter, trying as best she could to throw off her fatigue. "Juries do crazy things sometimes," she conceded.

"Furthermore, it's attracting far too much press. I've been getting some phone calls."

"Phone calls?"

"Phone calls, right."

"Influential people?" said Karen.

"People who tell me it's polarizing the city."

"Like who, for instance?"

"People tell me they're planning a demonstration in Harlem, for instance. Reverend Johnson. It could turn into a riot."

"So what you're saying is that we should do away with trials out of fear of riots," said Karen, and she added hotly, "and I say that's ridiculous."

They glared at each other.

"And in addition, you are no match for McCarthy."

This statement made Karen so angry that for a moment she was unable to speak.

"He's too good for you. It shines through the minutes."

"I always knew you didn't know how to read."

"The bottom line is, I'm ordering you to shut the trial down. Work out a plea with McCarthy, and let's get on to something else."

He was interrupted there. The door was thrown open and in walked Police Commissioner Malloy. He was surrounded by police commanders even bigger and burlier than himself, and he was beaming.

The PC had realized that he had only a few minutes in which to use the information at his disposal. Once the Albany press conference started, the news would be out and it would be too late. The best he could do with it, he had decided, was to serve as the messenger who bore glad tidings, which was what he was doing. He wore his grin as wide as it would go and played this role to the hilt.

"Let me be the first to congratulate you, Carrie."

Karen grimaced at this. No one had called her Carrie since she was a girl. "The trial's not over yet," she said.

She assumed he was talking about the trial. She was so angry at Harbison she was scarcely paying attention, and she looked across at Coombs who, like herself, was focused on Harbison's order to shut the trial down. She was trying to marshal arguments against Harbison even as this grinning buffoon of a PC tried to monopolize her attention.

"The news just came over the police radio."

"News?"

She glanced across at Coombs, then at Harbison, then at

the other police commanders. Every face was blank except Malloy's.

"What news?" she said.

"You and I will make an excellent team. Let me help you with the press conference. I'm more experienced in these things than you are."

No longer as mystified as before, Karen paid strict attention. "Press conference?"

"You'll have to have a press conference. But I'll be right here at your side. I'll tell them how we'll work together— like a well-oiled machine, that's how. Let me look at you: the new district attorney of New York County."

And so the news reached her. It reached everyone in the room, and a moment of total silence occurred. Karen, her mouth agape, stared at Malloy, and when that moment passed her eyes jerked around to Harbison. The acting district attorney looked stricken, and she felt an absurd desire to comfort him.

The others, led by Coombs, came forward and began to shake her hand. Then the phone rang and she picked it up, and the room went silent.

"Albany calling?" the others heard her say. "Yes."

Even as she waited for the governor to come on the line Harbison turned and started out of the office. Karen watched him go.

"Yes, Governor—" she said into the phone.

More and more people crowded into her office, and when she had hung up she was obliged to accept congratulations from everyone. "Thank you," she kept saying. "Thank you very much."

Many minutes passed before she was able to break away.

She went out and crossed the hall to the office of the district attorney of New York County, who was now herself.

Harbison was cleaning his things out of the desk. Karen entered and watched him.

"I don't know what to say," she said.

"Don't say anything."

Harbison went on packing.

Karen said: "I never expected—" She stopped. What was she apologizing to him for?

"I'll get the rest of this stuff out tomorrow," said Harbison. "I wish you the best of luck."

Carrying a stuffed briefcase and an armload of papers, he went out.

Karen picked up the DA's phone, her phone now, and dialed her husband.

"You're not going to believe this," she told him when the connection was made, "and you may not like it. I—I got the job."

She listened for a moment, then a big smile came on her face. "I love you too," she said.

She was sworn in by the governor on the steps of the original courthouse, the picturesque Grecian one next door to the one in which Karen worked. In design it related to civilizations of antiquity, rather than to violent, modern New York. Often the building had seemed to Karen pretty but irrelevant. Some days it had seemed absurd.

Today the old courthouse was to be as much a part of the show as she was, though this idea would not occur to her until later. It turned her swearing-in into a photo opportunity of the first magnitude. The press photographers and the TV cameramen wanted the great old building towering above and behind her. They kept moving her around because everyone wanted as much of it as possible in the frame, the obvious symbol of justice, and the Nikons and minicams all seemed aimed straight up her nose.

The wind was blowing her hair around. There was a crowd held back by police barriers, and many reporters and TV crews. A wooden lectern had been set up and the governor started a speech over a hastily erected public address system, and the wind blew his words around too.

"The skeptics and sexists were alarmed," the governor said in part. "Law enforcement is an all-male preserve, they told me, always has been. I told them, Open your eyes. Times have changed. Have you been watching this woman in court day after day? Is she qualified to serve as district attorney? Is anyone more qualified? Well, then, I'm going to appoint her. How about that? And she is going to make us proud of her— and proud of our city and our state."

He paused until the applause ended, then beckoned Karen to approach. This done, he looked to an aide for help. His next words, picked up by the public address, were not exactly immortal. "Who's got the Bible?"

"Here you are, Governor." An aide, someone Karen had not seen before, handed it to him.

The governor turned toward Karen, and his voice dropped to a whisper. But it was a whisper that chilled her. "I have great faith in Harbison," he said. "I've talked to him. He's willing to stay on. With him as your chief assistant, you'll do fine."

Karen gave him a look. Harbison's enmity from here on would be implacable. She had no illusions about Harbison, and none about the governor either. By forcing her to keep her enemy on as right-hand man, he was only signifying that although he had bet on her, these bets were hedged.

She looked into the governor's big smile and saw that it was meant more for the cameras than for her. "Ready?" he said. "Let's go then. Repeat after me. I, Karen M. Henning—"

Karen put her palm on the Bible and repeated the oath.

Her family was there, together with the mayor, the police commissioner, and other dignitaries white and black, and after the oath was completed and the governor had handed the Bible to someone, all crowded around her. She was hugged by her husband and children, and after that submitted to a good deal of kissing from men she knew barely or not at all, though if she had been a man herself, handshaking would have been enough. One of those who congratulated her was Reverend Johnson, and Karen was surprised. She did not think he belonged on this dais. She wondered who had invited him and why. The governor probably. The mayor perhaps. Some politician, anyway. As a sop to the black community without doubt. A white woman had just been appointed, and furthermore it was this particular white woman who was currently trying one of their own. Never mind that to invite Johnson conferred stature upon him that he had not earned. It acknowledged him as a legitimate black leader too, which to her mind he was not.

Karen at the lectern was grilled by reporters.

"Is this a dream come true for you?"

"Yes."

"Would you elaborate on that?"

She smiled sweetly and said: "No."

As she looked out over the crowd her eye was caught by Mike Barone, and it gave her a start. He was in the back of the crowd grinning, looking pleased for her. She watched him lift both hands high and mime applause. She gave a slight nod in his direction, acknowledging his congratulations, thanking him for it, as was only polite.

Barone thought she looked terrific. She was wearing a black suit over a red blouse. He was terrifically proud of her. The suit was tight-fitting, proof up there on the dais that she had a terrific figure too. *Terrific* was the only word he had that seemed to fit her.

This was the first he had seen of her family in person. Her daughter was a little shorter, a little blonder, but otherwise a clone of Karen. They looked like sisters, not mother and daughter. Her son was too young—you couldn't tell much yet. Karen's husband looked unimpressive to Barone, but she had married him, so he must have qualities. He hoped the guy appreciated the wife he had. Barone would certainly appreciate her, if he had her.

* * *

The wind had veered around. It was blowing Karen's skirt against the back of her legs. The reporters' questions continued.

"Will you run for a full term next November?"

"I don't know."

"What about policy changes?"

"I've been district attorney five minutes. I think I need more time than that, don't you? I also need to get back to court. I have a trial to prosecute."

"When does the Lionel Epps case go to the jury?"

The governor too looked interested in the answer to this one.

"A few more days," Karen said. She decided she could end the press conference on this note, before the silly questions started. With perhaps, on her part, a silly answer. "Thank you all for coming," she said. "Once the verdict is in, we can talk again."

Barone pictured himself walking down the street with Karen Henning on his arm—how all the heads would turn. Or walking her into a restaurant where maybe some cops would be. Not some seedy bar, a high-class restaurant. The mouths would drop open, and with good reason, a woman like this, and afterward the word would get around.

He was mooning over her like a teenager and, realizing this, he laughed at himself. She's not that kind of woman, he reflected, nor am I that kind of man.

Barone had felt many emotions over women, but never before such admiration. She was a woman who had everything. Up there on the dais she looked poised, absolutely sure of herself.

Karen, who had turned away from the lectern, moved to embrace her husband again, then each of her children. Behind her, she heard the governor's aides conversing almost in whispers.

"If she loses that case we're going to look pretty silly."

"The guy shot five cops. It's open-and-shut."

"Is there such a thing?"

No there isn't, Karen thought, and though it was not a cold day she felt herself begin to shiver.

As the ceremony ended Barone decided he might as well drive up to the Three-Two, see what had been going on up there in his absence. He had nothing else to do with the rest of the day and didn't feel like going home just yet. He watched Karen as she stepped down from the dais. More people crowded around her, congratulating her. He had decided not to approach her himself. She didn't need him up there. He would see her tomorrow in the office. For as long as the trial lasted he would see her every day.

He walked away toward his car.

— 17 —

Karen in the dark moved through her bedroom. She was trying to get dressed, trying not to disturb her husband. Moving as silently as she could, she found and put on a bra. There was almost no light. She found pantyhose too but could not put them on standing up and when she felt for the room's only chair it had a laundry basket on it, so she sat on the edge of the bed—gently so as not to wake her husband—and pulled and smoothed the hose up her legs. But Hank came groggily awake anyway.

"What are you doing?"

"Getting dressed."

Hank sat up in bed. "It's still dark out."

"I have to get to the office." She moved back to her dresser.

"Not this early."

"It's my first day."

Henry Henning switched on the bedside lamp and watched his wife, wearing a bra and pantyhose, slip her arms into a blouse.

"Come over here," he said, after a moment.

Looking dubious, Karen approached the bed. Hank in his tousled pajamas drew her face down to his and kissed her.

He made the kiss last longer than she wanted, then murmured: "I've never made love to the Manhattan district attorney before."

"I have to go, Hank."

"There's time," he murmured.

"Henry—"

Suddenly he wrestled her down onto the bed and though she struggled to get out from under, he began kissing her in earnest.

"Hank, stop."

But he didn't stop. It was almost like a rape. Her blouse was still unbuttoned. He had her bra pushed up and was dragging the pantyhose down her hips.

"I said stop."

She was so firm about it that his ardor cooled. She felt his arms loosen and she was able to stand up.

"I have to get to the office," she said, trying to rearrange herself.

"Karen—"

She had moved all the way across the room where she continued to get dressed. Presently she peered into the mirror over the dresser.

"Look what you've done to my hair."

Her husband sat on the bed staring at the space between his feet. She went over to him.

"Hank, it's my first day."

After a moment he said: "I'll drive you to the train."

She went to the window and looked out.

"You don't have to," she said. "My car is here."

The dawn would come soon. She could delimit her lawn, the street out front, the trees, the mailbox on its post. The DA's official limousine was waiting for her below; a reading light was on inside.

Henry stood beside her at the window. "My limousine won't be coming for me today," he said with attempted lightness.

Karen, as she continued to dress, gave him a worried look.

"I gave my chauffeur the year off," said Hank.

Sitting on the bed again, Karen reached to put on her shoes. So Henry is unhappy, she told herself; so I don't see what I can do about that now.

"You won't have to meet me at the station tonight," she said brightly. "That's another job you won't have to do."

"You don't understand," said Hank. "I liked meeting you at the station."

He put on his bathrobe and slippers, and followed her out of the room along the dimly lit upstairs hallway. Karen opened each of the two doors in passing and peered in on her sleeping children.

"You'll have to get them up in a few minutes," she whispered.

"I think I can handle it," said Hank.

They went down the carpeted stairs. Karen's bulging briefcase stood beside the front door. She picked it up and turned to face her husband.

"I'll have about an hour to try to take control of the office," she said. "Then I have to go to court."

She glanced back up the stairs. "Make sure they eat something."

"You should eat something," said Hank.

"I don't have time."

There was a pile of dossiers on a side table. She clasped it to her chest, then turned to kiss her husband. His arms went around her, but as an embrace it was unsuccessful. Her own arms were occupied, and all he could feel against himself were her wrists, her dossiers.

"Tonight, I promise you," she whispered in his ear.

"Good luck today," he said.

She felt him watching as she walked down the front steps toward the car. She felt him watch the chauffeur run around to open the door for her. The chauffeur said something to her and perhaps Hank wondered what it was.

He had merely introduced himself: "Detective McGillis, Mrs. Henning. I'll be one of your drivers."

Karen shook hands with him. "Nice to meet you, Detective McGillis."

"I drove the former district attorney eleven years."

It was a comment that seemed to call for a reply, but Karen could not think of any. The ones that came to mind were inane. Such as: I hope you'll drive for me that long. She opted only to smile at him, to say nothing. From now on she would have to be careful what she said to people, she realized.

Inside the car, waiting for her under the reading light, was Coombs. "Morning, Karen."

She felt suddenly alone. It was an emotion Coombs couldn't help her over, though if she told him so it would probably hurt his feelings. Her husband couldn't help her either. No one could. Perhaps it wasn't loneliness at all, but weight of responsibility. The two emotions were akin, after all. At times they were identical.

"It's awfully nice of you to meet me this early," she told the young man.

"Oh, come on, Karen."

"Well it is." After a pause she said: "What did you find out?"

The reading light shone down on the legal pad on his lap.

"You're about to learn what running the Manhattan DA's office is like."

She saw that there was a list, and she spoke to the chauffeur: "Would you put the partition up, please."

They waited until it was in place.

"To begin with," said Coombs, "your new secretary wants to retire."

"Betty? Why?"

"Loyalty, I guess you would say."

"Loyalty?"

"Loyalty."

"I always got along well with her."

"She says she served HIM—capital letters—all eight terms. She couldn't possibly serve anyone else."

"She was still working for Norm."

"For the few days. She had given him notice, apparently."

"How old is she?"

"Sixty-two."

"That's not so old."

"Listen, Karen, she was there all eight terms. She knows everything."

"Yes, I imagine she does."

"You have to keep her."

"All right, I'll see her first."

"After her the budget guy. Last night he was howling. The DA had been putting him off for a month. How are you on money?"

"Money," said Karen. How many millions of dollars was he talking about?

"Lots and lots of money."

"Henry always handled the money," Karen joked.

After flashing her a momentary smile, Coombs continued down the list. "Then Norm Harbison, as you requested. He'll probably quit. I know he had a big job offer downtown."

"No," corrected Karen. "Harbison is staying."

Coombs's eyebrows shot up. "Oh?"

"The governor said he was," said Karen in a flat voice. "The governor must know."

"The governor told you that?"

Karen nodded.

Coombs looked like a man with the breath knocked out of him.

"You're shocked," said Karen with a small smile.

"Weren't you?"

Karen said nothing.

"He promised him something," declared Coombs.

Karen thought this too, and she gazed out the window. The car moved slowly through the suburban streets in the direction of the parkway. "Wouldn't it be nice to know what," she said.

"You could ask him."

The streets were empty, the houses still dark. "I don't think he'd tell me." She paused. "And after Harbison?"

"You return about a hundred phone calls, then court. You have the chief administrative judge at six P.M. That will take about an hour. We can prepare tomorrow's testimony around him."

"An easy day at the office," said Karen with another small smile. "I wonder if there's someplace I could buy some flowers."

"At this hour?"

"The market might have some."

She leaned forward to tap on the glass partition.

"Detective McGillis," she said when it had come partway down, "could we stop at the Hunts Point Market on the way by, please?"

Hunts Point was the major wholesale market in the Bronx, maybe in the city. Though born and brought up in New York, Karen had never seen it. Neither had Coombs. Nor, it turned out, had McGillis.

At the entrance to the market the limousine was tied up in traffic as trucks of all sizes came and went. Finally Karen and Coombs got out and walked forward.

It was past 7 A.M and getting light fast. They moved through the market, dodging handtrucks and roughly dressed men, until they came to a flower stall. Karen handed money across and came away with a mixed bunch of cut flowers: gladiolas, carnations, roses. The two prosecutors came to another stall selling coffee and donuts. They could smell the coffee brewing. They could smell the donuts too.

"Do we have time?" asked Coombs.

"An easy day like this one?" said Karen. "Sure."

They stood sipping coffee. Karen held her flowers. The life of the market went on all around them.

Thirty minutes later she entered her new office. Betty was already at her desk. She looked prim, uptight, as if still in mourning for her late boss.

"Morning, Betty." Karen held out the flowers. "I brought you these."

A smile came onto the woman's face, but she quickly erased it, and she laid the flowers down on her desk.

"Thank you, Mrs. Henning."

"Yesterday you would have called me Karen."

"Yesterday you were not the district attorney."

"I'm still not," said Karen with a smile. "Only interim. I'm not the man who was here before."

Betty sighed. "He was a great man."

"It would take me eight terms to fill his shoes, and somehow I don't think I'll last that long."

There was a pause. Neither woman seemed to know what to say next.

"I never asked you," said Karen. "Do you have children?"

"I have a son. He's a teacher."

"My husband is a teacher." And then after a pause: "Betty, I don't know what your plans are, but I need your help. This is the biggest job any woman ever had in this city. I need your help so badly. If you retire or resign—if you leave me—I hope you'll stay. Please stay."

There was a long hesitation. Just then the budget man came into the office. His name was Werner, Karen remembered.

"Good morning, good morning," he said. "Carl Werner from budget and management, Mrs. Henning." His hand was out. "And congratulations on your appointment."

She shook his hand. "Thank you," she said.

Werner said: "And now I have some papers for you to sign."

Karen led the way into her new office. "Will you come in too, please, Betty."

Betty followed them in. Werner put a sheaf of papers down on Karen's desk and held out a pen. "You sign right here," he said, pointing.

Karen took the pen but protested immediately. "It's going to take me a while to read all this, Mr. Werner."

"If these papers are not signed, nobody gets paid this week."

She was not going to be pressured into signing she knew not what. "You can't expect me to sign without reading them," she said. When this sounded harsher than she intended, she added in a mild voice: "What would my lawyer say?"

"It's urgent, Mrs. Henning. It really has to be signed right now."

Betty had been studying the papers over Karen's shoulder. Karen, who didn't know what to do, looked at her, and she gave a nod. Karen signed and handed the papers back.

"Next time," she told Werner, "I'd like to have them well in advance."

"And so you shall," said the budget man. "Take a look at these now." He pushed other papers in front of her.

"I don't have much time."

"As a matter of fact, I need to sit down with you for a couple of hours."

Karen was looking over the second batch of papers. "Are these urgent too?"

"Well, not as urgent as the first ones."

"I really can't get to them immediately."

Werner frowned. "How soon can we arrange to meet?"

"Can it wait a week or two?"

"I'm sorry, it can't."

"All right. Work it out with Betty. Early morning or late at night. In between I'm in court, I'm afraid."

Werner gathered up all his papers. "Have a nice day, Mrs. Henning," he said, and went out.

Karen gazed down on copies of the papers she had signed and was uncomfortable. She had been a lawyer fifteen years. To sign something without reading it was unthinkable.

Betty appeared to understand what she felt. "The chief signed them once a month for all eight terms," she said encouragingly. "You don't have to worry."

Karen turned to her. "You see how much I need you, Betty. Please tell me you'll stay."

The two women gazed at each other. Then Betty gave a barely perceptible nod. Karen smiled gratefully, and they shook hands.

As Betty started back to her desk, Karen called after her: "When Mr. Harbison comes, please send him in."

Waiting, she stood over her desk still studying the papers she had signed.

Behind her back, Harbison entered. To attract her attention, he coughed.

"Oh, Norm. You startled me. Good morning."

Harbison only looked at her.

Through the open doorway she could see Betty watching them.

"Would you close the door please, Norm."

Harbison did so.

This was followed by a pause in which they eyed each other somewhat warily.

Karen needed to get a sense of the mood he was in. Why was he staying? What sort of understanding, if any, did he have with the governor? She wasn't sure what to say to him to elicit all this—how to phrase it. "You've been chief assistant since before I came to work here," she began.

Harbison, watching her, nodded slightly.

"The governor says you're willing to stay on," she said, and stopped, hoping he would volunteer something, but when he remained silent she was obliged to add: "If so, that's fine with me."

Again Harbison nodded slightly.

"Nothing would change," Karen continued.

"Nothing?" said Harbison. "Nothing, the lady says."

Karen colored, but recovered her composure quickly. "Your authority and responsibilities would remain the same. You would report directly to me. I would depend on you exactly as much as the old man did."

"More, I would think," said Harbison.

"At first, perhaps. Until this trial is over, anyway."

They gazed at each other.

"The governor thinks very highly of you," said Karen finally.

"Does he now."

"That's the impression I got."

"That's nice."

She stood in front of her desk, arms folded across her chest, rump resting on the edge. "He was full of praise for you at the ceremony yesterday."

Harbison did not rise to this bait either. He watched her and said nothing.

"Was there perhaps something you'd care to get off your chest?" she said finally.

"No."

"I don't expect you to be happy about what's happened. I do expect the same loyalty and dedication you gave to—my predecessor."

"Anything else?"

"No. I guess not."

Harbison nodded.

As he turned toward the door Karen experienced a sudden rush of fear. No, it was stronger than fear, it was terror. Here she was, district attorney, and she knew nothing about the job, she would be hopeless in it, she would be found out. Without Harbison she was lost. At any cost she had to keep him.

"There's an election in November," she said to his back. "You'll have another chance then."

Harbison turned and looked at her. "As you say, November."

She watched him go.

But after a moment the terror passed. It was replaced by a kind of fierce stubbornness. I will not be defeated in this job, she told herself. I will win the Epps case, and I will win the election in November.

With that, she picked up the sheaf of telephone messages from yesterday and began to thumb through them. More than twenty of the calls were from people she hadn't seen in years, or knew barely. People who wanted to congratulate her, no doubt. She was not a cynical woman—she hoped she wasn't—but she wasn't naive either. People who thought it worth making contact now, in case they needed a favor later. This idea gave her a sense of power, which in turn gave her confidence and lifted her spirits.

However, they were calls she was supposed to return. If she didn't, these people would think her rude. She didn't like to be thought rude. And another twenty similar messages waiting for her tonight, probably. Maybe more. Each call, if she returned it, would require her to chat. How long would it take to return twenty such calls? And what about all the other calls—there were at least as many—which required action, or were from people she cared about?

She began separating the messages into two piles, even as she glanced at her watch. Some calls she could try to make now, and she carried them out to Betty and asked her to dial them.

Coombs came in. "What did Harbison have to say?"

She started to answer, then stopped. Don't make this young man your confidant, she warned herself. He is not old enough, nor experienced enough, nor of enough rank.

Then she realized no one was of enough rank. She alone was district attorney. She was on top, and she was up there by herself.

"You met with him," said Coombs, "didn't you? How did it go?"

"We'll have to wait and see," she answered vaguely. From now on there were only certain people from whom she could afford to ask advice as needed, and no one in whom she could permit herself to confide.

"Don't turn your back on him," advised Coombs.

"Well, I don't have time to worry about that now."

Her calls began to come in. After a time she took her earring off from under the receiver. She often did this, forgot to put it back when she had hung up, and spent the rest of the day with one earring on, one off. Sometimes when she went looking, she couldn't remember where she had left it.

Around the phone calls she and Coombs began to go over today's list of witnesses and the testimony they expected.

Later they hurried down the corridor toward the courtroom. Both were carrying armloads of dossiers, and they had to dodge cops, jurors, witnesses, spectators, all waiting outside other courtrooms.

When they neared their own courtroom the corridor became even more crowded: great numbers of people were waiting in line to be admitted. Certain of them pointed her out to each other and called her name. The blinding lights came on and TV cameras filmed her as she and Coombs pushed their way forward.

"I've never seen crowds like this," said Coombs, once they were inside the courtroom.

Obviously Karen's appointment as DA had caused the TV crews to increase yesterday and today. As for the crowds, they had been big all along. Standing room only, like a Broadway play. Normally public interest fell off after the first week, and attendance with it, but that had not happened, presumably because of McCarthy's wild charges which he reiterated in interviews every afternoon on the courthouse steps. They weren't really interviews, they were more like speeches and they kept hitting the same point: corrupt cops trying to murder his client. He dominated the news broadcasts every night. Karen had been interviewed many times too. She had kept insisting that the case was being tried in court, not in the headlines, a much less sensational message to which the news media gave much less play.

"People wait for hours to get in," said Coombs.

And now that she was district attorney, the spotlight was on her and on this case even more than before. All of America was watching now, but without, probably, very much understanding of what was at stake. The split between blacks and whites already existed but there were tentative bridges across the void. If she lost, then in New York at least, and perhaps everywhere, the bridges would collapse. These were the stakes as she saw it. Hatred for the blacks whose streets they patrolled would run unchecked through the police department. Unchecked through most of the white city, too.

The blacks would match that hate, especially toward the white-controlled police department. This had happened in the days of the Panthers and the Black Liberation Army after all.

In addition a disastrous legal precedent would have been set. Whenever a similar case occurred, lawyers would claim self-defense like McCarthy, and sometimes, maybe even often, they would win acquittals, rendering the entire justice system even more ineffective than it was at present.

If she failed, Karen told herself, the bridges would have to be rebuilt from scratch at an enormous cost in money and pain.

And on a personal level, all of America would know she had failed. She had never had any right to lose this case, but if she lost now, it seemed to her, the degree of her humiliation would be like nothing she had ever experienced before.

A police officer in uniform, Schwartz, was on the stand.

"You were on the fire escape," Karen said. "Then what happened?"

"The defendant came running toward the window and—and—"

"I know this is difficult for you, Officer."

"—and he shot me. He nearly took off my arm. My right arm is paralyzed."

McCarthy began his cross-examination: "You fired first, Officer Schwartz, is that correct?"

"I have no recollection of firing at all."

"Excuse me, but according to the ballistics technician you did fire."

"His shot hit me in the arm."

"You meant to shoot first, though?"

"Before he shot me? Of course."

"You meant to kill him, but he was too quick for you? You went there with intent to murder him, to silence him once and for all, is that not correct?"

Karen's objections to questions of this kind had become so automatic and so frequent that she had had to begin to vary their tone. Sometimes she jumped up angrily. Sometimes she tried to sound bored. "Objection," she said now in a mild voice, and after Judge Birnbaum had sustained her she continued to speak, letting her anger build slowly for maximum effect. "Would Your Honor please remind the jury still again that these accusations by Mr. McCarthy are totally unsubstantiated, that if he made them outside of this court of law they would be libelous, that he would be sued, that he would be subject to millions of dollars in damages." By the end she was almost shouting.

McCarthy said: "I certainly intend to substantiate them, Your Honor."

"I'll bet."

"That's enough from both of you," said Judge Birnbaum.

McCarthy returned to his cross-examination. "Are you on terminal leave now, Officer?"

"Yes."

"You're retiring. After how many years' service?"

"Four years."

"After four years' service you're retiring on three quarters disability pay for life. How many hundreds of thousands of dollars does that add up to? Are you sure you have no feeling in your shooting arm, Officer?"

Karen jumped to her feet. As McCarthy walked away from the witness, she came forward.

"This time you've gone too far, Mr. McCarthy. Your Honor, I'd like to ask the witness to approach the jury box, to remove his uniform coat, and to roll up his sleeve."

This was done. A guard held Schwartz's coat.

Karen: "Officer Schwartz, please show your right arm to the jurors."

Schwartz walked along in front of the jury box. Much of the flesh of his upper arm was missing, what was left was still raw, and the jurors grimaced and turned away when they had seen it.

"Would Your Honor instruct Mr. McCarthy to approach the witness?" said Karen.

The judge nodded and McCarthy approached, but not too close. Karen removed a brooch from the front of her dress and held it, open, out to McCarthy.

"Please stick this pin into the witness's arm, Mr. McCarthy. Hold out your arm please, Officer Schwartz. Go ahead, Mr. McCarthy. Stick him. What are you waiting for? He won't feel a thing."

Karen and McCarthy stared at each other across the open courtroom. Karen was so angry her mouth was trembling, the brooch that she held out to him was trembling, and the jury saw this.

"Let the record show," intoned Karen, "that Mr. McCarthy has refused the brooch and turned back to his table."

An idea occurred to her at that moment—probably not a very good one, she conceded to herself—and when court closed she returned to her office where she summoned Tananbaum and three other senior prosecutors.

Suppose she put McCarthy on the stand as a witness for the prosecution, she told them. Suppose she swore him in and questioned him under oath about the insinuations and allegations he had been making in front of the jury for the last month and a half.

The idea evoked absolute silence.

"I don't think it's ever been done," said Tananbaum finally. "I think it's reversible error if you try it."

"The four of you constitute a task force," said Karen. "I want you to spend tonight and tomorrow scouring law books. I want you to find a precedent if there is one. Find me a precedent, that's all I ask."

* * *

Henry Henning was playing one-on-one basketball with his twelve-year-old son. The basket was on a pole opposite the garage door. It was getting dark. He let the boy score one on him, then came forward in his turn, dribbling. They were having fun. The kid was fast as lightning and darted in and swiped the ball from his father. Henry was giggling as he chased the boy to the basket.

When the ball came down he put it under his arm, and his other arm went around his son. "That's enough, Jackie, time for dinner now."

They started toward the house.

"Where's Mom?" Jackie asked.

"Working late. What would you like me to cook for dinner?"

"You're a good cook, Dad, but Mom is better."

—18—

But Karen was not working late. In an inflated bubble on a pier off Wall Street she was playing tennis with three other women. She was swatting tennis balls as hard as she could, running as hard as she could too, all in an effort to work off tension, but it wasn't working. The trial crowded her head and would not go away, and the balls she drove toward the corners or straight at her opponents would not stay within the lines. The air that kept the bubble inflated made an overriding soft whooshing noise that she had got used to, but the noise made by the airlock each time someone went in or out was distracting, everything was distracting, and too often she swung early, or else late, and the shot went wild, and she started apologizing.

When play ended she apologized again. The other women only laughed, insisting they had had fun, this wasn't the U.S. Open after all. Still hot and sweaty, they sat in the lounge and drank coffee, and talked about their husbands, and about sex.

"Last night I dreamt of my wedding again." It was a woman named Pearl talking. She had two sons, worked in a fashion design house, and Karen liked her more each week.

"I'm in church in my bridal gown. My husband-to-be has his fly open and I'm leading him up to the altar rail by a string around his dong."

It made the other women giggle.

"It's a recurring dream," Pearl said.

"That's about what weddings are," said Jill, who had been married three times and who worked for a company that managed apartment buildings.

"They ought to make it the official ceremony," said Pearl.

"We can petition Congress to make it the law," said Jill.

"I can just see myself," said the fourth woman, Marcia, who was personnel manager for a department store. "I'm getting ready for my wedding, and I can't find my string, and I say to my mother, Mom, lend me the one you used on Dad."

To Karen it was like conversations in dormitories late at night long ago. Funny, raunchy. She had not had any such conversations since and must have missed them more than she realized. She was enjoying herself.

She said: "On my honeymoon I had my hand on it and I said to Hank, That's what I'm married to, not you."

"How'd he take it?"

"He thought it was the sexiest remark he'd ever heard. Within seconds I was on my back."

The other women were laughing. It was a pleasure to make people laugh.

But what had made her reveal such an intimate detail of her marriage when she never had before?

"Sexually, men never get over being teenage boys," said Jill. "When they're over forty they're still voyeurs and masturbators at heart."

"Men never don't want to," said Pearl.

"The trouble with sex," said Jill, "is that it becomes a battleground."

This remark sobered Karen. "I must say that since I became DA I haven't been much in the mood."

"How does Hank take that?" said Jill.

She felt she had to defend Hank. "Oh, very well. He's very understanding." But she blushed as she spoke.

Pearl said: "Honey, they never understand."

"I've got an office to run, a trial to run," said Karen. "I wish I could just move out for a few days."

Pearl said: "If you want to move out, move out. He won't die."

"My children—"

"They won't die either."

"Move where?" said Karen.

"I have a suggestion to make," said Jill.

In bed, waiting for his wife to come home, Hank brooded about his marriage—and about his career too. No word had come from NYU. Meanwhile his wife seemed to have become a different person; somehow their marriage had gone terribly wrong. He didn't know what to do about NYU, or about his marriage either, and he searched his memory for something he might have done to Karen, or said to her, some explanation. But there was nothing he could see. He had done nothing wrong—nothing he had done any differently in the past. It was Karen who had changed. Her appointment as DA. That damned appointment.

In pajamas and bathrobe he went down to the living room to wait for her there, but fell asleep in a chair with the newspaper open on his lap. Only one light was on in the room. With the sound of the front door opening, he came awake. Karen, still in her coat, entered the room and they looked at each other.

Although Hank said nothing, the accusation must have been in his eyes, for he saw that she felt it.

"I don't have a grip on it yet, Henry," she said apologetically.

"You get home later and later."

"I'm trying. It will take time."

"The plumber was here this afternoon. Evidently you called him. I didn't know what you wanted."

"I'll call him tomorrow."

Henry nodded. They started up the stairs.

"I'll just look in on the kids," said Karen.

"They're asleep, Karen."

The spectator section was full, the well was full, but the jury box was still empty. At the bench McCarthy was addressing the judge, his voice low, almost hissing with anger. Karen listened with a bored expression on her face.

"They're trying to kill him again, Your Honor. Last night in jail they slashed his throat. They were trying to get his jugular."

"The defendant's neck was slightly cut on the edge of a chair," said Karen in a bored voice.

"He was beaten, his face is a mess. The guards did it. On orders from the police, no doubt."

"It was a fight with another inmate, Your Honor."

"Free my client before they kill him."

"I sent a detective up there as soon as I heard." She had phoned Barone at home. He had driven straight to Rikers Island, and within ninety minutes she had her report. She had Barone in the witness room in case he was needed. "The detective in question is standing by if you should care to talk to him, Judge."

Birnbaum, high on his bench, looked from one of them to the other. He did not ask to see Barone, but he was clearly waiting for more information.

"The fight was with an inmate named Willy Roper," Karen said.

"A sworn enemy of my client," charged McCarthy. "An obvious setup, Your Honor. A man who has attacked him before, who has sworn to kill him."

"Can we get on with the trial, Judge?" said Karen.

"What was such a man doing in an adjacent cell, if it was not a setup?" demanded McCarthy.

"Are you asking for another recess, Mr. McCarthy?" asked Judge Birnbaum.

"Bring in the jury," cried McCarthy. "Let them see what's been done to my client."

Karen perceived McCarthy's tactic and moved to forestall it.

"Maybe we better take a look at him first, Judge."

"There's no need to look at him," said McCarthy. "Let the jury look at him."

"No," said Karen, "I want to see him first."

Birnbaum peered at her over his glasses.

"I really must insist, Judge," said Karen firmly.

"Your Honor—" said McCarthy.

"Judge—" said Karen firmly.

Birnbaum looked from one of them to the other. At last he spoke to the bailiff. "Bring in the defendant, please," he said.

They waited while Epps was brought in in handcuffs. The jurors had never seen him in handcuffs, but they were not in the courtroom. His appearance was as Karen had expected. He looked like a man who had barely survived a plane crash. Above the usual Brooks Brothers suit, his face and neck were swathed in bandages, and in places blood appeared to have soaked through. Only his eyes, mouth, and hair showed. Over these bandages he wore his usual horn-rimmed spectacles, but with one star-burst lens.

"Can we have a doctor look at him, please, Your Honor?" said Karen. "I'd be curious to know if his wounds are as nearly mortal as we are meant to believe."

There was a long delay while they waited for the doctor to reach the courtroom. Karen spent it doodling on a legal pad. The jury box was still empty. The spectator section was now half empty, perhaps more. The people were out in the corridor or in the rest rooms.

The doctor finally arrived and was led to a side room where in the presence of the prosecution team, the defense lawyers, and the stenographer and four guards he examined the defendant. Working with extreme slowness, it seemed to Karen, he unraveled the various bandages. For Karen there was no suspense. Barone had described Epps's slight injuries to her, and she had believed him. At the end she saw what she had expected to see: a few small cuts and bruises.

"Very impressive makeup job," she said to him. "Who did it for you?"

Epps, his face now bare, looked at her with smoldering eyes.

Meanwhile, ignoring her and Epps both, McCarthy was staring out the window. It was as if the whole procedure was, and always had been, beneath him. She went over to him. "I think the judge should see this, don't you, Mr. McCarthy? I mean before we bandage him up again." She turned to one of the guards. "Will you ask the judge to come in here, please?"

But when she turned back McCarthy was gone.

"I think Mr. McCarthy should be reprimanded," said Karen as soon as Birnbaum had appeared. She had decided she had best treat Birnbaum gently; he wasn't going to do anything anyway. "I think you should threaten him with a contempt citation."

"I'll run my courtroom as I see fit, Mrs. Henning," said Birnbaum huffily. "You just worry about conducting your case."

For the moment Karen backed off, but when Epps was brought into the courtroom a second time, wearing much less prominent bandages, she went forward to the bench. McCarthy followed, and a colloquy ensued.

"Would you advise the jury that the defendant's injuries, such as they are, are extraneous to this trial," said Karen. She was putting pressure on the judge again and knew he would not like it. "The jurors are not to make inferences, suppositions, guesses—you know the formula, Your Honor."

"The press—" said McCarthy darkly.

Karen said: "Would you also admonish Mr. McCarthy that he is not to give inflammatory interviews about this to the press."

Birnbaum hesitated, looking from one to the other, but finally nodded his head. "So ordered, Mr. McCarthy."

"The press has its own way of finding things out," said McCarthy.

More juicy articles that the jurors are not supposed to read, Karen reflected.

"Maybe you better threaten him with contempt of court if he speaks to the press, Your Honor."

"I hardly think that will be necessary, do you, Mr. McCarthy?"

Karen went back to her table.

"You won that one, anyway," said Coombs.

Karen bent over her papers. "Did I?"

At lunchtime she went back to her office, where Tananbaum waited. He and his task force had found no precedent that would enable Karen to call McCarthy as a witness for the prosecution.

"In fact," said Tananbaum, "our research shows the opposite."

"I see," said Karen.

"We researched it pretty thoroughly."

Karen nodded.

"I wouldn't advise you to try calling him," Tananbaum said. "Without a precedent to go on, Birnbaum will never permit it, and just to make the attempt in open court is probably grounds for either a mistrial or a reversal later."

"Thanks for trying," said Karen.

"The rule exists to protect the defendant. Legal theory holds that the defendant is on trial, not his lawyer, and a man should not be convicted because his lawyer fucked up."

Karen said nothing. Tananbaum's report, though only what she expected, left her bitter and depressed. If she committed a procedural error, even asked the wrong question, she might win a guilty verdict but could be reversed on appeal. To avoid such error, she had to be incredibly concentrated, incredibly careful at all times. Whereas the defense attorney—McCar-

thy—could do or say anything he liked. If he won, he won.
A verdict of not guilty could not be reversed. If he lost, he
would appeal on the basis of her errors, or the judge's errors.
His own conduct would not be considered by the appeals
judges, it didn't count.

Karen went back to court.

Beside her in the big bed, Henry was asleep. From time to
time a snore escaped him. But for Karen sleep would not
come. Her mind churned, her stomach too, she was ex-
hausted, she reclined against the headboard in the dark, and
sleep felt as distant and unreachable as it had an hour ago.

She had been trying not to move, to stifle her sighs, trying
not to awaken Hank, but something woke him, for suddenly
she was aware that his eyes were open and looking at her.

"What time is it."

"About three thirty," she told him.

"Try to sleep."

"I can feel it getting away from me, Hank."

"Things always seem worse in the dark."

"I don't know what to do."

"The guy shot five cops. Believe me, you got nothing to
worry about."

"The jury doesn't believe my witnesses. McCarthy keeps
coming back to his single-minded argument, they were trying
to murder Epps."

Henry put his arms around her as if to shield her from the
dark. Then he began kissing her.

"It will help you sleep," he explained.

Without turning on the light they wrestled around for a few
seconds. But then Karen broke away.

"I can't, Hank. I'm sorry. I can't."

She hoisted herself against the headboard again, and sat in
the dark staring at nothing. Henry growled something unintel-
ligible, then turned on his side facing away from her.

Presently she went downstairs and put the coffee on. The

clock on the kitchen wall read 4:20 A.M. In bathrobe and slippers she paced back and forth, the coffee in one hand, sipping from time to time. She had become obsessed with the notion that she might lose the case. None of the previous cases she had tried had ever kept her awake like this. She had no idea what her jury might believe or not believe—which in itself was a bad sign. Surely if the jurors found her witnesses credible, or McCarthy's arguments incredible, there would have been some indication. She would have seen something, felt something.

At the edge of panic, pacing, she resolved to change her strategy. A number of cops from the shoot-out had still not testified. Barone was one. Toole, who had been shot, was another. She would call none of them, she decided. To call them would expose them to McCarthy's brand of cross-examination. He would ridicule them, insinuate that they were corrupt, turn them into would-be murderers. She did not know how they would stand up to it. Badly, probably, like all the cops so far. The jury did not need to see it. The jury had seen too much of it already.

So she wouldn't call the remaining cops and detectives at all but would call instead the men who had commanded the various police investigations. There had been three that she knew of. She visualized the three commanders parading to the stand one after the other, older men in uniform with gold braid on their caps. Men who had not been involved personally in the shoot-out but who had investigated it thoroughly, who had found nothing illegal or corrupt and who would so testify. McCarthy would not be able to accuse them of crimes or otherwise shake them. It would be testimony, she believed, that no jury could disregard.

She took her coffee into Hank's study, got the three signed reports out of her briefcase, and reread them. They were as she remembered. Next she paged through her police department phone book and, early though it was, called the three commands. She wanted the commanders telephoned at home or wherever they were. "At once," she said. "Wake them up if necessary." She poured herself another cup of coffee and waited.

The precinct commander called back within the hour. He sounded groggy with sleep.

"You're up early," he said.

She wasn't interested in what time it was. "Do you stand by the report you signed having to do with the Epps case?" she asked him.

"Yes of course."

"You found no evidence of corruption or illegality of any kind?"

"None whatever."

"All right. Be prepared to testify later today."

She had barely hung up when the phone rang again: the borough commander. She asked him the same questions and got back the same answers. He too was told he would testify later in the day.

She was dressed and ready to go out the door before the chief of detectives called.

"If you were writing your Epps report today," she asked him, "would you write it any differently?"

"No. What's this about?"

But she ignored the question. "Nothing new has come up, no new details? No allegations of any kind?"

"No."

She was about to hang up when she thought to ask him the final question, the one McCarthy was certain to ask on cross-examination. "There were just the three police department investigations, right? Yours, precinct, and borough. There were no others?"

"Internal affairs had one too, I think," the chief of detectives said.

"You think?"

"I know. Very hush-hush."

"You saw the report?"

"There may not even be one. I heard about the investi-

gation is all. Pommer is supposed to have done it personally."

All of the air seemed to go out of Karen. "I'll call him,"
she said. "I'll call you back later."

She had taken this call too in Hank's study, and when she
had hung up she sat for a time with her head in her hands.
After that she phoned internal affairs and ordered the sergeant
on duty to have Chief Pommer report to her office at 8 A.M.
Then she went out to her car and was driven to work.

"We haven't seen each other in a while," Pommer said, as
if they were old friends. He sat in uniform opposite her, his
cap in his lap.

"No we haven't."

"Those two ace detectives from the Three-Two," he
asked, "when will you be finished with them?"

She had been right to dread this meeting. "Which two?"

"Your chief witnesses, Barone and Muldoon."

Already on the defensive, Karen said cautiously: "I'm not
sure I understand what you're asking me."

"When will they be finished testifying?"

He's got something on them, Karen told herself. What does
he have on them? She said: "You've been conducting a secret
investigation having to do with my case, I believe."

There followed a short heavy silence.

"We do have a little inquiry going," Pommer conceded.

"Into the shoot-out?"

"More like into the two hotshots."

She did not want to ask anything more, or know anything
more. She wanted only to remain ignorant. Unfortunately this
option was not allowed her.

"I want a copy of your report. Immediately." A copy
would have to be given to the defense too, that was the worst
of it.

"There is no report. Not yet." Pommer must have known
that his investigation could sabotage the trial. He had been a
cop thirty or so years. He couldn't be that stupid.

"Nothing on paper?"

"No."

"At all?"

"Not really, no."

Probably this very meeting ought to be reported to the defense. "All right, what has your investigation turned up?"

"It doesn't really concern your case. It concerns some past cases. A few minor discrepancies here and there."

McCarthy, if she convicted Epps, would certainly appeal. If in the meantime Pommer had come forward with damaging charges against two of her most important witnesses, then the court could very well overturn the verdict.

Even if she won she would lose. She was twisting her wedding ring on her finger.

She was furious and trying to conceal it. "Please tell me what you're talking about."

"Nothing for you to get upset over. We looked into your case and found nothing significant."

"Nothing illegal? No evidence of corrupt acts of any kind?"

"No."

"McCarthy has been charging that the cops went there not to arrest Epps but to murder him to cover up drug sales."

"Yes, I read that in the papers. Nothing to it that we could find."

"You looked?"

"Of course."

"Hard?"

"I'm not in the habit of covering up for corrupt cops."

She felt renewed confidence. Perhaps she could put Pommer on the stand after all, and the other commanders with him.

"However," Pommer said, "some discrepancies in past cases did come to light."

"What discrepancies?"

"It has to do with internal disciplinary matters."

"That's all? You're sure?"

"Our inquiry is still ongoing."

"Nothing on paper?" she said.

"No."

"You're certain?"

"You'll be the first to know."

She wished she could order him to abort his investigation right now, whatever it was, but as an officer of the court she could not.

"Anything else you wanted?"

"No."

"You're missing an earring," Pommer said.

Karen's hand went to her ear. Then she glanced around her desk. Having found the earring beside the telephone, she clipped it on.

"Good to talk to you again," said Chief Pommer.

"Really?" she said, and he went out.

She sat for a moment at her desk, both hands on her blotter, breathing somewhat hard, picturing how McCarthy's cross-examination would go if she put Pommer and the other commanders on the stand. McCarthy would rub his hands together in glee, and then he would pounce. A secret investigation. No written report. Supposedly minor discrepancies. He would raise his eyebrows and turn toward the jury. Ho, ho, ho. What have we here?

She couldn't chance it, couldn't ask the commanders to testify.

So much for that brilliant idea.

She shook her hair out, resolved not to think about it anymore, picked up the folder on Toole, the last of the wounded police officers, and began to study it.

Late in the morning she called Officer Toole to the stand and he was sworn in.

She kept him there most of the rest of the day, making him describe in minute detail how the raid was put together, and then his own part in it. As he was trying to come in the window off the fire escape, he said, Epps had shot him. It was dark in the room behind Epps. Toole hadn't even seen him, just the muzzle blast as he fired, the white light many times repeated. Other cops had got him out of there and into the ambulance and then the hospital. He had come to with tubes in him, in terrible pain.

She turned the young man over to the defense for cross-examination.

"You look quite fit to me, Police Officer Toole," McCarthy began. "By the way, you filed a lawsuit against the city, I believe. Charging what, if I may ask?"

"Negligence, reckless endangerment. I don't know. My lawyer filed it."

"What damages are you asking?"

"I was shot in the groin and in the side. I spent a month in the hospital. Five million dollars."

McCarthy, playing to the jury, gave a low whistle. "Five million dollars. Not a bad month's pay."

Courtrooms are solemn places and often tense ones. Any untoward remark can evoke mirth, and this one sent the spectator section into gales of laughter. For as long as it lasted, McCarthy pranced around grinning. He played it like a comedian, and when the laughter began to diminish he started it up again by ostentatiously straightening his bow tie.

That the spectators had laughed did not much bother Karen. The spectators were no concern of hers. It was the jurors she watched; she scrutinized every face. To her relief no one had laughed outright. Nearly all, however, had been amused, and this was enough cause for concern. The average weekly income of these black citizens was how much? What did a number like five million dollars mean to them?

Finally McCarthy got back to business. "And did other police officers join you in your suit, Officer Toole?"

"The raid wasn't properly planned," said Toole evasively. "No one had time to get into position."

The previous laughter had had the additional advantage, from McCarthy's point of view, of throwing Toole even further on the defensive.

"How many others have sued?" persisted McCarthy.

"Three others."

"The raid was bungled?"

"Yes."

"Too much haste?"

"Yes."

"Because the object was not to arrest my client, but to murder him before he could get away, before he could talk, is that not correct?"

Feigning intense disgust, McCarthy walked away before the witness could answer.

Karen approached the stand, and Toole seemed relieved to see her. "Was the object to kill the defendant, Officer?"

"No it was not."

"Is it a crime to bungle an arrest of this kind?"

"No."

"Arrests are bungled from time to time?"

"It happens."

Karen: "Did any of the police officers commit a crime that night? Or talk about committing a crime, or suggest committing a crime?"

Toole: "No."

Karen, who was dressed for the office, and Henry, still in pajamas and bathrobe, sat at the kitchen table sipping coffee. Outside it was just getting light. "Do you remember Jill Herman?" Karen asked him.

"Your college roommate."

Karen had her hand on top of his. To anyone peering in the kitchen window it might have seemed an intimate scene between husband and wife.

"She and her husband are going to Europe for two weeks," Karen said.

"Husband number three," Hank said.

"I've seen her once or twice lately." Karen stopped. Hank didn't know she had joined Jill's tennis group, and she wasn't going to tell him now. I thought I was an honest person, Karen reflected. Now I've begun to lie and dissemble all the time. "Anyway," Karen finished, "she and her husband are off to Europe."

Karen bit her lip. Next came the hard part.

"She's offered to let me use her apartment," Karen told her husband. "It's near the courthouse."

She had intended to tell him at dinner last night—tell the children too. She had made a start at it but had been interrupted and when it became her turn again she found that the words were difficult to speak, and she had put it off.

Now she was about to leave the house as she did every morning, except that this time she had a bag packed at the door. It was now or never.

"I can have the apartment starting tonight."

"You're moving out," said Henry.

"Of course I'm not moving out."

Henry disengaged the hand that lay under hers and lifted his cup to his mouth. He said nothing, merely looked at her over the cup. She supposed he was either angry or hurt, most likely hurt. Or pretending to be hurt, which was a way men had when thwarted. Anything to make the woman feel like a shit.

"It will save me two hours a day commuting," she said.

He remained silent.

"Just till the trial ends," she said.

Still he made no response.

He feels rejected, she decided. Sympathy for him welled up, but she did not know how to express it. This is not a sexual rejection, she wanted to tell him. I'm not choosing someone else's bed over yours. But to voice such a denial would be to acknowledge that another man's bed was possibly real. It would make the rejection seem to him even more personal.

It was so complicated that her sympathy for him evaporated. He ought to understand what she was going through. It shouldn't be necessary to tell him. "I need time alone to write my summation," she said stubbornly. "And after that

I'll have to stand by 'round the clock until the jury comes in.''

Jackie entered the kitchen dressed for school, his hair slicked down. He kissed his mother.

"What's for breakfast, Mom?"

She was barely aware of her son's kiss, his question. Her eyes were fixed on her husband. "It's just for a few days, Hank."

Her gaze moved from her husband to the boy. "Jackie, I won't be home for the next few days. I'll be very busy in New York." Hillary came into the breakfast room, and Karen repeated this speech. When she had finished it her eyes met Hank's again, but there seemed nothing further to say.

—19——

McCarthy said to the woman in the witness box: "And did the day come, Mrs. Epps, when you visited your son in jail?"

"He's a good boy, and he's my son."

"Yes, and you visited him in jail?"

She was hefty, middle-aged, serious. "As soon as I found out where they had him, I went to bring him what comfort I could."

"And did you promise him something?"

The witness declaimed her lines like a revivalist preacher. "That the men who had done awful things to him would be brought to justice."

Karen's eyes went skyward. There was nothing even to object to. Questions and answers were equally pious and equally absurd.

"Awful things?" said McCarthy.

"Awful things."

"Brought to justice?" said McCarthy. "Meaning who?"

"Meaning the police."

Karen almost wanted to laugh. "Objection, Your Honor," she said mildly.

Judge Birnbaum said: "Let's try to stay closer to factual evidence, please, Mr. McCarthy."

Mrs. Epps was dressed in a severe brown suit that was clean and well pressed though not of the best quality. Probably McCarthy had picked it out for her. Karen could visualize him climbing the stairs in a Harlem walkup, going through her wardrobe, reaching in and saying: "Wear this." On second thought, he would never have bothered to go there himself. He would have sent one of those eager young law students who worked for him without pay.

But the image he wished his witness to convey was clear. This devoted mother was honest, hardworking, the backbone of her family, the epitome of the matriarchal Harlem society. Was the jury buying it? Harlem was a place of broken families. It was often described as a society without men. The jury knew this better than Karen. In many cases the women raised their children by themselves. This was considered normal, was almost expected. Women like Mrs. Epps were regarded in Harlem as pillars of the earth. How was she coming across to the jury? After six weeks, having called more than forty witnesses, Karen had rested her case. McCarthy had promptly called Irene Epps. She would be the first—and perhaps only—witness for the defense.

McCarthy as he paced remained closer to the jury box than to the witness. He was watching the jurors, not the witness, was asking his questions almost over his shoulder. Obviously he was trying to put himself as close to the jurors as possible so that subconsciously, subliminally, they would feel he was one of them. That he was as impartial as themselves. That his only object was the same as theirs: to see the truth revealed. Clearly he would have climbed into the box with the jury if allowed.

Karen thought this technique transparent. But perhaps the jury did not.

"And when you visited your son in jail," said McCarthy over his shoulder, his voice low and more pious than ever, "did he tell you who had fired first?"

It was an outrageous question. No ethical lawyer would have asked it. He was trying to introduce a mother's hearsay evidence on behalf of her son. Karen was on her feet: "Objection, your honor."

"Sustained," said Judge Birnbaum.

"He said the cops fired first." Ignoring the judge's ruling, speaking in a loud firm voice, the witness had answered anyway.

"Question and answer will be stricken from the record," said Judge Birnbaum. "Jury will disregard."

"He said they came to kill him," declared Mrs. Epps.

She had been, Karen saw, well coached. "Judge—" Karen cried.

"The jury will disregard," said Judge Birnbaum.

Sure, thought Karen. The jurors will erase from their heads what they just heard, the way one erases a cassette tape. Sure. Score another point for McCarthy. As he prepared his next question, it seemed to Karen that he was smirking.

"Do you know a detective named Muldoon?" he asked.

"Yes, sir."

"And how is it that you know him?"

"He came every week to my house."

"Every week?"

"Some weeks more than once."

"To see your son?"

"He would go into the room with Lionel and close the door."

"Close the door?"

McCarthy nodded knowingly. Had one or two of the jurors nodded knowingly as well?

"They would stay in the room for a while?"

"They would talk in low voices in there."

"Could you hear what they were saying?"

"I couldn't make it out."

"Did you ask your boy about it afterwards?"

"He wouldn't tell me, he was so ashamed. He would

say: Mama, don't make me tell. He was a good boy. I never seen him so ashamed as he would be after that detective left him.''

"Did money change hands?"

"Oh yes. Every time that detective leave, Lionel would have money.''

"How do you know this?"

"Because he would give me some to buy food for the table. He would say, You spend it, Mama. I don't want to touch it.''

McCarthy now looked positively triumphant. He was practically strutting. "And did something unusual happen one day?''

"It was about two weeks before the police tried to shoot my boy to death.''

"And what took place on that day?''

"Detective Muldoon came to my house. I told him Lionel wasn't there.''

"And then what happened?''

"He called me terrible names and threatened to kill Lionel.''

"What exactly did he say?''

"He said, I'm going to kill that bastard.''

"I'm going to kill that bastard,'' McCarthy repeated. And then again musingly: "I'm going to kill that bastard.''

The courtroom was silent. For more than a minute, which can be a very long time, McCarthy studied his witness. He let the woman's words drip like acid onto the jurors' minds.

A third time he said: "I'm going to kill that bastard.'' And then to the witness: "And what did you do?''

"Went downtown and filed a complaint with the civilian review board.''

McCarthy went to his table, rummaged among papers, and came up with a form which he asked to be marked for identification. "And is this a record of that formal complaint?'' He held out the form, waved it at the jurors, and handed it to Mrs. Epps.

The mother looked it over. "Looks like it."

Karen at her table had passed through a number of emotions, boredom, disgust, confusion, outrage, and then, as the complaint form was entered into evidence, an intense and passionate anger. Some of Mrs. Epps's testimony was no doubt true. The portion about the civilian complaint was certainly true. Karen had known nothing about it, had never been told.

"Did you know about this?" she hissed at Coombs.

He looked as shocked as she was. "No."

She was furious at Muldoon who, it seemed to her, had withheld information vital to her case. Verdicts had been lost over much less. Barone must have known also. How dare they not tell her?

"Go to my office," she told Coombs. "Make calls. Find Muldoon. Find Barone. Have them in my office when I get there."

Barone was at the Three-Two picking up his paycheck when called to the phone. It was Coombs. The conversation was abrupt and unfriendly: report to Karen's office forthwith.

"What's it about?" inquired Barone.

"Forthwith," said Coombs, and hung up.

Barone stared a moment at the dead phone, then shrugged and drove downtown.

He was sitting on a straight chair in Karen's anteroom when she came in. He knew she was going to be mad about something, but did not know what.

"We can't find your partner, where is he?" she demanded as soon as she came through the door."

"Danny's not working today," Barone said, and watched her.

"Come into my office. Do you know Epps's mother?"

The anger in her voice was barely repressed and Barone, trailing her, paused before answering.

"I've met her," he said cautiously. "I know the whole family more or less."

"Why wasn't I told?"

"We went over this for a week with Mr. Harbison at the very beginning. Before Coombs even came on the case. You mean he didn't tell you?"

He had suspected a quarrel between her and Harbison for a long time; this confirmed it.

"He hasn't been much help to you, has he?" Barone said.

She looked at him a moment, but did not answer. He was not surprised. She would consider the subject not his business.

"What's happened?" he asked. "Is there something I can do? Name it. Anything. You know that."

He did not like to see her worried. He tried to put as much sincerity as possible into his voice but she was in no mood for sincerity, or else it registered on her as something else.

"I want everything you have on Irene Epps, everything you can find out about her. Drop whatever you're doing and get on it." She was almost shouting at him. "If you need extra detectives, see Inspector Pearson upstairs. Tell him you're acting on my authority."

"All right," said Barone.

"And I want to see you and Muldoon tonight. Both of you."

"Look—" said Barone.

"I don't want an explanation. I want you to get on it. Go."

Barone stood his ground. "I know you don't like me but—" He stopped.

"I do like you," said Karen.

"You do?"

"Yes," said Karen after a moment, "I do."

It was an admission that caused a kind of surprised silence on both sides.

"There was a file on Mrs. Epps," said Barone. "Everything was in there."

"There's almost nothing in the file on Mrs. Epps."

"Mr. Harbison had it. I saw it."

"I don't believe you."

Barone forced a smile. "Usually I only lie when I'm on the witness stand under oath." But his smile faded and he said stubbornly: "Most of what was in the Rastar Williams file and the Irene Epps file I provided. Somebody's mislaid them both. What did Mr. Harbison say when you asked him about Rastar's file?"

"He said he knew nothing about it."

When Barone remained silent she added grudgingly: "By the time I asked him, Rastar was back in Attica, so I didn't press the point."

"But Irene Epps is still on the stand."

"I'm aware of that."

"So ask him about the Irene Epps file."

"I'll ask him tonight after court."

Seeing that she did not like the idea of confronting Harbison, Barone said: "Do you want me to ask him?"

"I'm quite capable of asking him myself."

"Don't get mad at me. I hate it when you get mad at me."

He was pleased to see a tentative smile. She said: "You sound like a little boy."

"When I'm around you that's what I sometimes feel like."

This caused another long silence.

Barone said: "I just thought that if I were the one to ask him it might be easier for you."

"No, I'll ask him."

"Because I'm the one who knew about the files, and it might seem less confrontational to him coming from a man instead of from a—" He stopped.

"—from a woman," said Karen. "Do you realize what an offensive remark that is?"

"Sorry."

"How truly ugly?"

"I said I was sorry."

They stared at each other.

Barone said: "You don't like the idea of asking him, do you?"

"Not particularly, no."

"If you want to ask him now," Barone said, "I'll go with you."

"He's at a bar association meeting at the moment, I believe."

"Do you have the keys to his office? You must have. Get the keys and we'll go down there and have a look."

"I said I'd ask him," Karen snapped. "I suggest you take care of the detecting and you let me run this office. Is that clear?"

"Perfectly," Barone said. "I'll have the information on Mrs. Epps by tonight. Do I bring it to your house in Bronxville, or what? Greenfield Avenue, isn't it?"

"How do you know I live on Greenfield Avenue?"

Barone was momentarily speechless, and they stared at each other.

"I'll be staying in an apartment here in the city," Karen said, and gave the address. "Bring it there."

The pious Mrs. Epps remained on the stand all afternoon. Around her McCarthy spun his web of half-truths, inanities, and lies, and Karen listened and fretted.

Harbison must have known about the complaint against Muldoon, but hadn't told her. Well, he hadn't told her much, just turned over a ten-inch thickness of files, one of which seemed to be missing. Two of which, maybe. A civilian complaint resulted in documents. It seemed inconceivable that Harbison had never sent for them. He must have sent for them. There was a file somewhere—or had been a file once—with those documents in them, and perhaps much more. Karen as she brooded was getting terrifically angry.

When court ended she went back to her office, where she telephoned Harbison.

As soon as he came on the line she said: "Did you know about this civilian complaint against Muldoon?"

"Of course."

"Where's the paper on it?"

"In one of the files in one of the case folders."

"No it's not."

"You have everything I had."

"Do I?" said Karen.

After hanging up she went out to her secretary's desk. "We have a set of master keys here someplace, don't we?"

"In the safe," said Betty.

"To the offices and to the filing cabinets too, don't we?"

At 6 P.M. Betty stuck her head in the door to say she was going home.

Karen said to her: "Leave the safe open for me, please. Good night."

Coombs came in. She told him to go home, she was too tired to work tonight, and was leaving herself in a moment.

So he too departed.

For another half hour, too tense even to return phone calls, Karen waited.

Finally she went out to the safe, selected the keys she wanted, and walked down the hall to Harbison's office.

His door was locked and when she knocked there was no response. Stealthily she put keys into the locks and walked in past his secretary's desk.

The light was on in his office, which stopped her for a moment. But his coat was gone and she did not see his briefcase.

The room was neat, everything in its place, the pencils lined up precisely, his telephone and desk calendar in line with the desk's edge. You've been in here before, Karen told herself, don't be so surprised.

There were four filing cabinets along the wall, four drawers each, sixteen drawers in total. She opened the first cabinet and went through the drawers one after the other, the last of them on her knees. The drawers were neat too. Mostly they contained case folders, each folder four or more inches thick, each one properly identified as far as she could tell, none of them relating to the Lionel Epps case. What she was looking for would not be that thick, only a few pages. If it was here. She parted each pair of expandable envelopes looking for something slimmer that would have been forced down in between and which would perhaps not be labeled at all. But she found nothing.

She kept listening for footsteps outside in the hall that might be Harbison returning. She could feel sweat trickling down her backbone, she was that tense. There was no way she could be sure her chief assistant had gone home, or would not come back.

The second cabinet was the same. And the third and the fourth.

She stood up and peered around. There were bookshelves which she approached, looking them over carefully. But they seemed to contain only books.

His desk then. She went and sat down in his chair and tugged at the drawer handles, but the desk was locked too. She sorted through the keys she had brought.

It was as she turned the key that unlocked the desk that she noticed Harbison's briefcase. It was in the kneehole, upright on the floor beside her shoes. Seeing it there gave her a terrific start, for it meant that Harbison was still in the building. Lawyers, Harbison in particular, almost never went home without their briefcases. He could be working in some other office, or he was in the men's room, or he had gone out for a quick bite to eat and would be back any moment. If she were to find anything she of course meant to confront him with it, but suppose he came back and caught her searching his office and she had found nothing. She felt like a burglar ransacking a room for valuables. She felt like a criminal must feel. Hurry, she urged herself, hurry.

There was nothing in the desk's middle drawer except paper clips, rubber bands, and such.

Nothing significant in the top drawers to either side, either: a tape recorder, batteries, packages of chewing gum, an adding machine. Old Christmas cards. More pencils. Stamps.

The two bottom drawers were file drawers. The one on the left contained more case folders.

Just then Harbison's briefcase tipped over onto her shoe. She dragged it out and rummaged through it. Some letters, some insurance forms.

Footsteps approached in the hall. She waited for them to pass by but they did not do so. A key was inserted in the outer door, and it stiffened her.

The cleaning woman perhaps. But she knew it wasn't the cleaning woman. There was no place she could run to, nowhere to hide.

She had found no evidence against Harbison and she was about to be caught rifling his briefcase. She preferred to be caught rifling only his desk. Thrusting the papers back any which way and the briefcase back under the desk, she sat up straight.

Harbison stood in the doorway.

"What are you doing in my office?"

She imagined her face had gone red. She could feel her cheeks burning and once again cursed her fair complexion. She took a deep breath, willed her heart to stop thumping, and looked up at him.

"I was looking for a certain file."

"What file?"

"There's a file missing in the Epps case. I thought you might have it."

"Get out of my office."

Instead of obeying, she yanked open the final file drawer and peered down into it. This was a defensive reaction only. She was trying to prove to him and to herself that she had a right to search his office and files if she chose because she was the boss. Because she was district attorney, and he was not.

"I'll go when I've finished," she said in a dogged, unsteady voice. "When I'm finished you can have your office back."

She no longer expected to find anything incriminating. She had been through the cabinets, the bookshelves, his briefcase, and most of the desk already. It was unlikely she would find missing files in the only drawer left.

In the drawer were folders marked *Personal*. Letters, she saw, some photos; his income tax files for the past several years. Finally she came upon a file marked *Miscellaneous*. In it she noted other, thinner files. They stood inside it and protruded slightly. One of them was marked *Williams, Rastar*, and she plucked it out and dropped it on the desk.

"What's this?"

Harbison picked it up and clumsily flipped through it. As he went to put it back on the desk it slid off and splashed to the floor.

"Pick it up," said Karen. "Now hand it to me."

As he handed it over he almost dropped it again. He said: "I have no idea how that got there, and Williams has already testified, so whatever is in this file is moot."

Karen went through it straightening pages until she came to a copy of her fax to the penitentiary at Attica asking that Williams be sent down to be interviewed by her prior to the trial.

And a second fax, also signed by her, canceling the first one. A cancellation she had never written or ordered sent. Which would explain why she had been unable to interview Williams until the day before he testified.

"Interesting," said Karen grimly, pushing it across the desk to Harbison.

She lifted a second folder out of the drawer. It was marked *Epps, Irene*, and she thrust it at him. "I bet this one is interesting too."

It contained, she saw as she paged quickly through it,

the civilian complaint against Detective Muldoon, the disposition of that complaint, and much more. Dropping the folder on the desk, she stared up at her chief assistant.

Harbison bit down on his lower lip.

"Was there some special reason you hid these two files?" she asked. "Did you pick them out at random, or what?"

It was such an unlawyerly thing to have done. She could hardly believe it of the man she had always supposed Harbison to be. How he must have resented her taking over his case, wanted her so much to lose. How he must hate her.

"I want you out of here tonight," she said.

"You can't fire me."

"Oh, no? I've just done it."

"The governor—"

"If you go whining to the governor, be sure to tell him why I fired you."

"He won't believe you."

She waved the two files at him. "I rather think he will."

"My secretary misfiled those files—"

"I want your shield."

Assistant district attorneys carried badges similar to police lieutenants'.

"Your shield and your keys."

Sweat had popped out on Harbison's brow. "Do I get a chance to explain?"

"No," said Karen.

"It must have been my secretary—"

"Clean out your desk," said Karen.

"My secretary—"

"Personal items only."

"Wait a minute," said Harbison, "wait a minute." But all the air had gone out of him.

"I want you gone."

"I've been here twenty-six years and—"

"Gone."

"You can't do this to me."

"Oh yes I can."

"Not like this."

"Just like this."

"Can I ask you something?"

"No."

"I need time."

"Your keys, your shield."

"Please," he said.

"Give them to me. Now."

Harbison put his shield and keys down on the desk. "A little time. Until Monday. Before you announce it. Can you please do that?"

"You're joking."

"I have a wife and children. Give me a chance to find something. You have to give me a chance."

"I don't have to give you anything."

"A few days."

He was begging. "That's all I ask."

His mood turned suddenly truculent. "I can turn this into a scandal."

He said: "You don't need that."

"It would smear you more than me," said Karen.

"Suppose I don't go to the governor," Harbison said.

Karen eyed him speculatively.

"Suppose I resign and I go quietly, no fuss."

The fierceness of her rage had surprised Karen. So had her ability to make her decision and fire this man, all in a few seconds.

She had no desire to destroy Harbison's family, and her emotion was already beginning to abate.

"Give me your letter of resignation," she ordered. And then in a milder voice: "Date it Monday if you like." A letter would tend to protect her with the governor. "Just as long as you're out of here tonight."

With this less than total victory, she decided to be satisfied. She was perhaps making a mistake, and she knew this. If so, she told herself, at least it was on the side of decency.

* * *

As she walked back to her office, she began to feel elated. She had prevented any protracted struggle by Harbison to keep his job. She had avoided the kind of juicy story the news media loved. Such publicity would have distracted her jurors, not to mention herself. And who knew, the media might even have taken Harbison's side, might have castigated her for days. She did not need that either.

Jill's apartment was on MacDougal Street in Greenwich Village. Karen let herself in. She was carrying her bulging case files and was trailed by her driver with her suitcase. She was still thinking about Harbison.

She said to Detective McGillis: "Just set it down any-where."

Peering around, she felt triumphant, happy and a bit flighty, as if she had come to this borrowed apartment for an illicit tryst, and was only waiting for her lover to appear. She put her briefcase on the kitchen counter, and when she looked up McGillis was still there, awaiting instructions.

"Thanks for your help," she told him. "I won't need you anymore tonight." She locked the door behind him. Three locks because this was New York City. She locked them all.

As she moved through unknown rooms she began to remember her teenage years when she used to baby-sit. She would enter each new house or apartment with a young girl's excitement. She would be eager to find out how two strange grown-ups lived. As soon as the couple had gone out and the child or children were asleep she could begin exploring. She would go to the bedside tables to see what kind of birth control they were using. She would look through the dressers, the closets, the jewelry boxes, the medicine cabinets. She would open and sniff the perfumes. Sometimes if the fit was right she might try on an article of clothing. She would examine the bookshelves, flip through some of the books looking for sexy passages.

She felt excitement tonight too, though it was of a different kind. In the bedroom she pressed down on the mattress, testing its firmness. In the living room when she turned on a lamp she noted an envelope with her name on it on top of the television set, held in place by a bottle of champagne. The message inside told her how to put out the garbage, and that one of the windows was broken and would not open. It advised her to enjoy the champagne, and her few days off from home as well. Karen smiled.

Having decided to call Hank she went to the telephone, but then put it down again because she was still savoring her conduct of less than an hour ago and was not yet ready to share it. Instead she went to the window, looked past her face in the dark glass, and watched the movement on the street below. She felt decisive. She felt somehow purified. Then she sighed and said to herself: "Get to work, lady," and she sat down on the sofa, and opened her briefcase. As she began studying the newly obtained *Epps, Irene* file, she became elated all over again. With what was in it she could destroy Mrs. Epps's testimony tomorrow, and McCarthy with her.

She closed the file and as she sat there she was almost gloating. Her enemy was gone. She had fired Harbison. She had never been a boss before, never fired anyone. She had not really had confidence in herself as district attorney, but she did now. I can do this job, she told herself. I'm more than a trial lawyer. I can run the office and win verdicts and manage the personnel too. Harbison had tried to destroy her, and he was gone and she was still DA, still in charge.

Presently the doorbell rang. She opened to Detective Barone.

"I've got most of what was in the original file," he said, "and a lot more besides."

He handed her some papers which she carried into the living room to the light.

He had followed her. "Did you talk to Mr. Harbison?"

She tried to keep from smirking. "I did, yes."

"What happened to the missing files?"

"Well, we found them."

"Good," said Barone. "At least you know I wasn't making it up. Where were they?"

Karen pretended to be studying the material he had brought. "They were in a drawer," she said.

"Misfiled?"

"Yes, misfiled."

"Misfiled on purpose, or what?"

How could he have known that, she wondered. "Of course not," she lied.

"I owe you an apology," she said. "I wasn't very nice to you before."

"When was that?" Barone said. "I didn't notice."

They looked at each other. "You have a nice smile," Barone said.

"So do you."

This exchange brought silence on both sides.

Barone said: "The mother's been arrested four times. She has four sons. Lionel is the youngest. His older brothers, half brothers I think they are, have done a total of twenty-six years in the can."

Karen glanced down at the papers he had brought. There was a richness of material here beyond even the contents of Harbison's file. Nonetheless, the cross-examination of Mrs. Epps would be delicate. "The mother's not on trial," she said. "She's his mother. I can't attack her too much or I lose the sympathy of the jury. Her other sons—I don't know. Where's Detective Muldoon?"

"I couldn't reach him. All I could do was leave a message on his machine. You'll have to be satisfied with me, I'm afraid. I can be very useful, honest I can."

Again the nice smile. It unsettled Karen. "We have work to do," she said. "Can I offer you something? I don't know what's here—"

She went into the kitchen, began opening cabinets, and found some tea. "Could I offer you a cup of tea?"

"Well," said Barone, "tea would be nice." He was standing in the kitchen doorway, watching her carefully.

"Start at the beginning," Karen said.

The kitchen was large with a nook containing a small table and two chairs. They sat at either side of the table and sipped the tea.

"When I got transferred to the Three-Two and met Danny, he was already using Lionel. How he happened to come across him I'm not sure. I think he caught him selling crack in a doorway. Some goddam thing. Kid was about fifteen at the time."

"Did he arrest him?"

"A juvenile? What was the point? It would just teach the kid that the system was nothing to worry about. Danny tried to frighten him instead, maybe slapped him around a little."

"Slapped him around?"

"Maybe," said Barone defensively. "I wasn't there."

"Then what?"

"After that he began using him. Lionel gave Danny the location of a cutting factory once. Another time, he put us onto a guy selling guns. Sometimes he told us where to find guys we were looking for."

Karen got up to get a yellow pad, after which she went into some of these cases in some detail, making notes.

They sipped their tea.

"You've been very worried these last few weeks, haven't you?" said Detective Barone.

"Yes."

"Because it isn't the open-and-shut case everyone thinks."

"It's a more special case than most people realize. A nearly all black jury. A demagogue like McCarthy playing to every racial fear and slight any of them have ever suffered."

"People look at the case," Barone said. "All they see is that the guy shot five cops."

"If I were to lose—"

He was listening, Karen noted. Really listening. People who listened were rare. She found herself wanting to trust him. Wanting to tell him how she had sacked Harbison. Wanting to bask in his congratulations. Stick to the trial, she told herself.

She sipped her tea and studied her notes. "How did you usually make contact with Epps?"

"There was a corner he hung out on. If he wasn't there, sometimes we went to his house."

"His mother testified you went there once a week."

Barone shook his head. "In the three years I've been in the precinct, five or six times at the most."

"Was he registered?"

"I don't know, you'd have to ask Danny."

"Did you pay him?"

"From time to time Danny did give him money."

"While you watched?"

"If we went up to his house I waited in the hall. Danny would go in and talk to him."

Karen was still making notes. "The tea is a bit cold," Barone said.

Karen looked at him a moment, then got up and put more water on to boil.

"The money you gave him, was it vouchered?"

"Getting money out of the department is really hard. I think sometimes it was department money. Usually it was Danny's."

"How could you give money to a thug like Lionel Epps?"

"In the detective business thugs are what you deal with. The parish priest is not usually present when criminals plan or commit their crimes." He paused. "You know that as well as I do."

They looked at each other. "Besides," Barone said, "Epps was not then what he later became. To us he was a small-time crack dealer. He gave up worse scum than himself, so we used him."

Karen studied her notes.

"The last several months before the shoot-out we couldn't find him. We heard he had moved across the river, that he was trying to take over a piece of the South Bronx. Then we heard that he was wanted by detectives over there for shooting some guy and wrapping him in a rug and setting him on fire."

"Yes," said Karen. "Everybody remembers that rug. It makes such a nice picture."

"So we thought maybe he had come back to our side to hole up."

"And you found him."

"Yeah, Danny found him. Danny went looking for Rastar Williams. He figured if he leaned hard on Rastar, Rastar would find him for us, and he was right. Danny's a pretty good detective."

He fell silent. She knew her color was high, her eyes especially bright. When she was as ebullient as this she was beautiful, and she knew it. She knew too that he was staring at her, and so kept her eyes on her notes.

He said: "You've looked so worried lately."

"I'm much less worried now." She held up the two new files, Harbison's and Barone's, and grinned. "You should come to court tomorrow, it's going to be a bloodbath."

Barone wore a nice suit. He had nice hands. She was surprised how comfortable it felt to sit with him at this table.

This notion made her get up, go to the stove and pour boiling water on top of new teabags, and bring the pot back to the table.

He said: "You must imagine that every woman in the city is watching you, cheering for you."

She did imagine this, especially tonight. They would all be cheering tonight. By firing Harbison she had struck a blow for herself, and for womankind as well.

Their knees under this too small table were probably no more than an inch apart. She was in a mood to flirt with him but cautioned herself not to. She wasn't a teenager and it wasn't fair to flirt with a grown man unless you meant it.

"I'll bet you're not sleeping well, having bad dreams."

This was true. By now she would have expected Barone to do or say something stupid, something that would put her off, but so far this had not happened.

"How did you know about my bad dreams? Does it show that much?"

"You look a little tired."

"There are lines around my eyes that didn't used to be there."

"Not true."

"I feel like I've aged ten years." She wasn't fishing for a compliment exactly, or was she?

He said: "You look terrific."

"I think I'll sleep well tonight though," she said, and tapped the two new files.

Barone said: "You have lovely eyes."

She gazed at him a moment in silence.

Suddenly he reached out and touched her face.

His touch brought her back to reality. My God, she told herself, he's making a play for me. She was not really surprised but to herself pretended to be. A street detective was making a play for the district attorney of New York County.

It made her think of the bed she would sleep in tonight. It was as if she could see through the kitchen wall into the bedroom on the other side. The bare pillows lay against the headboard, the clean sheets and pillowcases in a stack on top of the bare mattress—she was going to have to make the bed later. The most vivid image imaginable. Was Bar-

one able to put such ideas in her head without her even
knowing it? Was she supposed to ask him to come into the
bedroom with her and help her make the bed?

The idea almost made her burst out laughing. If she
suggested it, he would not, she was sure, turn her down.

She struggled to regain control of her emotions. Such a
possibility was out of the question. How did she let it even
come into her head? Her triumph over Harbison must have
made her giddy. Or else she was more tired, more stressed
out than she even imagined. She was certainly not going to
have an affair with Barone, and to make the bed up later
was just another chore facing her, the last of the day.

The phone rang. It was attached to the kitchen wall and
she reached for it, and it was Hank.

During the time she spoke to him Barone went out into
the living room to afford her some privacy, which was
thoughtful of him. Nonetheless probably he could hear her
from there so she avoided saying anything that might sound
intimate. She certainly didn't talk about Harbison. She
asked about Hank's day, and he about hers. She asked
about the children. The conversation then lapsed, and presently she was able to break it off and hang up.

Barone came back into the kitchen. I've got to get him
out of here, Karen thought.

"You've rested your case," he said.

"Yes."

"I've been expecting to testify, but you didn't put me
on."

"No." Though he waited for an explanation, she didn't
see where she had to give him one. Her strategy and tactics
were her own affair, not his.

But the silence continued. "I didn't feel your testimony
was necessary," she said.

And McCarthy might have mauled you, she thought as
they gazed at each other, how was I to be sure, so I never
put you on. "You were on the roof, not in the building,"
she said, "you didn't get shot—"

"True," he said, "Danny was more central to your case."

She got to her feet. "There's a Korean grocery on the corner," she said. "I have to get some things for the house." She moved past him out of the kitchen. "I mean, I can't just sit here eating up my friend's groceries." A rather long speech.

He made no protest, but followed her out to the street and into the nearby store.

It was like all the Korean groceries. Brightly lit interior, perfect pyramids of perfect fruit outside, all of it kept sprinkled as if with dew. The late hours of the Koreans were a godsend to busy New Yorkers who often needed to do their shopping at night. Karen bought tea, coffee, milk, bread, moving from shelf to shelf with Barone trailing and carrying the basket.

She paid and they moved back up the sidewalk with the detective clutching the bag of groceries to his chest. In front of her building she said:

"I'll take that from you now."

"Let me carry it upstairs for you."

"Oh, I can manage from here on."

She hoped he would accept the dismissal. She had enjoyed the past hour, and did not want it spoiled now.

"Thanks for bringing me that material," she said. She took the bag from his arms. "And for carrying my groceries." She smiled at him. "Now I'm going upstairs and to sleep. I'm so tired."

She saw him accept this.

"As the parties to the lawsuit said," he joked, "I'll see you in court."

He put his hand out, and she shook hands with him. But he held on to her, saying, "Can I kiss you good night?"

It was a line that might work with some silly girl, not with her. Her mood hardened. "What would you want to do that for?"

"I feel very close to you somehow."

They eyed each other. "Yes," she said dryly, "we understand each other, don't we?"

She presented her cheek, felt his lips briefly, said good night, and carried her groceries into the building.

— 20 —

Mrs. Epps was on the stand. Karen stood before her holding her rap sheet.

"And have you ever been arrested, Mrs. Epps?"

"Have I ever been hassled by the police? That's what happens to poor black folk. They get hassled by the police."

The reply stopped Karen for a moment. This was either an extremely skilled or extremely well-schooled witness, and she had best proceed with great care.

"Were you arrested in Macy's and charged with shoplifting?"

"The charges were dropped."

Karen concentrated on this arrest for thirty minutes, dragging the details out of the woman one by one.

"And were you arrested in your apartment building charged with assault on a neighbor?"

Stony silence from Mrs. Epps.

"The witness will answer the question," instructed Judge Birnbaum.

The answer when it came was a surly "Something like that."

Karen spent another thirty minutes eliciting details. "You stabbed her with a knife, is that not correct? And although you stabbed her, she failed to appear to testify, is that not correct? In fact she has not been seen since, is that not correct?"

Although worried about losing the sympathy of the jury, Karen was infuriated by this woman.

"And another time you were arrested and charged with receiving stolen property, is that not correct?"

Mrs. Epps did not answer.

"The police raided your apartment and what did they find?"

Karen had the police report marked for identification, showed it to McCarthy, and asked Mrs. Epps to read from it.

"I don't have my glasses," the woman said sullenly.

Karen said coldly: "May I remind the witness that she is under oath and must answer my next question truthfully. Has any doctor ever prescribed glasses for you, Mrs. Epps?"

"Poor people can't afford eye doctors."

"Do you wear glasses normally, Mrs. Epps? Have you ever worn glasses?"

"Sometimes I do," the witness replied after a long silence.

"All right," said Karen, "let me read it for you." And she read down the list of stolen property. "All of that was found in your apartment."

More silence from Mrs. Epps.

"There also was a sting operation and you were arrested for selling stolen property out of a storefront, is that not correct?"

Again Mrs. Epps did not answer.

"You were what is called a fence, is that not correct? According to the indictment, the property in question was stolen by your three older sons. Were they operating under your instructions, Mrs. Epps?"

The woman refused to answer.

"Where are those sons today, Mrs. Epps?"

When she still refused to answer, Karen answered for her. "Your son Simon is in Attica, convicted of murder," said Karen. "Is that not correct? And your son Charleton is in

Greenhaven, and your son Wilson is in the federal penitentiary in Atlanta, am I not correct?''

Karen was fed up with being careful. In attacking the
defendant's mother she was flying in the face of accepted
legal theory. But if the jurors were honest people, and she
was obliged to assume they were, she might win the case
right here, put the verdict forever out of reach of McCarthy.

And so she kept the woman on the stand, continued to
badger her, and by daring to touch on her relationship to her
four sons of course impugned her effectiveness as a mother.
She watched the jury's reaction throughout, but could not
read it.

''With a record like yours, Mrs. Epps, why should this
jury believe anything you say?'' Karen said rhetorically.

And there she stopped. ''No further questions, Your
Honor.''

When night came she left her office. In Jill's apartment she
ate a yogurt. Last night's elation had given way to new worries. Had she been too lenient with Harbison? Had she left
him room to retaliate in some way? She would have to replace
him as chief assistant, and soon, but with whom?

Had she been too rough on Mrs. Epps? Had she alienated
the jury?

Muldoon and Barone arrived as ordered.

''Please be seated,'' she said. It was not a social occasion
and she offered them nothing to eat or drink. ''You, Detective
Muldoon, I want to know when you first met Lionel Epps
and how. I want to know the details of every meeting you
ever had with him.'' She faced Muldoon directly. ''In the
morning you will be recalled and after I examine you, you
will be cross-examined by McCarthy, who will probably call
you a crook again.'' Her gaze swept around to include Barone. ''According to McCarthy, you're all crooks. I want to
hear some facts.''

Seeing Muldoon bristle she repented immediately. ''You
have to be ready to be called a crook,'' she said.

But for two hours she pressed them hard, until Muldoon got angry and started to storm out.

"Sit down," she ordered.

Barone looked from one of them to the other. "I think you should ease up on Danny a little," he suggested gently. "We're your friends."

"Sit down," Karen ordered Muldoon a second time, and he did. She had won the confrontation, but from then on he answered in monosyllables and stared at the ceiling, exactly as he tended to do in court.

No sooner had she shown them out than the doorbell rang. She had to reopen all three bolts. It was Barone. Muldoon, she saw, waited some distance down the hall.

"I think you should put me on the stand tomorrow, not Danny."

"I wasn't aware," Karen said, "that you were the attorney prosecuting this case."

Barone spoke urgently, his voice low enough so that his partner would not hear. "I can give you the testimony you want, and I can handle McCarthy on cross. He won't get under my skin the way he does Danny's."

"I'll keep your offer in mind," she said.

"He destroyed the testimony of all those other cops. He may destroy Danny again. With me that won't happen."

Karen was seriously worried about Muldoon as a witness, but he had to be put on. There was no alternative.

"You need me," Barone said.

"No, I need the proper answers from your partner."

"I can help you."

"The situation calls for Detective Muldoon. I explained to you why I elected not to put you on."

"I want to help you win this case."

"I'm sure you do," said Karen, and she began to close the door.

"You know you can depend on me."

"Do I?"

"You know me."

"I don't know you at all," Karen said.

She had hurt him, obviously. He looked away, then again met her eyes. "You need a strong witness tomorrow, the strongest possible and—"

"Good night, Detective Barone," she said.

"Karen—"

She closed the door on him.

The next day Muldoon again took the stand.

"About two weeks before the shoot-out," asked Karen, "did you call the defendant's mother some obscene names?"

"She abused me. I abused her back."

"Did you threaten the defendant's life?"

"No I did not."

"Did you say to her, I'm going to kill the bastard? Or words to that effect?"

"I told her he should give himself up to me before somebody shot him. I had information that a lot of people were after him."

"Police officers?"

"No. His colleagues in the drug business."

"His colleagues in the drug business," Karen repeated. And then again, musingly: "His colleagues in the drug business." She gazed across at McCarthy and thought: I can play the same dirty game you play, and I can play it just as well.

But she knew she couldn't. Wouldn't or couldn't, she was not sure which.

"His mother made an official complaint against you, did she not?"

"Yes."

"For threatening violence?"

"No."

"For using racial epithets against her?"

"Yes."

"Did the police department investigate her complaint?"

"Yes."

"And the result was?"

"I took a rip."

"A rip?"

"I got docked two days' pay for it."

Karen in front of the jury let her eyes move from face to face. To Muldoon she said: "You seem to have known the defendant pretty well."

"He was a regular informant."

"Which means what, Detective Muldoon?"

"He gave us information that resulted in the arrests of some very bad people."

"But I thought you understood him to be a very bad person himself."

"Not at first."

"You let him operate because he gave up more important wrong-doers than you thought him to be?"

"That's right."

"You talked to him once a week?"

"No. Not nearly that often. Once a month, maybe."

"You went to his house for this?"

"No. Usually I found him on the street. I'd make him a sign. We'd park around the corner, he'd come around, and I'd talk to him for five minutes in a doorway or an alley. We weren't making conversation. Five minutes was more than enough."

"But you did go to his house on occasion?"

"A few times. If something important suddenly came up that I thought he might know about. There was a triple homicide in a bar, for instance, and—"

Karen cut him off. The jury did not need to hear about extraneous cases. "How many times over the last three years did you go to his house?"

"Five or six times. He was a pretty good informant. His brothers were informants before him, but he was the best."

"His brothers?"

"By this time they were all in jail."

"He was a registered informant?" said Karen.

"Registered, yes."

"With the police intelligence division. Is this a record of his registration?" Karen waved the card at the jury before handing it to Muldoon, who looked it over.

"That looks like it, yes."

"Did you pay him?"

"Regularly."

"With police department money?"

"I have paid him with police department money, yes."

"Money that was vouchered, Detective Muldoon?"

"Money that was vouchered."

Karen walked back to her place and picked up a number of vouchers. As with the informant card, she had them marked for identification and afterward entered into evidence.

She began reading out dates and sums. "On December eighteenth, two years ago, did you pay the defendant $50?"

"Yes I did."

"And vouchered it?"

"Yes I did."

"And again on May thirtieth of the following year?"

"Yes I did."

Karen went through the rest of the vouchers, only two more in all, not many for such a long period. She decided she'd best continue along this same line of questioning, rather than risk McCarthy doing it on cross-examination.

"Sometimes you used your own money, is that correct?"

"Yes."

"Why is that, detective?"

"Getting money out of the department was too much of a hassle."

"Are you a rich man, Detective?"

"No."

"But you paid an informant with your own money?"

"It was easier that way."

"Money is money."

With downcast eyes Muldoon said: "I'm divorced, I have no kids. It was only five dollars, ten dollars here and there.

What else was I going to do with the money?" He became truculent. "It was my money. I could do with it what I liked."

He looked so abject, so hangdog, so alone in the world, that Karen felt a great outpouring of sympathy. Hoping the jury felt the same, she walked back to her place saying: "No further questions, Your Honor."

From her chair at the defense table she watched McCarthy move forward.

"What about the other money, Detective?"

Muldoon looked immediately wary. Once again he would not meet McCarthy's eyes. "What money is that, counselor?"

"Money from the drugs you cops forced him to sell for you. That's the real reason you went to see him once a week, isn't it?"

"Objection, objection," cried Karen. "He's doing it again, Judge."

But McCarthy simply overrode her. "To collect your money. That's what we're talking about here, isn't it, Detective?"

"Sustained," said Judge Birnbaum.

But McCarthy ignored the judge's ruling. His harsh voice was almost shouting. "He wanted out, Detective, so you decided he would have to be killed. Isn't that the truth of the matter, Detective?"

Karen was shouting too. "Mr. McCarthy continues to pollute this courtroom and to slander witnesses with accusations that are totally wild and without any basis in fact whatsoever."

Henry Henning was having dinner with Jackie and Hillary. Karen was not there.

"What do you think Mom is doing right now?"

"Writing her summation, I imagine. The case goes to the jury tomorrow."

"Can I light the candles, Daddy?" asked Hillary.

"Sure."

There was a candelabra in the center of the table. The girl lit each of the four candles in turn, then walked over and switched out the overhead light. After hesitating a moment, she went to the head of the table and sat down in her mother's place and grinned at her father and the three of them started to eat.

Harbison had that day called a press conference at which he announced that he had resigned as chief assistant so as to set up an office to run for district attorney in the fall; it would have been unethical, he declared piously, to continue to accept a salary when spending most of his time campaigning. He expected to be the candidate for district attorney on both the Republican and Conservative lines. If elected he would bring to the job both vast experience and unchallenged integrity. Without mentioning Karen by name he declared that the office of Manhattan district attorney was too important to be left in the hands of a political appointee whose credentials were meager and whose competence was doubtful.

In her borrowed apartment Karen watched part of this press conference on the television newscasts. I made a mistake, she acknowledged to herself. I should have just fired him. It was too late, she had missed her chance. No one would believe anything she might say now.

Well, she thought, I don't have time to worry about that. Alone in the apartment, she sat down on the sofa under a single lamp and began filling page after yellow page with what would be her summation.

But it was McCarthy's turn to sum up first, and he spoke for hours. He was quite eloquent, and the jury, from Karen's point of view, listened with too rapt attention. Mostly she doodled on her pad, looking up only from time to time, her glance moving from face to face as she tried to appraise the reactions of the jurors, of Judge Birnbaum, of Lionel Epps, even Coombs.

"How many police officers—white police officers—would you send to arrest one black youth?" demanded McCarthy rhetorically. "Would you send twenty? Does that seem normal to you? Or would you send that many only if the object was to kill him? Lionel Epps didn't want to die. He fired back, out of self-defense. Who else would defend his life? The police? The police wanted to close his mouth forever."

Nodding vigorously, McCarthy marched up and down in front of the jury.

"Twenty white cops. Would they lie to protect each other, to hide their own crimes? I don't have to answer that question. You will answer it as you see fit. There is no documentary evidence against Lionel Epps—excuse me, one piece: his registration card as a police informer. Are the police capable of inventing evidence like that? Of backdating records? Ha!"

McCarthy's arguments, to Karen, sounded preposterous. Did the jury find them so?

"No, they went there to kill him," continued McCarthy. "And he knew it. At the last extremity young Lionel Epps availed himself of the God-given right of all of us, the right to self-defense. He defended himself, and on that grounds you will acquit him."

McCarthy spoke so long that Judge Birnbaum adjourned the trial for the day. Karen went back to her office and after that to her borrowed apartment, where she worked over her summation still again.

In the stationhouse Muldoon and Barone went up the stairs to the fourth floor and pushed through the door. The lockers were in rows with benches down the middle. Muldoon's locker was in the third row about halfway along.

"What do you make of this?" he said. He held the ruined lock out from the door, then let it bang back.

"Somebody cut it open with a bolt cutter," said Barone. "What else am I supposed to make of it."

"IAD," said Muldoon.

Barone nodded.

"IAD guys come in the stationhouse," Muldoon said. "Middle of the fucken night. Fuckers had to go down and get the bolt cutter out of their car."

The locker room served 250 cops. During shift changes it was alive with boisterous, milling men. Most other times it was empty. Apart from Barone and Muldoon it was empty now.

Barone said: "If you'd had a combination on it like you're supposed to, they wouldn't have had to ruin your lock." In theory all 250 combinations were on file in the captain's safe in case the brass had to get into your locker for something. If you got shot and killed maybe. Or indicted for corruption.

"The desk sergeant mentioned it to nobody," Muldoon said. "So you know he was in on it. I mean, he had to have seen them. They walked right by him, three cops and a lieutenant."

"A lieutenant?" said Barone. A lieutenant was a lot of rank for something like this.

"How we found out about it," Muldoon said, "one of the radio car cops was out on the stoop waiting for his partner."

To send a lieutenant they must be serious, Barone thought.

"His partner was in the can the whole time taking a shit."

They meant business, Barone thought.

"I called you as soon as I found out," said Muldoon.

"How many lockers they go through?"

"I'm told about a dozen."

"Whose?"

"Random, it looks like."

"Those guys don't do much that's random," Barone muttered. He went over to his own locker, worked the combination, and pulled the door open. Inside was his uniform in a plastic bag, and his holster and gunbelt hanging from one of the hooks. He unzipped the bag and examined the uniform, then took out and studied the big service revolver, his eyes asking it questions. Anybody been checking you over lately? He hadn't used this gun in years. He hadn't worn a uniform in years but was obliged to own one in case he was assigned to riot duty or a parade. Or got flopped back to patrolman, he thought. On the shelf above was a box of rubbers. Had it been moved? He couldn't tell. He couldn't remember where on the shelf he had placed it, or even when. The seal was unbroken and he put it back where it was.

Had his locker contained anything else? Something that was not supposed to be there for instance? That was not there now? But he rarely came up here and could not remember.

"So what do you think?" said Muldoon at his elbow.

Barone said: "Captain give you a complaint for using a hard lock?" Though he made his voice sound casual, this was not the way he felt.

"Fucken captain," said Muldoon.

"So you take another rip," Barone said, watching his partner carefully. He sensed an agitation in Muldoon—much more agitation than actually showed. He had sensed it on the phone. He had been at home working on a stopped-up toilet. He had got into his car and driven the sixty miles back to the stationhouse. "A rip won't hurt you," he said. "Couple of vacation days. You don't go anywhere on vacation anyway."

But he saw that Muldoon was suddenly unwilling to meet his eyes. He knew what this meant, and it unnerved him. He said: "So what did you have in there you shouldn't have?"

There was a rather long silence. "Lotta crap," Muldoon said finally.

"Crap?" Barone was afraid he knew what was coming. "What kind of crap?"

"I think there may have been some stuff from old cases in there."

"From old cases?"

"Maybe."

"Evidence from old cases?"

"Yeah, maybe."

Like hypodermic syringes taken off junkies, Barone thought. Like vials of pills picked up at crime scenes and never carried to the lab to be analyzed. Like expended bullets handed over by the surgeon outside the operating room after he cut them out of some guy. Like knives or tire irons with blood on them.

"Stuff that didn't mean shit," said Muldoon vehemently. "Cases where the mutt pleaded out," he said defensively.

But evidence was to be vouchered and handed in to the property clerk, according to regulations, not kept in some detective's locker.

"Did you have any junk in there?" Barone demanded. "What about junk?"

It happened. Detectives who arrested junkies would sometimes hold back a packet or two of heroin, a vial or two of crack. You could pay off informants with drugs. It was easier than getting department money, and cheaper than using your own.

"I don't think so, no."

"You're sure?"

"Yes."

"That's a relief," said Barone. "For a minute there I saw myself visiting you in jail."

"There may have been a gun, though."

"Jesus," said Barone.

Muldoon said nothing.

"A gun," said Barone.

"Yeah, I think so."

"Where'd you get it?"

"Some crime scene. Five years ago, ten years ago. How the fuck do I know?"

Cops confiscated guns every day, so it was possible honestly to mislay one, or forget about one. Also, guns required paperwork, followed by a trip to the ballistics lab, and then to the property clerk's office, both of them downtown, with usually a long line at the window at one place or both. Arresting officers were sometimes overworked or lazy, and sometimes they waited too long to turn in the gun, and the case went forward without it, and then it was too late. If they turned it in now they'd be brought up on departmental charges.

And then there were the cops who liked to keep an unregistered gun around to drop on the body in case they shot somebody who turned out to be unarmed. Throwaway guns, they were called. These were the cops—and the guns—the police brass worried about.

"You really are stupid," said Barone shaking his head, not bothering to hide his disgust. "Don't you know better than to keep such things in your locker?"

Muldoon said nothing.

"You got problems, you know that. You got real problems."

"What the fuck," said Muldoon.

Barone might have problems himself, but wasn't sure yet what they might be. If internal affairs was coming after them for the shoot-out fiasco, which was what he supposed, he was not going to be as easy to nail as Muldoon.

Muldoon said: "There's a UF 49 on Pommer's desk right now. He's waiting to sign it. They're bringing me up on eighteen specifications."

Barone looked at his partner: at the protruding belly, at the soiled sports coat, the soiled tie. "How do you know that?"

"I called this guy I know."

"Who?"

"A friend."

Barone managed a grin. "I didn't know you had any friends."

Muldoon looked away.

"Except me of course," said Barone.

"He said they're going to try to fire me off the job."

"What are the other specifications?"

"Missing memo book entries. Failure to file some DD-5s. Missed court appearances. You name it."

If they were looking at memo books, then Barone's was a mess too. Every cop was guilty of paperwork discrepancies. And most cops now and then failed to appear in court, Barone included. They were busy on another case, or sick, or just forgot.

Muldoon said: "Even drinking on the job."

Barone looked at him.

"Fucken Ritter."

"You don't know that."

"Had to be."

"Everybody knows you get thirsty now and then."

They looked at each other in silence.

Muldoon said: "They went back six or eight years on me."

How far back would they go on Barone? "You'll take a rip," Barone said. He was worried about himself, but more worried about Muldoon. If their object was to dismiss Muldoon outright, they could do it. "A bigger rip than I said, but only a rip."

The fat man shook his head. "Listen, Mike—"

Muldoon prided himself on needing no one. Which was ridiculous, Barone thought. Everybody needed other people. Life was too tough. No one could get through it alone. The guy didn't even have any friends. All he had was the department. His life was the department. He had nothing else.

"Maybe," said Muldoon, "you could—" He stopped, and Barone saw that asking favors was not easy for him, even from his partner. But then he got the sentence out all in a rush: "Maybe you could talk to someone about me."

"Who'd you have in mind?"

"The DA, maybe."

"Her?" Barone visualized Karen Henning seated in his car, seated in her kitchenette, seated at her desk.

Muldoon waited anxiously.

"I don't know if I could do that," Barone said.

"Listen, Mike," said Muldoon, "maybe you've been fucking her, maybe you haven't, that's not my affair, but I know she likes you."

"How do you know that?"

"It shows," said Muldoon, nodding earnestly. "The way she looks at you."

Barone hadn't seen it, but chose not to say so.

"If it was the district attorney put in a good word for me,

the department would have to go easy. If you could ask her, Mike. Could you ask her?''

Barone looked into his partner's beseeching eyes. He saw such suffering there that he had to turn away.

''Could you ask her, Mike?''

''I don't know,'' he said, ''I'll have to think about it.''

''For weeks you have listened to Mr. McCarthy's charges, slurs, innuendos,'' said Karen in front of the jury. ''His accusations couched as questions. He has slandered every cop who appeared here without offering a shred of evidence. He would have you believe that twenty police officers formed a secret conspiracy to murder. That's quite a secret. A secret shared by twenty men. A secret guarded so closely that not one word leaked out. Is that possible? Could twenty men possibly keep so deadly a secret? Would you trust such a secret to nineteen other people, and imagine it would stay secret? With your career, your very life riding on it?''

Karen too marched up and down in front of the jury box, maintaining eye contact.

''The defense has offered no evidence, none, of police corruption relative to this case, none of police intent to murder the defendant, none that the police fired first, none of any legitimate right of self-defense by the defendant. Instead, consider the evidence you did hear. Evidence of a man so dangerous, surrounded by such an arsenal of guns, that twenty men went to arrest him. How many policemen have fallen in pools of their own blood because they attempted to make such arrests with too few men? Twenty men were necessary. This was normal police procedure. Ten were posted at the building exits, others were on the roof, the fire escapes, most of them not even in position when the shooting started. The defendant shot them down without warning, not in self-defense but solely in his frenzy to escape. If you acquit him now you send a powerful message to criminals——that when police officers come to arrest you for your crimes, you can shoot them down with impunity and afterwards claim self-defense, and get away with it. Ladies and gentlemen, if that is the message you mean to give, then none of us is any longer safe, and democracy itself is threatened. You have five counts of attempted murder of police officers to consider, and four counts of possession of illegal weapons. There is only one verdict you can give.''

She went through the evidence step by step citing the testimony in each case: how Epps was located, how the raid was planned, how it actually occurred, how the shooting started, how five cops were severely wounded by the defendant. She was lucid, vivid, forceful, she thought. She talked for two hours.

''Mr. McCarthy is asking you to acquit a man who happens to be black who shot down five police officers who happen to be white. A street thug who shot to kill five other men. He is asking for an acquittal which, if you give it to him on purely racial grounds, will set race relations in this city and country back twenty years. Perhaps more. I beg of you not to do it.''

She paused. ''The evidence against Lionel Epps is overwhelming,'' she told them. ''There is only one verdict you can give.''

When she had finished and sat down, flushed with her own rhetoric and with Coombs's whispered congratulations, she was able to convince herself that she had done her job perfectly, that a guilty verdict was the only one possible, that she had nothing to worry about at all.

Karen returned to her office where she chaired a meeting of her bureau chiefs. She listened to their problems, to suggestions for possible solutions, but couldn't keep her mind on it. She watched the clock. She watched the phone. Werner from budget and management came in after that. She could barely understand what he was telling her. If the case was really as open-and-shut as she hoped and believed, the guilty verdict might come at any moment.

But at 10 P.M. she was notified that the jury had retired for the night, with no verdict having been reached. She went down to the street and had herself driven back to Jill's apartment. It was too late to phone her children, and she had no great desire to talk to Hank tonight, she wasn't sure why. She took a long shower, then came out to the kitchen where she made herself a sandwich. She watched the eleven o'clock news: herself being interviewed in the corridor outside the courtroom. I look haggard, she thought. She turned off the set and went to bed.

—BOOK FOUR—

—21—

She was hanging her coat in the closet the next morning when Betty came in and read out the day's schedule.

"You have the corrections commissioner at eight thirty—overcrowding on Rikers Island. Deputy Mayor Blueberg is next, then the president of the bar association, then luncheon at Borough Hall in Brooklyn—"

"Better cancel the luncheon. The verdict could come in at any moment." A quick verdict was sure to be in her favor. Karen was still confident.

All day she waited, but there was no verdict.

Then it was night again. Wearing a bathrobe, hugging a pillow, she watched an old movie on TV. When the phone suddenly rang she rushed to pick it up.

"Yes, Larry, what's happened?"

The second day's deliberations were over, he said. The jury had again retired for the night. "So I guess we can retire too."

"Yes," said Karen. "Good night, Larry."

Having hung up she thought about calling for her car and going home. Instead she went into the bedroom and began to pull the bedspread down.

* * *

The next day, Saturday, she put on her sweat suit and sneakers and jogged west through Greenwich Village, past the town houses, the restaurants, the smart shops and the craft shops, the galleries. She jogged at a good pace, jogging in place at the corners until the lights changed, then jogging across, trying to jog off the tension and worry. She jogged all the way west to the river, her car trailing behind her, and then out along the long empty pier where she stood breathing somewhat hard and staring down at the water. The Hudson this morning was gray and choppy. She could see other piers up and down the river, all unused now, some of them rotting and collapsing into the water. They had been built for ocean commerce, especially the big transatlantic liners of the past. Nobody came out onto them anymore except joggers like herself, or dog walkers, or in the warm months, the homeless looking for a place to sleep. She remembered when she was a little girl standing up in the back of the car riding past the piers along the West Side Highway. Her mother and father, up front, paying no attention. The liners were moored side by side with only the piers in between, you could count the great smokestacks for block after block. Well, the liners were gone forever with nothing to replace them. You couldn't count the airplanes out at the airports. Her childhood was gone forever too, and there was nothing to replace that either. Having children of her own was not the same thing. And she ought to be thinking more about them, and less about herself.

Her confidence was gone this morning. The verdict should have been reached long ago. It was an open-and-shut case, was it not? And if the jury didn't see it that way, then she was in trouble. She was as low as she had ever been: not good enough to convict Lionel Epps, not good enough to be district attorney of New York County.

The water looked cold. There were no vessels on it anywhere, not even a sailboat. A magnificent natural harbor no longer much used. The calendar said it was now spring, but a cold wind bit against her face, blew through her hair, turned the sweat on her body cold. Turning, she looked back at her car waiting at the head of the pier, the patient Detective McGillis visible behind the windshield. He monitored the radio, and would signal her if her office signaled him. At any moment he might wave frantically, meaning that a verdict had been reached, and she would come running.

However, this did not happen.

There were gulls sailing around over the water, a few of them over her head. The sky was as gray as the water. Her hands were plunged into the pockets of her sweat suit. She did not mind the wind in her face. She kept turning around and looking at the car, reassuring herself that it was there, afraid to let it out of her sight.

Finally she jogged back to it.

"Anything come over?"

"Not a thing, Mrs. Henning."

She began to jog back to Jill's apartment.

Barone in a windbreaker on a ladder was repairing a rain gutter that had come down in a storm. He was brooding about Muldoon, about a man's responsibilities toward his partner. Presently he got down from the ladder, went upstairs, and changed his clothes. His wife found him standing half in his closet knotting his tie.

"I gotta go in," he told her.

"Hey," she said, "you were supposed to do some work around here today. The house is falling apart."

"I'll be back in a couple of hours," he said, giving her a smile and a squeeze on the bottom.

He drove toward the city at his usual speed and a state trooper came up behind him with the red light turning. He pulled over and got out of the car with his shield in his hand.

It made the other cop stop short, his hand on his gun. "Get back in the car," he ordered.

Barone showed his shield. "I'm a New York City detective."

He saw the other cop relax. "Okay," the cop said, "but slow down, for chrissake. You'll kill somebody."

"I'm in a terrific hurry."

"Even so."

They shook hands, leaned on Barone's fender, and exchanged names.

"Where they got you working?" the cop asked conversationally.

As soon as he could, Barone broke it off. Back on the highway again, driving as fast as ever, he was annoyed at the time he had lost. Getting stopped was always a pain in the ass. You had to chat with the guy. If it cost you only five or ten minutes you were lucky.

He parked beside the criminal courts building in a slot reserved for a judge and went in past the security desk and up to the eighth floor. The judges weren't working today and he had left his PBA card in the windshield.

He had expected Karen would be there waiting for the verdict, but she was not. Her office door was closed, and Coombs was seated at her secretary's desk going through the mail.

"What news from the jury room?" Barone inquired.

"Nothing. They're still at it."

"No rumors?"

"No."

"Where's Karen?"

"In her apartment, I think. Or in her car."

To approach Karen on behalf of Muldoon would not be easy. He had been brooding about it for sixty miles. He did not know how he would do it, he did not look forward to it, and he did not believe she would be receptive. She did not owe him any favors. She would not only say no, but would think less of him as well. But Muldoon had asked him to do it, and Muldoon was his partner. He had no choice. He saw no way out.

But she was not in her office, which meant he would have

to go to her apartment. She was Manhattan district attorney. He could not just knock on her door. He needed a pretext.

"She asked me to meet her," he told Coombs. "I guess she meant in the apartment. You got anything you want me to take over there?"

Coombs put together a whole manila envelope full of stuff, which was a great relief.

Karen showered, put on a bathrobe, and lay out on the sofa and tried to study dossiers relating to other cases, other office business. This was work she would have to do sooner or later, so she had brought it home with her, but to concentrate on it was impossible. She stood up stretching, trying to stretch away tension, boredom, worry.

Glancing around, she conceived the notion that the flat was filthy and that it was her job to clean it. At least it would take her mind off everything else. She went into the bedroom where she found a T-shirt and shorts belonging to Jill and changed into them.

The vacuum was in the hall closet and she dragged it out. She vacuumed the bedroom first, moving the furniture around, ramming the power nozzle as far under the bed as it would go. After that she did the main room. She worked mindlessly, once knocking a lamp off a table, catching it just in time. Even housework demanded a certain concentration, it seemed. She warned herself to pay attention, but couldn't. She began to vacuum the windowsills, the moldings, but the machine popped open because the bag was full and though she searched every closet and cabinet in the flat she could not find a replacement.

Which left her staring at the phone again. She began to pace, and as she did so she noticed things she had not noticed before, though she had already explored this flat thirty times. The breakfront in the dining room contained a tea service, a soup tureen, a chafing dish, some silver salt and pepper shakers, all tarnished. After staring at them awhile she got them out and ranged them on the dining room table. Gifts from previous weddings, probably. Hadn't been polished in years, probably. Who had time for polishing silver these days?

She found silver polish under the kitchen sink and began cleaning the silver, scrubbing hard. For the second time that morning she worked up a sweat. She worked clumsily, but realized it only when she broke a handle off the chafing dish. It made her curse.

"Damn," she said aloud. Which failed to express how she felt. "Damn, damn, damn," she cursed.

She pieced the pieces together this way and that, but of course they would not stick, which made her unreasonably furious at herself. She would have to take the thing to a silversmith, still another chore, and she did not have time for all the chores she had already.

At that moment the doorbell rang and she went to it, thinking it must be McGillis, for the car was still outside, ready to rush her back to the courthouse, if necessary. Probably he wanted permission to go to lunch—what time was it, anyway—and she threw back the bolts.

She opened the door and it was Mike Barone.

She faced him barefoot wearing shorts, with her bra showing through her T-shirt probably, feeling sweaty. It was not the way she wanted to see him or anybody else, and there was a moment when she did not know what to do or say.

"Oh," she said, "it's you."

He had surprised her, and she was discomforted by her appearance, but she was certainly not going to show this, much less keep him waiting outside while she ran into the bedroom like some blushing schoolgirl and changed clothes.

Good manners demanded that she invite him in, so she stepped back from the doorway and did so. "How are you?" she said curtly.

Surely he was here for some specific reason and would depart in a moment. She waited for him to tell her what it was.

"I'm sorry if I've surprised you," he apologized.

"You didn't surprise me."

He looked at her as if they had been friends for years, as if his knowledge of her was intimate. It should have been objectionable, but somehow was not, however uncomfortable it made her. She would have preferred a sexy leer which she could have dismissed by getting angry.

"You look nice," he said.

He was tall and wearing a suit and tie. She said: "I look awful."

"Not to me."

She was amazed to hear her voice ask: "How do I look to you?"

"Less like a district attorney, more like a woman."

Since she'd been appointed DA, most of the cops with whom she came in contact had taken, as it were, one or two steps backward, treating her with a deference that had not been there previously. Some were not at ease at all. Not Barone however. He seemed as comfortable in her presence as before.

She said: "You mean like women are supposed to look. Like a cleaning woman or a housewife for instance. Unthreatening to men."

"That's not what I mean at all." He smiled. "I just meant you look real. Earthy. Forgive me. I can't help responding to you."

This was not the type conversation she was expecting.

"I happened to be at the courthouse on another matter," Barone said. "I thought you'd be there waiting for the verdict."

"Well, I'm not."

"I stopped at your office to say hello," he explained.

"All right," she said, "hello." To stop in at her office was one thing, to seek her out here was something else.

"They had a lot of mail for you."

She didn't say anything.

"They asked me to bring it over," he said, and handed her the manila envelope.

"Thank you," she said, taking it.

"This waiting for a verdict is driving me crazy," he said, and stopped and looked at her, as if expecting a response.

"Yes," she conceded, "it's driving me crazy too."

"What do you think it means?"

"Well, you can't figure juries."

"This particular case is not just your case alone," he said. "It's mine too. Today is the third day the jury has been out."

When she made no answer he added: "When the jury stays out this long, it's probably a good sign."

"I don't know what to think." She put the envelope down on a sideboard. "Well," she said, "thanks for the mail."

"No one ever fired shots at me before. That's why it's so personal. I suppose that's the reason."

Perhaps the case was principally what interested him, not her at all. He had needed to talk to someone and had picked her.

To make conversation she said: "When you were on that rooftop and he was shooting at you, were you scared?"

"At the moment, no. It all happened too fast."

"Afterwards?"

"When I started down from the roof my knees turned to mush. I was trying to run down the fire escape. My knees were trembling and wouldn't hold me. I nearly fell down."

She laughed.

"I had hold of the iron banister and my knees let go and I sat down on the step."

She was laughing.

"It's true," he said.

She was touched that he would offer her so intimate a glimpse of himself.

He said: "He fired probably twenty-five shots altogether. He tried to kill us all. He deserves to be convicted."

"Yes."

They looked at each other. His eyes were dark brown, almost black. He had beautiful teeth.

He said: "I haven't been able to sleep through the night since the jury went out. You must be twice as worried. When I stopped at your office I thought maybe it would help me if I could talk to you, and that maybe it would help you too."

They were still in the entrance hall, which seemed to her impolite.

"The time must really be dragging for you," he said.

She nodded.

"Perhaps you'd like a cup of tea," she said finally. I'm always offering him tea, she thought. She didn't know whether to lead him into the kitchen or the living room—or what to do with him after that.

He seemed to sense her indecision. "Listen," he said, "why don't we go out and have lunch? I need some cheering up, and you probably do too."

Should she? It was a way of getting him out of this claustrophobic apartment. And herself out as well.

"There's an Italian restaurant on the corner," he said, but now he sounded much less sure of himself, as if convinced in advance that she would refuse. "Do you like Italian food?"

His discomfort was oddly pleasing. To put him at ease she smiled and said: "I like everything about the Italians." But when she realized how this sounded she was appalled at herself. "I mean—" But it was damage that could not be undone so she stopped.

"We can order a bottle of wine, and maybe we can make each other laugh." He added hesitantly, "And if we can't, at least we can talk about the case."

She said: "I'm not sure whether I want to talk about it or don't want to talk about it."

"Well, what do you say?" It seemed to her he was almost pleading.

For various reasons, sitting in a restaurant with him seemed unwise.

"I'm not exactly dressed for it." She looked down at herself.

He looked down at her too. Again it was in no way objectionable. He seemed to acknowledge who she was, what she looked like. In his eyes she read acceptance on her own terms.

This seemed to her exceedingly strange.

"Change into something. I'll wait."

McGillis was parked outside her door, and would see them come out together. She did not want that. If he had seen Barone come in, probably he had the clock on them already.

Her decision was not to go to lunch with him. Instead she should get rid of him as quickly as possible.

He said: "When we arrested Epps I was supposed to be sitting on the fire escape outside his window with my gun cocked. He wouldn't have been in a position to do anything except surrender. I never expected to meet him coming across a rooftop firing shots at me."

He looked away. "All the arrests I've made, I never was shot at. I've taken weapons off guys who were going at their wives in family fights. I've arrested many guys who were armed. One time we had a call. Stickup in a liquor store. I walked in on two guys with guns and disarmed both of them. Sure I was scared, but not like on that rooftop."

"Sit down," Karen said, gesturing toward the sofa, and she busied herself putting the vacuum away, the dust rag, the can of Endust. She put the silver back in the breakfront, and the polish under the kitchen sink. She sniffed the stink of silver polish on her fingers and put the faucet on and washed her hands.

All this time they talked of the trial, or rather Barone did, coming to stand in the kitchen doorway when she was in there, retreating when she came out. She had conducted the trial impeccably, he told her. Just because the jury had been out a few days was no reason to fear the worst, no reason to blame herself for some imagined failing in the way she conducted the trial.

Karen nodded, for this was what she needed to hear.

But the fact remained that there had been no verdict for three days. "Then why hasn't the jury convicted?" she asked.

"They will. Relax."

By now they were sitting on the sofa, their knees pointed toward each other but not touching. Suddenly he jumped up, reached down for her hand, and pulled her to her feet.

His touch had sent a jolt through her. My God, she thought, he's going to lead me into the bedroom. It's impossible. He's a detective and I'm district attorney of New York County. He wouldn't dare.

"Come on," he said, and led her down the hall. The bedroom was indeed the direction in which they were headed.

"Change your clothes, and let's go out to lunch," he said. He had stopped in the doorway, as if he planned to stand there and watch her do it. All she had to do was peel off her sweaty T-shirt. If she did, then whatever would happen, would happen.

"Lunch?" she said.

"It's not a fancy restaurant," he said. "You don't have to get dressed up. Pants and a sweater will be fine."

"The telephone. I mean—" Was he going to go to the closet, pick the clothes out for her, help her into them? She freed her hand. It was a long time since she had felt hunted, and she no longer knew how to handle it. "I really don't think I can leave the apartment," she said. "I mean I can't go out. I don't want to be too far from the phone." It was a long ragged speech. Avoiding his eyes, she tried to regain control of her breathing.

"Maybe I can fix something here," she said, moving past him out into the hall. "I don't know what there is. I mean—"

She was in the kitchen and he was right behind her. She was in shorts and a T-shirt and barefoot, and this strange man, this detective, was right behind her.

She opened the fridge and bent over to peer into it.

"Would you like a beer?"

"A beer would be nice."

He was at her shoulder, both of them looking into the open fridge. For some reason she was vulnerable today, she did not know why. She was reasonably certain he sensed it.

He said: "I don't want to put you to any trouble."

Not much you don't, she thought, and turned with the beer bottle in her hand and it slipped and she grabbed for it and missed and it crashed to the floor and exploded, soaking her to the shins.

She began pulling at the roller of paper towels. "I'll just clean that up, won't take a moment."

"It's my fault," he said.

"It's not your fault, I dropped it."

"Let me do it."

She was frantically sopping up beer. "I don't know what's the matter with me. I'm not normally a clumsy person."

He said: "Look at your feet." He tore off fresh towels. She felt his hands on her feet, her shins. It made her start blinking.

He stood up and they gazed at each other.

She looked away. She said: "It's going under the stove," and bent to stop it, and then began to push the shards of glass into a central spot, dropping wads of sodden paper into the sink. Barone in his nice suit was bent over beside her. But Karen's fingers had ceased to bend properly, she was working too fast, and she knew before she looked that a splinter of glass had become embedded in her thumb.

Finally the shards were in the garbage pail, the wrung-out paper towels as well. Barone washed his hands in the sink, and then she did.

"You're bleeding," he said.

She held her thumb under the water. "I think there's a piece of glass in it."

He held her hand and studied it. Finally she pulled her hand back, found Band-Aids and a tweezers in one of the cabinets, moved out to the living room where there was more light, and sat down on the sofa and tried to work on her thumb. Barone was beside her sitting almost in her lap. It was her right thumb, and she couldn't make her left hand work the tweezers properly, they seemed to be trembling.

He said: "I'll do that for you."

She said: "I'm not much good with my left hand, unfortunately."

With her hand gripped in his, he delicately probed her thumb. Their heads were very close together. It could not be helped, she could not do it herself, and the splinter had to come out, didn't it. In a moment he lifted the tweezers, holding up a sliver of glass to show her. "There."

He dried her thumb on another paper towel. She let him do it. He tore open a Band-Aid and wrapped the thumb tight, and that was the end of the waiting. His face got bigger and bigger, closer and closer, it was still not too late to change her mind, she might have turned away or stood up suddenly or even said something, but she did none of these things and he kissed her. The kiss went on and on. Her mouth opened of its own accord it seemed, she had been unable to stop it. By the time the kiss ended she was out of breath again, and she looked down at herself. His sleeve or wrist had been brushing her left breast and her nipple had popped up and was showing under the cloth, and the other one he hadn't even touched was showing too.

He stood up, taking her hand, murmuring something, she didn't know what. He had pulled her to her feet. All the strength had gone out of her, and it seemed to her there was nothing she could do to stop him, to stop herself.

In the bedroom she reached to pull the shades down, and the room became darker though not dark enough. Making love in the sunlight was for teenagers with their perfect bodies; she too had been practically new once but wasn't now, she had had two children, she was a woman not a girl. But he had turned her, was peeling the sticky T-shirt off her. Her bra came unstuck too. His head went down. She held his head in her hands and felt him sucking at her and she murmured: "I must taste pretty salty." She could smell herself, she was faintly embarrassed.

"You taste delicious to me." His head came up for a moment, then went back to what he was doing, which felt oh so nice.

It had always amazed her some of the things men liked about women, liked to do with women and to women. Icky things, she had thought at first. With their fingers, with their tongues sometimes. The first time a boy ever put his hand inside her underpants, which was where Barone's hand had somehow got to by now, she had nearly fainted with amazement or embarrassment, maybe both. Not now. She wanted to spread her legs wider, as wide as they would go, but with difficulty restrained herself, did not move.

He shucked his jacket. His hands went to his tie. His shirt came off. She raked her fingers through his chest hair.

She moved around the bed, first one side then the other, pulling the bedspread down. Even at times like this a woman had chores to do. Chores after, too, she would have to change the sheets. He had a nice body, what she glimpsed of it as she worked. She did not want to see too much. She didn't want to see what he had in store for her, she would feel it soon enough, it couldn't be soon enough. She folded the spread hurriedly, and lay back exposed, undignified, the longest wait of all. The most vulnerable moment of all. It had never happened to her, but a man could always walk out on you now, and how would you feel?

She should not be doing this, a dozen reasons crowded into her head in no particular order, all of them there at once. She was Manhattan district attorney, so how could she be lying naked on a bed being gazed at by a detective she hardly knew. And if he talked, as he would, as all men did, it would be worse, she would have no reputation left. Even if he kept silent, McGillis downstairs would not, why should he, something as juicy as this. She was a public figure, and also a woman. A man, a politician for instance, might be seen in her current role, here on this bed, and no one would notice, much less be shocked. But in the case of a female district attorney, the first one ever, the news might sweep the city, Hank would hear, the voters would spurn the adulterous wife and in November vote her out, as Hank might too, she did not think so, but he might.

What about Hank? He was conducting swimming practice at the moment, she believed, would not burst in on her, she was safe on that score at least. There was no way he could find out unless she told him, which she would never do, unless she threw it in his face during an argument someday, but she would never do that either. She was going to take what she wanted, what at the moment she needed. It was her right. She had paid her dues. This wasn't the Middle Ages anymore.

There would be no interruptions unless the telephone rang with the verdict. At the moment she did not care about the verdict, not one bit, all that worry was gone, the nicest feeling of all.

Barone had turned away from her, was tearing something open. She knew what his furtive movements signified, and before he had completed them sat up, breasts swinging, took the half-opened package from his fingers and put it on the bedside table. It signified still other reasons why to do what she intended to do was dangerous and absurd. "You don't need that," she said, feeling for a moment how she felt men must feel: much of the excitement, maybe almost all of it, was in the risk.

"I hate those things," she said.

He studied her with some care. "You're sure?"

"If you are."

Barone could be the most dangerous problem of all. How did she get rid of him afterward? Or even worse, suppose she didn't want to? He embraced her, sweaty breasts tight against his scratchy chest, kissed her as if he were in love, which he could not possibly be, though she herself was, in a way, and that seemed to her still another amazement. She wanted to murmur endearments but stopped herself, said only: "You have no idea how much I want you right now."

When he knelt between her knees, his fingers went to his mouth, and she saw him gathering saliva to lubricate himself with, and she said: "You don't need that either," feeling herself sopping, gaping even, and proud of it.

"You are the most delicious woman," he said. He was

smiling, rearing up in two senses, all of him, and all of a
sudden she thought of Hank again. It was inevitable, and it
made her catch her breath. Where Barone now knelt no one
but Hank had knelt since she was eighteen years old.

He came down over her, and in a moment had reached, it
seemed to her, as high as her heart.

The campus pool, five lanes wide, twenty-five yards long,
was in a long, low-ceilinged room. The water was kept at
sixty-eight degrees, considered the optimum temperature for
fast times, so this was the air temperature as well. A boy was
swimming for the wall. Above him, wearing a sweat suit,
stopwatch in hand, breathing the moist, chlorine-laden air,
waited his coach, Henry Henning.

The boy hit the wall, and Henning, leaning down, showed
him the face of the stopwatch.

"Not bad," Henning said.

The boy lifted himself out of the pool. "No better than last
week," he complained. "I've got to get it down." He thought
about it a moment, then said: "Professor Henning, suppose
I shave off all my body hair like they do at Ohio State and
the other big schools?"

"All your body hair?" Henning nodded thoughtfully and
wondered what to do or say next. The boy's name was Gilfoyle. There were other boys in the pool or standing near the
edges who needed his attention, in one way or another problems every one, but none as immediate a problem as the one
represented by Gilfoyle. Putting his arm around the boy, he
led him off into the corner.

"My head, my eyebrows, everything," said Gilfoyle earnestly.

The room was of course extremely humid. In places mildew
showed on the ceiling or high on the walls. The odor of
chlorinated water hung heavy in the air.

"Shaving off all my body hair ought to be worth at least
three tenths of a second," Gilfoyle said.

This was a small college and the boy was no world-record holder.

"Well, what would your parents say?" Henning hedged.

"I won't tell them."

"Maybe they would guess," Henning said, studying him. "You could eat dinner with your hat on, I suppose. But if you have no eyebrows they might get suspicious."

This was just a kid seeking the approval of his teacher. Henning felt he had to be careful. A boy this age was vulnerable, easily crushed.

"Have you thought this out?" he said carefully. "For instance," he said, reaching for arguments, "how will your girlfriend react?"

"I don't have a girlfriend right now."

Did Henning detect a wistful note? Not every kid was able to make a connection with the female sex, whatever the mores of the times. Older people, Henning knew, imagined that college kids fucked like rabbits. They had no idea what actually went on. The insecurities of the age group had not changed all that much. A boy like Gilfoyle, inexperienced and suffering from acne, was possibly afraid to approach girls at all.

"I know you'd like to have a girlfriend," Henning told the boy. He was speaking slowly, thoughtfully. "And I worry that all the girls on campus might begin to call you Skinhead, and refuse even to date you."

This argument appeared to stop Gilfoyle, though only for a moment. He said: "But I can't think of any other way to get my time down."

Seeking approval, the boy looked at the man and found resistance instead. It shook him, and he began to have second thoughts. "Don't you like the idea?" he asked.

"The season's not nearly over," said Henning. "You're getting stronger every day. Why don't we wait a couple of weeks until you stop improving. Then you can shave your head, shave off your body hair, and if your time drops as a

result, we'll know why, and maybe I'll ask all the other kids
to shave themselves too."

The boy was nodding. He seemed even a bit relieved.
"That sounds good, Professor Henning. You'll tell me when
to do it?"

"Sure will. Now get back in the tank."

Another crisis averted, Henning thought, and he wanted to
smile but couldn't lest Gilfoyle think he was laughing at him.
All he could do was call out to other swimmers. "Tancredi,
Mulligan, Revet, in the tank. Ten laps flat out."

He had no way of knowing what his wife might be doing
at that moment but thought that when he talked to her tonight
on the phone—unless she came home which she probably
wouldn't—tonight on the phone, then, he would describe this
conversation with Gilfoyle, it would make her smile, he was
rather proud of the way he had handled the boy.

Barone proved to be nothing special as a lover. If she closed
her eyes she could easily imagine that the man on top of
her was Hank. It was herself who was different, her soaring
sense of power, this reveling in herself, her body, her
sensations, her excitement. When it was over there was
even a faint disappointment. On the basis of this new experience and very little else she concluded that men were
pretty much all the same, there was nothing different out
there.

Nonetheless, she was still on a high, still pleased with
herself, excited, almost light-headed, nothing to hold back
anymore, no dignity or ceremony to stand on now, nothing
to hide from herself, nor from him either, certainly not her
naked body which he had gazed upon from every point of
view, and she jumped out of bed saying: "And now if you
don't mind I'm going to take a shower."

He reached up for her. "Don't leave me."

"Can't you smell me? I stink."

"No you don't. I love the way you smell."

But she laughed and as she crossed toward the bathroom wiggled her bottom at him.

She did not lock the bathroom door. He would have heard that, and the idea seemed to her under the circumstances rude. In addition perhaps she knew what would happen if the door were only closed, not locked, perhaps even wished it to happen. She had the curtains shut, the water hitting her straight on top of the head and coursing down her flesh. Her eyes were closed, a half smile on her face, and she heard him spread the curtain and step in beside her.

"I need a shower too," he said, "move over."

He began to soap her back, and then the rest of her too, in a friendly, familiar but nonpassionate way. "I have a confession to make to you," he said conversationally. When she looked sharply up at him over her shoulder, he added: "It's not about this. I never dreamed this would happen. I still can't believe it actually did. It's about something else."

She liked his hands on her.

"I want to ask a favor of you."

Her eyes were already closed and she was scarcely listening.

"It's about Dan Muldoon."

Again she half turned and looked up at him.

"They're going to bring Danny up on charges," he said. "I was hoping you could do something for him."

"Charges?"

"Bullshit things."

She was offended at the word—it made her feel common. It seemed to show a lack of respect for her office, for her personally as well. It seemed to proclaim an intimacy which did not exist between them. Yet how much more intimate could they get? These were thoughts that did not make much sense to her. She was confused. She did not really know this man. She should not be standing in a shower with him, he should be calling her Mrs. District Attorney from the witness box, or from the other side of a desk.

While she tried to puzzle all this out, Barone was describing the department's case against Muldoon. "It's all bullshit," he said. "If you were to go to bat for Danny the department would pull back completely."

She was annoyed that he would ask such a thing. It was as if on the basis of a few minutes in bed he had asked to borrow money. But at the same time she was inclined to admire his loyalty, his earnest defense of his friend.

"I can't do that," she said.

"Why not?"

"Because I can't."

"You don't want to."

"All right, I don't want to."

He studied her face long enough to know how serious she was, then grinned at her. "Forget I asked," he said.

She wished he would get out of the shower now so she could get out herself, and that he would get dressed and leave. Instead he began soaping her body again. He had pulled her to him again, her back to his front, her shoulder blades against his chest. He was soaping her breasts, the insides of her thighs, he was soaping her all over, with the inevitable result. First her eyes closed and then her heart began to thump in her chest, and then she realized she had got all excited again, uselessly so, she supposed, for he could not possibly be, not so soon, and being unable to do anything he would leave her unfulfilled in this new state of tension. His knees were pressing against the backs of her knees, she felt that, and then she felt another pressure, pressing against the cleft of her buttocks.

"Well, well, well," she said. "What have we here?"

He half carried her out of the shower. They didn't bother to dry off but began again on the bath mat beside the tub. The mat was none too thick or comfortable, and the water continued to pound down inside the curtain beside them.

"So will you at least think about Danny."

It felt like he was driving her into the floor. "Shut up," she said.

They moved back amid the tangled sheets only when she protested that the floor was too hard. In bed he went on pumping away, he was quite remarkable she supposed, even as she began to get sore, until finally she said, "Stop, that's enough."

She stood up. "It's late, you better go."

He took it well. "Yes, I don't want to be late getting home."

She put a bathrobe on and left the room, having no desire to watch him dress, and afraid he might want to start up again. When he came out he was knotting his tie and he reached to kiss her. She permitted this, why not, it was much less trouble than refusing and having to explain her newly found reluctance, which she herself didn't understand.

"I think I'm in love with you."

"That's nice," she said, meaning the opposite. "Do you always fall in love so easily?"

"It's not so easy. I've been fighting it for months."

This declaration produced a kind of elation in Karen, a warm rush of affection for him too, reactions that shocked her. A declaration of love meant, or at least implied, that now he would pursue her, try to make her love him back. It was impossible. Frightening too. It was simply not possible.

"You're a remarkable woman."

"Thank you."

"Can I come back tomorrow?"

"No you can't." She led him to the door, where she hesitated a moment before speaking again.

She picked up an accordion envelope full of papers from the sideboard. "It's my turn to ask you a favor."

"I'm crazy about you," he said. "You can ask me anything you like."

"My driver is waiting down in the street. You've been up here two hours or more. I'd rather he didn't get any ideas." She thrust the envelope at him. These were documents she had hoped to work on this weekend. She knew she would never get to them now. "Maybe my driver's asleep, but if he sees you come out carrying papers, maybe he'll imagine we were working hard up here."

Barone smiled. "And so we were."

This response annoyed her. "Take these papers back to my office and put them on my secretary's desk."

"That's all?"

"They have to go back anyway." They didn't, but what did he know? "Someone's coming by to get them later." Also a lie, but it was the best she could think of. It was all she could think of.

He said: "It's a pretty easy favor."

She wanted to tell him to please not brag to anyone about what had happened, but could not speak the words such a request required.

"Danny's in pretty bad shape," he said.

"I can't help that."

When she had let him out into the corridor he glanced hurriedly around, saw that it was empty, and took her in his arms and kissed her again. This time she did not respond.

"Think about Danny."

After closing the door she sat down in the living room and stared at the walls. Her entire body ached. Her body revolted her. Her conduct revolted her. She heard herself muttering endearments to this man she hardly knew. She had assumed every obscene pose he'd requested. She had moaned and groaned and begged. Why? It was not sexual ecstasy, she had had that before and knew very well what it was, but sexual delirium, which she had never had before. What had made her behave that way? Nor did she know what she felt for this man now. At a certain moment she had wanted to cry out: Oh I love you, I love you. The words wanted to burst out of her of their own accord. She had barely stopped them.

Thoughts of the trial came back, the absence after three days of any verdict. What could the jurors be thinking about, what were they talking about? They must want to get it over with as much as she. What was there to decide? Epps had fired on cops, wounding five. This had never been disputed.

So why was there still no verdict?

She went into the bedroom to strip the sheets and on the bedside table saw the half-opened condom. She stared at it a moment before bending to tug off the sheets. She stuffed them into a pillowcase, threw the bundle on the floor of the closet, and remade the bed, and when she had finished the condom was still there beside the lamp. Perhaps she should pin it to her chest like a soldier's medal. Or they could have a ceremony in which Barone could do it. Memento from combat. Distinguished Service Cross. Bravery in the face of the enemy. To her it seemed a memento not so much of shame as of what lawyers called procedural error, an irreversible one. Sex: the world's greatest narcotic. Better than alcohol, better than drugs, because it absorbed one's total concentration, and for a while at least made everything else unimportant. It could take you up high, though at times like this it could drop you even further. She touched the condom with one finger. He could have infected her with some disease, even AIDS. Unlikely. And at this moment she certainly felt healthy enough. Or suppose she was pregnant. Unlikely also, it was the second day after her period. She wasn't going to think such thoughts. She turned them off. She had enough to think about. She picked up the half-torn package, carried it by one corner into the bathroom, and flushed it down the toilet.

She wanted to go home but her arms and shoulders ached, and her crotch, and probably there were bruises on her body that she would not be able to explain. Her face felt raw too. So she could not go home. In addition she could not have faced Hank. She had never understood adultery before, hardly believing it to be the crime the law pretended, that people pretended. Gave lip service to, anyway. She saw the gravity of it now. It was not the acts one performed with another, but the degree of intimacy one permitted another, the turning of one's total being toward another, so that for a time the old marriage ceased to exist, as hers did not exist at this moment. The old marriage would have to be remade later, if possible.

It could be remade if one party never found out and the other could succeed at pretense. It would take time, and there would be a strangeness that the betrayed party would certainly feel. And the result would be a marriage different from what it had been.

At suppertime she called home. Hank answered. Even speaking to him across a telephone line was hard, and the conversation was brief enough. She spoke to each of her children, trying to be interested in what they told her, trying to be cheerful.

"When are you coming home, Mom?"

"Soon."

That was Jackie. But Hillary asked the same. "When are you coming home, Mom?"

She had never imagined she would be gone this long. "Soon. The jury can't stay out much longer."

She ached to hold them in her arms, as if this might make her feel more like a mother again, if not a wife. Instead, after a few minutes' conversation, she hung up the phone.

She prepared supper for herself, but ate very little. At nine o'clock her office called: the jury had retired for the night.

"All right," she said, "dismiss my driver." She might have gone downstairs and dismissed him herself but chose not to. In a sense she was hiding from him too. Let the office do it by radio. "Tell him to be back at nine A.M. tomorrow."

She went to bed, but got little sleep.

The next morning, Sunday, she looked at herself in the bathroom mirror and saw, or thought she saw, dark circles under her eyes. She got dressed and went downstairs and her car was there. She leaned in the window. "I'm going to church."

"Get in," said Detective McGillis. "I'll drive you."

Karen had no desire to get out of a limousine in front of the church. She said: "It's two blocks away. If anything comes over, come in and get me." Nothing would come over this early. The jury was in a hotel and had first to be driven back to the courthouse. They would be brought coffee, and only then begin to deliberate. Obviously they were still far from a verdict. If they had been at all close they would have come to it last night and announced it so they could go home.

People had congregated outside the church. They were filing inside. She was immediately recognized. People nudged each other. She heard the whispers, sensed the stares. She went in, sidled into a pew, knelt down and tried to pray, or perhaps only communicate with herself. The new her. It seemed to her that she now existed on a different level from yesterday. If she was capable of yesterday with Barone, what else was she capable of? She felt she had committed a great evil. If betrayal of a loved one, and of a duty, was not evil, what was? She felt severely shaken, and prayers would not come. As a girl she had been devout. She had loved the white dresses and veils, the clasped hands, the sound the organ made. Nowadays, apart from midnight mass at Christmas, which she liked, and high mass at Easter, which she also liked, she did not go to church very often, and did not insist her children go. In a world where countries continued to blow each other up every year, in a city where Harlem teenagers machine-gunned each other to death every day, the church seemed increasingly irrelevant. To a mother trying to raise her children, a celibate clergy had nothing to say.

Nonetheless, she was hoping for a message of some kind, she supposed, but people stared at her throughout the mass and the meaning of the prayers continued to elude her.

"Lord, I am not worthy," the priest intoned, and the congregation, Karen among them, responded: "Lord, I am not worthy."

The mass ended and she walked back to the apartment and began to wait.

Noon came. Nothing. Two P.M.

She phoned her office seeking news, any news, even rumors. To her surprise she got Coombs.

"What are you doing there?"

"Biting my fingernails, what else?"

"Go home. Go to a ball game. Watch television. Don't hang around there."

"I couldn't help it. I had to come in, find out if anyone knew anything."

"All right," said Karen. "What's the latest rumor from outside the jury room."

"They've asked to see the guns again. And the documents."

"The guns? What for?"

"Who knows?"

Another hour passed. She turned on the television. The Yankees were playing somewhere. It was cold, wherever it was, and the wind was blowing. She watched a few innings, then turned it off again. Hank was taking his team to a swim meet in Albany today. He was lucky, he was a man with something to occupy his time.

She had postponed thinking about Barone. He would come here again tonight, she was certain of it. This thought became more and more insistent. She got more and more tense. Because she had told him not to come he would not call first. He would simply come to the door. The bell would ring and she would open it and it would be him. He would reach for her, probably imagining he could tear her clothes off and she would love it. If she knew him at all, that's the way he would think.

Her reaction would be—what?

She had no intention of repeating yesterday. It would be better if she were not here at all. She could go down to her car, go for a drive. She could go out to the movies. The trouble was she did not know what time he would come, and in fact was surprised he had waited this long. How much longer would he wait, make her wait? If she went out, he could be waiting when she came back. She would have to come back sometime. By going out she would have accomplished nothing.

She was not afraid of him. She was not going to run away.

She would face him when he came. She would invite him in and tell him firmly that yesterday was a mistake, that she would not see him again, please go home.

Would he accept that?

He was not a violent man. Of that she was sure. He was really rather gentle. He was really rather sweet.

When it was dinnertime she found she could not eat.

Her office called. The jury had retired for the night.

She was as certain as before that Barone would come, and that when he did she would send him away. The only question was when would he come. She wondered what was keeping him. She took a shower, bathing herself carefully, and afterward put on a satin dressing gown her children had given her on her last birthday. She liked the way it molded her body. She liked the way it felt on her bare skin. She saw no reason why it should give Barone ideas. She could tell him no just as successfully this way as fully dressed, and then, as soon as he had gone, go to bed and to sleep. She began pacing up and down. What was keeping him?

The doorbell rang. She went to it. Her heart was pounding. It seemed to be pounding not only in her chest but in her ears, behind her eyes. She opened the door.

"Hi there," he said, "can I come in?"

— 22 —

Assistant DA Bill Schroeder spoke: "The deceased was an eighty-three-year-old woman who was known to keep large sums of money in her apartment. She was found stabbed and slashed. Yeah, I went up there. It was pretty bad."

This was the weekly meeting of the chief homicide prosecutors. A dozen young assistants sat around the conference table. This group was no longer Karen's business except in the broad sense, Tananbaum was in charge now, but she was there, a legal pad in front of her, because the alternative was to sit alone in her own office worrying about a jury that was still nowhere near a verdict apparently, worrying even more than that about herself and the acts—she thought of them today as crimes—of which she had proven to be capable.

"The crime took place where?" she said.

"The East Side," answered Schroeder.

Karen was surprised. "Not Harlem?"

"No, no. Rich man's country."

For such a vicious crime, this was rare.

Karen wore a freshly pressed green suit over a white blouse that she had ironed carefully this morning, and more makeup than was for her normal, her face carefully made up to conceal what she considered to be the ravages of last night.

"Continue," Karen said.

"The two defendants, a man and a woman, are both white, both addicts," Schroeder said. "The man, known as the Slasher, has a record of prior arrests and convictions that runs to five pages."

To sit at the head of the table which, over her protests, was where the others had made her sit, had raised Karen's spirits somewhat. That all of them continued to defer to her made her feel better. Hundreds of people worked for her. She was district attorney of New York County.

The meeting had been going an hour. Although the crimes described had been heinous one after the other, there had been many laughs, but no one was laughing now.

"Needing money for drugs," Schroeder said, "the Slasher and his girlfriend worked out a plan. The girl, a friend of the old lady's granddaughter, would go up to the apartment, knock, and go in. Before the door closed, the Slasher would run in with his knife, threaten the old lady and rob her. That way the old lady would not know they were together. But what actually happens is a little different. The girl does enter the apartment, calling out: Nanny, I've come to visit you. But the Slasher walks in with her."

"They didn't keep to the plan," murmured Karen. No matter what one's mood or physical condition, the business of the office went on.

"This is my brother, says the girl. Well, it was the best she could think of on short notice. The so-called brother then grabs the old woman from behind, tries to smother her, then knifes her." Schroeder looks up from his notes. "He also broke her jaw and her shoulder."

Karen winced.

"They threw their bloody gloves into the bushes outside the house," said Schroeder, "then went up to 105th Street to buy heroin—"

"Heroin or cocaine?" asked Karen.

"Heroin. This is not your most modern up-to-date slasher. So they buy the junk, and then go to a hotel where they meet the old lady's granddaughter, who is the lover of both of them, by the way, and everybody shoots up."

The tale was becoming grotesque and around the table the smiles had come on.

"Next they go to an Irish bar to celebrate, where the Slasher decides that his prints might be all over the old lady's pocketbook. So he returns to her apartment—walking in and out past the tenant patrol."

Everyone laughed, even Karen, though this day she would not have imagined herself able to laugh at much.

"After putting the old lady's pocketbook and jewelry into a plastic bag and dropping the bag into the river, where it was later found by police divers, the happy trio returns to the same hotel and they shoot up again. After they were arrested, each of the defendants accused the other of being the actual killer. Both were apparently trying to protect the granddaughter."

"What's the granddaughter like," someone asked.

"She's everyone's ideal of what a granddaughter should be," Schroeder said. "Sweet, fragile—what can I tell you."

When the laughter ended this time, Schroeder said: "The question is, what do I do now?"

The question was not addressed to Karen, or to Tananbaum either. Schroeder didn't know whom to address it to, apparently.

It was Karen who answered. "As overloaded as we are," she decided, "we have to have two trials." It's not your bureau anymore, she told herself, let Tananbaum decide. "The irony is that it makes no legal difference who the actual killer is," she said. "They are both guilty of felony murder under the law."

She said: "I want no plea-bargaining in this case." The killing was too vicious. "Take this one all the way to trial," she ordered.

To Schroeder it was obvious that Karen had taken over the meeting. "Do you want me to indict them jointly, Karen?"

"My preference is separately. I don't want the two defendants talking to each other."

There was a buzz of talk around the table. Such indictments might puzzle the juries involved, someone suggested. Yes, someone else said, each jury would hear testimony about the accomplice, but the accomplice would not be on trial and would be nowhere mentioned in the indictment.

"Juries get confused easily," Tananbaum suggested.

It brought Karen's own jury to mind. You're telling me, she thought.

"Is indicting them separately worth the risk?" said Tananbaum.

Karen threw the matter to a vote. All but two of the lawyers sided with her. Well, what had she expected? She was the boss and if you voted with the boss you couldn't go wrong. Even the two who had voted against her quickly added that they really had no strong opinion.

"All right," said Tananbaum, "call it unanimous."

Was irony intended? Karen didn't know and didn't care. For as long as she was in charge they would do it her way. "Who's next?" she said.

The meeting lasted all morning, relentless descriptions of outrageous crimes followed by discussions of the legal problems they engendered.

Karen's mind wandered. She became fixed on herself again, on the jury that did not come in, on her still-unexamined conduct last night, on what her conduct would be this night to come. She sat with a blank, expressionless face, contributed nothing, and Tananbaum, surprised that she allowed it, took over the meeting once more.

"The murder took place in the apartment of the deceased and his common-law wife, with whom he had been living for the past five years, except for the eighteen months he was in jail."

The speaker was Assistant DA Ron Murphy, the newest and youngest of these elite prosecutors.

"During the time he was in jail," Murphy said, "his common-law wife and the defendant had been, as they say, seeing each other."

Deceased, defendant? What did any of this matter to Karen? Really matter?

"The three adults are in one bedroom, and the three children of the wife, all by different men, none of them present, are in the other bedroom."

Karen tried to force herself to pay attention.

Murphy said: "The three adults get into an argument, during which the common-law husband punches his common-law wife in the stomach.

"She says: You shouldn't hit me in front of company.

"That's all right, the other man says, I'm leaving anyway."

Tananbaum murmured something Karen didn't catch, and everybody laughed.

"Well," Murphy said, "the common-law husband walks the other man to the door, at which spot the other man shoots him. Pulls out a revolver and shoots him. Not once but many times. The children heard much of this, and saw some of it. They saw the bullet flashes. They ran past the body of their common-law father into their aunt's apartment in the same building."

After a pause, Murphy said: "The common-law wife later told the detectives she didn't see anything, didn't hear anything, and didn't know anything. The only witnesses I have are the kids."

"The kids are going to take the brunt of this one," someone said.

No one was laughing now. "The defense lawyer is asking to get at them," said Murphy. "I don't think I can prevent him from talking to them."

"No, you can't," said Tananbaum. "Where was this?"

"Lenox Avenue in the Thirty-second Precinct. The detective who has the case was terrific with the kids. I watched him work. You know him, Karen, he's part of your case too, the big fat guy, Muldoon.''

Karen had looked up.

"He had them up in the stationhouse," Murphy said. "He calmed them down, fed them ice cream, got a coherent story out of them. He did a good job.''

Karen, who was in no mood to hear about Muldoon, excused herself and left the room.

During the afternoon she interviewed a succession of young men and women who wished to become assistant district attorneys. Their credentials had been scrutinized at a level much further down, they had survived a number of previous interviews, and it was her job to talk to them now because her predecessor had always done so for thirty-two years. It had become the tradition of the office.

Allocating a minimum of fifteen minutes to each candidate, she put forth her questions, watched how they responded, made notations in their folders, walked them to the door, thanked them, told them they would be notified, and asked her secretary to send in the next name on the list. The final decisions must not seem to come from her. The bureau chiefs would do it. As district attorney she must cultivate a certain aloofness. She could not afford to seem any future employee's friend or sponsor.

From time to time there were interruptions, one of them a phone call from her husband. He had had a call from NYU, and wanted to share the news.

"Hank, that's wonderful," she told him.

"They asked if I could come in and talk to them a week from Monday. Dean Blake, the president, everybody.''

"What do you think it means?''

"I know what I hope it means.''

"I have someone in the office," she said.

"I didn't mean to disturb you. Are you coming home tonight?''

She told him she was not. "I have so much work to do." The jury would deliberate until 10 P.M., she said. "I better stick around."

When this left a glum silence on the other end of the phone, she added: "That's really terrific news, Hank. I'm so happy for you and proud of you."

At 6 P.M., however, instead of sending out for dinner, the jury asked to be returned to the hotel, and the notification went out that deliberations were over for the day. With four unexpected hours in hand, Karen could well have gone home. Instead she had herself driven back to her apartment, where she dismissed her car, telling Detective McGillis she would not need him anymore that night.

She made herself a sandwich and drank a bottle of beer, and after that she paced, and waited for Barone. Though nothing had been said last night and they had not communicated during the day, she knew that he would come, and her whole body was tense with waiting. She knew approximately when to expect him, for he was working a 2 to 10 P.M. tour. The drive downtown would take him about twenty minutes. Say ten twenty. Ten thirty at the latest. McGillis was gone. There would be no one to witness whatever happened next. Of course Barone might leave work early. It was not impossible that the doorbell would ring at any moment, and she had begun to jump every time she imagined she heard movement in the corridor outside.

After about an hour of this her mood turned to acute nervousness, and an hour after that to irritation. By then she had broken out a deck of cards, was playing solitaire on the coffee table, and was brooding about herself uninterruptedly. There was no way she could condone her recent conduct, or consider herself an honorable person. She was not an honorable person. She had betrayed her husband, her family, herself, her station as district attorney. She had behaved like a cheap slut with a man far below her in rank, and she was waiting around in this dismal little apartment for it to happen again.

Her body tingled nonetheless, and she could see Barone's

shoulders, his hands, and wished he would come through the door quickly, make it happen quickly, because her revulsion with herself was getting out of control, and she worried about it turning into a greater force than any of these others that for so many days had been battering her psyche.

It wasn't self-revulsion that got her finally to her feet, that sent her into the kitchen to the phone on the wall. Rather it was the habits of a lifetime reasserting themselves. If she were here when Barone showed up, then what would happen would happen, she would be unable to help herself. Her only hope was to be somewhere else.

She called her office and when the duty officer came on the line asked that McGillis be contacted, that her car be sent around to take her home. After that, she said, if the office needed to reach her, home was where she would be.

It was then quarter to ten. "Ask McGillis to hurry," she ordered. "Tell him I'll be waiting out front."

Pacing, she waited ten minutes inside the apartment, then went downstairs and out onto the stoop where she peered up the street for the car that was not there and that for an eternity did not come. She kept checking her watch. She was biting her lip too, as nervous as she had ever been. Now it was after 10 P.M. Barone would be here any minute. Suppose Barone got here first, then what? Suppose the two cars arrived simultaneously? She saw herself, with McGillis as a witness, striding back into the flat with Barone.

That she would ever do such a thing was not possible. But she might do it. She didn't know what she'd do. As far as Barone was concerned she felt a total weakness of will. However much she told herself that she wanted only to go home, Barone had only to show up to stop her. Or so she feared.

At last she saw headlights coming down the street. She went down the steps to the sidewalk, and it was McGillis, and she tugged open the door of the car.

A second car had come into the street. It stopped a short distance behind McGillis. The streetlight fell on the windshield and she saw that the driver was Barone. They stared at each other, and for a moment she froze where she was. Then she gathered herself and stepped into the car assigned to the district attorney of New York County. She didn't know what Barone thought, what he would do. But she was free of him, at least for tonight. She slammed the door and settled back in the seat. Had McGillis seen him?

"Take me home to Bronxville," she ordered, and made herself small in the corner so that not even her head showed in the rear window.

An hour later McGillis pulled up in front of her house. She thanked him and got out. She had her key ready. She got the door open and went in. She had already forgotten McGillis, remembering him only as she heard him drive away. She went up the stairs.

Henry was sitting up in bed reading a magazine. Karen came into the room and they gazed at each other.

"Come to bed, Karen," Hank said.

"Just let me look in on the children first."

She went into Hillary's room. During the time she stood looking down at her the girl slept soundly and did not move. The door to the hall was closed all but a crack. Karen glanced around in the dim light. The room was a mess, clothing strewn everywhere. She gave a rueful smile and went out.

Jackie, when she bent over to kiss him, came sleepily awake. Though he did not speak, his arms came up and went around his mother's neck, and he clung to her even as he slid back down into sleep again. She remained bent over him, breathing on him, for some time, then disengaged the small arms and left the room.

She lay against her husband in the dark and said: "I'm sorry, Hank."

"There's nothing to be sorry about."

"You must be sex-starved, I've been gone so long."

"You too."

"Intellectually I want to, but my body just won't respond."

"The jury's been out how long, five days? You're under terrific strain, that's all."

"I feel like such a flop. The case is lost. You know it and I know it. And now I'm not even any good as a wife."

"You haven't lost the case. Not yet, you haven't. And you're a wonderful wife, and I'm happy to have you home and to be in bed with you."

For some reason this made her start to cry. She lay in his arms sobbing, and he kissed the tears away. He kept saying: "Hush now, hush, go to sleep, hush."

23

The jury returned its verdict late the next afternoon.

There was the inevitable delay as the lawyers were notified and the prisoner was brought in from Rikers Island. Word that the verdict was coming had spread through the halls of the courthouse and through the district attorney's floors. People gathered outside the courtroom, mostly lawyers working in the building and hurrying newsmen, but also Reverend Johnson's civil rights group, which had kept a vigil in relays on the courthouse steps during the six days the jury was out, and very soon Reverend Johnson himself. All these people began to file through security inside, and after them came others, and the courtroom was full as the forewoman of the jury stood up in her place and the judge addressed her, intoning his words into a kind of religious hush.

"On count no. 1, attempted murder of Police Officer Wiendienst, how say you?"

"On count no. 1, we find the defendant not guilty."

A shout went up. Religion went out the window. There were gasps, moans, squeals. Someone cheered. Someone else burst loudly into tears. Judge Birnbaum was already banging his gavel for order. The liturgy would continue, had to continue. There were four more counts of attempted murder to come, and lesser charges after that, judge and jury were not finished. But to the multitude the suspense was over, the trial was at last over, the remaining parts of the verdict as obvious to all as if known in advance. Those stupefied by what they had heard remained in their places. The rest spilled toward the door, and Judge Birnbaum on his bench banged repeatedly for order.

Finally, with the courtroom more empty than full, order was restored.

"How say you as to count no. 2, attempted murder of Police Officer Schwartz?"

"On count no. 2, we find the defendant not guilty."

The judge and the forewoman carried their ritual to the end, but the solemnity was restricted to the two of them.

At the prosecution table District Attorney Karen Henning stared at her hands and did not once raise her eyes. Justin McCarthy was grinning and slapping Lionel Epps on the back, but she did not see it. Reporters were pushing their way out of the courtroom to get to the phones, or else were pushing forward to interview the principals as soon as the judge would have left the bench. She did not see that either.

At the pay phones in the corridor a reporter had got through to Norman Harbison in his campaign office, asking for a comment. "What?" said Harbison. "What?" To the reporter Harbison's voice sounded gleeful. But it quickly became dolorous. "I am of course very disheartened by such a verdict. However, it goes along with what I have been saying about incompetence. Well, the voters will have a chance to change all that in the fall."

The reporter as he broke the connection did not see the big grin that came onto Harbison's face, did not see him stand up, come out from behind his desk, and clap his hands together with pleasure. But he imagined it and he thought: That will be tomorrow's story, Harbison would be worth talking to tomorrow.

Though the courtroom had almost completely emptied out, Karen and Coombs sat in stunned silence at their table.

"It was an open-and-shut case," Coombs said. "Open-and-shut."

Karen, who was close to tears, shook her head. She said: "Let's go." They gathered up their papers and made their way up the aisle.

Outside the courtroom they saw that the mob of reporters had surrounded McCarthy, who was giving an interview in the grand manner. A little way off Reverend Johnson was giving another.

"I find it the obvious verdict, the only fair verdict," they heard Johnson say.

"Justice, being destroyed, will destroy," McCarthy said. "Being preserved it will preserve."

"The jury has proven its wisdom," said Johnson, "and the perfection of the democratic way."

The reporters around McCarthy all began shouting at once so that no single question could be heard. The lawyer cupped his ear as if straining to hear, though why, Karen wondered bitterly. He wasn't answering questions, he was making an oration.

"Justice is the soul of the universe," he said. "Justice alone satisfies everybody."

"Is this your sweetest success?" a reporter shouted.

This question McCarthy heard. Or else he had a speech ready on the subject and had been waiting to get it in: "Success is a good thing," he declared. "Honor is better. But justice excels them all."

"What does this verdict mean?" a voice shouted.

"Does it send a message?" shouted another.

"The message," said McCarthy, "is that white cops can no longer shoot down black youths without a response. Write it down. It is a message you must broadcast to the world. No more black power. From now on, black firepower."

Karen had got out the courtroom door and ten feet further on but there her progress stalled, the mob around McCarthy had somehow enveloped her too. Unable to move forward or back she was obliged to listen one after another to his pronouncements. They made her flinch and though she tried to push her way into the clear, this proved impossible. She managed only to get further into the mob and soon was surrounded so closely that Coombs beside her fought to give her room to breathe.

McCarthy noticed her. She saw him lunge in her direction, his arm snaking around her shoulders as if she were his girlfriend, and he bent to whisper in her ear. She shook free of him, her face dark with anger, and resumed pushing forward.

"What did you tell her?" screamed the reporters.

She heard McCarthy laugh. "I offered her my condolences. She is a gallant opponent and a gallant lady. It is not easy to lose."

Now she had left him behind and was striding down the corridor, but suddenly the reporters abandoned McCarthy, swelling around her instead, again impeding forward movement, bombarding her with questions that were so many and so loud as to be incomprehensible. Microphones were thrust into her face. It was her turn now to make pronouncements and she realized it. She could make any speech she cared to. She might talk about justice, might weep for justice. She might weep for racial understanding, for opportunities lost again today. She might speak of a divided America, for that's what today's verdict was about. Of a people who are exiles in their own country and who, increasingly, won't play by the common rules. She might cry out a warning: Don't you see what this verdict means? Don't you see what is happening in this country? That blacks hate whites and vice versa, that it is getting worse, and if this goes on there is no hope for any of us. This was her chance to say something brilliant, she told herself. But in America brilliance was reserved for winners. People would see only her pain, and for this reason would scoff at any words she might speak. There were no brilliant losers. And so she opted to say nothing. She opted for dignity and restraint, and this proved less difficult than she would have imagined, for there was no other course open to her.

She could not decode all the voices, had no idea what anyone was asking her. "The jury has decided," she said. "The jury has decided," she said again. She kept saying it. "Under the American system, there is nothing more to say."

She kept pushing through the crowd. She wanted only to get away. When she was nearly clear a single question did pierce the noise, and other voices took it up.

"In the light of today's verdict, are you going to resign?"

"Yes, are you going to resign?"

"Will you turn in your resignation?"

And for a moment all fell silent and waited for her reply.

Karen said nothing, merely kept pushing forward. At last she was free of them, with a clear view down the immensely long corridor, but there was another smaller group off to one side, a different interview in progress; one of the jurors was explaining the verdict, it seemed. She didn't want to hear this, what difference did it make, but the juror's voice was loud, she could not escape it.

"Are there rogue cops?" the voice asked rhetorically. "Could those cops have gone there to murder the defendant?" It was the forewoman of the jury speaking. Her name was Wilkins, Karen remembered. She was a welfare clerk. She had a husband and children. "Could the defendant have shot those police officers in self-defense?" Mrs. Wilkins asked rhetorically. "Could it have been like Mr. McCarthy said? Maybe. We had a reasonable doubt, and that's what we voted."

Karen boarded the elevator, got out on her own floor, and as she walked down the corridor people commiserated with her. They came out of their offices to do it. She did not respond.

In her own office she and Coombs sat staring at each other across the desk.

"What did McCarthy say to you back there?" Coombs asked her.

"He said: Don't worry, you'll get him next time, he can't help himself."

"And he's a lawyer."

"Yes, he's a lawyer."

"It was a racist verdict, and you should denounce it as such," Coombs said.

She said nothing.

"The evidence was overwhelming," he burst out. "How could the jury disregard it?"

"I don't know."

"The jury system failed."

"Yes, this time it failed."

Her chief public relations officer came in. "I'm getting a lot of calls," he said hesitantly.

"I suppose you are," Karen said.

His name was Bert Pinckney. "There's a rumor spreading that you intend to resign," he said.

Karen did not respond.

"They're all calling up about it," said Pinckney apologetically. "I don't know what to say."

The door to her office was open. She had resolved that she was not going to hide from anyone. She saw the police commissioner enter her anteroom, accompanied by several of his commanders in uniform, and although Betty tried to stop him, he strode in on her.

"This is an outrage," the PC said. "I'm outraged. There will be thirty thousand cops outraged as soon as they hear."

Karen said: "I'm outraged myself, Commissioner."

"Five cops shot, two of them disabled for life, and the assailant walks."

"He won't walk, Commissioner. He was convicted of the gun charges. He'll do time."

"A year?" the PC sneered.

"Several, I think."

"What do I tell my men? The prosecution was incompetent. The DA sold you out."

Karen's restraint was beginning to desert her.

The PC said: "I don't see how you can look me in the eye, look any cop in the eye."

She began to get angry. "Did it ever occur to you that maybe you lost that trial, not me?"

"Are you going to resign? Or wait for the governor to fire you?"

"Lost it last week when the black kid stealing oranges was shot by the cop."

The PC said defensively: "It looked like he had a gun."

"Lost it last month when cops killed the deranged black woman."

"She came at them with a knife."

With increasing intensity Karen fought back. "Lost it with years of racial slurs and humiliations, years of corruption and brutality."

"Lady, I have thirty thousand cops. There's no way to eliminate that entirely."

"There are cops in the ghetto precincts who behave like an army of occupation," Karen said. "Whose fault is that? Cops who have contempt for the people they serve. Cops who are not trained well enough, not supervised well enough. Whose fault would you say that is? Who's responsible for the climate that exists between the people and the police? Is it me?"

"This is preposterous," the PC said.

"You're not leading your department, you're just sitting on it."

"Don't you talk to me like that."

"Cops also do hundreds of brave and generous acts each day and no one even hears about it. They ought to. That's your fault too. Lionel Epps shot five cops and the jury didn't see it as a crime. I can't beat that. I can't go into the jury room with them. Unless you lead the people back to the cops and the cops back to the people, you're going to get plenty more verdicts like this one. Now get out of my office and don't come back until you're ready to apologize.''

The PC and his entourage stormed out. Everything Karen had said was to her absolutely true, and for a moment she seemed to see the verdict in perspective. She had lost a skirmish, not the war, and on a personal level she had driven the police commissioner from her office. If there had been any audience besides Pinckney and Coombs, it might have stood up and cheered.

"What do I tell the press about your future plans?" Bert Pinckney said apologetically, and it brought Karen back down to earth. The police commissioner was gone. Her moment of triumph was over. It had been short-lived. The PC was all of it. She gazed at Pinckney. Her rage was gone. It had left her drained and near tears. She went behind her desk and scribbled a few words on a letterhead.

She handed it to her press officer. "Please forward this to the governor.''

Pinckney read it, shook his head sadly, and left the office.

"What did you write?" asked Coombs.

"I hereby offer my resignation as Manhattan district attorney.''

"Oh, Karen.''

"The PC's right. Everybody's right. I should have found a way to win.'' She paused and looked at her young assistant. "I don't have any choice, don't you see?''

She began thrusting things into a briefcase. Her eyes were moist. Coombs saw this and came forward to embrace her, but she shrugged him off and started out of the office.

"I'll go with you," said Coombs. "I think you need company.''

She shook her head: No. She went out.

McGillis drove her back to the borrowed apartment. As she let herself in, the phone was ringing but she did not answer it. She went into the bedroom and began throwing

things into her suitcase. The clock beside the bed said it was
5 P.M., which made Karen stare at the television set. There
would be news broadcasts starting on all the networks. Finally
she switched the TV on, but instead of watching it went to
gaze out the window. Behind her an anchorwoman read the
news. The Epps verdict was the lead item.

". . . There are unconfirmed reports that Manhattan District Attorney Karen Henning has offered her resignation following . . ."

Karen switched off the TV. The phone began to ring again.
She did not answer. A little later the front doorbell rang.
Barone, she thought, and did not answer that either but instead
went back to the window. Presently she saw him come out
of the building and get back into his double-parked car.

It got dark in the room. Karen, who had stopped packing,
sat on the bed beside the open suitcase and stared at nothing.
The phone rang several times more. The dinner hour came
and went. She was not hungry and did not move from where
she sat.

Still later she stood at the window sipping tea. When the
doorbell suddenly rang, she gave a start of surprise. Putting
her cup down she went down the hall, peered through the
peephole, then threw the various bolts and opened the door.
Outside were her husband and children.

Hillary said: "Hi, Mom, how're you feeling?"

"We've come to get you, Mom," said Jackie.

She embraced her children, and then her husband.

"I've offered my resignation," she said.

Hank grinned at her. "The governor rejected it."

Karen tried to absorb what this meant.

"We heard it on the radio coming down. He denounced
the jury and the verdict."

"You know what he said, Mom?" Jackie piped up.

"That law enforcement wasn't a football game," Hillary
said.

"Yeah," said Jackie, "you don't fire the coach every time
you lose."

"He said you had done a fine job and he was asking you to stay on," Hank said.

Karen was under no illusions about the governor. To accept her resignation would be to admit that he had made a bad appointment. He had appointed her so recently that his own prestige was tied to her. In defending her he was only defending himself. He had had no choice.

"I didn't do a fine job," she said.

"Shall I call him up and tell him to reconsider?"

She had detected pride in Henry's voice—pride that his wife had the governor's support, pride that his wife was district attorney.

"Oh, Henry," she said.

He was a teacher. He didn't understand the degree of her humiliation. The people she dealt with would feel sorry for her. He didn't see how difficult it would be to carry on in her job, even to meet anyone's eye.

"Get your things, Karen, and let's go home."

And what about the election in the fall? She didn't even know if she wanted to run, but she wanted to be asked and now probably would not be. When some other candidate was selected everyone would know she had been passed over, would whisper behind her back, her ignominy compounded. She wouldn't even be able to resign but would have to stay on in office until her successor arrived, Harbison probably, then slink away shamed.

Hank carried her suitcase down to the station wagon. The children got into the back and they started home. Hank was at the wheel driving one-handed. With the other he held her hand, and she thought of Barone, who would have to be dealt with, still another problem, and not the least of them. And so she stared straight out over the headlights and suffered. Whatever was to happen, she deserved it. She had brought it on herself. But there would be nothing left of her. In the back seat Hillary was leaning forward, her face between her parents. Jackie was standing up, his arms around his mother's neck. The family was all together for a change and that was very nice, and Karen was trying to concentrate on how much she loved them all, each of them smiling happily every time she looked at them, and from time to time she managed to force herself to smile in return.

— 24 —

Everywhere Barone looked he saw Karen. He wanted to comfort her, to hold her, to be with her, and if this was not possible he wanted to talk to her at least. But when he phoned she did not take his calls, nor did she return them.

Every time he entered the squadroom he sang out: "Any messages for me?" He made his voice sound cheerful, which he wasn't. The answer was always the same: No. Finally he drove downtown from Harlem and as he rang the bell of her apartment he was as nervous as a teenager.

A strange woman peered at him through the peephole. He had to show his shield before she would open up. She was the apartment's owner, apparently. She was just back from somewhere, apparently. At this time of night, she said, Karen was probably in bed in her house in the suburbs. What time was it, said Barone. Nearly midnight, she told him. He apologized profusely and backed away.

He resolved to forget Karen, and tried but couldn't, and didn't know why. After a few days, he went down to the courthouse, entered by the district attorney's door on Leonard Street, and took the elevator up to the eighth floor to her office. Her secretary, who was used to seeing him, said she was down the hall somewhere. Barone went looking for her.

He looked into every office on the floor, and after that loitered in the corridor. Presently he saw her get out of an elevator. She was talking to someone as she approached and at first didn't see him. When she did he thought she faltered for a moment, a good sign, but her greeting when she reached him was cool, as was the smile that went with it, and instead of stopping she continued into her office as far as her secretary's desk, where she turned and said:

"Well, Detective, what can I do for you?" She was standing beside the desk shuffling through telephone messages.

The hallway would have afforded some privacy. In here there was none.

"Can I see you in private?"

Law enforcement was a place of so many confidential investigations that a request of this kind raised no eyebrows.

She said: "What's it in reference to?"

When he did not answer she bent over her appointment book. "I'm pretty busy today," she said. "Maybe tomorrow or the next day. Work it out with Betty."

She started into her own office but stopped in the doorway. "Nice to see you again," she said, and closed the door on him.

Betty looked up from the appointment book. "How about the day after tomorrow at four o'clock."

"I'm working at four o'clock," Barone said, gazing at the closed door. "Look, I'll have to call you."

He went down to his car where he sat behind the wheel staring out through the dirty windshield. His sense of loss was the most acute of his life. He went back to the precinct where he tried to write her a letter on one of the Selectrics with the broken keys. The machine could type out words like *perpetrator* and *aforementioned* all by itself or so it seemed, but not what he wanted so much to tell her, and in any case he was interrupted by a serious commotion in the street, and he went to the window to see what it was.

Reverend Johnson had decided to march on the Three-Two Precinct.

The holy man was in possession of a permit allowing him and his demonstrators to march from 125th Street (now officially Martin Luther King Boulevard) up Lenox Avenue (now Malcolm X Boulevard) as far as 135th Street where the buses they had come in would be waiting, and where they were supposed to disband and go home. Johnson had had his permit for some time. It was pure coincidence that it carried a date so close to the end of the trial, when passions were still so high. Logically the verdict should have come days previously, and logically Epps should have been convicted. But it hadn't and he wasn't.

Seeing no need to waste a perfectly good permit, Johnson had decided to stage the march anyway. He had chartered the buses, had rounded up his core demonstrators, and in a state of triumph and general euphoria, with the usual banners waving in the breeze, the march had got under way only about an hour late, moving uptown between two files of policemen in riot helmets who had been drawn from other parts of the city and who were under strict orders not to confront the demonstrators.

It was a mild early-spring afternoon and television crews filmed the march, and hundreds of people lined the sidewalks watching and cheering.

The permit did not allow the marchers to cross 135th as far as the stationhouse itself, as this seemed likely to provoke a confrontation with Three-Two cops, which Johnson said he didn't want, and which the police department certainly didn't want. With five of their number shot and the assailant acquitted, there would be no telling how Three-Two cops would react.

Upon reaching the prescribed end of the march the demonstrators coagulated around the buses, handed their signs to Johnson's men, and began to climb on board, and the riot police relaxed and began to look away or even walk away. But some twenty or thirty young men suddenly took off running, sprinting west across town in the direction of the stationhouse.

The riot police were commanded by a captain. His orders

had been to contain the line of march, and he had done it. He had not been ordered to send his cops running after a group of young men who already had half a block's head start. This would have looked unseemly, cops chasing people they couldn't catch who were not breaking any law anyway. It was undignified. It would look very bad, and would probably have been ineffective as well. Black kids, in this captain's experience, could run like the wind. Faster than cops, certainly. So he let them go.

Many of them were not kids. When they realized there was no pursuit they slowed to a kind of loping walk, and as they passed in front of all the idlers standing on doorsteps and on corners, they began to recruit them: Come on in with us, man, we are not going to obey any regulations laid down by the city, by the poh-leece, we are going to march right up in front of where they live and see how they like it.

By the time they reached the stationhouse in the middle of its block there were over a hundred of them.

On security duty on the stoop stood a single cop. There were eight cars on patrol at that hour, all of them out in their sectors, plus two detective cars which were out also. The stationhouse itself was manned by a handful of administrative cops. Upstairs in the squadroom were four detectives, one of them Barone.

The mob, and by now it could qualify as a mob, was not led by anyone. It had coalesced around an idea rather than a person, a somewhat complicated idea with several facets, all related. Part of the idea was to celebrate the great victory won in court, and part was to rub cops' faces in that victory; part was to prove that today's marchers, in the light of that victory, could go anywhere they wanted to go; and part was merely to taunt and deride any Three-Two cops who could be found.

All of this was unspoken. In many heads it was only vaguely realized or not realized at all. The idea was to affront the Three-Two cops, not confront them, but no one had worked out how this was to be done. A mob after all is a mob, and by definition has no common focus, no sense of responsibility, and it recognizes no limits. The individuals composing this particular mob only wanted to let off some steam, holler a bit, and leave. But the mob as a whole had a different dynamic.

The mob flowed along the street, and in front of the stationhouse stopped and began chanting slogans. A number of cops came out from inside. Barone was among those who came down from upstairs. They stood on the stoop watching. The precinct captain came out, saw the size and mood of the mob, and decided his stationhouse was about to be stormed. He ran back to the desk and ordered a sergeant to call in the sector cars as reinforcements.

There were about ten cops and detectives on the stoop by then, and with such an audience to play to the mob found that mere slogans were insufficient. The mob's mood changed from one second to the next. The slogans became curses, vilifications. Men taunted the cops, dared them to react. Men shook their fists.

Fine, thought Barone watching carefully. So far, no problem. He was not armed except for his short-barreled revolver in its holster in his belt, but so far nothing about this mob worried him, much less frightened him. There was not even any traffic tie-up to worry about. Very few cars passed in front in the course of the day because fifty yards further on was the park, and because nearly every building on both sides of the street, apart from the stationhouse itself, was burnt out and empty.

The sector cars began to arrive, sirens wailing. Some of the drivers as they climbed out left their sirens on. Instead of frightening the mob, this noise seemed to inflame it.

It could be said that the mob consisted of two parts, those at the front who directed their emotions toward the cops on the stoop, and those at the rear who, lacking direct contact with all that, were somewhat bored. They felt ignored. This rear part of the mob, glancing idly around, noticed the row of cars backed against the curb behind them—the cops' personal cars. They could see the police cards in the windshields, and in any case in such a street who else's could they be?

These men at the rear felt both protected and obscured by those in front, and one of their number grasped the nearest car by its bumper and started it rocking. This seemed an excellent idea and in a few seconds others had this first car by its bumpers and fenders, the rocking increased, and in a moment the car went over onto its side. A second car went over all the way onto its roof, and a great cheer went up.

At first no one up front realized what was happening, not the cops on the stoop or getting out of the sector cars, not the demonstrators facing forward, all of whom now turned to see what this commotion in the rear might be about. The demonstrators liked what they saw. Tipping over cars looked interesting, it looked like fun, and it seemed a fit expression of their mood as well, and groups of men spread out among the entire row of cars, rocking them, flipping them over, smashing windows with boards or rocks found in the street.

Most of the sector cops had been standing by their cars waiting to be told what to do. They imagined they were controlling the mob in an enclosed space. They couldn't see the first cars go over but the cops on the stoop could and they started pointing and screaming. Some of them rushed inside and came out with night-sticks, and they jumped down into the street to defend their cars. Among them was Barone, for his own car, he had seen, was already surrounded and rocking. He moved into the mob flailing, trying to reach his car. He and the cops around him were using their sticks like machetes to cut a swath to their cars. They laid open some heads and men went down, but in other cases the sticks got ripped out of their hands and were used against them, and they themselves began to go down and, once on the pavement, to get beaten or trampled.

One of the cops fought his way back to his sector car and called in a signal ten-thirteen, assist police officer, which caused police cars to come pouring in from every corner of the division, sirens wailing, more and more cops jumping out into the melee, their clubs swinging. What was later described as a police riot was now well under way.

But the forces of light, as they saw themselves, were badly outnumbered still, and getting the worst of it from the forces of darkness. Inevitably a cop drew his gun and fired. He fired into the air, only a warning shot, but warning shots were strictly forbidden by regulation because studies showed that they not only did no good most times but often started everyone else shooting too, frequently with tragic results.

Which was what happened here. Many guns came out, including some from the pockets and waistbands of the demonstrators, and when one man showed what looked like a gun—the later investigation showed the "man" to have been seventeen years old and the "gun" to have been a pair of sunglasses—a cop shot him dead. Barone's gun too was in his hand by then for he had lost his nightstick and was using his short-barrel .38, his finger outside the trigger guard, to club open people's heads.

About ten shots were fired in all, and they ended the riot. The demonstrators took off running, except those dazed or unconscious or shot on the ground, all of whom except for the dead man were wrestled into handcuffs and arrested. Other arrests were made later in the emergency rooms of the two local hospitals where demonstrators had gone with bullet wounds, or to get broken bones set or wounds stitched up.

Breathing hard, his hair in disarray and his nose bleeding, Barone stood in the now silent street and pushed his gun back into its holster. Then he went over to his car. He had not managed to reach it in time. With the help of four other cops he got it back on its wheels. Its roof was caved in and one window smashed to smithereens. He looked down at himself. His suit was ruined too, great tears in the left sleeve and the right knee. A $500 suit with one knee showing through. He signed out and went home, and this would prove to be a mistake because investigators from Division, and an hour later from internal affairs, descended on the scene and began checking cops' guns, collecting all those that had been fired. Four cops were in the hospital by then, two with broken hands, one with a broken leg, and the fourth one shot in the side; but the only other cop not still present, and whose gun therefore could not be checked, was Detective Third Grade Michael J. Barone.

Earlier a single television crew, three men from Channel 7, had followed the demonstrators across from the buses on the off chance that something might happen. They had jogged part of the way but the cameraman and the soundman, both lugging heavy gear, could not run very fast very long so they were late getting to the riot. However, they knew what to do when they got there. The soundman got on top of a car with his microphone. The cameraman shinnied most of the way up a lamppost and made footage he hoped might win him a prize or at least a raise. The reporter was as close to the action as he could get, his back to it, facing the camera, doing his stand-up with a riot going on behind him.

Most of this footage would be shown on Channel 7 that night. A number of faces were identifiable, one of them Barone's, and one of the most vivid sequences showed him swinging his gun, which he held cupped in his hand, into faces as he fought his way to his car.

This riot, which had been provoked by the police, according to Reverend Johnson, of course caused a great furor in the city, one that did not die down because Johnson kept giving interviews that threatened new demonstrations, and because Channel 7's footage, which some commentators said in voice-over showed the unprovoked clubbing by the police of peaceful black demonstrators, was quickly licensed to other stations, where it was shown and reshown over and over again for a week. There was no way any regular television viewer could avoid seeing it less than four or five times.

Newspaper editors and editorial writers would not let it be either. Some favored the police account of the event, some were against. The mayor was under terrific pressure, and so therefore was his police commissioner. The mayor wanted a decisive investigation and people punished, and he wanted this fast before the whole city blew up. With his job on the line, Malloy had to come up with something, and he called in Chief Pommer.

Pommer said he could serve up Detective Muldoon's head on a platter, if the PC wished, that work had already been done, but anything else would take time, the cops were all lying, protecting themselves and each other, and he needed a copy of Channel 7's film to check the faces and the stories against and they wouldn't hand it over.

Malloy told him for chrissake tape it off the TV and make something happen. And as for Detective Muldoon, what the hell did he have to do with the riot, he hadn't even been working that day.

"Muldoon was at the root of the Epps case," explained Pommer, "and the Epps case was at the root of the riot."

The PC grew thoughtful. "All right," he said, "what do you have on him?"

Pommer outlined what the charges against Muldoon would be.

"Paper discrepancies," said the PC. "Unvouchered evidence. Jesus."

"Missed court appearances, the gun in his locker, those things are potentially serious," insisted Pommer.

"What do you have on the other guy, his partner? The two of them together might have some impact."

"Not enough."

"You're some investigator."

"I had a man in their car for months."

"I thought I told you not to do that?"

"You told me they were heroes until the trial was over. Well, it's over."

The PC realized he had been disobeyed, but he knew better than to go into that now. He couldn't afford to fight Pommer too. He would take care of Pommer some other time. His problem right now was something else and it was pressing. His thoughts returned to Muldoon. Finally he said: "You got charges against him that have nothing to do with the Epps case, and nothing to do with the riot either.''

However, the more he thought about it, the more Pommer's suggestion seemed sound. Muldoon had become a name because of the trial, and to sack him for whatever reason might relieve the pressure a little. It was action and it was quick. It would buy him some time.

So the next day Pommer filed charges against Detective Third Grade Daniel Muldoon. There were fourteen specifications, fewer than Muldoon had thought on the day he had sought help from Barone, none that Muldoon had not expected. According to Pommer these charges were grave ones, entailing upon conviction possible dismissal from the department with loss of pension, and he ordered Muldoon busted to uniformed police officer and suspended without pay awaiting departmental trial.

At the stationhouse former detective Muldoon's gun and shield were taken from him. He was ordered to clean out what remained in his locker. As he left the stationhouse the cops on duty at that hour were lined up to shake his hand in sympathy, but he was unable to meet anyone's eyes. There were tears in his eyes he was trying to hide and he did not or could not speak.

He went immediately to a bar where he began to drink himself insensible. Barone stayed with him as long as he could.

"Fucken departmental trial," Muldoon muttered once. "They'll fire me off the job. You know they will."

Barone did know. No one got acquitted when it had gone as far as this.

"They can't take your pension away from you," he said. "The charges aren't serious enough."

"They can do anything they fucken want to do."

This was true too.

"If they do it, you can sue and get your pension back."

"Fucken lawyers," said Muldoon.

Barone could do nothing except give his partner's shoulder a sympathetic squeeze.

"How about laying off the sauce now," said Barone. "You've had enough."

But Muldoon wouldn't, and eventually Barone had to leave him and go to work.

The suspension of Muldoon did not calm the city, nor ease the mayor's pressure on the police commissioner, or the PC's on Chief Pommer, and five days later Pommer filed new specifications charging unauthorized use of weapons and other breaches of department regulations against seven cops whose faces were identifiable on the Channel 7 tape, the best known of whom, because of publicity connected to the Epps trial, was Detective Mike Barone. All seven were similarly suspended without pay.

Karen was distressed to learn of Barone's suspension. She could not stop worrying about him. With no money coming in as he waited for trial, how would he support his family? What was he to do if dismissed from the department? How much did being a cop mean to him? She realized that she didn't know him well enough to say.

She supposed he would come to her for help. She expected her phone to ring; she would have to take the call. He would put her in an impossible position. It was help she would be unable to give. He must see that, she told herself, but felt sure he would not. He had asked her to help his partner, and now would ask for help for himself. But the days passed and no call came. She found this admirable. She was both surprised and impressed, and almost wanted to phone him up and thank him.

A grand jury had been empaneled to investigate the cop's fatal shooting of the teenager. Tananbaum was in charge, but Karen considered the case so important that she wanted regular reports. The grand jury, twenty-three people almost evenly divided between men and women, whites and blacks, was meeting twice a week to hear witnesses and consider evidence.

Now with Barone and the six others suspended, these cases were put before the grand jury too.

At once Karen stepped back completely, ordering her press office to release a statement to this effect to the media. Inasmuch as the recent Epps trial had involved certain of these same police officers, her statement read, she was recusing herself; she would have no further contact with the grand jury or its deliberations.

A week later she happened to meet Tananbaum in the corridor. The grand jury had just voted not to indict anyone, he told her. The shooting was justified given the conditions under which it occurred, and against the other seven cops there was no evidence of wrongdoing at all. ''The riot was caused by the demonstrators, not the cops. The charges against the cops stem from the police brass going into hysterics,'' he said.

Karen knew how worried all eight of the cops must be, snapping at their wives and kids, not sleeping nights. Nonetheless she ordered Tananbaum to hold off his announcement until next week; she would give the city one more week to cool down lest the grand jury's decision start some new disorder.

So that's the way it was done. The city took the news calmly, even in Harlem, which had drifted back into the apathy in which the poor all over the world sought refuge. The community still believed that an outrage had been committed against it, but what was one more among so many? Anger had all been dissipated by then, the fire had gone out.

Muldoon went on trial in the fourth-floor trial room at police headquarters before the deputy commissioner of trials who would serve as both judge and jury. This was not a criminal trial and the burden of proof had shifted from the prosecution to the accused. Muldoon would have to prove that the charges against him were not true, and he did not know how; or perhaps, given his overpowering contempt for headquarters and for the police hierarchy, he chose not to bother. His lawyer, provided by the police union without charge, was unable to influence Muldoon's conduct.

Based on the testimony of Chief Pommer's witnesses, the deputy commissioner found former detective Muldoon guilty on twelve of the fourteen counts and recommended that he be dismissed from the department with the forfeiture of all pension rights.

Anxious to show the mayor that he could be stern when the situation required it, the PC approved this recommendation as soon as it reached his desk, and Muldoon was so notified. After twenty-six years he was no longer a cop.

Next would come a similar trial involving Barone and the other seven accused—for the cop who had killed the teenager had now been charged too.

Two days before this trial was to start Karen wrote a letter to the police commissioner. She wrote it out by hand. The charges against Detective Barone, she wrote, were twofold: improper use of his firearm, but the grand jury had found no proof that he had fired it; and leaving the scene of an investigation, which had been perhaps only an accident. She said that in her opinion the police department could not afford to lose an officer of Detective Barone's caliber. She said she had worked with him on two major cases, and both times he had been of inestimable help to her. She described him as shrewd, hardworking, dedicated, in every way honorable, and altogether one of the best detectives she had met. She hoped the PC would take this letter into consideration when he ruled on the case.

It was all she could do. She did not expect Malloy to acknowledge the letter and he did not. She did not expect it to have much effect either. Malloy probably thought he could afford to ignore her, and that he was nearly rid of her altogether, for the Conservative Party had now formally announced Norman Harbison as its candidate for district attorney in November. Harbison was the Republican Party's choice too. He would have to run in the Republican primary but was considered such a strong candidate that no one else of consequence was entered.

That left only the Democratic nomination undecided, and Commissioner Malloy probably thought she was out of that too.

Although she had received a number of phone calls from party leaders, and had even met with them over dinner, Karen had as yet made no public announcement of her intentions. Nor at any of the meetings did the leaders, Kauffman and O'Reilly, offer her anything. They were just sounding her out, they said.

She was busy reorganizing the Manhattan DA's office, Karen told them. This was true. It was taking most of her time, she told them. Her office, which had not been reorganized in over twenty years, had to be made to work more efficiently. She had not yet given a thought to the election, or to her future, she said. Hadn't had time. This was a lie, but she told it with a smile, and perhaps they believed her. She was certainly not going to beg them to put her on the ballot, and she continued to watch and to wait.

So word circulated that she did not want to run, that she did not see herself as a politician, that she could not face the weeks, even months, of campaigning. Family problems were hinted at. Karen saw this happening and decided to do nothing about it.

Her office had grown enormously in the last several years as hundreds of new prosecutors were added. The divisions had become huge and were almost unmanageable. Beneath them the bureaus had become so big that unimportant cases sometimes got mislaid, lost. She studied the problem, then persuaded senior supervisors to break most of the divisions into smaller parts, adding bureau chiefs and section heads as needed. Once this was done she instituted in each bureau a training program for newly hired young lawyers.

She added an intelligence unit whose job was to identify habitual criminals; she wanted prosecutors to know who they were prosecuting. The complaint and indictment bureaus, which were where every case started, had become bottle-necks; she beefed them up. Soon cops were wasting less time in the complaint room; indictments began coming down quicker. She reinstituted the old elite homicide bureau, reasoning that it was good for any organization to have an elite unit to which everyone else could aspire.

She ordered every assistant DA on a regular basis to visit not only Rikers Island but the upstate penitentiaries too; it seemed clear to her they should know firsthand what they were condemning defendants to. She sent out teams to the universities, and to the major law firms as well, to recruit more and better blacks, Hispanics, and other minority lawyers.

Her confidence increased every day. According to Tananbaum and others around her, morale was greatly improved, the office was working better, and she was gratified one day to pick up the *New York Times* and read an editorial about what a fine job she was doing. She loved her job and had decided that she was good at it.

She wanted to keep it.

But it was not certain she could. Kauffman and O'Reilly had begun casting about for a candidate among state senators and city councilmen. When their search turned up no one of stature, Karen received additional phone calls from them. But they still did not offer anything, or make their intentions clear.

In the face of this she continued to make bland answers to their overtures, if overtures they were. Did this make them somewhat frantic? Did she detect anything in their voices, in their questions? If so, it was perhaps not so surprising. She remembered being importuned for dates as a teenager. This was perhaps similar. Politicians in the role of suitors. The more she put them off, the more attractive to them she became. So she hoped.

Muldoon's trial had lasted two hours. Barone's, since there were so many other defendants, lasted three days. But the verdict was the same: dismissal with loss of all pension rights. Well, Barone had had no pension rights to lose, having served only twelve years so far.

The news, though she knew it was coming, upset Karen more than she had ever expected, and it pushed her toward a decision of her own. She closed the door to her office, asked her secretary to hold all calls, and for some minutes sat brooding. Barone was out of law enforcement now, but she was not. Not yet.

Picking up her phone she made some calls and some appointments, one of them with the governor.

She met him two days later in an office he kept in the World Trade Center.

It was a big office high up in the south tower with a sofa and chairs by the window and a splendid view over New York Harbor. A male secretary showed her in. The governor came toward her all smiles and outstretched hand, but before withdrawing the secretary said: "You have ten minutes until your next appointment, Governor."

"Sit down," the governor said, leading her toward the sofa, "take all the time you want."

Nice trick, Karen thought. All the time I want for ten minutes. I'll have to remember that trick.

"So nice to see you again," the governor said, sitting across from her, "how can I help you?"

She had not seen him or communicated with him since her swearing-in ceremony, and so she began by thanking him for his support when the Epps verdict was announced.

He nodded. "You didn't come over here just to thank me," he said, and he gazed at her with those dark brown eyes.

"I have something to tell you," she said, "and then a favor to ask you."

The governor waited.

"I've decided to run in the Democratic primary. As a courtesy I thought you should be the first to know."

"It's pretty late," he said. "Is there still time?"

"I've checked on that. There's still time."

He nodded. "And the favor?"

"I'm asking for your support."

"Does that mean without my support you won't run?"

"No. If you oppose me, that would make it harder. My decision would not change."

They gazed at each other. "I've heard all kinds of things," the governor said. "I've heard you were having trouble at home."

"That," Karen said, "is not one of your concerns."

"No, of course not." The governor paused. "I don't know what you think I can do for you."

"You're head of the party in New York State."

"I'm the governor. Kauffman and O'Reilly run the party."

Karen smiled at him. "Do they still take your phone calls?"

To her relief the governor smiled back. Though she might look to him relaxed she was as tense as she had ever been. To have any chance of winning she needed endorsements. If she could get the governor's, others' would be easy. The next few minutes were vital.

"In a primary I really shouldn't support anyone," he said. "It's up to the voters to pick a candidate."

"In a primary mistakes can get made. A candidacy can get undermined either accidentally or on purpose. I would like to eliminate those possibilities as much as possible."

The governor had both hands flat on his knees. He looked defensive. "They might have other ideas over at party headquarters. They might ask me why I'm supporting you."

"You appointed me," said Karen. "You want to see the voters validate your choice."

"It's not in my interest to back a candidate who might lose," the governor said.

"I'm the obvious candidate," Karen told him, "and also the most attractive one. The one most likely to beat the Republican candidate. You must have thought that too when you appointed me over him."

Abruptly, the governor said: "What happened between you and Harbison? Did he resign or did you fire him?"

The male secretary stuck his head into the room.

"Governor—"

The governor waved him out again.

"He resigned," Karen decided to say.

"The reason I asked him to stay on originally was because I thought he had experience running the office that you did not have. That you needed him."

"I think I've proven that I didn't need him."

"He's already blaming you for losing the Epps case. Blaming me for appointing you as well. If you run against him," the governor said, "that will be his whole campaign. Most of it anyway."

They gazed at each other. Karen's eyes did not drop.

"I've heard rumors," the governor said, "that he tried to sabotage your case against Epps."

He waited, but Karen said nothing.

"Missing files, that sort of thing."

Still Karen said nothing.

The governor got up and peered out the window. "Information like that—if it's true—leaked to a serious investigative reporter, could have an impact on the election." He turned and faced her.

"So it could," Karen said. "If it's true."

They studied each other. "Without me," Karen said, "the party could well lose the election, couldn't it?"

The governor sighed. "Tell me why you want the job."

This was a political negotiation. It was not the time or mood for Karen to expose her deepest feelings to this man. "You were an assistant DA yourself years ago," she said. "You know what the office is like, what law enforcement is like. I want to make a difference. You know very well why I want it."

The governor nodded. He was perhaps remembering the earliest years of his career. "Yes," he said, "I guess I do."

There was another long silence.

"I liked the way you handled the grand jury in that riot situation," he said finally, and he nodded at her several times.

"So do I have your support?"

The answer, it seemed to Karen, was a long time coming. As she waited, she had to force herself not to squirm.

"All right," the governor said, "I'll make some calls in your behalf."

"Thank you," said Karen, and she could not stop a smile coming on. Neither could the governor, apparently, and for some seconds they stood there smiling inanely at each other.

She met with Kauffman and O'Reilly and signed the papers that same afternoon, asking only that no announcement be made until the following day.

The problem now was to inform Hank. She had once thought her marriage invulnerable but had learned this was not so. It had become as fragile as anyone else's. There was a crack in it that had not been there. She did not know how big a crack, but she felt it was no longer something she could base her life on. There was no one she could depend on now but herself.

Although she was going forward into the election no matter what, she wanted to stay married as well, if she could, and she went home and cooked dinner and afterward sat down with Hank in their living room and told him she was thinking of entering the Democratic primary.

His assistant professorship at NYU had recently come through. He would start with the fall semester. He was feeling much better about himself lately, she believed. There was a new confidence about him, and this was something she was counting on. "It has to be a joint decision," she said. "It can't just be me."

Hank's reaction was to laugh. "You don't like Harbison, do you?"

"No, but it's not only that."

"What is it then?"

To work in law enforcement was to work for the common good at its most basic level, she said. There were tremendous satisfactions.

Here she faltered. How was she to say what she felt? She

hadn't tried to explain herself to the governor and wasn't sure she could make even her own husband understand. Law enforcement was a place where one lived in constant contact with the extremes of human conduct, she said. Emotions were touched over and over again that a woman didn't even know she had. One felt on the side of the angels every day. One helped hold society together. She did not want to switch now to the defense side of the law and find work in a law office defending criminals, which is what she would have to do if Harbison was elected. Her thoughts came spilling out in no particular order, and only the plainest of them, she supposed, made sense to Hank. Having once served as district attorney, she could not just step back into the ranks of assistants and stay on, she said. That was asking too much. No one would know how to treat her, she wouldn't know how to behave herself, and Harbison would never permit it anyway. If she was defeated for election she would be out of law enforcement forever on January 1, and she did not want to be. She would be out of work altogether, and this had to be considered too.

Again her voice faltered. It was complicated, she said.

"You like your job," Hank said. "It's as simple as that."

"Yes, perhaps it's as simple as that."

So far Hank was offering less opposition than she had dared hope.

He said: "You'd have to run twice, first in the primary, then in the election itself."

"Yes."

"You'd have to campaign," Hank said. "You'd have Harbison campaigning against you."

"I realize that."

"You know how politics is these days."

"Yes."

"He'll fight dirty."

"Probably."

"He'll subject you to all kinds of scurrilous attacks."

"Yes, I imagine he will."

"He'll attack you personally."

"On what grounds?"

"He knows all about you."

"He knows nothing about me."

"He'll find something in your past."

"There's nothing to find," she said.

"You'd be amazed what people can dig up."

She took her husband's hand. "There's nothing there," she said.

"If you run it will disrupt our lives," he said after a pause.

"I'm aware of that."

"Well," Hank said finally, "I have the impression you mean to run whatever I say."

Karen said nothing.

"If you want to run," Hank said, "I think you should do it."

She met Barone one time more.

It was summer by then. He was coming out of a courtroom on the fourteenth floor. They nearly bumped into each other and it stopped them in their tracks, both of them startled, even shocked, neither one sure what to say. Then a smile came onto Barone's face. Karen thought it the warmest, most loving smile anyone had ever given her. His face was wreathed in it, and his hand shot out and she took it.

He said: "I certainly am awfully glad to see you again."

Of course she was moved by such a reaction. How could she not be? "Me too," she said.

This was followed on both sides by embarrassment.

Barone gestured toward the courtroom behind him. "I was in there testifying."

Jurors, spectators, lawyers moved by them along the hall.

"And you," Barone said. "What are you doing up on this floor? Not still trying cases, are you?"

"It's a Mafia guy," Karen said. "We want him held without bail. We thought maybe if I appeared personally it would carry some weight with the judge."

They nodded at each other.

It was an extremely hot day. Karen was wearing a short-sleeved linen suit, blue with green piping. She had on medium-high heels and carried the inevitable dossiers in her arms.

Barone wore a lightweight tan suit over a pink button-down shirt, and a dark brown tie. Still the sharp dresser, Karen thought.

She said: "So what are you doing these days? When you're not testifying, I mean."

"I took a job with a construction company near where I live. We build schools, shopping centers. We're pretty big. I meet with customers, plan jobs."

He saw that she had been concerned for him. He said: "I'm doing fine."

"I'm glad, Mike."

"You can cross me off your list of worries."

He gave her another fond smile.

"It was an auto theft case," he said, gesturing at the courtroom behind him. "I think it was the last case I had left."

Karen digested what this meant. After today there was nothing to bring him to this courthouse, or even to New York City. Most likely they would not meet again.

"By the way," Barone said, "I want to thank you for the letter you wrote the PC on my behalf."

"You saw that?"

"It was introduced by the department advocate at my trial. The PC must have sent it over."

Karen was surprised. Malloy had not seemed to her that fair a man.

"I wanted to do more than just write a letter," she said.

"There was nothing you could do. You probably shouldn't even have written the letter."

"I wanted to help."

"You did help. More than you know."

Karen gave a wry smile. "I didn't do any good at all."

"Your letter meant everything to me. It was the only thing got me through that trial."

Again both of them fell silent.

"How's your wife?" said Karen. "How are your daughters?"

"Fine. How is your husband and your children?"

"Fine."

Barone did not know what to say next, apparently. Neither did Karen.

He said: "I read that you're going to run in the primary."

"Yes. I've never run for office before. I don't know what kind of politician I'll make."

"Well, you've got my vote."

She laughed. "You don't live in the city. You don't have a vote."

"You know what I mean," he said. "You'll always have my vote."

This caused another silence.

"Harbison is a stiff," Barone said. "You'll beat him easy."

"You think so?"

"Absolutely."

"You don't know a thing about it," Karen said, and they both laughed.

They looked at each other.

"Do you ever think of me?" Barone asked.

"No," Karen lied.

"It wouldn't hurt," Barone suggested. "Just once in a while."

"I'll try."

They stood smiling at each other. "I have to go," Karen said. "I was due in court ten minutes ago."

"I have to go too. To be this close to you and not grab you is agony."

She was surprised at how nice this was to hear. But she was careful to give no reaction. Instead she put out her hand. "Good-bye, Mike."

"Good-bye, Karen."

He started away from her down the corridor but she called after him. "Thank you for your vote."

He gave a smile and a wave, and continued toward the elevators. After a moment Karen opened the door and went into the courtroom.

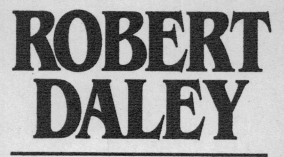